JESSIE KEANE

STAY DEAD

PAN BOOKS

First published 2016 by Macmillan

This edition published 2017 by Pan Books
an imprint of Pan Macmillan
20 New Wharf Road, London N1 9RR
Associated companies throughout the world
www.panmacmillan.com

ISBN   978-1-4472-5434-8

1 3 5 7 9 8 6 4 2

A CIP catalogue record for this book is available from the British Library.

Typeset by Ellipsis Digital Limited, Glasgow
Printed and bound by CPI Group (UK) Ltd, Croydon, CR0 4YY

Visit www.panmacmillan.com to read more about all our books
and to buy them. You will also find features, author interviews and
news of any author events, and you can sign up for e-newsletters
so that you're always first to hear about our new releases.

STAY DEAD

Jessie Keane is a *Sunday Times* top ten bestselling author.
She's lived both ends of the social spectrum, and her fas-
cination with London's underworld led her to write *Dirty
Game*, followed by bestsellers *Black Widow*, *Scarlet Women*,
Jail Bird, *The Make*, *Playing Dead*, *Nameless*, *Ruthless* (the
fifth book to feature Annie Carter), *Lawless* and *Dangerous*.
Jessie's books have sold more than 750,000 copies.

She now lives in Hampshire. You can reach Jessie on her
website www.jessie-keane.com

To Cliff
Yo, Bitch!
What a year, eh?

ACKNOWLEDGEMENTS

Thanks go to Jane Gregory of Gregory & Co and to the Pan Macmillan team. A special mention here for my editor, Wayne Brookes, whose skill and patience has helped catapult my books into the *Sunday Times* Top 10 bestseller list.

Thanks to White & Co who helped me move vast piles of books and waterlogged belongings this year, and to James Colville who guided me through the whole process of (finally) moving home while writing this book at the same time.

Last but never least, thanks to all the supermarkets and stores and bookshops who stock and sell my books – and all my readers, bless you! Big thanks too to all my Facebook and Twitter friends, followers and fans. It really wouldn't be the same without you.

OMERTA

(The Mafia code of silence)

PROLOGUE

Outside the Shalimar nightclub, London, June 1994

Annie Carter had lived through her fair share of bad days, but this one had to rank among the worst. She had only two close friends in the entire world. One of them had just told her to piss off, and the other one was dead – and that broke her heart in two. She came out on to the pavement fighting back tears, unable to fully believe what was happening to her life. She didn't know where her husband was, or what he was up to, but visions of naked sweaty limbs and glam young girls danced in her brain day and night, like fairy dust or a gigantic snort of coke.

Added to all *that*, she had a secret, a big, big secret that she'd been carrying around with her for years. The burden of it was heavy, and terrible. She couldn't share it with a single living soul. And she feared there was worse to come.

She was coming out of the Shalimar, one of three lap-dancing clubs owned by her husband Max, the other two being the Palermo and the Blue Parrot. She was looking a million dollars because she always did, even when she was feeling like shit. She was wearing a Gucci black skirt suit, white chiffon blouse and Italian-made high-heeled boots, and her long chocolate-brown hair bounced on her shoulders. Even in the depths of emotional torment, Annie

Carter took trouble over her appearance, and she'd slicked on red lippy and a flick of black mascara.

Right now, Annie felt like her whole world was caving in on her. People who had once treated her with respect were behaving toward her as if she was diseased, dirty. Ellie and Chris Brown. Steve Taylor. Gary Tooley. Even Tony, who had been first Max's driver, then hers, and then Dolly Farrell's.

Maybe they know, whispered a voice in her brain.

The thought of that sent a vicious, bone-deep shudder of dread through her.

No. Impossible.

They *couldn't* know.

Could they?

She stood there in the dismal drizzling rain. Summer in England. A bike shot past. Then a long dark car swerved into the pavement with a screech of brakes. Horns tooted, taxi drivers hollered out of their windows and waved their fists. Annie walked on, uncaring, thinking about Dolly, feeling the awful gnawing grief grip her, shutting off the world around her, filling her whole being with blackness. Suddenly there were two big men standing on either side of her and one of them was shoving what felt like a knife into her side.

'In the car,' said the one with the knife. She looked up into a big plug-ugly face with a bulbous nose dotted with blackheads, mean piggy eyes and thick curling black eyebrows that met in the middle.

I know you, thought Annie.

He jabbed the knife deeper into her side. 'Don't fuck me around,' he warned.

Annie saw that the other one was shaven-headed, his tanned face pitted with adolescent acne.

'Do it,' said Eyebrows.

Annie got in the car, and off they went.

Baldy stopped the motor by a warehouse down by the docks and together him and Eyebrows dragged her out. Annie's heart was pummelling her ribs like a drum, but she thought the best thing would be to front it out.

'You don't know what you're playing with here,' she said, gulping and breathless.

Ridiculously, she heard the next phrase coming out of her mouth, a phrase she openly laughed at when it was uttered by politicians, film stars, people who were so far up their own arseholes that they had lost all sense of reality.

'Do you know who I am?' she said.

Eyebrows looked at her. Baldy's face was like stone.

'Yeah, we know who you are. And *what* you are too.'

'I'm warning you—' started Annie, and Eyebrows slapped her hard across the face.

She flew backward as if shot from a cannon. The stinging pain of the blow was shocking. She tottered unsteadily on her feet and grabbed her face as if checking it was still attached to her head. She couldn't take it in. This *fucker* had the nerve to hit her – *her*, Annie Carter. She drew in a breath. Her eyes were watering. She started to speak again, and Eyebrows came in close and punched her mid-section.

All the breath went from her in one almighty *whoosh* of exploding air. She fell to the ground and lay there, unable to breathe, her mind in shock, her body clenched, her stomach a fiery ball of agony.

You bastards! You can't do this! I'm Max Carter's wife, are you fucking mental . . . ?

Her mouth formed the words but she couldn't speak. She had no breath to speak *with*. Groaning, face screwed up in pain, she tried to crawl away, thinking *this can't be*

3

happening. Eyebrows kicked her hard in the ribs and there was a snap and unbelievable pain rocketed through her as she felt something give. She went face-down into the muddy gravel, the rain washing her hair into the dirt, covering her clothes with yellow slime.

She was choking, half-vomiting with the anguish of it, crawling, trying feebly to get away. It wasn't possible. They were following her, both of them. Kicking her in the guts. And in the end it was easier to just stop moving, to just hope that it would end.

It *did* end, eventually. In this century or the next, she wasn't sure. But not before she'd passed out; not before she'd prayed for oblivion, even for death, just to make the pain stop.

Help me, she thought.

But no one came.

Oh yes. It was a bad, bad day.

PART ONE

1

February 1994

The calls started late one night, waking Gary Tooley, the manager of the Carter-owned Blue Parrot nightclub, from his peaceful slumbers alongside his latest squeeze, Caroline Wheeler.

'What the *fuck*?' he asked, because actually it wasn't even late one night, it was early the next morning.

To be precise, it was three o'clock, and he was pissed off to be woken up like this. He'd had a crazy Friday night, punters kicking off and complaining left, right and centre, staff arsing about and people shooting up in the toilets, and all he wanted now was some kip. Was that too much to ask?

Of course Caroline, the idle bitch, didn't lift a finger to answer the phone. She'd been working the bar a couple of months when they'd started getting friendly, and friendly had quickly turned into fucking the life out of her down in the stockroom, then in the empty bar, then in the cellars, then in bed.

Now here she was, snoring like a hog and taking up most of the quilt. Christ, he would *really* like his own bed to himself for a change. Caroline was good in the sack –

she was even good on the *floor* – but sometimes all a bloke wanted was some sleep. He leaned over her huddled form and snatched up the phone.

'What?' he demanded.

And then came the voice. Female. Foreign accent. But speaking English. Saying that there was a crash, she knew about it, Constantine had planned it.

What the hell? wondered Gary, brain fogged with sleep.

'Who is this?' he said, when she'd babbled on for a full five minutes.

There was a long pause. Then a decisive: 'I am Gina Barolli.'

'OK. Right. And why are you phoning me in the middle of the night?'

'You work for the Carter family.'

'I do. Yeah.' Gary scrubbed a hand wearily over his face. Caroline snored on, undisturbed.

'It was all for *her*. Annie Carter. The crash.'

'The what?'

'The plane crash.'

Gary's attention sharpened. Was the mad old bint talking about the plane crash in the seventies, the one that should have put an end to those mad cunting Irish the Delaneys forever? Sadly, it hadn't. Redmond Delaney survived. Gary knew all about the plane crash; all the trusted people close to Max Carter did. So what?

'My brother, Constantine . . .' she said, and paused.

'Yeah. Your brother. What about him?'

'I'll tell you everything,' said the woman, and the line went dead.

That was the first call. And then came others, and that made Gary think. Maybe it was time to cash in on some of this info. Caroline had expensive tastes and he had a bit of a gambling habit, loved the dogs and the horses; a bit more wedge would come in very handy right now. And he knew exactly who he was going to get it from.

2

It was a pity, Redmond Delaney thought, that he'd been ousted as a priest. A real shame, because the priesthood had suited him nicely, given him a standing in the community that he'd missed after being forced to abandon his previous existence as an East End gang leader.

The Delaney mob had ruled Limehouse and Battersea, back in the day, and people had treated him with respect, treading very carefully around him. Cold and controlling, he had relished his position and his fearsome reputation. It had amused him to see terror in people's eyes when they came face to face with him. How ironic, that the roles of gang boss and priest should turn out to have so much in common: extracting confessions from sinners, doling out hellfire and damnation to wrongdoers . . .

Both jobs had similar perks, too. Gang groupies had flocked to him when he'd run the Delaney mob. Church groupies had twittered around him when he ran his parish. Ah, so tempting they were, all those shy, bored housewives who were dazzled by this stunning red-haired Adonis in his black soutane and pristine white collar. *Too* tempting, that was the trouble. Easy meat, really. One after another he used them, and every time he'd prostrate himself before the altar afterwards and say, 'Sorry, Lord, but I am only flesh and the flesh is weak. Forgive me.' And every time he'd be forgiven, his sins wiped clean . . . until the next time he weakened.

He'd been busy indulging the flesh again the morning his career as a priest came to an abrupt end.

The woman had come to him with a personal problem – something about a bored husband who she believed was straying. Redmond had listened, or appeared to, while thinking: Tasty. Blonde. Curvy. Quite delicious. A little morsel for him to gobble down at the first opportunity.

'Drop by the presbytery, we'll discuss it,' he said, thinking that she was very angry, very hurt, about her husband's extramarital activities, and that anger and hurt would make her vulnerable. He couldn't wait.

The minute she set foot inside the hall and the door closed behind her, Redmond put his tongue in her mouth and slipped a hand under her dress to touch a silken cool thigh. As he kissed her, his hand went higher, delving deeper.

'Oh God . . . oh, Father!' she gasped in shock and delight against his lips.

'You've been driving me insane,' he said, and kissed her again.

He said this to all of them, of course, all the little titbits he enjoyed, because it fed their female vanity, made them proud. They'd turned a *priest*, sworn to celibacy, their charms so overwhelming that even fear of God left him unable to resist.

She was Sally Westover, who was married to Bill Westover, who almost certainly *hadn't* strayed because he was such a dull bugger, but Father Delaney wasn't going to tell her that. Instead he took her upstairs to his single priest's bed and gave her the hammering of her life.

Then . . .

'Oh God, the phone. . .' she moaned.

Damned thing was ringing, right by the bed.

'Don't stop,' he ordered her, snatching it up. 'Yes?' he said.

'Is that Redmond Delaney?' asked a male voice.

'Who wants him?' asked Redmond, watching Sally's large pendulous nude breasts bouncing around above him while she straddled him, impaling herself repeatedly on his manhood and wheezing like an asthmatic chimpanzee.

Oh, she's a good one, he thought.

Later he was going to indoctrinate her properly into the ways of the flesh. She'd barely touched the surface, he could see that. She was a keen amateur, that was all. After this afternoon she would be full of remorse. She was a wife, a mother (he could tell that because she was quite loose), and she would be so guilty. He would tweak that guilt, hang his head in shame, say she had made him commit this sin, betray his vows.

Oh yes. Such fun and games he would have with Sally Westover. He would introduce her to the delights of pain and ice and fire, to bondage and choking, all those darker aspects of sexuality that were his preferred territory.

'This is Gary Tooley,' said the voice on the phone. 'You don't know me, but—'

'The one who runs the Blue Parrot?' asked Redmond, thinking that Sally was banging away so hard now that it was getting difficult to maintain his control. He remembered Tooley. Redmond had a good memory, a very fine brain in fact, and he knew that Gary Tooley worked for the Carters.

He wondered – briefly – how Tooley had got hold of this number. He didn't like people tracking him down; as a rule, Redmond liked to do the stalking if there was stalking to be done. In fact, he enjoyed it.

'Yeah, that's me.' Gary sounded surprised. 'I've got some information for you.'

'What information?'

'You won't believe it,' said Gary.

'Tell me.'

'Nah. Not over the phone. We need to meet up.'

'That's not convenient.' Sally gasped and Redmond raised a finger: *shush.*

'It will be when you hear what it is.'

'All right.' Redmond was mildly intrigued. 'When and where?'

Gary named a place, a time. Redmond said: 'This had better be worth my while.'

'It is,' said Gary, and put the phone down.

'This is so good,' groaned Sally, bouncing, bouncing, bouncing . . . and then all at once it was too much, and Redmond grabbed her hips and came.

At the same moment, as he gasped and writhed and thrust at Sally with abandon, there was a knock and the bedroom door opened.

'Sorry, Father, I forgot the shopping list and I thought I'd better ask—'

Redmond's housekeeper, Mrs Janner, stopped dead in the doorway and stared at the naked couple on the bed, her face a mask of shock. Sally daintily put her hands up to cover her breasts. Redmond just lay there, thinking, *Well, that's that then.*

That was the day Gary Tooley first got in touch with him, the same day that Mrs Janner phoned the bishop, the same day that Redmond Delaney was summarily dismissed from the priesthood.

Pity, really, because he had liked it.

While it lasted.

3

The Palermo Lounge nightclub, June 1994

The uniformed police got the call at 11.24 on a Friday morning, and by 11.42 they were there, talking to an hysterical young barman called Peter Jones.

'She opens the front entrance door at eleven, every day. But today I got here and it was still locked. I thought she was ill in bed or something, so I used my own key. She don't like me doing that, but what else could I do?'

'Why doesn't she like you doing that?' asked one of the uniformed police, his weary sigh and set face saying he'd seen it all before, and then some.

They were standing in the big bar, backlit with blue fluorescent lights, and all was serene down here. As in the other Carter-owned clubs, the Blue Parrot and the Shalimar, there was lots of gold leaf on the walls, and angels and cherubs flying around the ceiling, dark tobacco-brown carpeting underfoot and about a hundred chairs decked out in faux tiger skins set out around circular tables. There were teensy little podiums with poles for the dancers. Gold chain curtains concealed exits over at the far right-hand side of the vast room; and there was a staircase, roped off and leading upwards, on their left. Neither of the two cops wanted to go up that staircase.

Pete was dragging his hands through his close-cropped blond hair, over and over, like he wanted to rip it straight out of his head, and his baby-blue eyes were reddened with tears.

'She's a very private person, she *lives* here,' said Pete. 'Up there. That's her flat. I went up as soon as I came in, called out to her, asked if she was OK. She didn't answer. So I knocked at her door, still nothing. I tried the handle and it was open. I went in. And I found her. Then I phoned you.'

Tears were slipping down Pete's face. The female cop touched his arm, guided him to a chair. The male cop looked up at the staircase. Then, with a heavy sigh, he went over there, and began to climb the stairs.

An hour later, CID arrived in the unsexy buttoned-up form of DS Sandra Duggan, whose honey-coloured hair was scraped back to display knife-sharp cheekbones and eyes that viewed the whole world with hostility. With her was DCI Hunter: tall, dark-haired, grave-faced – *literally* grave-faced; everyone down the nick said he ought to be a fucking undertaker with a boat like that – with a down-turned trap of a mouth and inky-brown eyes that scanned everything around him like a computer.

CID spoke to Pete and then went upstairs with Pete trailing behind them.

'Fuck,' said Sandra as they opened the door to the flat and entered the little sitting room straight off it.

Hunter and Duggan stood there and assessed the situation. The dead woman was sprawled out on the thick shag-pile carpet, which was a soft dusky pink. Her head was on a white sheepskin rug by the unlit gas fire, and some of the rug had turned to red where blood had spilled out of the bullet wounds to her neck and forehead.

'Not pretty,' agreed DCI Hunter with his usual formal manner. Neither he nor his companion moved further into the room; they wanted to preserve the crime scene.

'Oh God,' moaned Pete, looking past Hunter's shoulder and then just as quickly looking away.

The woman's eyes were open and already glazing over with the film of death; they stared up at and through the ceiling, blank as a china doll's. She was wearing a strawberry-pink boucle skirt suit that looked expensive, maybe Chanel; an inch of a paler pink silk lining was visible where it had rucked up over her knees.

Nothing special about the woman at all; a bubble-permed blonde of around forty or fifty, pale almond-shaped blue eyes, a round and maybe even pretty face if it hadn't been for the blood and the brain matter. She looked good for her age, that's what Hunter thought; and very, very dead. He sighed for all the loss and grief and anguish in the world, for the evils that were done every day to women, and men, and children.

'What's her name?' he asked Pete, whose face was now firmly averted from this horror.

'Dolly,' said Pete, and started to cry again. 'That's Dolly Farrell.'

4

Limehouse, 1945–55

Dolly Farrell went to the bad early on in life, but when she was born, a blank page for history to write on, she already had one major distinction: she came into the world just as Adolf Hitler left it. She was yanked, already screaming, from her mother's body on the same day the beaten Führer, trapped in his Berlin bunker by the oncoming Allies, decided that the party was over, and put a bullet in his brain.

'And not a minute too soon. Fucking shame the crazy bastard didn't do that five years earlier,' said Sam, Dolly's father, as he heard the news while smoking a celebratory Player's down in the sitting room of their rented terrace house. He could hear the new baby bawling its head off upstairs and thought in admiration, Jesus, the mouth on that kid.

My son, he thought, and smiled to himself.

The Farrells were Catholic; not practising as such – there was no church on Sundays for them, no confession – but more or less going by the Catholic creed they'd been raised with. Which meant that this first child, now Dad was demobbed and home from the war and wanting to work on the railways like his dad before him, was going to be followed by many more.

Sam went up after the midwife had done the necessary, cleaned all the muck away, and there was his wife Edie,

17

looking flushed and exhausted, holding the new baby in a blue blanket. Of course it was blue. The blanket was blue because Sam had wanted a boy and refused to countenance anything else. He'd been convinced that the bulge on Edie's front contained his son, who would play footie with him and be a big healthy lad, take after his dad.

'My son's in there,' he'd once said happily, ecstatic that his wife had got pregnant so quick after he'd come home from the war. Hadn't expected to live through it, not really, Adolf throwing so much shit at them all, but he had, and he'd climbed down off the train, come home, dropped his trousers and bingo! There was Edie, pregnant.

She'd wanted a girl, of course, but he'd said, 'No, it's a boy. Course it's a boy,' and he wouldn't let her get pink stuff for the spare room, only the blue, he was that certain he was right. Sam was always right.

And now look at this. A fucking girl.

Edie's face was sheepish; she knew he'd be disappointed.

'It's a girl, Sam,' she said quietly.

'Ah, never mind,' said Sam, fag still in hand, exhaling an irritable plume of smoke all over the new baby as he peered in for a look. 'Ugly little runt, ain't she?' he joked with a grin. Then he looked at Edie and gave her a quick peck on the cheek. 'A boy next time, eh?'

Edie did have a boy next time – two years after Dolly arrived – and Sam got royally pissed down the Dog and Duck celebrating with his mates and then reeled home and clouted Edie when she commented on the state of him.

It was a lesson learned – after that, Edie didn't say a word when he got drunk, which he often did after a hard day on the railways. He'd started in the signal box after the war, but it was all hours and he didn't like being cooped up in there, pulling levers and listening for the many different-sounding bells. It was all too complicated. So he applied for another job and went out on to the tracks as a wheeltapper. He liked that, all his mates were around him and they toasted him, slapped him on the back, said what a great feller he was.

Sam thought he was a very great feller indeed. After the boy was born – Nigel, they named him – Sam lost no time in climbing on board Edie and impregnating her a third time. A girl this time, Sarah, and then he got to work on Edie again and – at last! – another boy to be proud of, little Dick. After that, Sam put his own little dick to good use, and then along came Sandy, who was a boy but a bit sickly, prone to the sniffles.

'She shouldn't have many more,' said the midwife, who'd attended all five of Edie's births and could see that it was dragging the poor cow down. Not only having the kids, but on a railwayman's wage it was a fight to keep them all clothed and fed. Edie was struggling, anyone could see that. If they wanted to. Which Sam didn't.

Sam wanted a big Catholic family, seven minimum.

'Mind your own fucking business,' he told the midwife.

Who'd asked for her opinion anyway? He was keeping the kids fed, just about, although of course he had to have his fags and beer first. After all, he was the breadwinner, wasn't he? There had to be something in it for him.

After Edie's fifth pregnancy there was a stillbirth, then a miscarriage, then another stillbirth. Tired, depressed, Edie finally said to her husband, enough. He would have to use something if he wanted to go on enjoying marital relations. That earned her another clout around the ear. He was from a good Catholic family, Sam told her in a rage; what she was talking about, wasn't that a sin?

'I can't go on with it, Sam,' said Edie in tears. 'It ain't fair.'

'It's God's will,' said Sam, and that was an end to it. He was doing well on the railways, he was responsible for a small

gang of men on the tracks now, his pay was better than before. There was no reason he shouldn't enjoy his own wife and have the big Catholic family he wanted. No reason at all.

'I'm so tired,' whinged Edie.

He was sick of the sound of her voice, always whining on about what a hard life she had. He supported her, didn't he? Treated her all right. Wasn't that enough?

Nothing would deter Sam from making her perform her wifely duties. Back from the pub, he would fall into bed and right away he'd be on her. Sometimes she protested, and then it turned into straightforward rape, but if ever Sam felt a twinge of conscience over that he salved it quickly – because he knew that a man could never rape his wife, he had legal rights over her. Conjugal rights, wasn't that a fact?

There came another miscarriage.

Another stillbirth.

Edie seemed to shrink into herself, become like a shadow. She lost weight and her face was pale with misery; she was no longer the pretty, engaging and hopeful girl he'd married, and Sam felt cheated.

'I don't know what the fuck you want from me,' he raged at her. 'You've got a bloody good earner looking after you, you've even got help around the house now Dolly's getting older. What the hell do you want?'

Edie never answered that question openly, but in her head she did: she wanted him to leave her alone. She wanted him to go out one day and never come home. That was what she wanted, and if she said as much he would kill her stone dead. So she didn't; couldn't. Worn out by the misery of endless pregnancies and bloody miscarriages and devastating stillbirths, she stepped back from the world. And in her heart she grew to hate him, her Sam, once her best love, her only love. All that had turned to dust.

5

Limehouse, 1955–57

When she was ten, Dolly Farrell considered running away from home. She was at primary school with her friends, and she liked primary school and never missed a day because it was much nicer than home. The school was a small Catholic-funded centre of education, and it looked like a church; in fact it had been built in the same year as the Victorian church just up the road, beside the recreation ground with its huge, terrifying slide for the kids to play on.

For Dolly, primary school was an escape. It felt safe and there were big brightly coloured posters up all around the room she sat in every day, saying *A is for Apple* (a big rosy-red apple to illustrate) and all the way through the alphabet to *Z is for Zebra* (a striped horse on this one). Even the teachers she hated weren't too horrible. Mrs Lockhart took the kids for maths and clonked you on the head if she felt your work wasn't up to scratch. Mr Vancy, who taught English, lobbed a rock-hard oblong blackboard duster at you if you chatted at the back of the class during lessons; and Dolly, who didn't much care for education, was always chatting at the back of the class with her mates Vera and Lucy.

Dolly loved being a milk monitor and handing out the bottles from the crates to the younger kids, and having biscuits

21

at break time, and the meals were okay, even if the cabbage was boiled to fuck and the custard was thin as cat piss.

She liked the priest, Father Potter, who came in every Friday and gave the kids a sermon in assembly. He played lovely classical music to them, saying in his super-posh voice that he wished them to learn a love of fine things, of beauty, and to go out into the world the better for it. She liked walking along the road in a crocodile-line of two-by-twos with all the other kids, one teacher at the front, another at the back, all the way to the church to sing hymns about praising the Lord.

She didn't think she had much to praise Him for, not really, but she liked being in the church, she liked the stained-glass windows and the big angels with their luminous green and red feathered wings and the dumpy little cherubs with floaty hankies over their bits; it felt safe.

Then one day it was Lucy's birthday and she and Vera were invited back to Lucy's house for tea and cake. Lucy's house was in between Dolly's and the school; Dolly would call in there in the mornings, trailing her younger sister and her brothers behind her – eight-year-old Nigel, seven-year-old Sarah, little Dick and the youngest and frailest boy, Sandy, the poor bastard, who was always smothered in pungent Vick and goose grease over the winters to keep him from catching colds. Neither the Vick nor the goose grease seemed to prevent illness in Sandy, but Mum gave it a go when she was well enough to bother, which wasn't often; so usually the task of greasing him up fell to Dolly.

Dolly and Vera and Lucy had a whale of a time at Lucy's birthday tea, and Vera went home clutching a slice of sponge cake in a brown paper bag. A few minutes later, Dolly trailed out the door. Her brothers and sister had gone on home earlier, straight from school, and now the light was starting to fade as the sun set in the west, lighting the winter sky up like a huge apricot-coloured lamp.

Dolly stared at it, thinking it was the most beautiful sight she had ever seen. Clutching her bag of cake, she sighed and started homeward, and was passing the recreation ground when she saw the slide there. She ambled over, pulling out cake crumbs from the bag and eating them, and calculated that she had time for a go on the slide before going home.

But what if she didn't go home?

The thought entered her head and for a moment she felt a lift of the spirits, like those mighty angels' wings had gently pushed her upward. The thought of that . . .

Oh, the thought of that was wonderful.

When she thought of home, she thought of Mum sitting slumped and staring into space in a chair at the dirty kitchen table, of Dad roaring about the place the worse for drink. It made her guts crease up in anguish. She would never be able to invite Lucy back to hers for tea, that was for sure. She would be too ashamed. It would be all round the school in no time that she lived in a filthy hovel with cockroaches crawling around the floor and you wouldn't want to eat your tea there or even touch anything in the bloody place, it was all sticky and grubby with filth.

Dolly tried to help her mum around the house, she really did. But with five kids and two uncaring adults, the place was a tip. And now they'd started giving her homework and saying that soon she'd be off to big school, so she had to be prepared to work harder.

God, angels, are you listening? she wondered as the sky deepened to rose-gold. Streaky charcoal clouds drifted through it, like thick pencil-marks on a page. How the fuck can I work any harder? Don't I work hard enough now?

She was the one who had to get her younger siblings ready for school in the mornings; she was the one who had to get in from school and cook something for the family. She was the one who did just about everything there was to do, and more besides.

Through it all Mum just sat there, ignoring the housework, barely even touching the food Dolly put in front of her. The doctor had given Mum some pills, but they didn't seem to be working. Every morning when the kids set off for school, Edie would be slumped at the kitchen table, and when they got home she'd still be there, in the same chair, as if she hadn't moved an inch all day. And Dolly thought she probably hadn't.

Dolly finished off the cake, screwed the bag into a ball and threw it down. Then she climbed up the slide, ten steps. It had taken her years to overcome her fear of the slide; it was slippery as polished glass going down, and you shot off the end of it in the most fearsome way. If you weren't careful, you'd fall awkwardly and break your leg – it had happened last year to one of the younger kids. And Dolly didn't want to break her leg.

But then, if she did she'd be taken to hospital, and that would be good, better than home. Wouldn't it?

It was nearly dark now.

Dolly released her grip on the hand-holds at the top of the slide and whizzed, flew, cannoned down it and whirled off the end almost laughing, breathless, exhilarated.

'Dolly!'

She stiffened. Turned. Dad was pacing toward her, coming quick, and there was something angry about every short, bandy-legged line of his body. Suddenly all the magic of the day dropped away as if it had never been.

He bent over, enveloping her in the smell of Old Holborn and gamey unwashed clothes. She thought he might be reaching for the bag she'd tossed on the ground, but he wasn't. He grabbed her arm, hurting her, and bent and slapped her hard across the legs, twice. It stung like hell and she let out a cry.

'What the fuck are you doing, worrying your mum like

this?' he shouted. 'Come on!' he said, and started dragging her off the field and back to the road, back to home.

For a while, she'd almost felt free.

But it didn't last long.

It never did.

6

Dolly hated secondary school. The primary had been nice, tucked in near the church. It was small. But big school was just that: too damned big. She didn't know anybody there because Lucy and Vera were put in the top stream and to her embarrassment she was put in the bottom, along with all the other no-hopers who had home troubles or who never paid attention in class.

OK, she admitted it; she'd never worked much at primary school. She'd mucked about and enjoyed it; it was a relief to be at school and not at home. Now, she was paying the price. Lucy and Vera had somehow cracked on, worked harder than her; but then, they had good backgrounds, nice parents. She didn't.

Well, Mum was nice, to be fair. She just couldn't cope, that was all. Edie was under the doctor now, taking a lot of pills and sometimes she'd be carted away in an ambulance. Dad had gathered the kids together the first time and told them that Mum was getting some treatment for her nerves, that it would help her, make her better.

For a while, it did. It was usually about three months, Dolly reckoned, before the wheels came off the truck in Mum's brain once again. Then it was just her sitting in the chair all day, crying, and then it was off in the ambulance for another course of 'treatment'.

'What do you think they do?' asked Sandy, the youngest, eyes wide with terror. 'Do they strap her to a table or something, inject her with stuff . . . ?'

'Plug her into the mains, that's what they do,' said Dick, looking quite excited.

'No, they don't,' said Dolly, although it was true, more or less. Dad had told her, because she was the eldest and she was his special girl, his favourite, that the treatment Mum got at the hospital was electric shock therapy. But Dolly clouted Dick upside the head because he had a big mouth and couldn't he see that Sarah was frightened?

'They do! Straight into the fucking National Grid,' persisted Dick, rubbing his ear and grinning.

'It's a very mild thing,' said Dolly firmly to Sarah, although she knew different. She had seen her mum brought home after those 'sessions', babbling and crying in a state of confusion and vomiting her guts up. Sarah hadn't seen any of that. 'It's hardly a shock at all. And it puts things right in Mum's brain.'

But they all knew that the treatment had no long-lasting effect. It was just Mum. She couldn't help it.

Dad still had his job on the railways, but he was off the wheeltapping now. They'd made him a shunter, put him in with a new gang of men. He was doing well, so at least they never went hungry.

Dolly tried to keep the house tidy, but being naturally untidy herself, and hating housework, she found that she just couldn't manage it.

So their house was dirty. Often, the kids went unwashed and their clothes were threadbare and filthy. Sandy wet the bed; he was nervous, highly strung like Mum. But so what? None of the families in their street were much different. All around them on the council estate there was junk piled up in front gardens, mange-ridden dogs endlessly barking, grubby *kids sitting out on the front step watching the world go by when they should have been at school, studying.*

Nobody around here gave a flying fuck about education, about making a better life for themselves; it was just the way it was. Vera and Lucy were exceptions to the rule. Around here, you knew your place, you didn't go giving yourself any stupid airs and graces, trying to be all la-di-dah. Try to make something of yourself and you'd get laughed at or beaten up, or both.

For the boys, the future probably held a job on the railway like Dad. Nigel, the eldest boy, was prudish and formal; he hero-worshipped his little strutting bantam-cock of a father, and was sure to follow in his footsteps. For the girls, there would be marriage and kids.

But whenever Dolly looked at Mum, she wondered about that. Marriage and kids? It hadn't done Mum any fucking favours. Everyone was talking about how the actress Grace Kelly had found her prince, like in a fairy tale; she'd married Prince Rainier the Third of Monaco.

'Gawd, innit lovely?' all the girls were saying.

It was in all the papers, it was even on the telly, they said, the actual honest-to-God ceremony had been filmed.

Dolly was pretty sure that she wouldn't want to go down that road, not now, not ever. She was troubled by her own feelings about it, though. What else could a girl do? Men earned the money, women had the babies. It was set in stone. But the very idea of it turned her stomach.

7

Sometimes Dolly thought it started when she was ten, just before she considered running away. But no. Actually, when she really thought, it started a year or so before that, with him giving her little gifts.

Whenever she thought about it in later life – and mostly she tried not to – she always thought of the story about the frog put into cold water that was heated until it boiled to death. Had it been put in boiling water to start with, it would have jumped out. But death was slow, insidious; it crept up on the frog and lulled it; and that was how Dolly's downfall came about, too.

The first time Mum went away to get her 'treatment', Dad brought Dolly a box of chocolates.

'Got to spoil my best girl, haven't I,' he said gruffly, shoving the gift into her hands. 'Don't tell the other kids, they'll all be wanting stuff, and that's just for you, because you're special.'

Dolly was delighted and flattered. She felt important, because Mum was away and she was in charge of the house, even if she was a lousy cook and an even worse cleaner. She tucked the chocolates away in a recess of the wardrobe in her and Sarah's room, and ate them whenever the others weren't around.

Dad loved her, she thought as she ate the chocolates; she was special. She bunked off big school – no one cared, anyway – and spent more time in the house, trying to hold back the tide of mess and failing. But she was appreciated, she was loved. Missing her mum, she liked that.

When Mum came home, looking like one of the zombies in those comics Dick loved so much, Dolly was relegated to second place, and Dad didn't pay her much attention at all. So Dolly began to look forward to Mum going away, because when she did, there was Dad with gifts for his special girl: a tortoiseshell comb, a music box with a twirling ballerina inside, more chocolates.

And when Mum wasn't there, when the other kids weren't around, he cuddled her. She liked that, at first.

'Come and sit on my lap, Doll,' he'd say, and she would, to be enfolded in a hug scented with Old Holborn and beer-breath, the unwashed bristly skin of his chin nuzzling into her neck. It was lovely, comforting somehow.

The cuddling became tickling, and play-fighting, and one day down in the sitting room Sam was laughing and Dolly was giggling wildly and they rolled on the grubby carpet, her and her dad, and his hand came to rest on the small barely formed nubbin of her breast. It stayed there, rubbing, and Dolly's giggles faded in her shock and confusion as she felt her nipple harden.

'They're getting bigger,' he said, and she didn't know where to look or what to say, she was that embarrassed. It felt nice, the pressure of his hand there. Nice, and somehow very wrong. Shameful. 'Now look what you've done,' he said, and took her hand and placed it over his trousers. She felt something hard there, and jerked her hand away and sat up.

'You know the facts of life, don't you, Doll?' he asked, sitting there on the floor staring at her. 'You started your bleeds yet?'

Dolly didn't know what to say. Was he telling her she was going to bleed from somewhere, like a nosebleed maybe? Was that somehow connected to what men and women did, how they had babies? The thought made her shudder.

Dad put his hand on her shoulder, slid it up to caress her cheek.

'You know what men and women do together, don't you, Doll?'

She wanted him to shut up. This was horrible. She thought of the angels in the stained-glass window of the little church, the beauty in them, the goodness. This wasn't good. This was awful and evil. She knew it somehow, deep in her soul.

'You know the man puts his thing in the lady?' he said, and he was whispering now, leaning closer, his breath tickling her ear.

Dolly said nothing. She was frozen there, rigid with disgust and disbelief that her dad was saying these shocking things to her. She wanted to stand up, to run, but she was afraid he'd stop her if she moved. Or touch her again in that bad way.

'He puts his thing right in her, and it feels good,' he said, and he was touching her hand, grasping it, bringing it back to that strange hardness at his crotch. Cringing, Dolly tried to pull her hand free, but she couldn't. 'You're my best girl,' he said, and his voice caught as if he was breathless. 'There. You see? It's going to be so good for us.'

So, after Lucy's birthday tea, Dolly almost *ran away. As far as the rec, anyway. But Dad brought her home again, and when she got home there was Mum sitting in her chair at the kitchen table – and Dolly thought that, while Mum was here, she was safe. Dad wouldn't try to do the man-and-woman thing with her, not while Mum was here.*

8

Annie Carter dreamed of him again on the night it all kicked off. Constantine Barolli – the godfather. Him of the all-American tan and the armour-piercing blue eyes, the startling white hair, the sharp suits. It was as if he was there, he was so real. Smiling at her, telling her he loved her.

Once, long ago, Constantine could make anything right. Could make her feel enfolded, protected in the safe cocoon of his love. She turned over in the bed, her eyes opening to blackness, the last insubstantial filaments of the dream floating away into the air around her. Her and Constantine, walking on the beach at Montauk on Long Island, the millionaires' playground, hand in hand. She could feel his strong grip on hers, could see the sun on his hair, the crinkling of the lines around his eyes . . . but it was fading, fading . . . and then it was gone. *He* was gone.

Coming back to full wakefulness, Annie felt the cool blast of the aircon and she shivered, blinking, pulling the sheet over her body. She awoke to blackness, to an empty room, an empty bed. No Max. And now, as the dream ebbed away, as she came back to herself, she thought, *No Constantine either.*

Annie sat up, pushed her hair out of her eyes, clutched at her temples. *Jesus, these dreams.* Recently she'd had them over and over again. She was with Constantine – Constantine as he had been so long ago – they were happy, as they had been all those years ago. It was all so real, *disturbingly* real, and strange – and then she woke up and felt bereft, abandoned, as cold reality crept back in.

And now Max was gone too.

Annie hauled herself up in the bed, reached over, her eyes becoming accustomed to the darkness so that she could see outlines, discern dim shapes. She groped for and found the glass of water on the bedside table, took a sip, and tried not to think about all of it.

But she did.

She couldn't help it. How could she *not* think about it?

Twenty-three years ago, it happened. Constantine had been her second husband. Way back then – believing Max to be dead following a gangland hit – she had married Constantine, and was pregnant with his child when *it* happened. The explosion. And after that? The dreams.

Ah God, those dreams!

At first they had not been sweet, happy dreams like those she was experiencing now. They had been *hideous* dreams, waking nightmares in which Constantine appeared before her in the night, wrecked, smouldering, dead and yet *not* dead, holding out his ruined arms to her. Those dreams had been terrifying. She had wondered if she was losing her mind.

Annie flicked on the bedside light. Light flooded the room and drove back the shadows. Nothing sinister here, she reassured herself, looking around and sternly getting a grip on her wayward imagination. There was no mouldering remnant of a man she had once loved, come back to haunt her.

And Max? What about him?

Annie frowned, her guts tightening with tension. Max was off in Europe on business. He'd taken off a week ago, without any real explanation. *What* business, he had refused to discuss with her, even though she had asked. He had just said he had stuff to do, and left.

Max was a law unto himself. He never explained, never apologized, never kept her in the loop. He had things to do, that was all he'd said, and he'd just . . . gone.

Leaving her here, alone.

Which was OK. She was fine on her own, usually. But not this time.

Because you think he's having an affair, don't you? You don't think he's doing business at all, you think he's doing some tart.

It was true that Max had been cold, distant to her before he left. That had worried her. Usually, if Max had something to say to you, he'd say it to your face, get it off his chest. Not this time, though. This felt *different*. And now she wasn't sleeping well, and she was having these *fucking* dreams. Somehow they made her feel almost that *she* was the unfaithful one. The one who cheated. The very thought made her frown, made a shaft of uneasiness pierce her gut, hard. She had lost Max once, but found him again, and she was so lucky to have done that, so incredibly lucky to have him back in her life after all they had been through. She knew it. She didn't want to lose him again.

But these *dreams*.

They were so vivid, so colourful, so convincing in their reality, that when she was asleep she was actually *there*, once again. In her dreams she was once again Annie Carter-Barolli, a Mafia queen, cosseted and powerful, married to a man whose word was life and death, whose name struck fear in everyone on the streets of New York.

Sighing restlessly, Annie glanced at the alarm clock. Two in the morning, and she was wide awake. There was no chance she'd get back to sleep. She never did, not after one of the dreams. They churned her up, made her think: What the hell is this, have I got a problem here?

Do I need to see a shrink or something?

Around the time of the Montauk explosion, way back in the seventies, she knew she'd had some sort of a breakdown. Was her mind slipping out of her control again, was that what this was all about?

But everything was good now. She and Max were OK. Weren't they? Her daughter Layla and Constantine's son Alberto were cruising the Caribbean islands, touching base rarely, but they were fine. Layla contacted Annie and Max whenever she could, even sometimes arrived unannounced on the doorstep, much to their delight.

Yeah, everything's fine, Annie told herself. But there was that niggling sense of trouble looming she couldn't deny. The dreams. This *feeling* of something bubbling away under the surface, sending up noxious dirty little *plops* now and again to her brain – something bad. Max had been so cold to her recently, looking away from her, leaving her without a kiss, without even a single civil word.

Yeah, you need a shrink, she told herself, almost laughing at such self-indulgent weakness. She was Annie Carter, she was rock-solid, a strong and single-minded woman. So why was she letting her imagination run riot? Yes, she had secrets – *guilty* secrets. And . . . maybe now he had one too.

Shut up, you silly cow, she told herself, lying back down, flicking off the light.

He's at it and you know it, said the voice in her brain. *He's screwing around. He's tired of you. And maybe that's what you deserve because you've been keeping secrets from him,* bad *secrets, and maybe he's found out.*

That was when the phone started to ring in the living room.

9

Sicily, June 1994

Max Carter was fed up to the back teeth when he flew into Catania. He left his two travelling companions at the airport with a promise that he'd be in touch soon, and picked up his hire car. In a sour mood, he then took the coastal road to Syracuse. He checked into the Grand Hotel Villa Politi, and waited. He waited for over a week, eating fine Sicilian food and drinking a little Strega – not too much, he didn't want to risk getting pissed and losing focus – and *still* the woman was dicking him around.

Bloody women.

She was capricious, imperious, but he was used to that in women – he was married to Annie Carter, for God's sake. But *this* woman was proving even more difficult than Annie. It didn't surprise him, given the way the two women had clashed in the past over who was the queen bee. It was a game Annie would always win at, hands down.

First the woman said they would meet in the Politi's lounge. And she didn't show up. One of her lackeys phoned, said she was indisposed, so sorry. Then the venue was rearranged to Taormina, a picturesque town set high on Monte Tauro. They would meet for lunch at the Belmond, overlooking the twin bays below. Come alone, they said.

Max drove there – alone, as agreed – and waited. Another phone call to cancel. She didn't want to meet there after all, she'd changed her mind. She would prefer to see him somewhere away from prying eyes. Her lackey suggested a place not far outside Syracuse, could he do that?

Max gritted his teeth, punched the wall, and said yes, that would be fine. It would *have* to be.

His senses were alert now. Something was wrong with all this. The woman was dancing around him like a ballerina, and he was wondering why. Maybe she had changed her mind about what she'd said when she'd spoken to Gary Tooley on the phone. Maybe she regretted her actions. Maybe she'd been drunk or drugged at the time and in the clear light of day she'd sobered up, come down off cloud nine and reconsidered.

Having *spoken* those words, though, the deed was done. The secret was out. Perhaps she wanted to put it back in its box. And the way to do it? By now he thought he knew the way she might choose. Whatever was going on with her, he meant to find out the truth – and meeting face to face was his best chance of doing that, even if without his back-up he risked ending up dead. If only the devious bitch would actually turn up one of these days.

In his hotel room on the morning of this *new* meeting, he got up, showered, called the hotel where his men were staying and told them what was going on.

'You need us up there?' asked the one who picked up.

'No,' said Max. 'But be ready. I'll call. Looks like this is it, finally.'

He dressed in a cool white linen shirt, cream cords, brown loafers; then he slipped on his gold ring with the lapis lazuli square set into it, added a Rolex and a couple of other items and looked in the mirror, running a hand through his thick, black and slightly too long hair to tame it into shape. He could almost pass for a Sicilian himself; his old mum Queenie had always called him her 'little Italian'. He was powerfully built and tanned, with a piratical hook of a nose and deep, dark navy-blue eyes.

The heat was climbing and the sun was pouring molten lava down upon his bare head as he walked out into a perfect Sicilian day and got into his car. Max hated hats. He liked the sun in his eyes and the wind at his back. He started the engine and drove up the dusty track to the agreed meeting-place, passing tiny small-windowed white villas, uniform rows of vines, olive groves. Potato-shaped peasant women dressed in black were sitting outside their doors, lemon trees overhanging the walls of their houses, skinny dogs wandering free in the street.

He wound down the window and let the hot air blow through, thinking of Annie, who would probably be asleep right now in their villa up near Prospect on Barbados. It was a peaceful place, set above a thin crescent of white sandy beach, away from the luxury hotel complexes and shaded with palms and manchineel trees. They both loved it there. But *this* was more important. This would have to be addressed before it drove him stark staring mad.

The *suspicions*.

Had his wife betrayed him?

Everything had been fine until the woman called the Blue Parrot club in London and talked to Gary Tooley. Gary had relayed the news to him. Max hadn't *asked* for any of this. But he had it. And ever since Gary had passed on the woman's words, he'd been having sleepless nights, tormented days. He thought that it couldn't be true, could not be possible. But . . . *what if it was*?

That nagged at him, wouldn't let him rest. If it was true and not the ramblings of a drunkard or a fool or a crazed cow off her head on nose candy, then there would be big trouble and he was going to kill some cunt. But he could handle trouble. It was uncertainty that sent him mental.

He drove, trying to clear his mind, determined not to let the fury take hold again, not to let it all pile in on him and fog his brain. He drove past the lines of olive trees heavy with fruit, past thin goats and their kids, past plodding donkeys laden with hay coming back with their owners from the parched yellow fields.

Finally he reached the place she had chosen.

It was a disused amphitheatre, a crumbling old wreck well off the tourist trails, built by the Greeks or the Romans – he didn't know which and he didn't care. He got out of the car, hearing nothing but the silence of the hills and the mad chirruping of the crickets, seeing nothing but dust and heat-haze and the purple-sloped hugeness of Etna lowering over the scene. No car here, not yet.

He wasn't early.

He looked at his watch.

He was on time.

A hard sigh escaped him. She wasn't going to show today, either. He knew it. Swearing, the dust-swirling wind buffeting him, he strolled off toward the remains of the theatre, entering the sheltered boiler-room heat of the big sand-covered circular arena where once life and death had been played out for real. Max walked out to the centre, under the full super-heated blaze of the Sicilian sun, and looked around.

In the echoing silence he could imagine the ancient crowds up on the stands, howling for blood; huge lions imported from Africa and starved to make them even more ferocious running loose; gladiators in body armour and fearsomely crafted helmets and shields wielding maces and swords, battling it out with the big cats and each other.

That world was gone, but close your eyes and you could see it, taste it, almost *hear* it. He could still feel danger in this place, and bloodshed, and tragedy. It was so quiet here; eerie.

Good place to get rid of someone, he thought. No one ever came up here. It was the perfect spot to dispose of an enemy, leave them for the crows to dine out on.

Then he heard the car. He looked in the direction of the entrance where he'd come into the arena and saw the plume of dust as a motor climbed the hill toward it.

At last.

She was coming.

Game on, he thought, and his heart started to beat more quickly.

10

Across the other side of the Atlantic Ocean, Annie's heart was beating quickly too. She grabbed her robe, threw it on. Ran through to the living room and snatched up the phone. 'Yes?' she said.

It couldn't be good news. Not at this hour. Or maybe she was just panicking over nothing, coming out of that stupid damned recurring Constantine dream all hyped-up with worry when there was no reason to be. Maybe it was Max phoning home, forgetting the time differential. Time was a flexible thing in Max's world. He was late for everything. It was a standing joke between them.

Her husband was powerful, tough, independent. He was still essentially the man he had been back in the sixties, when he had run a lucrative protection racket around the East End. He'd made a fortune, and he'd been bright enough to never get caught doing it.

That was it. This was Max, calling home. Suddenly she felt hopeful.

'Max?' she asked. She could hear breathing on the line. 'That you?'

'Mrs C?' asked a male voice.

Not Max then. Annie felt her spirits droop. 'Who's this?'

'It's Tony.'

She clutched a hand to her brow and closed her eyes.

She had *hoped* it would be Max, even if he had ballsed up the times. When he'd left, he'd been . . . well, so *odd*. Removed from her. She didn't like that. It made her very anxious.

'Tone?' Into Annie's mind flashed an image: big eighteen-stone bruiser Tony, bald, besuited and with two gold crucifixes, one in each cauliflower ear.

Tony had driven Max around the London streets for a long time, and then her; he was a dedicated member of the Carter team, which had evolved over the years so that now it was almost entirely legitimate. Once, things had been different: in the sixties, Max Carter and his boys had rivalled the Krays for sheer honest-to-God fear factor. Back then, big gangs had owned the streets – the Frasers and the Richardsons from South London, the Regans from the west, the Foremans from Battersea, the Nashes from the Angel, while the Krays held Bethnal Green and the Carter boys had Bow and a bit of Limehouse.

Slowly, things had changed, though; now the Carter operation was clubs and security, and nearly 100 per cent straight. *Nearly*. But Max was still the boss, and Max was always a wild card; unpredictable. This latest departure was a classic example; she didn't know what the hell he was up to.

He's having an affair, you silly bitch. Because he knows. He's found you out and he's having a revenge fuck. He's sticking it to someone new and – oh yeah – someone younger.

'What you phoning for at this hour? It's two o'clock here,' she asked Tony.

'Mrs C . . .' Tony started, then hesitated. 'Is Mr Carter there?'

'No, he's not.' Annie frowned. 'What's up, Tone? What is it?'

'I got bad news for you, I'm sorry.'

Annie slumped down on to the sofa. Outside, she could hear the faint dull rhythmic roar of the ocean, pounding up on to the warm white sands of the beach below the villa. Her heart clenched with fear. *Max?* she thought.

'Tell me,' she said.

'It's Dolly, Mrs C.'

'Doll? What about her?'

'I'm sorry,' he said. 'She's dead.'

11

Max watched as the man – who was short but powerful-looking, dark-skinned and wearing a cream Panama hat – unloaded the woman from the car.

Unload was the word. Max had expected that she might be frail, but there was this whole business going on, the man taking the wheelchair out of the back of the car, bringing it to the front passenger door, nearly *hauling* the woman into it. Then he backed the chair up, closed the door, fussed over her, settled her comfortably, draped a pale-blue blanket over her lap to cover her bony knees and her bright red pleated skirt; then he pushed the wheelchair containing the bent old woman toward the arena where Max stood waiting.

Max watched them coming, watched the dust-devils whirl around them, the man and the woman in the wheelchair. They vanished into the deep shade of the entrance, then reappeared into the vivid sunlight in the centre of this decrepit old place. The woman was wearing a huge broad-brimmed straw hat, pulled low over her face. Her hands were tucked in under the blanket, and her feet were big, clad in sparkling white trainers.

They approached slowly, and man and chair came to a halt six feet from where Max stood waiting.

The man gave a grin and said: 'Mr Carter?'

Max nodded slowly.

'I am Antonio, I will interpret for Miss Barolli,' said the man, and he reached inside his shirt.

Max dived to one side and a spring-loaded knife concealed in his shirt sleeve dropped into his hand. He threw it as Antonio pulled the gun out, and the knife hit the man's wrist with a hollow *thunk*. Antonio let out a high shriek of pain and shock and the gun fell into the dust. He collapsed to his knees on the ground, clutching at his bleeding wrist with the knife deeply embedded there. Max moved forward quickly and kicked Antonio under the chin, sending him flying backward. Max was on him in an instant, but he was out of it, unconscious. Max yanked his knife loose, ignoring the sudden arterial spurt of bright crimson blood, and turned to the wheelchair. Its occupant was struggling upward, tossing aside the blanket.

Max came up behind the chair and rammed the bloody knife against its occupant's throat.

'Hold it,' he said, pressing hard, and the woman in the chair froze, held her hands up. Max pulled off the hat to reveal a man's haircut, and threw it aside. There was a gun in the 'old woman's' lap, which had been hidden beneath the blanket.

'Gina Barolli don't need an interpreter,' said Max. 'She speaks perfect English. I know that because I've met her before. And you, my friend, are not Gina Barolli. And you've got bloody big feet for a woman, haven't you.' Max pressed harder with the knife. 'In fact, you're a bloke. Enough of this fucking around. Tell me where she is, or I'm going to cut you a new arsehole.'

The man started babbling in a thick Sicilian dialect. *This* one maybe did need an interpreter.

'Shut up,' snapped Max. 'Speak English.'

More Sicilian.

'Mate, you're going to lose a lot of bits if this goes on,' said Max. 'Now come on. It's an easy question. Where is Gina Barolli?'

And then the man did a surprising thing; he lifted the gun in his lap . . .

'Don't,' said Max, pressing harder with the knife. A thick thread of wet red trickled down on to the baby-blue blanket.

The man ignored Max. He raised the gun to his temple, crossed himself, and blew his own brains out.

12

'What did you just say?' Annie Carter slumped down into an armchair, still clutching the phone in her hand.

'Dolly's dead, Mrs C. I'm sorry,' said Tony's voice.

For a second Annie had a wild hope that maybe *this* was all part of a damned dream – that she was still asleep, that this wasn't real. But the sound of the waves on the shore was real enough. The sadness in Tony's voice was real, too. Terribly, horribly real.

Annie gulped. Her mouth was dry and she had trouble getting the words out. 'What happened?' she asked faintly.

She thought he would say *heart attack*. Something sudden, something unexpected like that. Dolly was a fit middle-aged woman. But shit happened; Annie knew it.

Instead, he said: 'She was shot. Killed. In the flat over the Palermo.'

Annie stared numbly at the phone. She couldn't believe what she was hearing. Dolly, *shot*?

'I'm sorry,' said Tony again when Annie said nothing.

'What . . .?' Annie croaked. She coughed, cleared her throat, tried again. 'What the hell do you mean, she was shot? Who shot her?'

'We don't know. Pete on the bar came into work and she hadn't opened up. He thought that was strange – you know what she's like, always up and at 'em . . .'

Annie knew. Dolly was a morning person; she was not. Back in the day when they'd both lived at Aunt Celia's place in Limehouse, there Dolly would be, irritating as hell, whistling at seven o'clock in the morning while everyone else nursed sore heads and growled at each other.

'. . . He used his own main door key, went up to the flat and there she was. Dead.'

Annie still couldn't take it in. *Dolly*. For God's sake. She thought of her friend – her oldest, dearest friend – full of life and coarse jokes. Once the roughest of rough brasses, Dolly Farrell had evolved over the years into a very efficient club manager, a pivotal member of the Carter workforce.

And now Tony was telling her that she was *dead*? That someone had *killed* her?

'Why would anyone want to hurt Doll?' she asked, pulling a shaking hand through her hair. Across the room she could see herself reflected in a big driftwood-edged mirror that she'd picked up on a trip to the market with Max – a lone woman in a red silk robe, slumped in the seat as though she'd just been knocked sideways. Her hair was mussed up from sleep, her tanned face was grey-tinged as the shock set in, her dark green eyes were shadowed with pain.

'I don't know. I really don't,' he said.

'The police . . . ?' she asked.

'They've been. Done their stuff. Dabs. Pictures. The usual.'

'When did it happen?'

'Thursday night.'

'It's Saturday. Why the fuck didn't you call me sooner?' Now anger was overriding the anguish.

'What could you have done?' Tony was silent for a beat. Then he said: 'Mr Carter's not there with you?'

'No. He's not.' But she was used to coping without help,

even without hope. *Dig deep and stand alone*, that was her motto in life. So far, it had served her well. She had come through storms before, had soaked it all up and she was still standing. But this . . . this was the bitterest of blows.

'Have the Bill got any leads?' she asked, thinking, *Not Dolly, no, make this be a bad dream, please* . . .

'That's what I'm asking our tame coppers, right now. Not getting any answers yet, but I'll keep asking.'

'Who the hell would *do* this?' said Annie, suddenly springing to her feet, clutching at her head. 'What had she— I mean, what's been happening with her? Was there a man involved with her, anything like that?'

Even as she said it, Annie thought that it was a stupid question. Dolly had never, to her knowledge, had much time for men. She had a troubled past, and Annie knew that men had been a large part of that trouble. So far as she knew, her friend had been happiest living a celibate life.

'I'm asking the questions. I thought of that. But you know Dolly. Don't seem like her style somehow.'

Annie was pacing around, pulling the phone cord along with her. 'What the *fuck*?' she raged, feeling helpless, thinking that this couldn't be happening.

'You want me to do anything?' asked Tony.

Annie was having flashbacks. Dolly drinking gin and tonic in the bar, laughing at some off-colour joke one of the punters had told. Dolly hauling Annie's arse out of bed after she'd split from Max back in 1980, pulling her back to her feet with the force of her will, *making* her carry on even when she didn't want to. She felt her eyes fill with hot, painful tears – and she *never* cried. But this was Dolly. Dolly was her best mate. And now . . . oh fuck, how could this be? – Dolly was *dead*.

Annie blinked hard, gulping back her tears until all she

felt was that cleansing rage again. She kicked the coffee table, hard. Then again. Then again. Shells skidded over the surface and dropped to the floor. Anger rushed through her in an unstoppable tide. Whoever did this, they were *finished*. She would see to it.

When she spoke again, her voice was harder, steadier. 'Ask the questions, Tone. Ask as many as you can. See nobody rests. Keep doing what you're doing.'

There was a silence at the other end of the phone, all those thousands of miles away, in London. Then he said: 'What you going to do?'

Annie drew in a breath.

Composed herself.

'I'm coming back,' she said.

13

For long moments after the man in the wheelchair killed himself, Max stood there in awe. He'd heard of it, but never seen it up close and personal. *This* was the type of loyalty these people commanded, with their *omerta*, their code of endless silence. To death and beyond.

He stared down at the corpse still half-propped in the chair, leaning way over to the left. The bullet had been high-calibre, and there was a lot of damage; death had been a certainty, no chances taken. Blood and bone and brain matter had spewed out of the shattered skull in a fountain. Rather than talk and disgrace himself, betray the Mafia code he'd sworn to uphold, the man had taken his own life.

Crazy bastards, thought Max as he took wheelchair man's gun.

But you had to admire them somehow.

Antonio was moaning now, starting to come round.

Max forgot wheelchair man and walked over to where Antonio lay bleeding on the ground. He picked up his gun, tucked it into the waistband of his trousers with the other man's gun. Knife in hand, he approached the man and looked down at him.

Antonio stirred, his eyes flickering open. Crying out in

pain, he put his right hand over his left wrist, where the blood was still pumping out.

Max poked him with a toe and Antonio stared up at him with the pain-warped ferocity of a rabid dog.

'My friend,' said Max, 'you're going to bleed out in about forty minutes. You understand me, yeah? Because you were going to be the interpreter for that sack of bones in the wheelchair. Right?'

The man said nothing. His eyes flicked sideways, took in his dead companion slumped over in the chair, then back to the man standing over him.

'Unless I get you to some help, you're going to die,' said Max. Judging by the way the other one had reacted, he didn't hold out a lot of hope for this plan, but he had to try. 'So tell me where Gina Barolli is, and you'll get it.'

The man spat at Max.

'That's not nice,' said Max, and put his foot hard on the place where the blood was spurting out. The man on the ground shrieked.

'Tell me,' said Max.

The man writhed and cursed in Sicilian.

'Don't fuck me around,' Max advised him. 'Speak English. Tell me where she is.'

'She's in hell and so will you be soon,' he sobbed.

'She's not in hell,' said Max. 'She's been making phone calls, saying things. And I'm here to see her and find out what she's on about. Only she never shows, does she. Instead, she sends you two clowns – one dressed up like a pantomime dame and you without a fucking clue – to finish me off. Now why would she do that?'

Antonio said nothing.

'This is going to get very painful for you if you don't start talking,' Max warned with a sigh. 'I'm going to see

Gina Barolli, one way or the other. So you may as well make this easy for yourself.'

'Fuck *you!*' shouted Antonio.

Max leaned down over the man and opened up his other wrist, too. The man screamed like a little girl as blood spurted. 'Now look. You've got trouble. Twenty minutes tops, I'd say. People can live after this. If they get the right medical stuff done to them, and quick. But leave it too late, and you know what? Even in this hot sun, you're soon going to start feeling very cold. First comes the shivers, and then you're weak and disorientated, and then you pass out and the next thing is – you're dead.'

'Jesus . . .' the man wept, rolling from side to side while the life's blood flooded out of him and was sucked up by the sand.

'It don't have to be that way, though,' said Max. 'Tell me where Gina Barolli is, and help's on its way.' Max frowned. 'Think I can do a bit of first aid, patch you up good enough to get you to the hospital. If you talk, that is. If you don't, forget it.'

The man's dark eyes were glaring up into Max's. 'I will *never* talk,' he said.

'Now see, that's annoying,' said Max, wondering what a Sicilian male would place more value on than loyalty. He thought he knew. He leaned down and unzipped the man's fly.

'What are you—' the man babbled, bleeding, squirming.

'What, you're like your mate in the wheelchair? You're prepared to die to keep her secret?' asked Max. 'Then you're going to arrive in hell minus your prick, you cunt. Now talk, or things get ugly. That's a promise.'

14

Oh, the fucking rain. How could she have forgotten about the rain? And the grey skies. A year in Barbados, and now Annie Carter's default setting was blue skies, white sand, vivid sunshine. *This* was strange to her, but the damp air and the cool wind reminded her forcibly that this was home, where she was born, where she had spent most of her life. London. Traffic swooshing by in the downpour as she sat in the taxi from the airport. Grimy buildings looming like canyons overhead as the car edged along in thick traffic, the windscreen wipers sweeping back and forth in a sleep-inducing rhythm.

She'd love to sleep. She hadn't slept on the plane, although she'd tried. Her brain just kept churning over what Tony had told her on the phone the day before yesterday – that Dolly was gone, lost to her, dead and never to return.

It choked her up, every time she thought about it.

And she thought about it all the time.

She hadn't even spoken to Dolly recently. They called each other maybe once a month, just for a chat. Annie would ask how the business was going, and Dolly would always say fine and tell her what the girls in the club had been getting up to. There was always some funny story with one of the punters, Annie always put the phone down laughing.

The last time they'd spoken had been about a fortnight ago, and then there had been no suggestion that anything was wrong, and Annie had been blissfully unaware that that was the last time she would ever talk to her friend.

She just wished that she had been able to speak to Max before she left Prospect. She'd left him a note in their usual place, told the maid where she was going, and to tell him when he got back, but . . . she'd really needed him there when she got that awful news. And as usual he was away, busy, doing something that didn't concern her.

A spasm of hurt lanced her as she thought about that. He was so secretive these days and she was thinking more and more . . . trying not to, but she was thinking that her gut feeling was right, that he was having an affair. Why else would he not tell her what he was doing, where he was going?

She was trying not to be all little-wifey and clingy and *needy* about this, but for God's sake, he never told her anything! So yes, she felt hurt. And angry. And guilty and afraid, because she had secrets of her own. And on top of all that, now she had this to deal with – and where was he?

He's fucking another woman . . .

Stop it!

Her mind was all over the place. Even things that should have been straightforward, like deciding where she was going to stay in London, had her going round in circles. The Holland Park house was standing empty, closed up, unstaffed and unwelcoming since Rosa, her old house-keeper, had retired. The Carter firm still owned the three nightclubs – the Palermo Lounge, the Blue Parrot and the Shalimar – and each had a flat above the premises. But Annie didn't feel strong enough to go near the Palermo, to set foot in the place where Dolly had been murdered – not yet, at any rate. Besides, the Bill would have the flat cordoned off as a crime scene; most likely they'd have shut down the club too.

The Blue Parrot was being run by Gary Tooley, a tall blond vicious man who'd been one of Max's most trusted foot soldiers for years and who cheerfully hated Annie's guts, so he wouldn't be putting out the bunting for her anytime soon. She didn't like Gary, and when he phoned Max in Barbados she always left the room. And she'd noticed of late that after these calls Max was always cold and uncommunicative toward her. But then, Gary had never missed a chance to put the knife in where she was concerned. He was always ready to drip poison in Max's ear about her.

Having ruled out Holland Park, the Palermo and the Blue Parrot, she'd booked herself into a hotel. Only now that she was back in London and the reality of Dolly's death was beginning to sink in, the last thing she wanted was to be all on her own in a hotel room. For a moment she considered going to stay with her sister Ruthie in Richmond, but then dismissed the idea. Ever since they'd been kids their relationship had always been difficult, edgy.

In the end she'd told the cab driver to forget about the hotel and take her to the Shalimar club instead. First things first: she needed to touch base with Ellie, who together with her husband Chris Brown, ran things at the club. Ellie had been Dolly's friend too. Once, she'd been a working girl just like Dolly, and they'd lived together at Aunt Celia's Limehouse knocking shop. They'd both worked for Celia, and then for Annie. Ellie would understand how devastated Annie was feeling.

'Here we are then,' said the driver, pulling into the kerb outside the Shalimar. He was a big bluff Cockney in a red anorak who'd chatted to her all the way from the airport. She couldn't remember a single word he'd said, and she didn't know what she'd said back to him either. Her mind was fogged with grief and weariness.

Annie paid him and got out into the rain, dragging her case and hand luggage with her. The cab pulled away. Almost instantly she was drenched, and she stood there with the cold rain battering down on her upturned face, looking up at the Shalimar sign, grey now in the noonday gloom, all its bright red neon lights turned off. She looked up and down the soaked street, traffic nudging along, jostling pedestrians with umbrellas held low against the gusting downpour, trying to avoid the puddles on the glimmering wet pavement. For better or worse, she was home.

'Annie?' asked a female voice.

Annie turned, and there was podgy, dark-haired Ellie, standing in the rain clutching a pint of milk, her neat two-piece burgundy suit darkened with moisture around her shoulders. Dolly, Ellie and Annie – over the years they had become a trio of mutual cheerleaders. Now, one of them was gone. Annie watched as Ellie's face crumpled.

'Christ,' said Ellie, and threw herself sobbing into Annie's arms. 'Can you believe it?' she choked out. 'Dolly!'

Annie hugged her tight in the pouring rain.

15

Gina Barolli looked out of the window and saw the car coming up the drive toward the big sprawling villa, churning up a yellow dust-cloud as it came.

So it was done. It was put right.

Two of their best had gone to correct the mistake she had made; she couldn't remember their names and that was annoying, but they had gone, she *knew* that, and she knew that everyone was very agitated and angry about it all.

She couldn't remember what her mistake had been.

She knew she'd made it, yes of course she did, she wasn't a *fool*, even if the people here treated her like one sometimes. Shouting at her, saying why did she do that, why did she make these stupid mistakes?

Ah, none of it mattered now anyway. The car was coming, and she craned out of her wheelchair, using the windowsill as a support, to see it pull in at the front of the building where the lavender grew thick and violet-blue, heavy with bees and a delicious fragrance. A man got out, black-haired, darkly tanned. She didn't recognize him and that puzzled her. Where were the other people, *her* people? He looked like one of the Cosa Nostra, the brotherhood; but she didn't know him. Two more men followed – bigger, bulkier men than the first one. She didn't recognize them, either.

Or . . . she didn't *think* so.

Of course, sometimes nowadays she didn't know *any-body*, and that irritated her; so perhaps he was one of hers after all. Who knew?

God, old age was a curse; things slipped away from you – your strength, your health, even your mind, until finally what was left? Nothing except a pile of bones in a casket. But – and now Gina smiled to herself, a secret, triumphant smile – sometimes you could cheat old age. Sometimes you could even cheat *death*.

Then the smile faded as she remembered. The *mistakes*. Oh yes. Lots of them. Her big, dreadful mistakes. Suddenly she grew agitated, trembling, trying to hoist herself from the chair. No, perhaps the man wasn't one of her own. Now she remembered what had been happening but it was all a jumble, none of it clear. She'd been phoning someone in London. She knew she had. But who? She couldn't remember. And then this *man* had started calling the number she'd left – *this* number, and she had said she would meet, talk. She'd been putting him off because she had no idea what this was all about, but she knew it couldn't be good.

The only thing she remembered clearly was the furious reaction when they found out what she'd done. She'd heard shouting outside her room and women sobbing – someone calling the nurses silly bitches, demanding to know why they hadn't done as they'd been *told* and kept her away from the house phones, telling them they were fired. But when they came in to see her, their voices were calm, telling her what to do. Stall him some more, this Max Carter person.

That was his name. Max Carter. She'd remembered!

So she'd stalled him. Told him she would meet him to

discuss it here, then here, then here. And she hadn't shown up, and then Antonio . . .

She'd remembered that too! Antonio!

Antonio had said, We will sort this, once and for all. We will go out, Bruto and me, and Bruto will pretend to be poor old Gina in her wheelchair, and all will be well. Tell him the old amphitheatre, and we will finish him there, Antonio told her, his voice as patient and soothing as if he was talking to a naughty child. Yes, she had made some silly mistakes, maybe a *lot* of them, but there was nothing too impossible to sort out. *He* was going to sort it.

Gina frowned as she heard doors slamming downstairs, raised voices, the sounds of a struggle, things crashing to the ground. Anxiously she twisted around in the chair to look at the open doorway leading out into the hall. She tried to get up from her chair – she hated the thing, she spent so many hours confined to it – but she was too weak. With her skinny, shaking, blue-veined hands she fumbled with the chair's wheels, and managed to turn it so that she was facing the door.

'Fidelia!' she called in her querulous voice, a voice that had once made people snap to attention. Once she had been respected, even feared, because of her family connections. Not any more.

Fidelia didn't come.

Suddenly, all was deathly quiet in the villa. Stillness. Silence. And then she heard it. The stealthy tread of footsteps approaching. Frozen there, her heart stuttering in her chest, she clutched at the blanket over her knees and anxiously watched the open door.

'Fidelia?' she called again, quieter, her voice trembling.

Then a man stepped into the doorway. He was carrying a gun. He was compact, muscular, with black hair and dark navy-blue eyes. He was aiming the gun steadily, straight at her. As he moved, he left faint bloody footprints on the marble floor. Two other men appeared behind him, both of them armed, both of them looking dangerous.

'Who are you?' she asked the one in front, her voice hardly more than a whisper.

'I'm Max Carter,' said the man, coming into the room. 'You wanted to speak to me, didn't you.'

'No, I . . . it was a mistake. That's all.' She looked bewildered, then she remembered. A faltering smile lifted her lips back from her yellowing teeth. 'Antonio has put it right.'

'No. He hasn't. Antonio's in the hospital,' he said.

Gina said nothing. If I say nothing, she thought, then I can't do anything wrong. I can't make another *mistake*. This mistake was clearly a bad one, far worse than everyone had previously thought. Antonio was in the hospital. For a moment, groping around in her mind, she couldn't remember who Antonio *was*, and then she had it. Antonio was the one who had got very angry with her. Antonio was the one who said he'd put it right.

Max stepped further into the luxuriously appointed and sunlit room. He didn't lower the gun. He was looking at a helpless, confused old lady in a wheelchair, but seeing something very different: the latent, deadly power of the Mafia. The old woman had secrets and in her confused state she had spilled them – and those secrets were dire enough to make her send two men to kill him so that they would never be revealed.

He moved closer to where Gina sat. Leaning in, he grabbed the blanket and threw it aside. Helpless old woman or not, he wasn't taking any chances. But there was no weapon hidden there; no knife, no gun. He knew these people were dangerous, unpredictable, like scorpions. The sting was in the tail, and the tail would strike when you least expected it.

Max stepped back again, watching her like a hawk. She looked bewildered, but it could be an act; he didn't trust it. He put himself out of kicking distance, and placed himself so that he could watch her and at the same time not block his back-up's view from the open doorway.

'Tell me your name,' he said.

'My name . . . ?' she echoed faintly. Gina stiffened. A shot of pain, a bolt of white heat, went through her chest and she put a shaking hand there.

'Yeah. I want to hear you say it.'

'My name . . .' For another of those frustrating, maddening moments she couldn't remember. It would come to her. Be calm, be calm . . . but how *could* she be calm when this man, this stranger and these other men were here, pointing guns at her head? And this pain! Worse than any she'd had before, it was nagging, growing, spreading.

But was the man a stranger, really? She seemed to know his face, his manner. And the name. She felt she knew that, too. But she could be wrong. She was wrong about so much, these days.

The name.

Her name.

All at once, she had it. 'I am Gina Barolli,' she said, grimacing. The pain was increasing. Her left arm was beginning to tingle.

Max was nodding. 'You may not remember me, Miss Barolli, but I remember you.'

'Do you?' For a moment she looked pathetically hopeful. Then she winced.

Is she ill? wondered Max. *Or just bluffing?*

'Yeah, I do. You're Constantine Barolli's sister.'

16

Up in the kitchen over the Shalimar, all was quiet except for the radio playing; the girls weren't in yet to get ready for the evening's trade.

'Chris is down the wholesaler's,' said Ellie, taking the teapot off the dresser, which was loaded, as always, with her 'crystals' as she called them; gemstones and glassware fashioned into dainty swans, penguins, dragons. She made the tea and put the pot and two bone-china cups on the table. 'Take the weight off, Annie,' she said, and Annie sat down and watched as Ellie took a seat opposite and poured the tea out.

'This is awful,' Annie said, voicing what they were both thinking. 'I can't believe it.'

Midway through pouring the tea, Ellie slapped the pot down on the table and put her head in her hands. 'Shit,' she muttered, and groped for a hankie, found it. Red-faced, eyes wet, she blew her nose hard, tucked the hankie back in her pocket and looked at Annie.

'Dolly! Why, for God's sake? What did she ever do to anybody?' Ellie gasped out.

Annie reached for her hand and patted it. 'I don't know. Have the police been here yet? Have they asked you anything?'

Ellie shook her head. With unsteady hands she picked

up the pot and took another stab at it. This time, she got the tea into the cups. Slopped in milk. Pushed one cup across to Annie.

'Thanks.'

The news came on the radio. Ellie jumped to her feet, went over to it, turned it off.

'They keep talking about it. It's horrible. It was such a *shock*,' she said, and her voice was steadier. Then she looked at Annie. 'I thought Mr Carter would come with you. Being as it's Dolly, being as it's such a terrible thing to have happened.'

'He's away. Busy,' said Annie.

Yeah, busy doing what? drifted through her brain. Didn't they say you should always trust your gut feelings? But that he was having an affair – *that* was too horrible, too devastating, to take in.

But it's possible, yes?

Yeah, it was. Max was a handsome man, charismatic; he drew women to him. Annie had seen it happen. Had actually *seen* the cheeky cows ignore her, standing right there beside him, and zoom in on him like a missile. She had even laughed about it to herself, secure in the knowledge that Max would never stray. But now, well, who knew? She was eleven years younger than him, but she was in her forties now, and loads of wealthy men in their fifties went for girls half their age. Young and nubile, the girls flattered them and looked so good as the men flaunted them in front of their jealous friends.

He wouldn't be the first man to do it, and he certainly wouldn't be the last. All those secret trips to Europe, those covert chats to Gary on the phone . . . But maybe some of those calls hadn't been from Gary at all. The way he'd pulled away from her, detached from her, getting up and going into another room, closing the door, talking low. And afterwards, he'd been different with her, there was no denying it. She wasn't imagining it; he'd been cold to her.

So was he really *talking to Gary?*

Or was he talking to some other woman?

'Annie?' said Ellie, seeing she was miles away.

'Yeah,' said Annie, coming back to the here and now. She took a swig of the tea, picturing the girl. She'd be a brunette, twenty-ish; keen-eyed and sniffing out wealth, power . . . and of course she would be gorgeous. Annie had seen it all before. The young Eurasian beauty on the arm of a decrepit but wealthy-looking old man in Kingstown. The glamorous blonde flirting with a man twenty-five years her senior in the Sandy Lane restaurant. She and Max had been sitting at the next table, had even smiled at each other, sharing the unspoken thought: *there it is again*. Blondes had never done it for Max. No, it would be a brunette. Like her, only a lot younger. The pain of it clamped at her guts, made her feel sick.

'You know what?' Ellie was saying, hands clasped around the teacup as if trying to get them warm. 'I spoke to Doll last Monday on the phone. We were going to meet up next Thursday at the Ritz, our usual thing.'

Annie nodded: she knew. Tea at the Ritz. Once, she had regularly joined them there.

'Now she'll never make it,' said Ellie, her face dissolving into tears again. 'Sorry,' she muttered, going to the work-top and tearing off a hank of kitchen roll. She dabbed at her eyes and blew her nose, chucked the tissue into the bin. She came back to the table and sat down with a shuddering sigh, then stared at Annie with reddened eyes. Ellie's mascara was all down her cheeks, she looked a mess.

'Who the fuck would do a thing like that?' asked Ellie. It was a howl of protest.

'She was shot, Tone said when he called me,' said Annie, swallowing past a painful lump in her throat.

'That's right. She was shot. God, poor Dolly.' Ellie's eyes were bright with tears. She gulped and stared at Annie's face. 'I thought Tone would've collected you from the airport. You came in a cab.'

Annie shook her head, trying to think past this huge obstacle in her brain. *Dolly was dead.* Truth was, she'd been so devastated by what Tony had told her on the phone that she hadn't thought to mention transport to him, and he hadn't offered. Which, now she thought about it, was odd. Usually, Tone was on the ball with such things. But then, he'd had a shock too.

'You got a spare bed, Ellie?' she asked. She felt weary, right through to the bone.

There was a flicker of hesitation before Ellie recovered herself and said, 'Course. There's always a place for you here.'

Of course there was. Annie was the boss's wife, after all. Right now, she was wondering how much longer that was going to be the case. It made her feel sad, hurt, angry. She and Max had been through so much, and she didn't want it to end this way, with him having a hole-in-the-corner affair and her having to cope all alone again.

She *loved* him. Worshipped the bones of him.

She drank the tea and let out a heartfelt sigh. 'I need a kip. After that, maybe this is going to make some kind of sense.'

But I doubt it, she thought.

'Come on, I'll show you to your room,' said Ellie, standing up. She paused there, clutching at the kitchen chair. Her tear-reddened hazel eyes met Annie's. 'They'll find out who did it, though, won't they? The Bill, I mean,' said Ellie. 'They've *got* to.'

Annie nodded. 'They will,' she said.

Or I will, she added to herself.

17

'I do remember you,' said Gina Barolli, her face screwed up, her hand still clutched to her scrawny chest.

Max moved a little closer – not *too* close – and he kept the gun trained on her.

Gina's mouth trembled. The pain was bad, and growing. Then she said: 'You're the security man. In London. You called yourself Mark something then. You were guarding *her.*'

Max stared at her, wondering at her thought processes. So she remembered that time after Constantine's death, when Annie had moved back to London to escape the poisonous influence of his eldest son Lucco. But it seemed she didn't remember what had happened later, in New York, when Max's true identity had been revealed and Alberto, Constantine's youngest son, had taken over the reins as the godfather.

'Where is Fidelia? And where is Antonio?' Gina demanded.

'Fidelia's tied up right now,' said Max. 'And I told you. Antonio's in the hospital. He had an accident. You've been phoning one of my clubs in London, the Blue Parrot, talking about your brother.'

Had she? Gina couldn't remember doing that, and if she had she ought to be *ashamed*, because that was a stupid thing to do, and dangerous. *Omerta* demanded her silence. She knew that. She had lived by that code all her life.

'I didn't phone anyone,' she said, her lips trembling as the pain clamped her chest tight again.

'Yeah, you did.' Max glanced back at the two men standing silent, watching, from the doorway. 'Wait outside. Close the door,' he said, then returned his attention to Gina as they obeyed. 'You spoke to Gary Tooley and you said something very interesting. You said that my wife ain't my wife at all. You said that she's still married to your brother, Constantine.'

'That's right.' Gina's chin set suddenly in a stubborn line. 'That's the truth.'

'That *ain't* the truth,' said Max. 'Because Constantine is dead. He died in an explosion years ago, in Montauk.'

Gina raised a trembling hand to her brow, closed her eyes. Then she opened them and stared malevolently at Max. 'How dare you come here. Constantine will see to you, my friend. You can be very sure of that.'

'That would be a hell of a trick. The bastard's dead in a box in a New York cemetery.'

Suddenly Gina was clutching harder at her chest. 'Can you fetch Fidelia . . . ?' she said, her voice little more than a whisper.

Max moved in a little. 'What is it?'

'Get Fidelia. I feel . . .'

The only sound in the room for long moments was Gina's laboured breathing. She was slumped further over in her chair now, holding her chest. All at once, huge globs of sweat were popping out on her face.

Christ, she's not faking it.

Max ran to her chair and pulled her upright.

'Gina? Miss Barolli? Come on, you old fuck, don't

bloody die on me now!' He patted her thin cheeks, looked at the blue-tinged lips and thought, *Shit, that looks bad.*

Her eyes were flickering closed and her brow was soaking wet and creased with pain. Then the eyes, dark and hate-filled, fastened on his and she spat at him. He pulled his head away sharply, as if drawing back from a striking snake, and now she was *smiling* although he could see she was in agony.

'She's not your wife at all,' she gasped out, having to pause between each word to catch her faltering breath. 'She's his. She has always been . . . she will always be . . . *his.*'

Max put a hand to her chest. He could hardly feel a heartbeat and suddenly he thought of mummies, ancient mouldering Egyptian mummies, coming to life after thousands of years. He'd always laughed at horror films, but he was living one now.

'Constantine Barolli is dead,' he said between gritted teeth. This mad old *bitch*, what the hell was she saying?

Now she really was smiling, although the smile became a twisted grimace of pain.

'He's not dead,' she said, so low that Max had to strain to hear it. 'He's *alive.*'

'He died in the explosion at Montauk,' said Max.

She was shaking her head, laughing at him, crying out in pain, but still mocking him, jeering at him.

'He didn't die. You can't *kill* a great don like Constantine . . . oh . . .'

She was wincing, clawing harder at her chest, kneading frantically at her left arm.

'He died,' said Max.

'He didn't die,' she gasped out. 'And she knows it.'

'She?' Max stared at the contorted face.

'Annie Carter. *Her*. The puttana. The bitch. She's . . . always known.'

With those final, damning words, Gina Barolli took one last halting breath and her eyes closed. She slumped, lifeless, in the chair.

And Max knew at last.

Gary Tooley had been telling the truth.

Annie *had* betrayed him.

18

Limehouse, 1958

Turned out, Dolly was wrong about the safety thing. While Mum sat like a vegetable in the rocking chair up in the bedroom and the younger kids were at school or out playing, things would happen. Mum was becoming more and more cut off from reality. Dad would come in from his job and while usually he just had a wash-down with a flannel, occasionally he would bathe in the tin bath in front of the fire. Dolly would fill the bath for him with endless heavy kettles of water off the stove while he sat at the kitchen table watching her. More and more he was doing this, taking a full bath – and she knew why. She always went off into the sitting room and let him get on with it.

'Dolly girl!' he'd call out.

It was the shout that filled her with fear. She would creep to the closed door and say: 'Yes, Dad?'

'Come and scrub my back, there's a good girl,' he called back to her.

'I'm doing my homework, Dad!' she shouted back, although that was a bald lie, she never did homework. If they put her in detention for it – and they did, often – she was pleased, because that meant she wouldn't have to come home until later. She never wanted to come home, not now.

'That can wait! Come on.'

What else could she do? This was Dad.

Trembling, she opened the door and stepped into the kitchen. In front of the fire, there was Dad sitting naked in the tin bath. He was bulky, hairy. She stood there, undecided, until he looked back at her over his meaty shoulder and said: 'Come on then, girl. Soap my back for me.'

Dolly thought she might be sick, and if she was sick then she hoped it would choke her and end all this weird, claustrophobic misery and torment. But she went over and took the soapy flannel from his hand and started scrubbing her dad's back. She kept her eyes firmly on his back, hotly and horribly aware that he was undressed and that this was wrong. But he was her dad and he loved her, didn't he?

So was it wrong?

She didn't know, and there was no one she could talk to about it. The teachers? Impossible. A friend at school? She no longer had any friends there, she'd drawn away from people, thinking they might guess her dirty secret and be disgusted with her just as she was disgusted with herself.

Her brothers and sister? No, she couldn't tell them. They would be jealous of the gifts, they wouldn't understand. Already Sarah was acting strange with her, being cool and offish. She thought that Sarah might know what was going on, and a hot tide of embarrassment flooded her at that thought. Mum, then?

No. Not Mum. Dolly was Mum's rival for Dad's affections, she could see that. And somewhere in her heart she relished it, felt a certain twisted, ghastly pride at the feeling. She wished Mum was normal like other mums, that she wasn't a head case, that she would be here, really here, and shield Dolly from these things that shouldn't be happening.

So she couldn't talk to anyone about it. And anyway, this was Dad, and Dad loved her. She soaped his back, and then he caught her arm and took it down the front of his body. He leaned back in the water and pressed her hand to that long white hard thing that loomed out of the soap suds. Horrified, Dolly thought she might scream but instead she cut off from the here and now and thought of the stained-glass angels in the little church near the primary school she had loved so much, of how happy she had been then, when she had been innocent and untouched; before she knew about the man-and-woman thing and everything had turned bad.

Desperately she tried to blank out what he was doing, moving her hand up and down, faster and faster until his whole body stiffened and she thought he must be having a stroke or something. She hoped he was. Then the hard thing went soft, and finally Dad sighed and relaxed and let go of her arm.

'You're my special girl, ain't you?' he murmured, lying back, eyes closed.

Dolly hugged her arm, which felt bruised. She let the flannel drop into the soap suds with a shudder of horror. Then she turned, and saw Mum standing at the bottom of the stairs, watching them.

19

Dolly was shamed to her soul by Mum seeing what was happening in front of the fire. Her face, her whole body, burned with embarrassment and guilt that her mother had seen her doing the bad thing with Dad.

What Dolly expected was that Mum would shout and scream, that she would cuff Dolly around the ear, and she deserved that . . . but none of that happened.

Dolly would never forget the image of that room: the hot fire blazing, her mother standing on the bottom step, staring; and Dad's head slowly swivelling around as he saw Dolly's horrified face turned toward where Edie stood.

Sam Farrell stared at his wife, and said nothing. After long, long moments Edie simply turned and went back upstairs. Dad sat back in his bath. And Dolly fled the room.

Dolly thought that after the bath thing Edie would talk to her husband, angry words would be exchanged; but again she was let down. If anything, Mum seemed to withdraw even more, only sometimes Dolly caught her mum staring fixedly at her, saying nothing, just looking at her daughter as if she was looking at a stranger.

Then one Saturday Dad came in from the pub. Mum was in the kitchen in her usual seat, staring at nothing in particular, and the kids were out playing. Dad came in, weaving a *little on his feet, slightly drunk, and looked at his wife slumped there. His expression was one of impatience and disgust.*

'Going to sort out the box room,' he snapped at his wife. Then he turned to Dolly. 'Come on, Doll, you can give me a hand.' And he headed for the stairs.

Dolly looked at Mum, but Edie's eyes remained resolutely on the floor. What was he talking about, the box room? The tiny room was a tip, everything went in there, all the shit in the entire world it seemed, so why was he talking about sorting it out? Dad never bothered himself with stuff like that.

'I said come on – you deaf?' Dad snarled at Dolly from the bottom of the stairs.

Confused, Dolly followed him up. But instead of going left to the box room, he went into the bedroom he shared with Mum. Her heart suddenly in her mouth, Dolly hesitated at the door and he took her hand, pulled her inside, shut it. He passed a hand over his face and she thought she saw a flicker of something like despair there before it was gone, quick as a flash, and then he was smiling.

'You're my best girl, ain't you, Doll?' he said, and his voice was almost whining, almost pleading, as he led her to the bed.

'What about the box room?' Dolly blurted out in terror, her face red with shame because she knew what he was going to do, he was going to do the man-and-woman thing to her, she knew it . . .

And Mum knew it too.

That thought cut into her, sharp as a knife. Mum was sitting downstairs letting him do this, because it kept him away from her.

'That'll keep. Lay down there, Dolly, there's a good girl.'

What could she do? This was wrong, but it was Dad, and she loved him, of course she did. So she lay down on the bed and when he lay down next to her she didn't bolt for the door.

It took willpower not to, but this was her dad. He loved her. She had to keep reminding herself of that, she had to.

Down in the kitchen, Edie heard her daughter's piercing scream.

'Oh Christ in heaven,' she said, and as Dolly screamed again she put her hands over her ears and rocked backward and forward in her chair, crying. 'Forgive me,' she moaned. 'Please forgive me.'

20

After that first time, it happened again and again – so many times that Dolly lost count, and she tried to count, to think that some day she might reach the end of this, that it might stop. But it didn't.

Mum knew.

That was the bit that really choked Dolly. Mum knew about this, and she didn't intervene, didn't give a monkey's. She was just relieved that Dad's attentions were elsewhere. But maybe this was normal? Maybe this was just one of the adult things that Dolly hadn't previously known about, and which she had to learn? She didn't know.

Time and again she thought of the angels in the little church, of how stupid and innocent she had been to think that there was beauty in the world. She remembered the sweet-faced old priest with his fine words about God and redemption. But the priest had been wrong, so wrong. There was no beauty. There was nothing in this world except filth and degradation.

Beauty?

What a laugh.

It didn't exist, not in her world. Nothing worth a flying fuck did.

Mum wouldn't look her in the face any more, Dolly knew that much. And more and more they carted Edie off to the hospital to get 'zapped', as Nigel mockingly called it. Nigel thought Dad could do no wrong, but Mum? He'd grown critical of her, aping his father's attitude. When Edie got home, it was Dolly who had to put her to bed, clean up the sick, deal with her vague, mad statements. It always took a day or two for Edie to come back to herself, and in between she was lost to them. Not a mother at all, really, just a thing in a bed, babbling nonsense, poor cow. Dolly saw how Edie cringed away from her husband whenever he came near, and she didn't wonder at it. She felt rage and bitterness toward her mother, no love at all now, but in the cold logical core of herself she could see Edie's viewpoint. She could see that Edie had chosen to sacrifice her eldest daughter and save herself.

So it went on, months and months of endless torment. Dolly ate chocolates, the guilt-gifts she got from her dad, and she grew fatter, comfort-eating. Home was a war zone and she was just spoils, to be enjoyed as the man of the house thought fit.

It went on, and on – until she was ill.

Everyone was ill that winter; the flu bug was doing the rounds and sure enough the whole bloody family went down like nine-pins. First it hit Edie, who'd been in the hospital again getting her brain fried, and her usual sickness and nausea when she came home just went on and on, until they had to call the doctor out.

'Influenza,' he pronounced, and left. 'Bed rest, liquids, warmth.'

Then little Sandy, the weakest and youngest of the kids, fell victim, then Dick and Nigel, and finally Sarah, who'd been helping Dolly care for the whole damned lot of them. Inevitably, Dolly herself got up one morning and fell back on to the bed, too hot and dizzy to stand. For two weeks it was Dad who had to do the honours, stopping off work to heat up soup to feed them all and carrying buckets and bowls to and *fro to all their sickbeds. Dolly was viciously glad to see him having to empty the shit and vomit in the khazi out in the back yard.*

Served him right.

And there was a bonus to being ill; Dad didn't come near. Didn't want to catch a dose of the dreaded lurgy like she and the others had.

The Devil looks after his own, thought Dolly as she watched her father faffing around the house, moaning like a drain about having to fetch and carry for them all. He didn't get ill, the bastard.

But soon the family recovered. Sarah started making cups of tea and helping again, Edie crawled from her bed to the rocking chair and then downstairs to the kitchen to flop into her usual seat there. The boys went back to school and Dad to work. But Dolly remained unwell; the flu didn't seem to want to loosen its grip on her, and she was usually the strongest, the fittest of the whole family.

Eventually, Edie stirred herself enough to call the doctor out again. Dolly hated the doctor with his pompous air, she hated seeing the disgust on his face when he came into the house, into the bedroom she shared with Sarah. He prodded her with a stone-cold stethoscope, had her sit up, pressed the cold horrible thing to her chest and back, told her to breathe out, breathe in. Then he palpated her abdomen, looked at her face. He drew back, repacking his stethoscope in the Gladstone bag.

'Do you have a due date?' he asked.

Dolly stared at him blankly. What the hell was he talking about?

'How old are you, girl?' He sounded exasperated.

'Thirteen,' said Dolly. She felt like she was about to be sick again. Every morning, she was sick as a dog, it was wearing her out.

'*You know who the father is?*' Now he looked truly disgusted, like she'd crawled out from under a stone.

'*I don't know . . .*' She had no idea what he meant. The father? What father?

'*You're pregnant,*' said the doctor, and Dolly's whole young world imploded.

21

She should have been able to turn to her mother at a time like this, but she couldn't. Edie scarcely talked or moved or took any interest in anything these days. Talking to her was like talking to a wall. You got just as much sense out of either one.

To Dolly's utter shame and humiliation, it was Dad the doctor talked to after his visit to her sickbed. She watched the two men conversing out on the landing, glancing back in at her, and she saw the exact moment when Dad got the news; she saw all the colour leave his face in an instant, and despite her own shock and devastation she felt a stab of evil gladness. It shocked him, did it, what he'd done to her? Well, good.

After the doctor left, Dad came back upstairs. All the kids were out at school. Edie was off having her brains adjusted, there was only the two of them in the silent messy house, this awful place that had become Dolly's own private corner of hell over the last few years.

He came and stood at the end of the bed and he looked awkward, his eyes shifting around the room, as if trying to avoid fixing on Dolly, lying there in the bed. Maybe he was disgusted too, like the doctor.

But he did this to me, she thought.

Sam's lip was curled like there was a bad smell under his nose. She'd let him down, she could see that, and somewhere inside her that hurt; he was her dad, and she loved him. But she hated him too, and now the hatred was growing stronger, like this thing he'd planted inside her.

'The doctor said . . .' she started, and she had to stop, she didn't know how to go on with it. Embarrassment flooded her cheeks with red and she faltered to a halt.

'I know.' His eyes wouldn't meet hers. It was almost comical, only it wasn't very bloody funny at all, really, was it? Not when you got right down to the facts of the matter.

'We'll sort it out,' he said, and without another word he turned and left the room.

One week later, Dolly was still in bed, feeling fragile. Timid little Sarah came in with soup and tea and chatter, as she did every day, doing her best to keep Dolly's spirits up.

'This flu's a bugger, but you'll be better soon, don't worry,' she said.

Then Dad came in from work that evening and said: 'It's all fixed up, we'll go tomorrow.'

His eyes were doing that slip-sliding thing again, going around the room, not looking at his daughter, and he was sweating. Fix what? wondered Dolly. As soon as he'd gone, her hands wandered to her stomach, feeling the slight alien curve of it. She'd seen pregnant women; she'd be like the side of a house soon, and there would be things to buy, nursery stuff, she supposed. That must be what Dad was talking about. And at least this thing inside her meant that he wouldn't touch her any more; there was that to be thankful for.

The next day Dad stayed off work. Dolly got up, ate breakfast, spewed it back up, then cleaned herself and they caught the bus over to Aldgate. Maybe there was a shop there with kids' stuff, she didn't know and she didn't ask. Dad didn't talk to her on the journey and Dolly was glad of that. She felt both queasy and numb, all at the same time. The numbness, the *distance from the real world, had started the first time he'd played the man-and-woman game with her, and it had stayed.*

When they got off the bus, they walked a couple of streets along lines of identical Victorian semis. Dad opened the gate of one called 'Swanlea' and Dolly trailed after him up the little chequer-tiled path, feeling almost faint. Dad knocked on the door and in a minute or so it was opened by a middle-aged woman so heavily made up it looked like she was wearing a clown's mask. Her eyes were huge and fringed with blackened lashes. Her darkly tinted red hair, all the life coloured out of it so that it had the texture of a Brillo pad, stood out around her face like a frazzled scarlet halo.

'Mrs Averly?' asked Dad.

'Yeah. Mr Farrell, is it?' she said, fag in hand. She squinted first at him and then at Dolly. 'Come in then.'

They moved into a grubby hallway that stank of cabbage and cat piss, and the woman shut the door behind them.

'First things first,' she said, and held out her hand.

Dad rummaged in his billfold and pulled out a fiver. He placed it in her hand, and she nodded with satisfaction and quickly tucked it into her bra.

'That's fine. You can wait down here.' She turned to Dolly. 'Come on then, girl, up the stairs.'

This wasn't a shop with baby clothes. Bewildered, Dolly followed the woman up. They went into a tiny box room; inside there was a fold-up bed stashed against the wall, hectic violet wallpaper with sprigs of heather rampaging all over it. In the centre of the room, on the scuffed and worn purple carpet, was a yellow washing-up bowl steaming with warm water and frothy with soap suds. Beside it was what Dolly recognized as an enema, and an open packet of Omo.

'We'll soon have you straight again,' said the woman, crossing to the fold-up bed and stubbing her cigarette out on an overflowing ashtray perched there. 'Don't you worry.'

Dolly had no idea what she meant, but she was a kid and this ugly gorgon of a woman was an adult; it wasn't her place to question.

Then the woman turned back to her with a thin smile. 'Right then, lovey. Slip your knickers off and stand over the bowl.'

22

Dolly didn't know how she got back down those bloody stairs and out of that place in Aldgate. She was in agony. From the moment the woman had started pumping that Omo mixture into her, she'd been doubled up with pain.

'Don't you worry about that, you'll come away, that's what matters,' said the woman in an irritated tone of voice because Dolly had the gall to complain and start to cry.

Dolly didn't even know what that meant. Come away? Come away with what?

'All right then, Doll?' asked Dad when she came back downstairs, and he looked sheepish when he saw how white she was, her face twisted up with pain, before his gaze skipped away from her again.

'Thanks,' he said to the woman, and they left.

Dolly, standing at the bus stop and trying not to pass out, couldn't believe it. Her dad had taken her to that horrible ugly frightening cow and let her do that dreadful thing to her. As they waited and the rain drizzled down, a young mother with a child in a pushchair stood nearby and the child howled its head off.

Shut up, you little shit, thought Dolly, looking daggers at the tiny thing, feeling she could hardly bear to have that near her, not when she'd had all this done to her.

'Dad . . .' she moaned, clutching at her stomach.

'Bus'll be here in a mo,' he said brightly, smiling at the young woman with the kid, everything normal here, nothing to see.

Eventually the damned bus came, and they all piled on. Dolly didn't know how she made it the whole length of the journey without shrieking out loud. Finally they were home, and Dad helped her up the stairs to bed and then left her there, closing the door behind him.

'Dolly's not well, but she'll soon feel better,' she heard him saying to Sarah out on the landing. 'Don't go in, Sar, she's having a kip.'

Dolly writhed on the bed in fearful agony all the rest of that day and all night. She couldn't sleep through the pain, it was awful. When morning came and it got light she tried to get up, to get dressed. She could hear the others, her brothers and her sister, getting up, going downstairs to the kitchen, but she could hardly move, the pain was too great.

Somehow she got herself up on to the edge of the bed and hauled herself to her feet. It was then that she felt wetness and saw her nightie was soaked with blood. Another hot bolting spasm of agony shot through her and as she tried to stand up she felt something warm drop down between her legs.

Gasping, crying, she got the pot out from under the bed and crouched over it, and then it happened: the baby came away and fell straight into the pot with a sticky, stomach-churning slurp. Staring at it, Dolly nearly screamed but she didn't, she couldn't rouse the rest of the household, what would they think?

She'd been quite far along. In her innocence, she hadn't known what the fuck was happening, but she could see it was a girl, fully formed and hanging by the cord, still joined to her. Horror gripped her then. It was a girl, a real child, and they'd sluiced it out of her like it was nothing.

'Oh Jesus, oh angels,' said Dolly, crying, desperate. She

looked at the poor little kid's face and nearly fell to the floor in shock. She'd committed a mortal sin, this was a human being and she'd killed it.

Another cramp sent the afterbirth sploshing down on to the floor. Dolly let out a scream then, she couldn't stop herself.

Presently, as she stood there staring down at the abomination in the pot, there was a tap at the door. She cringed with panic. 'Who is it?' she shouted.

'It's me, it's Sar. You all right, Doll?' came her sister's voice.

Christ, she couldn't let poor little Sarah see this!

'Fetch Dad will you, Sar?' she called, and stepped away from the pot, wetness trailing down her legs and making her shiver with revulsion. She toed the pot under the bed and got back between the sheets, feeling blood sticking to her, messing up the bed. It was a horrible thing she'd done and she was shivering now, bleeding, feeling sick at what had just happened.

Dad was up within a couple of minutes, and came in the room, closing the door behind him. He stood there, and said: 'Has it come away then, Doll?'

Dolly couldn't bear to look at him. She nodded, swiped at her tears.

'Under the bed,' she said, and Dad moved forward, delicately stepping around the afterbirth, and pulled out the pot. Dolly heard him draw in a sharp breath.

'Doll?' he said.

Dolly turned her head and stared at her father. His grizzled face looked sweat-sheened and white; he looked like he was about to puke his guts up and Dolly knew why: he'd seen what she had seen – that the tiny dead girl had his face – the same chin, the same nose, everything.

'You all right then, girl?' he asked, and his voice shook.

Something hardened in Dolly then. She stopped crying, and

nodded. 'I'm fine,' she said. 'But the sheets are dirty and so's my nightie, I'll need clean.'

He was nodding too. With a shudder his eyes went back to the tiny dead thing in the pot. 'I'll see you all right,' he said.

Before he'd taken her to that ugly cow in Aldgate, Dolly would have believed that.

Now, she didn't.

23

London, June 1994

'Fuck, it's you,' said the man.

Annie turned. It was the day after she'd got to Ellie's. She'd overslept so she had a quick bath, dressed, skipped breakfast, said hello to Chris, Ellie's husband, who was sitting at the kitchen table and who grunted a reply. She braced herself and took a cab over to the Palermo Lounge to see what was happening there.

Answer? Not much. The big double red doors were closed, the neon sign was switched off, there were police tapes strung up and a beat copper was standing there, staring impassively into the middle distance. And now this *other* man had arrived, one she recognized. He was about six-three, with straight dark hair and dark hard eyes that endlessly scanned everything around him. He was formally dressed in a black suit, white shirt and tie. His downturned solemn trap of a mouth didn't lift in a smile.

'Oh! DCI Hunter,' she said vaguely, and went back to staring at the front of the building.

He stood there with her, silent for a moment. Then he said: 'I thought you might show up. A bit of a shock, yes? You knew her well.'

'I've known her for years,' said Annie, and she had,

since way back in Limehouse when Auntie Celia had held sway over the best whorehouse in the district and Dolly had been the brassiest of the brasses who worked there. Dolly had come a long, long way since then. They all had. And to see it end like this was damned near unbearable.

'And how is *Mr* Carter?' asked DCI Hunter.

Annie's face was set as she turned her head and started at him. Years, the Bill had been trying to pin stuff on Max. But he was always too sharp for them. Too sharp for her, too. She wondered what he was up to right now, and again her mind filled with images of tangled limbs, hot and heavy sex, some anonymous *younger* woman greedily, eagerly, taking her place. Quickly, she dragged her mind away from that. There was nothing she could do about it.

There's nothing you can do about this, either, said a voice in her head.

But she couldn't, wouldn't ever, believe that. She'd come back to find out what had happened here. And she meant to do that.

'You got any leads on this?' she asked him.

He gave a tight little smile. 'None that I am inclined to share with you.'

Annie shrugged. She'd find out anyway. From way back, before the Carter gang became *almost* legit, running not only the three London clubs but also a lucrative security firm whose territory encompassed a hefty chunk of central London and deep into Essex, they'd had tame coppers tucked away in the Met, people who were on their payroll and kept them up to speed with whatever was going down.

'She was shot, I was told,' said Annie.

'If you know anything else about this, you should tell me,' he replied, neither confirming nor denying it.

'How the hell would *I* know anything? I've been abroad.'

'Disgruntled customer? Lover?'

'Dolly didn't have lovers.'

'She was never married?'

Annie pursed her lips. She felt she was giving away more than she wanted to, but perhaps he could help. Perhaps he could even nail the lowlife who'd done this. 'Dolly didn't care for men much,' she said.

'Women then?'

'Dolly? Nah. Dolly was no lezzie. Dolly was . . .'

Had been . . .

Self-sufficient best summed it up, Annie supposed. Some people might say she had a cold core, but that wasn't the case. Once you were in with Dolly, you were in for life and she'd do anything for you. But . . . no lovers, male or female. She liked cats, Annie knew that. But not kids. She could vividly remember one of the girls' sisters bringing in a tiny baby to the Limehouse knocking shop, and all the girls cooing over the infant – but not Dolly. Never Dolly. She didn't want to hold the child and she seemed uninterested in it. If anything, she seemed relieved when the girl left and took the kid with her.

'Friends?' asked Hunter.

'She had friends all right. Close friends. Ellie at the Shalimar. And me.'

'Relatives?'

Annie squinted at him through the rain. It was coming down harder, sticking her hair to her head. Jesus, she hated the rain. All at once she had an urge to run back to the airport and get on a plane, escape to her carefree sunlit life, to Max.

'How should I know?' she asked. She didn't know a damned thing about Dolly pre-Celia, and that had been the sixties. Dolly had never spoken about brothers or sisters, or her mother and father.

'What, you've known this woman for a long time, been friends with her—'

'Best friends.'

'And you don't know whether she has any relatives? Don't that strike you as strange?'

Annie took a moment, considering this. 'Sometimes you know when a person don't want to talk about something. They don't have to tell you, you just know. Dolly didn't want to discuss her past. And I never dug around in it because I got the message loud and clear, OK?'

'Would Ellie at the Shalimar know more?' he asked.

'She might . . .'

'I'll talk to her.'

'. . . but I doubt it.'

Hunter was silent, staring up at the Palermo Lounge's façade. They were both getting soaked to the skin. Then he stirred and let out a sigh. 'I'm going inside,' he said, and moved off toward the PC standing at the door.

'Can I come?' asked Annie, following.

Hunter stopped in his tracks. 'For what?'

'I might be able to see if something's wrong. You never know,' said Annie.

'I don't think so.'

'I could help you,' she said.

Hunter turned and looked at her.

'I have contacts. Lots of them,' said Annie.

'I know that. I know what *type* of contacts too, Mrs Carter. Keep out of this.'

Annie stared at him. 'Anything I find out, I'll share with you. That's a promise.'

He paused, gazing at her hard-set face, drenched in tears or rain, or both. He really couldn't tell. In that moment, he thought she was beautiful, formidable. He'd always thought it, and it annoyed him. Annie Carter had been many things in her life – a Mafia queen, a gangster's moll, a madam in a Mayfair whorehouse. When he looked into her eyes he saw a steely determination and a strength that was alien to most women. She was a bad lot. *Not* the type of woman that any self-respecting, straight, top-class copper should go thinking thoughts like that about. But she was right: maybe she could help.

He stared at her for another moment. Then he said: 'You don't touch anything. Not a damned thing. You understand me?'

Annie nodded.

'Come on, then,' said Hunter, and led the way inside.

24

Inside, the club was dark; it was a place built for the night, not the day; there were no windows. It only came alive in the evenings, but for now it was spookily still, empty. The atmosphere was chilly.

Annie reached out to the wall on the right of the closed door, switched on a bank of lights. All at once the big room sprang into focus: acres of brown carpet, faux tiger-skin chairs and deep chocolate-brown banquettes tucked away in quiet, private recesses. And everywhere, there was gold. On the walls, the ceiling. Great gilded angels were spreading their wings; golden poles were set into tiny podiums, gold-framed paintings adorned the walls.

'What did I just say?' asked Hunter.

'Dunno. I wasn't listening,' said Annie, and walked over to the bar and found another switch. The blue neons flickered and flared into life.

'I said *don't touch.*'

Annie was looking around her. Over to the right were the private dancing rooms behind gold beaded curtains. And to the left? The stairs up to Dolly's flat. Her eyes went there, and stayed.

'You're sure you want to do this?' said Hunter, watching her face.

Her eyes met his. 'There's nothing there, right? She's gone.'

Hunter nodded and turned to lead the way. He unclipped the rope at the bottom of the stairs and started up. Annie followed, not wanting to. All right, she wasn't going to see Dolly there, but this was where she'd died. If spirits did linger, then surely Dolly was up in the flat now, waiting for them, waiting for *her*. Waiting for someone to find her killer, take revenge, let her rest.

Hunter stopped at the top of the stairs and pushed open the flat door, which was covered in grey dust where the technicians had collected fingerprints. He stepped inside. This room was brighter than downstairs, with an outside window; but the light filtering in through the closed curtains was drab. Hunter flicked on the overhead light and everything came to life. Pink everywhere, Dolly's favourite colour. Cushions and doilies and stuff, this was very much a woman's room. And . . .

'Fuck,' said Annie faintly, her eyes fixed on the rug in front of the gas fire. The off-white sheepskin was soiled with a dinner-plate-sized splodge of blood. *Dolly's* blood. There were streaks of blood on the wallpaper beside the hearth, on the mirror over it, and on the fireplace itself. There were little numbered pointers that had been placed here and there by the crime scene boys.

'You all right?' he asked.

'Fine. I'm fine,' said Annie, drawing in a shuddering breath. Now, at last, she could believe it. Dolly really was dead. Here was where it had happened, where some *creep* had snatched her life away. Grief and anger warred inside Annie. Anger won, just. It took an effort of will to hold her voice steady, not to shout or cry. 'You got any idea who did this? *Why* they did it?'

'Well, it wasn't robbery,' said Hunter. 'The safe in the

office hasn't been opened, and all Thursday's takings were still in there, untouched. The keys were in her handbag. So was her cash, and credit cards. Nothing taken out of the bag at all, so far as we can see.'

Annie nodded. It would feel better if money had been the motivation. The fact that it wasn't made it more personal. Or maybe this was just some random nutter at work. Then she had a horrible thought.

'She wasn't . . . ?' she started, and then found she couldn't say it.

But Hunter understood. 'No evidence of sexual assault. It was quick, Mrs Carter. Almost instantaneous. We've fingerprinted all the staff and Ellie and Chris Brown, and if you would come down to the station later we'll take yours too.'

'I haven't been here recently,' Annie pointed out. 'And my dabs are on your files, anyway.'

Hunter gave her a long look. He knew her history; she'd been busted for running that disorderly house in Mayfair. 'I'd like to take them again, even so.'

'You're looking at the nearest and dearest, right?' said Annie. 'Close friends, close family. You look to them first to find killers.'

'Sadly, we do.'

Annie stared at him steadily. 'You've already checked whether I've been back here in the past few months. Checked with the airlines?'

'Yes. I have. And you have, haven't you? Brief stops in London, then on to the States or up to Scotland. What were you doing up there, Mrs Carter?'

Annie shrugged. 'Just playing tourist. I like it up there,' she said, hoping he'd drop it, hoping he hadn't delved too deeply into any of it.

He was moving around the room, looking at the rug, the

door. He bent down and stared closely at the blood on the hearth. Then he looked up at her. 'You're sure you know nothing about her relatives?'

'Nothing at all,' said Annie, stifling a wave of guilty irritation. Of course he'd had to check. What else did she expect? And she'd fronted it out, anyway. It was OK.

'Any lovers at all? However far back in the past? Anyone?'

Annie shook her head. 'You know her background, don't you?'

'Refresh my memory,' he said, standing up.

'I first knew Dolly when she worked at Aunt Celia's. They called it a massage parlour, but that's just a fancy name for it. It was a whorehouse near the docks in Limehouse. In those days, Dolly was aggressive, rough around the edges. Then time moved on and she softened a bit . . .'

Annie was thinking back to those times, thinking of the friends she'd made in that most unlikely of places, thinking of Darren, and Aretha, Ellie and Dolly. Back then, she and Dolly had been at each other's throats. They had been enemies first, friends later.

'You're smiling,' said Hunter, watching her face curiously. 'What is it?'

'Nothing. Just thinking that those were good times.' Now the smile was gone and she just looked sad.

'In a Limehouse knocking shop.' His tone was cynical.

'Believe it or not, they were. The best.'

'Paying protection to the Delaney mob, I believe.' Hunter eyed her sharply. 'What about them? Is there any connection now?'

Annie bit her lip. Not too long ago, she'd had trouble with the Delaneys – and at that point, she'd thought they were done for. And most of them were. Tory, Kieron, Orla . . . Once, the Delaney gang had been powerful and frightening. They were now part of the past. But . . . she knew that the scariest Delaney of all was still alive.

Redmond.

She felt a shudder go straight through her at that thought. A big Irish Catholic family, the Delaneys had struck terror into the streets at one time. All gone now, history – except Redmond. And the thought of him could still frighten her. She'd seen him in the flesh a few years ago. Hadn't thought it was possible. She'd been off her head at the time, and had half-believed that she'd dreamed his being there . . . but afterwards she had known. Afterwards, she found proof of it. Redmond wasn't dead. He was *alive.*

'There's no connection that I can think of,' she said. And she hoped, *prayed,* that was true.

25

Annie was ticking things off her mental checklist. She had checked in with Ellie; she had forced herself to visit the scene of Dolly's appalling murder at the Palermo; she had called in at the cop shop and let them take her prints again; and now she was on her way to the Blue Parrot. She wasn't looking forward to it, but it was something that had been chewing at the edges of her brain, gnawing at it the way a rat would chew on a piece of rancid meat.

Calls from Gary.

The calls from Gary were what seemed to have brought about the change in Max. Assuming the calls were indeed from Gary, as Max claimed, and not from some grasping little tart intent on stealing him away from her. So, *if* Gary was calling Max – why so frequently? With Max out of reach, the only way to find out was to speak to Gary.

Tony was nowhere to be found, Chris was still out and about on some sort of business, so Annie took a cab over there. It was late afternoon, and still raining. The sky was a grey upturned bowl darkening steadily into night, the traffic was thick, swooshing through the streets, headlights cutting through the gloom, wipers running at top speed.

Fucking England, she thought.

As the cab wove its way through the traffic, she thought of Layla and Alberto, her daughter and her stepson, cruising the Caribbean; they might be fugitives but they were in love and free as birds. She couldn't help envying them; it broke her heart to think that she and Max had been like that once – obsessed with each other, always wanting to be together. Now . . . Annie's throat clenched with misery . . . *now*, he couldn't seem to wait to get away from her. And he didn't even do her the courtesy of being upfront about it. He just *went*.

When they got to the Blue Parrot she paid the driver and hurried inside. The bar staff were getting ready for the evening's trade: polishing glasses and bringing up crates of mixers from the cellars. Like the Palermo Lounge and the Shalimar, the décor in here was dark chocolate and gold, angels and cherubs, faux tiger skin on the chairs and some of the banquettes. In fact, all three clubs looked damned near identical.

But there's a difference, she thought as she stood there in the big room that constituted the main body of the club. At the Shalimar, Ellie's motherly presence gave the place a warm ambience. And at the Palermo, Dolly had imbued her territory with a brassy sweetness. Here, there was only Gary and a coven of ever-changing girlfriends to run the place. The atmosphere was not cosy, not welcoming. Strictly business.

'Shit, not you,' said a male voice from behind her.

Annie turned around and there he was: Gary Tooley. Over six and a half feet tall, and so skinny it was as if he'd been stretched on a rack. His eyes were devoid of any humanity; she'd always thought that and clearly nothing had changed.

Gary Tooley looked like what he was: a vicious thug. His straight straw-blond hair had been restyled since she'd last seen him; he now wore it swept straight back, giving him an even more hawkish air. He was wearing a dark designer suit, a white silk shirt open at the neck. Working for Max had given him a good lifestyle; he'd come from the East End gutters, but today he looked rich and she knew that would please him, because Gary loved money – it was his god, the only thing that mattered to him.

'Hi, Gary,' she said, and then her eyes went to the minuscule blonde at his side. Big calculating blue eyes rimmed with black lashes, a sneer on a face plastered with too much fake tan and make-up, and a too-short pink leather dress showing off a taut little body.

'And who's this?' asked Annie.

'I'm Caroline,' said the blonde. 'Who the fuck are you?'

'This is my girlfriend,' said Gary to Annie. Then to Caroline he said: 'This is the boss's wife, hun.'

The woman linked both arms possessively through one of Gary's. 'Gary and me, we're together.'

Looks like a match made in heaven, thought Annie: *a horrible cow and a soulless, sadistic bastard.* Ignoring the blonde, she addressed Gary: 'You heard about Dolly?'

'Yeah. Big friend of yours.'

'She was. Yes.' He didn't say sorry for your loss, what a nice woman she'd been, nothing; but then, Annie hadn't expected that. Not from him. She diverted her gaze, glancing around the place in case he should see any weakness in her eyes at the mention of Dolly. You didn't show vulnerability in front of people like Gary, they'd eat you whole. She knew that.

The club was starting to come to life: lights flicking on over the bar, doormen arriving, giggles and chatter from girls heading to the dressing room to get ready for the evening. There was a female cleaner working late, moving in and out of the chainmail curtains over to the right of the room, pushing a vacuum cleaner. There was a smell of lavender polish in the air.

'So how's business?' she asked, looking back at Gary.

'Good,' he said, and his eyes were wary.

'A private word?'

'About what?'

Annie looked pointedly at Caroline, clinging on to him like ivy on a wall.

Gary stared at Annie for a moment, unblinking. Then he patted Caroline on the backside and said: 'See you at six thirty, babe. OK?'

Caroline gave Annie one last look and moved off toward the door. Then Gary said, 'Gimme a moment,' to Annie and followed Caroline's wiggling leather-wrapped arse over to where the doormen were standing. He saw Caroline out the door with a peck on the cheek, then spoke to the men there. One of them handed him a newspaper. After a couple of minutes, he headed back to Annie. 'Come on up to the office,' he said, and turned to lead the way.

26

Once inside the office, Gary went around the desk and sat down. He gestured for Annie to sit, too. She did. They could hear the DJ firing up his decks now, could hear Queen thrumming up through the floor, Freddie Mercury's superb voice singing 'A Kind of Magic'.

'So what's on your mind?' he asked her, throwing the paper on to the desk.

Annie glanced at the front page. O. J. Simpson had been charged with the murder of Nicole Brown Simpson and Ronald Lyle Goldman outside the Simpson home. And a hacker had been charged for wire and computer fraud. It all seemed removed from reality, about a million miles away.

Gary looked pissed off to see her. His loyalty was to Max; they'd been part of the same gang since school. For as long as she could remember, Gary had despised her. Gary screwed women but hated and mistrusted all of them – and he viewed any deep involvement with them as foolish. Annie wondered if Caroline knew that yet. Well, she'd find out. Gary had always seen Annie in particular as a female bloodsucker, a vampire who would draw the life out of Max, weakening and sapping him. Well, *fuck* Gary.

'You've been phoning Max a lot lately,' she said, by way of openers.

'Have I?' He leaned back in his chair, linked his hands behind his head, very casual, and stared at her with that pale blue unblinking gaze.

'Yes, you have. And I'd like to know, about what.'

Now he was smiling, a flash of teeth that was more like a snarl than anything else. 'You better ask Max, not me.'

'I can't,' said Annie.

'Why's that then?'

'Because Max has gone somewhere. Left with no explanation.' Annie leaned forward in her chair, her eyes holding his to emphasize her point. 'He's just *gone*. Said he had stuff to do, and took off. I don't know where to or for what reason, but what I *do* know is that he's had a lot of calls from you lately. And so the question remains – what's he been talking to you about?'

Gary straightened and shrugged. 'This and that,' he said.

'Yeah? Can you be more specific?'

'Private stuff. You know. Man to man.'

Annie nodded slowly. 'Private? Well, we're married, Max and me, so I think you should make an exception.' Her eyes were hard dark green pebbles as they held his. 'So tell me what the *fuck* is going on, Gary, will you?'

'Hey.' The smile dropped from his face. He sat up straight and leaned both hands on the desk and stared into her eyes. 'Don't come in here flinging your weight about. I run this place for Max, not you.'

'You run it for both of us, Gary. I told you. We're married. Joined at the hip.'

'Yeah, like fuck! He's gone and you don't even know where.'

'Do you?'

'What?'

'Know where? Only, what with all those phone calls, I've got a feeling that if anyone knows, it's you.'

Gary shrugged but his eyes were steely as they stared into hers. 'If you want to keep Max sweet then you ought to start bloody behaving yourself.'

Annie's jaw dropped and a skitter of fear shivered up her spine. 'What the fuck's *that* supposed to mean?'

'It means this conversation's over,' he said, and stood up. 'I don't have to take any of your shit.'

She started shaking her head. 'No. *No!* You tell me what you mean, Gary. You can't just say a thing like that and think I'm going to leave it there.'

Gary came around the desk. To Annie's shock, he grabbed her arm and hauled her to her feet.

'Now you listen to me,' he hissed into her face from inches away. 'I *told* you, this conversation's done. I got nothing to say to you. Now *get*.' And he shoved her toward the door.

Annie stared at him. *Fuck it, he knows*, she thought. 'You're going to be sorry you did that,' she said flatly.

'Yeah? We'll see about that. Now get the fuck out of here.'

Annie left him there and went back down the stairs. She stepped outside the club. It was still raining. Traffic flowed past and she saw the yellow light of a taxi and stuck her hand out. It pulled in to the kerb. 'Shalimar club,' she told the driver, stepping into the back.

Once buckled in, she sat there, her mind racing. Dolly was dead. It was so painful to think of her gone, it broke Annie in two. And it galled her that someone was walking about free when they should be punished for that. And Max . . . oh God, Max! What was going on with him?

What Gary had said chilled her. Nerves were crawling

in her stomach as she thought of the one thing she had never told Max. The one thing she *couldn't*.

If he knows . . .

No. He couldn't.

But she couldn't make herself believe that.

27

'Ellie, I need a word. Seriously,' said Annie.

They were in the kitchen of the flat over the Shalimar; Ellie's domain, hers and Chris's. They ran this club and so far they'd run it well. Annie had always believed that Ellie and Chris were her friends. That she could depend on them. But since she'd been back, she wasn't so sure. She knew she wasn't imagining it — there was a strange wariness in Ellie's face, and Chris? So far, he hadn't spoken a single word to her, and that bothered her. Particularly after what Gary had said today at the Blue Parrot.

So here she was, doing what she thought of as *testing the water temperature*. And so far, it was icy.

'Can't it wait? I'm up to my arse here, we'll be opening soon,' said Ellie, pausing at the cupboard.

'No. It can't. Spare me a minute.'

Annie could see the reluctance on Ellie's face as she sat down opposite her at the kitchen table.

'What is it?' asked Ellie.

'Gary said something odd to me,' said Annie.

'Oh? What?'

'That I ought to behave myself.'

'*What?*'

Annie nodded. 'I don't know what he meant by that,

and he wouldn't explain. Do *you* know what he meant, Ellie?' She was gazing intently at her friend's face.

Ellie's eyes slipped down and she shrugged. 'Gawd knows. Gary's never liked you. You know that.'

Chris passed by the open kitchen doorway.

'Chris!' called Annie.

There was a moment's delay, then Chris appeared. *Sheepish*, she thought. *That's how he looks. Like he don't want to see me here. Like he don't even want to know I'm breathing.*

'Can I have a word?' she asked.

Chris looked at Ellie, not Annie. 'I'm busy,' he said, and walked on.

There was a tense mood in the kitchen now as the two women sat there. Ellie was staring down at the tabletop, Annie was staring at her friend.

'Ellie,' said Annie.

Ellie didn't glance up.

'Ellie, what the fuck's going on?'

Ellie stood up suddenly. She pushed her chair in, her eyes everywhere but not once resting on Annie's face. 'I can't,' she said, and seemed about to bolt from the room.

'Wait! All right. Forget about that. But look – Dolly. Do you know anything?' Annie stood up too, and looked urgently into Ellie's face. 'Come *on*, Ellie. This is Dolly we're talking about. The police want anything we can give them. We have to give them *everything* we can.'

Ellie paused. Her eyes flicked to Annie's face and then away.

'All right,' she said with a sigh.

'Her family – can you think of anything about them? Any little detail, no matter how small? If you do, tell me.'

Now Ellie did look at Annie. 'Why? So far as I know,

she wasn't even in touch with them. Hadn't been for years.'

'Does she have brothers, sisters? What about her parents? Are they still alive?'

'I don't know. I'll have to think. Now I really must . . .' And she was gone, bolting for the door, leaving Annie sitting there alone.

Next morning, after a sleepless night, Annie got up and was out of the club before anyone else had stirred. She hailed a black cab and went to an address across town and mooched around the shops on the high street until she saw a BMW pull into a space. A man got out – squat, solid as a tank, dark-haired, and dressed neatly in a black suit, pale blue shirt and matching tie. Annie walked over as he stood at the door of a shopfront, over which the logo *Carter Securities* was emblazoned in gold on a black background.

'Hi, Steve,' she said, and Steve Taylor, Max Carter's right-hand man, once his most dangerous attack dog, turned and looked at her with mud-brown eyes as he shoved the key into the lock.

'Fucking hell,' he said.

'Nice to see you too,' said Annie.

When they were inside, Annie asked him the same question she'd asked Ellie.

'Going on? What do you mean, what's going on?' Then he changed the subject. 'You heard about Dolly?'

'Yeah. Tone phoned. Where *is* Tone, by the way?'

'About.' Steve shrugged. 'Don't see much of him these days.'

'I can't get my head around it. That happening to Dolly.'

'Tragic,' he said. 'I thought you might come back, thing like that happening.'

Annie stared at him for a beat. 'Well, at least you're talking to me,' she said.

'Shouldn't I be?'

'Gary gave me the heave-ho from the Blue Parrot. Ellie's acting weird. And Chris won't say fuck-all.'

He shrugged again, remained silent.

'Do you know what's going on?' Annie asked. This was *Steve*. He'd been her ally for years. Surely he hadn't turned against her now? Why would he?

'No,' he said. 'I don't.'

He's lying.

Still, he was talking. That was something.

'Steve . . . is there anything you can tell me about what went on with Dolly? I mean, who would do that to her?'

'Christ, how would I know?' Steve looked exasperated. 'I was as shocked as anyone. Thing like that happening, who wouldn't be?'

'Have you talked to Max recently?'

'No. I think Gary does, more than me. The clubs get more problems – mouthy gits out on a Saturday night getting tanked up on champers, you know the sort of thing. I pretty much run the security side of things myself now.' He looked at her. 'Max trusts me to do that.'

Meaning what?

There was some barbed point being made here, and she was afraid that she knew what it was. Steve wasn't talking to her as Steve always had. Before, there had been respect; now there was a veiled *something* going on.

Disapproval?

Mistrust?

'You've done well for yourself out of the firm,' said Annie, standing up and strolling around the office. Plush carpet. Expensive buttoned leather chairs. A big mahogany desk.

'Meaning?' asked Steve.

Annie turned and looked at him coolly. 'Oh, I don't know. We're all speaking in fucking riddles these days. You keep in pretty close touch with Gary still, do you?'

'Gary?' Steve shrugged. 'Not much. As I said – he runs the club, I run security.'

Annie thought. 'What about Jackie Tulliver? Where's he got to these days?'

'Jackie?' Steve let out a *humph* of disgust. 'Jackie's a piss-head. Don't see him, not now. He's probably already drunk his stupid self into the grave.' He sat back in his chair. 'Listen. I'm sorry as hell about your friend, but it's nothing to do with me. I know sod-all.'

Annie leaned in over the desk and stared straight into his eyes.

'I think you're holding back on something,' she said. Her eyes narrowed. 'And if I find out that you are, you'd better fucking well watch out.'

'You do?' Steve stared up at her, and his eyes were distinctly unfriendly. 'Prove it,' he said, and picked up the phone, dismissing her like she was nothing.

28

When Annie got back to the Shalimar, the place was in uproar. Chris was out on the pavement, twitchily smoking and pacing around. A Samsonite suitcase and a couple of bags were on the pavement beside him, and one of the bags was split open. They were *her* bags, she realized. And that was her suitcase.

'What's up?' asked Annie, paying off the taxi and approaching.

She glanced from Chris to the bags. They were Louis Vuitton, and one of them was wrecked, spilling a couple of lightweight dresses out on to the wet dirt. She bent, tucked the items back in, gathered up the bags. She had known Chris was unhappy having her here for some reason, and it was clear he was chucking her out of the club, but he didn't have to go and break her damned bag.

'What's *up?*' Chris turned to her with a snarl on his lips and his eyes spitting venom. '*You're* up. *You*, coming back here. For fuck's sake, I *told* her, I *warned* her, but did she listen?'

Annie stepped back, shocked by this onslaught. This was *Chris*. He'd always liked her. Now, he was staring at her as if he'd like to kick her straight up the crotch.

'What are you doing, breaking up my bloody bags?'

He looked down at them. 'I didn't do it.' He flicked his

head up and let out an angry snort of smoke. 'They chucked them out the top window. Go and have a fucking look, you *cow*,' he said, and turned his back on her.

Annie flinched in surprise. Aggression from Chris was shocking. He was one of *hers*, one of her oldest and best allies. Now he was looking at her like he hated her guts. She went into the club, taking her bags and case – which was still intact – with her. She held her breath and looked around – but everything was OK. In fact, it all looked neater than neat in here. Chairs cleaned, carpets immaculate, bar lit up ready for trade. Not a soul about down here, though. No bar staff, no hostesses, no DJ warming up his decks, nothing.

Which was odd.

When she'd left the club, everything had been running like clockwork, getting ready for another busy evening. Now, the place looked dead. But she could hear noises coming from upstairs, angry voices, shouts, cries.

Annie went across the empty club space and turned left. A girl in tears hustled past her, shouting something over her shoulder. Annie left the case and bags at the bottom of the stairs and trudged on up, getting a bad feeling about this. When she got to the top she saw Ellie standing in the hallway, arms wrapped around herself, turning this way and that, her eyes frantic. They settled on Annie, and then Ellie let out an angry breath like a bull about to charge and vanished through the door to the right, the one that led into the kitchen.

Letting out a sigh, Annie followed, and it was then that she saw, and understood. All Ellie's glassware, her precious crystals, were in bits on the floor. The dresser with all the crystals on it had been tipped over. The kitchen table was a pile of splinters, the chairs were matchwood. Food had been scooped out of the cupboards and now sauce and ketchup decorated the formerly pristine walls. Ellie, the neat freak, stood in the middle of it, tears pouring down her face.

'Oh *shit*,' said Annie, halting in the doorway.

'Look at this! Just *look*. They done the office too – poor Miss Pargeter's going spare in there. Her papers are all over the damned place. And the girls' changing room, and some of the bedrooms . . . yours included. They tossed your stuff out the bleeding window, said if I let you stop here they'd come back and do it all over again, only worse.'

Annie gulped in a breath. 'They? Ellie, who?'

Ellie shrugged. 'I don't know them. They had masks on.'

'Didn't Chris try to stop them?' asked Annie.

Ellie turned to her in temper. 'Don't be fucking stupid! There were six of them, bloody great blokes in boiler suits with pick handles. He'd have only come off worst.'

'This is because I'm here?' said Annie numbly, staring around at the devastation that *she* had brought down on Ellie's head.

'Yeah,' said Ellie tearfully, picking up a beautifully crafted glass swan with its wing missing. 'I should never have let you stay. All this is my fault.'

'I'll go,' said Annie.

Ellie turned brimming eyes on her. 'Chris is hopping bloody mad at me over this.' Ellie's stare hardened. 'Christ, it's *you*, isn't it – you attract trouble like flies on shit.' Ellie gulped. 'Where will you go?'

'I don't know. Over to Holland Park maybe. Or a hotel. Anything.' *And it's best you don't know where, with all this kicking off.*

Ellie stared at her. 'Whatever you've done, it must be something pretty bad.'

'I haven't done a thing.'

'Maybe they shot Dolly because of you.'

'*What?*'

'Who knows?'

'I'll go,' said Annie. Her brain was spinning. Then she had a thought. 'Ellie, did you think any more about what I asked you? If there was anything you knew about Dolly's family, or friends, or anything . . . ?'

Ellie rushed at her and for a moment Annie thought she was going to get a belt around the ear. But Ellie stopped inches away. Breathing hard, she stared into Annie's eyes.

'You come back here and all I get is trouble!' she burst out. 'Chris is mad at me, he thinks this is *my* fault because he said I wasn't to let you stop here, but I insisted. I told him, whatever she's done, she's still my mate. And now look! It's a fucking disaster!'

'Ellie . . .' It *was* a disaster. There was no arguing with that.

'Fuck off out of it!' shrieked Ellie. 'Just. Fuck. Off. You hear me? Just *go*.'

Annie nodded. She went out of the wrecked kitchen and along the hall.

At the top of the stairs, Ellie called: 'Wait!'

Annie stopped walking. Turned.

Ellie stood there in the hall, clutching her head as tears washed her mascara down her face. She blinked at Annie, and then she blurted out: 'Doll's family. They used to live Limehouse way, I remember she told me that once. Quite a way from Celia's place. And they were Catholics. You know . . . you heard about her dad interfering with her?'

Annie nodded. She remembered – vividly – her Auntie Celia once telling her about that, and that Doll had suffered through a nasty backstreet abortion because of it.

'Well,' said Ellie, 'there's more. Back in the sixties at the knocking shop, I . . . I heard Dolly telling Celia that she wanted a hit on her dad.'

'You *what*?' Annie's mouth dropped open.

'It's the truth. I heard her say it. Well, I *overheard* her.'

Annie remembered Ellie as she had been then, insecure, always skulking in hallways, listening at doors.

'What else did you hear?'

'That she wanted the Delaney family to see to it. You know what? Once I asked Doll why she didn't go to church, to Mass, like Catholics always do. You know what she said?'

Annie shook her head.

'She said it was because the church told lies. It said there was beauty in the world, and there wasn't. I never forgot her saying that.'

29

Outside, she found Chris gone and DCI Hunter getting out of a black car at the pavement.

'You sure you want to go in there?' she asked, dropping her bags into the dirt again. She took pride in her appearance, and that extended to her accessories too; but what the hell – the bags were fucked, anyway, one scuffed, the other torn. Only the suitcase had stood up to the scrum.

'Why? What's up?' he asked.

'The place has been bulldozed. Six men went through it like a bloody hurricane.'

He stared at her face. 'And why's that?'

'What?'

'People don't do things like that for no reason.'

'I don't *know* the reason.' She kicked one of the ruined bags irritably. 'How's *your* day going, Inspector? You got any news for me?'

'Like what?'

Annie felt her hackles rise at his calm tone. 'Oh, let me think. Like who killed my best friend, and why, and what the fuck's going to happen about that?'

'The investigation is ongoing,' said Hunter.

'You're very bloody annoying, you know that?'

'Heard it said.'

'I need to get to the bottom of this. I *have* to,' said Annie fiercely.

Hunter leaned in. 'No, Mrs Carter. What *you* have to do is assist the police in the course of this investigation, in any way that you can. Don't give me any of your shit. Is that understood?'

Annie was silent, glaring.

'*Is* it, Mrs Carter?'

'Fuck off,' she said, and turned and walked away.

30

The Grapes was busy at lunchtime. For many years, this pub had been the place where all the Carter boys went to meet up and get their jollies, a real old spit-and-sawdust alehouse in the heart of the city with a host of hard-eyed regulars keeping curious tourists at bay.

Annie stepped into the main bar and thought that it had hardly changed at all. The Southern Comfort and Bushmills mirrors hanging on the dingy nicotine-stained walls, the rows of small flasks of Wade pottery, with Gin, Sherry, Port and Whisky labelled on each one. There were bigger barrels too, in mint greens and iridescent pinks, and huge oak casks cut through and turned into seating for the patrons.

On one of these big cut-down barrels sat a small gnome of a man, plug-ugly and wearing a stained pale blue denim jacket. A cloud of cigar smoke enveloped him, and a tumbler of whisky sat in front of him on the table.

Despite all the hustle around him, and the happy chatter at the bar, he sat alone, drank alone. Annie stood there inside the door for a moment, looking at him while Amazulu cranked 'Too Good to Be Forgotten' out of the juke. Max had always said drinking a few pints was OK, but if you were down in the dumps you never wanted to get started on shorts. Jackie had obviously got started on the shorts a long time ago. As Annie watched, he threw back the amber liquid remaining in the glass and gestured to the barman, a big handlebar-moustached ex-RAF type, for a refill.

Annie walked over and slid into the seat on the other side of the table.

Jackie Tulliver looked at her like she'd landed from another planet.

'Hiya, Jackie,' she said.

'Holy fuck.' He wheezed and a splodge of ash fell from the cigar he'd just clamped back between his teeth. 'What you doin' here?'

'Looking for you.'

Now Annie had found him she was wondering if it had been worth the effort. She was – literally – scraping the bottom of the barrel with him. Jackie was a mess. He had a three-day white-whiskery growth of beard on his skinny chin, his cheeks were sunken, his complexion yellow. He'd never been a beauty, but now he looked fucked. He looked two steps away from a cancer ward and a terminal prognosis, and his head was weaving about in that characteristic drunk's nod that made her think for one moment, horribly, of her own mother, Connie, who had always been pissed on the sofa and who had died of the drink.

'Jesus, the state of you,' she murmured.

'Get you a drink?' he asked, as the barman came over and plonked another whisky down in front of his best customer.

'No. Thanks.'

Even before the barman turned away, Jackie fell on the whisky like a desert dweller on a watering hole. He threw it back, smacking his lips with relish, emptying half the glass in a single gulp.

'Jackie,' said Annie.

'Yeah. What you doin' here then?' he asked, obviously forgetting he had just asked her the same question.

'Jackie,' said Annie again.

'What?' he slurred.

'Steve was right then.'

'Steve?'

'Steve. He was right. You *are* a pisshead.'

A hint of annoyance went chasing across Jackie's face, then it was gone.

'You got no call to speak to me like that,' he whined.

Even the tone of his voice reminded her of Mum, lying drunk and shouting pitiful rants while the rent man hammered at the door and Annie and her sister Ruthie cowered in fear of eviction.

'No? You're saying you're not a pisshead then? Only the evidence says different. It's one o'clock in the afternoon, and you're downing whiskies. You're drunk. You're unshaved. You're not even *washed*, I can smell you from here, you stink like a polecat.'

'Now hold on . . .' His watery eyes were blinking at her.

'No, *you* hold on. I need some help, you berk. Steve's not going to provide it, Gary Tooley's told me to sling my hook and Chris at the Shalimar is running scared because someone's just done his place over. Tone? I don't even know where the fuck he *is*, but the way things are going I won't be getting big hugs and kisses from there, either. You know what this is about? Why everyone's acting so damned weird?'

He looked at her. Then he shook his head gingerly, like it might drop off his shoulders and roll on to the floor.

'You heard about Dolly Farrell?' she asked. 'You know about that, do you?' *Or about anything?*

'Course I do. I'm not a fucking fool. I heard it. It was on the news, in the papers.'

'Good. Then you know we've got work to do, you *know* that. But for fuck's sake! You don't look capable.'

He said nothing. Stared at her dully. Then he reached for the whisky again. Annie snatched it from his hand and dashed it on to the floor. Several of the other patrons turned and looked.

'Hey!' Jackie started up, his face twisting in rage.

'Oh, that got through, did it? Taking your dummy off you, that hurt?'

'You got no call—'

'Oh shut up, you're a bloody disgrace.'

'You don't know what I been through . . .'

'No, I don't, and what's more I don't bloody care. *Do* you know anything about why everyone's acting strange?' She was almost sure she knew the answer to this question herself now. But she hoped – she *really* hoped – that she was wrong.

'What . . . ?'

Annie stared at his blank expression. No, he didn't know a thing. He didn't know because he wasn't being included, or even contacted, because Steve was right; he was a useless drunk. But at least he wasn't reacting to her the way everyone else had.

'Jackie, we got things to do,' she said, calmer now.

'What . . . ?' He was looking at the empty whisky glass, wishing it full again. She could see it.

'Yeah, we got some work. Remember that? Come on. Follow me.'

Annie stood up, gathered up her case and bags, then walked out into the street. Jackie followed behind her. And at that point, the fresh air hit Jackie Tulliver like a round-house punch, his eyes turned up in his head and he slumped straight into the gutter and lay there, out cold.

'*Fuck,*' said Annie loudly. She stayed there for a

moment, staring down at him; then she let out a sigh, hefted her bags and suitcase, and hailed another cab. She didn't bother trying to wake Jackie up; it was a waste of time.

As usual, she was on her bloody own.

31

As soon as she'd checked into her hotel, she got a call put through to the villa in Barbados, praying that Max had returned home and had got her message. But the cleaner answered and told her Mr Carter was still away.

Yeah, but where? With who? Doing what?

'Thanks,' said Annie. She replaced the phone on the cradle and fell back on the bed.

The skies outside her window were dark and pouring with rain, so she reached out and switched on the bedside light.

Loneliness settled over her like a black cloud. She had got used to being with Max, living with him, loving him. Their relationship had always been stormy, but she had never doubted his love.

Now, she did. And she felt abandoned.

Where the hell had he gone? Why hadn't he told her?

It made her uneasy and sad, this enforced separation. And alone, *truly* alone, with no one standing firm beside her. Not Chris, not Ellie, not even Steve. Tone? Who knew. She'd find out soon, but she had a horrible feeling that the news wasn't going to be good on that front either. Jackie Tulliver had turned out to be a dead loss. And now, on top of all *that*, there was this terrible business with Dolly.

She buried her face into the pillow and let out one deep,

heartfelt sob. She didn't cry. She *never* cried, but this pain was so great, her heart seemed to seize up in her chest, stopping her breath, making her squeeze her eyes tight shut like a child who can only pray the monsters will go away.

This monster wouldn't.

Dolly was dead.

Annie had few friends, but those she did have were precious to her. Like Ellie – who seemed to have turned her back on her. And Dolly, the feistiest, the best of them all, was gone.

Into Annie's mind came images of her old pal; Dolly laughing, moving briskly about behind the bar of the Palermo, snapping orders at the bar staff one moment then roaring with laughter with them the next. She remembered how delighted Dolly had been when she'd left Tony the driver and the Jag for Dolly's own personal use around town. Dolly, who according to Annie's Aunt Celia had struggled so much in her youth, who'd had it really hard, was now queening it around the place, a woman of means, a woman *in charge*.

There were more images parading through Annie's brain now. Dolly getting rat-arsed at their habitual meetings at the Ritz, her tongue running away with her even more than usual. But that was Dolly, wasn't it. All attitude, that was Doll. She'd suffered in her life and her stance had become: don't fuck with me, or you'll be sorry. She was loud, coarse and impulsive; Annie was the exact reverse. Maybe that was why, after their initial skirmishes, they'd got on well and stayed friends ever since.

Christ, how could that happen to Dolly? Annie wondered, thinking of some scumbag walking into the Palermo, up the stairs, into Dolly's little flat, her treasured pink-toned haven, and shooting her dead.

I've got to do something, she thought, and then, exhausted, still fully dressed, she fell asleep.

The phone woke her, breaking into a dream about Dolly and Celia. She opened her eyes, which felt gritty. It was bright, morning. *No*, it wasn't. The light was on, glaring. She was . . . she didn't know where the fuck she was. She sat up. There was a small brass carriage clock on the bed-side table, it said one-fifteen in the morning, and— Oh God, now she remembered, she was in London, every-thing had gone tits-up, and Dolly was dead.

Her heart sank again as that realization hit her. But the phone kept ringing. She reached out, pushed the hair off her face and snatched it up.

'Yeah?' she snapped.

'Mrs Carter, there is someone in reception. I'm so sorry to disturb you at this hour, but he insists it's urgent.' There was a hushed conversation, then the receptionist came back on. 'It's a Mr Tulliver.'

Annie let out a quivering sigh. 'Send him up,' she said.

Jackie Tulliver was in a foul mood when he got to Annie's door.

'Where'd you go?' he demanded, bustling past her into the suite.

'You know where I went. I went here.' Annie looked at him. He might be a godawful mess but there were still a few brain cells rattling around in that thick skull of his because here he was; he'd found her. 'And you tracked me down.'

'No big bloody trick. Holland Park's all closed up, I remembered that. You weren't at the Ritz. You've stayed here before, you're a creature of habit, right? So you had to be here.'

He'd sobered up a little.

'I don't know what happened,' he said, examining and then opening a TV concealed inside a large ornate Georgian doll's house. 'I was with you in the pub, then we went outside . . . Jesus, look at this. Ain't that neat.'

'You passed out in the gutter. And you know what? It suited you so well, I left you there,' said Annie, sitting down on the bed.

He turned and looked at her. 'Thanks for fuck-all then,' he said. 'Anything could have happened. I could've choked, or died of the cold.'

'It's June, and you were spark out, on your side. Not choking.'

'You wouldn't give a toss if I was.'

'So true. So what do you want, Jackie? It's the middle of the night, in case you haven't noticed.'

'You got any drinks in here?' he asked.

What the fuck. If he wanted to kill himself, she wasn't his damned mother, was she? Annie sighed and pointed to an antique writing desk. Jackie went over, found and opened the fridge concealed there. It was stuffed with chocolate bars, miniature whiskies, brandies, vodka. Jackie grabbed a whisky with an unsteady hand, didn't bother to enquire about a glass. He unscrewed the cap and necked it in one swallow.

'That crap's going to kill you,' Annie told him.

Jackie shrugged, lobbed the empty bottle in the waste bin, and swiped another full one before closing the door.

'Look, I'm makin' an effort here,' he said, coming and sitting down on the bed. He bounced up and down a couple of times. 'What size is this? It's comfy.'

'Jackie.'

'Hm?'

'Watch my lips. If you're up to it, we have things to do. Never mind the damned décor.'

'What things?' he asked, his eyes wandering around the room.

Jesus, is this it? wondered Annie. *Is this the best I've got to play with?*

The answer was yes.

'Important things. Things that require you being sober, not pissed out of your head.'

'Yeah?' Jackie looked at her, his face working. 'You think I'm a loser, don't you?'

'You got *that* right.'

'I'm not,' he said.

'Oh really? Prove it.'

'How the fuck am I supposed to do that?'

'First you get on to our tame coppers in the Met. There's still a few on the payroll. Tone's on it too, but turns out he's unreachable right now, and anyway two heads are better than one. See what's cooking on Dolly's case. See what the narks are telling them.'

'I can do that,' said Jackie. 'I can be your strong right arm, count on me.'

Annie looked at him. 'The only strong thing about you is your smell. Just fuck off and do it, will you?'

32

Limehouse, 1958

Dad got rid of the aborted baby. He brought up newspapers and wrapped the thing up and took it away. Then he came back with clean linen and a bowl of hot water, flannel and towels, and left Dolly to make the bed and clean herself up.

Still in pain, she slept after that; no one came near. She slept all through that day and into the next, and when she woke at last the pain was gone, the enema had finished scraping out her insides and she had nearly stopped bleeding too.

It was over.

Dolly felt huge relief at that, along with massive guilt. She thought of the stained-glass angels in the church windows again, but her mind shied away. She ought not to be thinking of those angels, not her, she was wicked, bad to the bone.

But . . . was it really over?

The baby was gone, but where did that leave her?

Dad had looked as sickened as she did when the baby came away, she knew he'd seen himself, his own features, in the poor kid's face. Well, good. He ought to suffer. Christ knew, she had suffered enough and none of it was her fault. Or . . . was it? Was it something she had done, trying to make herself look pretty maybe, had that somehow forced him to do the man-and-woman thing with her? Was it her fault, really? Had her wickedness infected him, made him do those bad things?

And there was something even worse loitering at the back of her mind. Once she was up and about and well again, would he pick up where he'd left off, start all that again, maybe even – and now she sat up in the bed, horrified – would he make her have another child, take another trip to the Aldgate woman? Would she have to endure another day and night of agony, only to deliver another dead horror?

It could happen. Dolly thought it really could. This awfulness could happen again and again until she went like Mum, totally off her head. And she couldn't allow that. She wouldn't.

Dolly's mind was spinning in small trapped circles. Terrified though the idea made her feel, she knew she had to do it. It was the simplest of plans, really. And she didn't have a choice in the matter, not any more.

She gave it a couple of weeks, enough to get her strength back, to return to her usual robust state of health. All the while, she was careful to tell Dad how rough she felt, that her insides hurt, just in case he should think of resuming the stuff he liked to do with her upstairs. She told him about the washing powder in the bowl and the enema, and could almost have laughed to see how it turned his stomach. He was revolted by female stuff, the mess and gunk that came with periods and babies and the results of him having his fun.

Then, late one night when Sarah was fast asleep and the whole household too, Dolly dressed, picked up the bag she had already packed, and left home. She was nearly fourteen.

33

It was summer, so life on the streets wasn't quite so bad as in wintertime. You could sleep in doorways and the coppers didn't bother you much if you kept out of their way. And Dolly saw there were others doing this too. She bought cakes with what little money she had, and bottles of pop. She washed in the ladies' loos in the town centre. Kept herself nice, or tried to. But it felt awful, being without a home. It made her sick with anxiety. Still, when she thought of what she'd left behind, she could only be grateful not to be there any more.

When the money ran out, she started to make a living for herself giving hand and blow jobs to strangers down the alleys. All you had to do was keep your mind blank while this went on, and she was good at that. She'd had plenty of practice. She did it, took the money. Fed herself. Then sat on the pavement outside the shops during the day, watching the world go by, watching people, lucky people with homes to go to.

Men brushed past her, women clattered by on stiletto heels; one of them, in a sharp mustard-coloured skirt suit, holding a fancy cigarette holder in her hand, paused in front of her and then, to Dolly's surprise, tossed a few coins into her lap. Dolly looked up. The woman's button-black eyes were warm and twinkling; then she moved on.

Dolly had been on the streets for a couple of weeks when she was approached late one evening by a tall skinny man *wearing eagle-tipped shoes. She looked up, up, up and saw there was a scar running down the length of his cheek. She'd seen him about before; he was flashily dressed and looked a nasty piece of work, she thought. Dolly had just been thinking of going back to her usual sleeping spot, but now here he was, planted on the pavement in front of her, looking her over.*

'What you doing out here?' he asked, his voice faintly foreign.

Dolly didn't answer. She stood up, gathered her things together. He grabbed her arm.

'You on the game here? This is my patch, my girls work this street.'

'I'm not on the game,' said Dolly, who had a pretty good idea what he meant by that now. He meant the man-and-woman thing. So far, she'd avoided that, used her hands and mouth instead. She'd seen his 'girls' – most of them middle-aged and shivering the nights away on the streets with short skirts and high heels, poor cows. They'd given her looks – not friendly ones.

'You better not be,' he snapped. 'I'm Gregor White, I own this patch, all right?' And he walked away.

The woman with the posh fag holder and the twinkling eyes came by again a couple of times in the week after that. She never spoke, but always she tossed a couple of quid in Dolly's lap and then walked on. Dolly watched her along the road until she turned the corner and was out of sight. Then she sighed and gathered up the notes. Money was getting very tight. Soon, she might have to go the whole hog, do the man-and-woman thing. She hated the thought, but at least while she was being poked she would be getting paid more, there was that to be thankful for.

Once or twice she got the bus and went and stood at the end of the road where the family home was. She stood there, half-hidden behind a garden wall, and watched her dad go to work with his jaunty bow-legged stride; saw formal, upright Nige and pale, skinny little Sand come out, saw mad Dick go barrelling out the gate all dirty and dishevelled with his satchel flying, on his way to school. Once she saw an ambulance pull up, saw Mum being wheeled out in a chair to go and get her brains unscrambled. But she couldn't feel sorry for Mum any more. She could only hate her.

When the money got really short, she did it; one night a stranger walked by and paused and asked how much for full sex. She thought of a figure, doubled it, and then she went into the alley with him and did the thing. It didn't hurt, not like when Dad had done it the first time, and the stranger was worried he'd catch something off her so he wore a Johnny, so no worries about pregnancy and little dead bastards.

It was easy, really. She just took her mind off somewhere else while it happened, that was all. Easy. Or at least it was – until Gregor White, the tall man with the scar and the fancy shoes, came back.

'My girls been watching you, bitch,' he said, nudging her with his toe. His shoes were clearly expensive, with fancy metal toecaps beaten into the shape of two eagles. He was very flashy in his dress, doing well out of what his girls brought in. Girls! Most of them were old enough to be grandmothers. Dolly felt sorry for them, being at the mercy not only of punters but also this creep. Men? They were all arseholes and she detested them.

'So?' asked Dolly.

'So you shove off now,' he said, leaning into her.

'Or what?' asked Dolly.

The first punch knocked out one of her teeth. The second sent her sprawling sideways on to the pavement and she lay there, winded, shocked beyond words, as the fancy shoes with their metal tips battered her legs. She curled into a ball to try to protect herself, but he was in a fury and he kept kicking at her calves and thighs until she felt herself blacking out with the pain. The world faded, and that was good; that was a mercy.

34

'She'll be all right in a sec,' a female voice was saying. 'Gordon Bennett, poor little tart! Who'd do a thing like that? There'll be a few scars to show for this on those legs. She's only a kid.'

Dolly didn't open her eyes. One eye hurt too much to do that, anyway. And she was frightened. Who knew what awaited her when she actually faced it? Coppers or something, wanting to take her straight home? Who knew? She couldn't go back there. She wouldn't.

'How old you reckon she is then, Celia?' asked another female voice.

'God, I dunno. Twelve, thirteen? Poor mare.'

'We'll wait downstairs,' said a male voice.

'Thanks, Darren. You are a love.'

Dolly stiffened. Her face where he'd punched her felt like it was on fire, her legs hurt like a bastard and the slightest movement sent it all dancing around, jittering along her damaged nerve-endings, the pain, the anguish. She heard the door open and close. She was lying on a bed, she could feel it soft beneath her. Over the past weeks she'd got used to pavements. Stone-hard, cold, painful on the joints; she'd staggered about during the day like an old woman. She knew it would wreck her health eventually, sleeping out rough like that.

There was a gentle hand smoothing her brow, but she didn't dare open her eyes, just in case she was mistaken and the man *remained there, inside the room, in case it was a trick and the woman was in on it.*

Mum had been in on it. Mum had let Dad hurt her. So why not this one?

No. Safer to keep her eyes closed, play possum. When she got her chance, she'd creep out, get away.

'You awake there, girly?' asked a voice. Female. Soft.

But she didn't answer.

Safer that way.

But where would she go this time?

The answer to that was easy. Another street, another part of town. Keep out of the way of the prossies and their pimps. She was learning, and learning fast.

'Girly? You there?' The voice was light, teasing.

Dolly kept still. Safer.

When at last she was sure the woman was gone from the room, she opened her eyes. Or one of them, anyway. She lifted a hand to her face and felt the swelling there, the soreness. When she lifted her arm, it hurt. Everything hurt, but her legs were the worst. Groaning, she hauled herself up in the bed and looked down. There was a bandage around her left leg, on the calf, and a huge red-spotted plaster on her right thigh.

She was in a bedroom, in a double bed with lace on the pillowslips. There were pink cabbage roses on the walls, and some nice furniture. She could see herself reflected in the big triple mirrors on the dressing table, where there were brushes and combs, perfumes and make-up.

Jesus! She stared at herself. Her left eye was black and swollen shut. Her lip was split where the pimp had knocked her tooth out. She probed the gap with her tongue – it was quite far back in her mouth; it wouldn't look too bad if she didn't grin like a loon, and she had little reason to grin.

Then to her shock the door swung open. She flinched and

strained back against the pillows, but it wasn't a man. It was
the dark-haired woman with the twinkling eyes and fancy fag
holder, the one who had passed her so often out on the street.
She was wearing a red wool skirt suit this time. She smiled to
see Dolly sitting up.

'All right then?' she asked, and stepped into the room,
closing the door behind her.

Dolly said nothing.

The woman walked over and stood beside the bed. 'Blimey,
you ain't half been in the wars,' she said. 'What was it, then?
One of them nasty bastards, them pimps?'

Dolly said nothing.

'Beat you up bloody good, didn't he. Was that it?'

Slowly, Dolly nodded. It hurt. She winced.

'You know his name? Could you point him out?' asked
Celia.

But that might mean more trouble. Dolly kept quiet.

'I'll bring you up some aspirin in a second,' said the woman.
'I'm Celia. Celia Bailey. What's your name then, girly?'

Dolly only stared at her.

'You got a name?' persisted the woman. 'Come on, what's
up? Cat got your tongue?'

'Dolly,' said Dolly slowly. It hurt to speak.

The woman's face lit in a smile. 'Dolly! Well that's nice. We
thought we might have to cart you off to the hospital first off
when I found you, but Darren carried you up here and I had
a look at you and I think you're going to be just fine. Nothing
broken. Not too much damage. You might have a small scar or
two on them pins, but I think you got off pretty light really.'

Dolly was going to be out of here the minute she could get
on to her feet. You didn't trust people, you couldn't even trust
family. She expected attack at any moment; she'd got used to
that.

'D'you know who did this? Can you give us a name? Describe this person?'

Gregor White with his eagle-tipped shoes.

But Dolly wasn't going to tell. Telling would bring retribution, Dad had always told her that. So she shook her head, then winced because it hurt so much.

'Never mind. But if you do think of anything, at any time, you tell me, OK?'

Dolly nodded again. She wouldn't.

'I bet you'd like a cup of char, wouldn't you?' asked Celia.

Slowly, painfully, Dolly nodded a third time.

'I'll bring you some cake and a cuppa, wash down the pills.' Celia patted Dolly's arm, very gently. 'Don't you worry. You're safe now.'

It was all lies; Dolly knew it.

35

For a few days Dolly felt too ill to move, much less leave. So she stayed. And Celia breezed in and out of her room asking questions about where Dolly had come from, where were her parents? Dolly didn't tell her in case Celia thought it would be a good idea to ship her back home. She missed quiet little Sar, dour prim Nigel and impetuous Dicky – even sickly Sandy. But she despised her mum for letting things happen to her, horrible things, and her dad? Whenever she thought of him, she wanted to puke.

'Ah, when you're ready,' Celia would say, very relaxed, and then she would spoon-feed Dolly morsels of food just like she was a baby, dabbing her chin with a napkin when she was done, and Dolly would sleep and dream of nothing.

Only the noises disturbed her. The doorbell seemed to ring constantly, day and night. And there were always people coming up and down the stairs, bedroom doors closing, people giggling and sighing and moaning, and the headboard in the next room kept thumping against the wall.

Cocooned under the covers while her cuts and bruises healed, Dolly decided to close her mind to it all. She could do that. It was better here than on the streets, that was for sure. Days turned into weeks, and she was able to get up, get dressed. Celia had seen to cleaning her clothes for her, and although the mirror in the bedroom told her that her face still looked a fright, all yellow and purple with bruising, she could open both eyes properly now. She brushed out her short mousy hair, which was straight as a yard of pump water, and went downstairs into the hall. She could hear voices.

Dolly went along the hall and opened the door at the end of it. The volume of the chatter shot up and she was confronted by a collection of girls – there was one boy among them – all sipping tea and smoking fags. The air in the room was blue, warm and fuggy. Conversation stopped short as Dolly appeared there.

'Oh, hello, Dolly love,' said Celia, getting to her feet. 'Come and join our merry little band, eh? Tea, ducky?'

Dolly nodded. 'Thanks.'

'You're looking a bit better now,' said Celia, as she went and boiled up more water. Slapping the kettle on the hob, she turned to the room at large and said: 'I told you, didn't I? One of those bastard pimps beat her up, poor kid.'

There were murmurs and 'Ohs' all round the room.

'Here's a seat,' said the handsome blond boy, standing up and grabbing another chair, pulling it into the table beside his own. 'Come and sit down, lovey.'

So this was Celia's family, thought Dolly. They seemed a nice bunch; friendly. She sat down beside the boy.

'I'm Darren,' he said, and held out a soft, slender hand. 'Glad you're better.'

'Dolly,' she said, and shook it.

'This is Ellie,' said Darren, pointing to a fattish brunette across the table.

'She does the chubby chasers,' said a hard-eyed blonde.

Ellie paused with her hand in the biscuit tin. Her face reddened. 'Oh, very fucking funny,' she said.

Dolly didn't have a clue what a chubby chaser was.

'And that's Aretha.' Darren indicated a gorgeous black dreadlocked woman at the far end of the table. 'That's

Cindy . . . ' That was the hard-eyed blonde. 'And that's Tabs.'
Tabs was a vivid redhead.

Dolly nodded to all of them to be polite, but these couldn't
be Celia's family, could they? Aretha was black. Tabs was red-
haired. Darren himself was blond and so was Cindy. There
was no family resemblance between Celia and any one of these
people – not even Ellie, who at least shared the same hair
colour. Dolly's own family looked somewhat alike, with pug-
gish noses, round faces, and blondish or mousy hair. They were
none of them beauties, nor ever would be, but you could see at
a glance that they were kin. These people clearly weren't.

Well, she thought as Celia placed tea and biscuits in front of
her, it was none of her business. And before long, she'd be out of
here anyway, it wouldn't matter. She'd be back on the streets.
Then she thought of the pimp who'd beaten her up, and shuddered. She'd have to find another spot to work. That was all.
Make sure she didn't fall foul of him again.

'Nice to see you up,' said Celia, sitting down at the table
and daintily tapping the ash off her cigarette into a glass ashtray with a Capstan logo on the side of it. Dolly watched her,
fascinated. With her sharp suits, fully made-up face, scarlet
fingernails and ivory fag holder, Celia certainly had style.

The front doorbell rang, and Tabs the redhead went to
answer it. When Dolly heard a man's voice out there, she
thought of her dad. Maybe he was looking for her. She felt sick
with fear. The kitchen door opened and she jumped as if she'd
been shot. Aware of Celia watching her, she picked up her
teacup with a shaking hand, and drank.

Tabs poked her head around the door. 'Customer for Aretha,'
she said, and the beautiful black woman uncurled her six-foot
length from her chair with a grin.

'Some of us, we just so in demand,' she purred, and headed
out of the kitchen, closing the door behind her.

'Yeah, yeah,' said Cindy.

Tabs sat back down.

Customer? thought Dolly. She heard people going up the stairs, heard a door open and close overhead. No one else seemed to be taking any notice. The chatter resumed. She picked up a biscuit and bit into it and let the warmth and the camaraderie in the kitchen wash over her. It was comforting, somehow. Not like home. Presently Darren stretched and said he'd better make tracks, and Cindy and Tabs said they were off to the shops. Celia said she was expecting Billy, so would Ellie see Dolly back up to her room?

There was another knock on the front door when Ellie and Dolly were out in the hall heading for the stairs. Ellie let in a vacant-looking man in a deerstalker hat, clutching a briefcase.

'Hiya, Billy,' she said, and he walked past her without a word.

'You think you'll be staying on?' asked Ellie as they went up the stairs and stopped outside Dolly's bedroom door.

'Nah,' said Dolly. She could hear a strange sound coming from the room next door to hers. Like someone being beaten or whipped, she thought. Only it couldn't be. Could it? Surely Celia wouldn't allow anything cruel to go on, not in her house? Maybe she'd been wrong about Celia, though. Maybe the streets would be safer after all.

'That . . . noise,' she said to Ellie.

'Yeah? What about it?'

'Do you think we ought to help . . . ?'

'Help Aretha?' Ellie laughed out loud. 'Oh no, I don't think so. Aretha can handle herself, no bother. It's the client that's in trouble, not her.'

'What?' Dolly stared in bewilderment. Aretha was beating someone up? But why?

Ellie rolled her eyes. 'Jesus, you're a little innocent, ain't you? Look, Aretha's a dominatrix. Do you know what that means?'

Dolly shook her head.

'It means she beats the crap out of the customers because that's what they want her to do. They love it.'

'Customers?'

'Yeah, customers.' Ellie lightly tweaked Dolly's nose. 'This is a knocking shop.'

When Dolly still looked blank, Ellie raised her eyebrows and puffed out a sigh. 'A fuck-shop. Full of whores. Got it now?'

36

Dolly's first instinct was to run. Ellie's words shocked her, but she understood them. She understood plenty now. Ellie meant that people were doing the man-and-woman thing right here, under this roof. Money was changing hands for services provided. And how long would it be before she got dragged into it, made to do it with some bastard she didn't want?

She seriously thought about it, just upping and getting gone. But over the weeks that followed, Celia made no demands. She continued to be kind to her, and seemed perfectly willing to go on providing bed and board. And the place was happy. Despite all the comings and goings, despite what really went on here, the place was orderly, neat, run on a strictly businesslike footing.

No one hurt her. Celia took her up West, bought little bits and pieces for her, fussed over her in a way that Mum had never done. She'd missed that, and had never realized it until now. But Celia had a hard side to her too; she could be firm with the girls and tough with the punters. One day Dolly walked into the kitchen when Celia was sitting at the table having tea and biscuits with that bloke 'Billy', who looked like a dimwit in his deerstalker, his briefcase on his lap like a shield against the world.

Now she saw Celia's tougher side. Celia's face hardened when she saw Dolly standing there. She stubbed out her cigarette in the Capstan ashtray and hissed out a stream of smoke, while giving Dolly a look.

'Give us a fucking mo, will you, Doll?' she snapped. 'Clear off for a second, OK? And stick the bloody wood in the hole.'

Surprised, Dolly backed out of the kitchen and closed the door. She went through to the empty front room. Her mother had a front room a bit like this, the best furnished room in the house but mostly unused.

Dolly sat on a plush sofa and thought of Mum. That fucking front room at home had never been used, to be honest. For years Mum hadn't behaved as a true mother should. Mum had just sat in the kitchen and stared at the floor, and let Dolly be picked on by her dad. Her heart twisted with sadness as she thought of little Sand, and Nige and Dick, and quiet, obedient Sarah, and wondered what was happening with them these days.

Suddenly, the door opened and Celia stood there.

'There you are! He's gone now, you can come in the kitchen, all right?'

Celia led the way into the kitchen and Dolly followed. Celia started putting used cups in the sink and getting out fresh ones. She put the kettle on to boil. Then she turned and smiled at Dolly.

'That was Billy,' she said. 'Sorry, did I snap at you? Only he's very important, Billy.'

Dolly was bewildered by this statement. The long-faced git looked like an idiot, how could he be important?

While the kettle boiled, Celia leaned back against the worktop, folded her arms and looked at Dolly. 'We pay up to the Delaneys, Dolly. Do you understand what that means?'

Dolly shook her head.

'It means they take a slice off the top of what I bring into the house with my girls and Darren,' said Celia. 'And in return, they keep me and my lot safe.'

'Billy works for them, does he?' asked Dolly.

'Billy? Nah.' Celia spooned tea into the pot and poured the water on. 'Billy works for the Carter boys, but Billy's been coming round here ever since he was little and Billy don't break his habits. Of course, there's bad blood between the Carters and the Delaneys, and it's getting worse all the time, but Tory Delaney says it's OK, so everyone makes an exception for Billy. He's a bit simple, poor duck. There but for the grace of God go all of us, that's what I say.'

Celia came and sat down at the table.

'So what you going to do now you're all better?' she asked.

Ah. So now she was going to be put back out on to the streets. Dolly wasn't that surprised, not really. Celia had been good, keeping her here for so long. She couldn't expect it to last forever.

Dolly opened her mouth to speak, but Celia said: 'Of course you can stay here if you want. You're very welcome, I'm sure. And you needn't worry. I run a respectable household. I won't allow anyone under sixteen to get fucked in it.'

Dolly didn't know what to say. She was floored – not for the first time – by Celia's weird mix of no-bullshit earthiness and pristine elegance.

'You can help out around the place, if you'd like to. Clean up, you know. Earn a bit of pin money that way, how about that?'

Dolly swallowed hard. She was touched. No one in her own family had ever been so kind to her as Celia was.

'I'd like to stay, and help out,' she said.

Celia tucked a fag into the ivory holder. She lit it, then gave Dolly a squinting grin through the smoke. 'Bloody good show,' she said. 'Let's drink to it.'

37

London, June 1994

Annie was down the cop shop first thing Thursday morning, pushing her way through the sorry remnants of the night before: the drinkers, the prossies, the dazed druggies. When she got to the counter, she asked for Hunter.

'He's not in,' said the sergeant behind the desk, swatting away a drunken man's hand from his pen and pad. Wafts of unwashed flesh, vomit and hard liquor were coming off the man in great crashing waves.

'Will he be in soon then?' Annie was trying to hold her breath and talk at the same time.

The sergeant shrugged. A woman passed by Annie. She was plain as a pikestaff, with scraped-back honey-brown hair, no make-up, a mouth as thin and hard as a steel clamp. She wore a cheap-looking navy suit made for comfort, not elegance. The sergeant lifted the flap in the counter for the woman and she was just about to go through it when Annie stopped her with a hand on her arm.

'DS Duggan?' she said. It was Hunter's sidekick, Annie knew it. She remembered her from when it had all blown up with Rufus Delaney.

'Something I can help you with?' asked DS Duggan,

drawing to one side, well away from the stinking drunk. The desk sergeant sighed and dropped the flap.

'I'm looking for DCI Hunter.'

'He's out.'

'I know. But you'll do,' said Annie.

'In what way?'

'In the way that you can tell me how it's going with the investigation into the death of my friend.'

Sandra Duggan's thin lips drew into a straight line. 'You're talking about a police investigation, Mrs Carter. We don't discuss such things with members of the general public, I'm afraid. If we have questions to ask you, we'll be in touch.'

'No.' Annie was shaking her head. 'You see, *I* have questions for *you*. I want to know if you've got anyone for this yet. Any suspects. Anything.'

Duggan stared steadily at Annie. 'I think we just covered that,' she said, and went to turn away, toward the desk.

'Whoa.' Annie caught her arm again.

'Take your hand off me,' said Duggan.

Annie did. Her hand lingered on the fabric. First impressions had been right. Those threads *were* cheap and nasty.

'Look. Any information would be welcome,' said Annie, lowering her voice so that none of the other people in the front office could hear her. 'It would be received confidentially, of course. No questions asked and nothing ever said about it. And there would be payment.'

The thin mouth opened in a soundless O of surprise. Then a small laugh escaped Duggan as she stared at Annie.

'Are you trying to bribe an officer of the law?' she asked.

Annie stared back, hard-eyed. 'Perish the thought,' she said.

'Only if you *are*, I have to say that's a very serious matter.'

Annie nodded slowly. 'Understood,' she said. Well, it had been worth a try.

'If there's nothing else . . . ?'

'No. Nothing at all.'

Annie walked out of the cop shop and into a dazzling sunny morning. For the moment, she was at a loss. Jackie – hopefully – was on the case, doing what she wanted. Hunter was off doing something, she didn't know what. Maybe things were moving, but it didn't feel like it. She wished he'd get his finger out of his arse and do something positive about finding Dolly's killer, before she went shrieking mad with frustration.

And it was then, right then, that she saw a familiar and very welcome sight. A face she knew. A *friend*.

38

A bulky man was getting out of a sleek black Jag and crossing the road to go into a newsagent's a few doors down.
The bald gleaming head, bronzed from some foreign holiday, the twinkling set of gold crucifixes, one in each huge
cauliflower ear, the immaculate suit pulling tight over
eighteen stones' worth of solid muscle. Annie was a woman
spotting a life raft in a stormy sea.

'Tony! Tone!' she yelled out, smiling suddenly because
she had never seen a prettier sight than this big ugly
bastard.

It was Tony – first Max's driver, then hers, then Dolly's.
He'd been her greatest supporter through many a battle.
He turned his head and she waved madly. People were
looking, staring, and Tony stared too. He paused mid-
stride and then she saw the change come over him. His
face hardened. And then – to her shock – he turned back,
away from her, and kept walking.

'What the *fuck* . . . ?' she said angrily. She wasn't about
to let this go.

Annie ran after him and followed him into the newsagent's. Inside the tiny shop a tired-looking man in a flat
cap was dispensing the day's news to his punters. When
Annie caught up with Tony, she grabbed his arm.

'Tone? Didn't you see me?'

But she knew he had. Of *course* he had. He had seen her, and chosen not to. It gave her the creeps. All right, she hadn't expected flags and banners from Gary, but Chris? Ellie? Steve? And now even Tone, who had been the one to phone her, the one who had told her all this was going down?

They know, they all know, and Max, where's Max right now, who's he with, what's he doing, and oh God, does he know too . . . ?

She took a deep breath, tried to calm herself, but she had a real case of the jitters. The way he was *looking* at her – Tone, her old mate, who'd stood in her corner on more than one tricky occasion, who'd always backed her to the hilt.

'Mrs C,' he said, with a cool nod of the head. At the same time, he was rootling in his pocket for change, looking at the headlines about Labour winning sixty-two seats in the election and still looking for a party leader after John Smith's untimely death. In the running for leader was Margaret Beckett, John Prescott and someone called Tony Blair. Tony kept his focus on the news, showing her no interest.

'Tone, what's going on?'

Tony was silent.

'Come on, say something, even if it's only bollocks!'

'I don't know what you're talking about,' he said, his eyes avoiding hers. He paid at the till, tucked the paper under his arm, left the shop. Annie trailed behind him. She was having to half-run to keep up with his long stride. He was walking back to the Jag. Finally she grabbed his arm again. Tony halted. Looked at her. Seemed to look straight *through* her.

'What?' he asked.

'*What?*' Annie echoed, half-laughing although it wasn't

funny, not in the least. 'Is that all you've got? For fuck's sake! Dolly has been *shot*, and you act like you don't care.'

'That's not true,' said Tone. 'Of course I bloody care.'

'Good! Then will you please stop walking away from me?'

'I got nothing to say to you.'

'Are you *kidding* me?' Annie raised her fists to her head and was actually wrenching at her hair with her hands, she was so exasperated. 'Dolly is *dead*, Tone. And you were her driver, her minder, you were supposed to look out for her, and what the fuck were you doing? Were you off somewhere having a wank? Because it's pretty clear you weren't doing your job!'

That did get a reaction. Tony's brows drew together and he looked thunderous.

'Look,' he said sharply. 'I drove her last Thursday afternoon, up West. She wanted to go shopping, that's what she always did on a Thursday afternoon if she wasn't meeting Ellie Brown at the Ritz. I dropped her back at the Palermo at about four, and she went into the club and I went home. When I went to check in with her Friday lunchtime, she was bloody dead. More than that I can't tell you. I wish to God it hadn't happened, and if I find whoever did it before Old Bill does then they're up to their mangy arses in trouble and there won't be no nice civilized trial or a cosy cell to lie in, they'll be fucking *gone*, you got me?'

Annie was silent; their eyes were locked. Tony swallowed hard, then looked away.

'I liked Dolly,' he said. 'You know that. To think of some scummy bastard doing that, it makes me sick to my stomach.'

'And that's all you know?' asked Annie quietly.

'It's all I know.'

'I need help, Tone. I want to find out who did this and I

want to deal with it in *our* way. You're right – no cosy cells, no trial. Only justice. *Our* sort of justice. Will you help me do that?'

Say yes, she thought. He would say yes, he had to say yes.

'No,' said Tony, and turned away from her.

Annie caught his arm again. Tony paused, looked back at her face. Annie released him, her shoulders sagging. 'Do you know what happened to Jackie?' she asked.

'What?' He looked at her blankly.

'Jackie Tulliver. He used to be sharp as a razor, now he's drowning himself in the bottle day and night. What happened?'

Tony shrugged. 'His mum died,' he said. Then he turned his back on her and walked over to the Jag. He didn't look back; not once.

Yeah, he knows, she thought. *They all do.*

39

Annie stood there staring after him. Something bad was happening here, something *terrible*. She longed for Max, for a friendly face, for things to be as they used to be, when she was treated with respect, when all the boys knew that she was *Mrs Carter*, and you had to tread softly around her, or else. Now, she was nothing but shit on their shoes, and she didn't like that feeling at all.

'There you are,' said Jackie, wandering up to her, a fat cigar clamped between his yellow teeth. Annie almost groaned. *This* was all she had to work with. This *wreck*. He was staggering a little, and his hands were shaking. He was unshaven, unwashed. As usual.

'Yeah,' sighed Annie. So his mum had passed on. Was that really an excuse for *this*? 'Here I am.'

'I've talked to our people in the Bill, they don't know nothing. Not yet, anyway.'

'Right.'

Jackie coughed. Looked at her.

'What?' she asked.

'A little dosh up front would be good,' he said, his eyes straying to the off-licence over the road. 'Got a couple of contacts you might want to speak to. Might be worth your while.'

Ah, what the hell.

Annie handed over a tenner and off he went, weaving through the traffic, people honking their horns at him but Jackie taking no notice, intent as a bloodhound on the trail. She followed him slowly, her mind on Dolly, on Tony, on the whole flaming awful mess this was turning out to be, and as she did so a cyclist came past her, skidding to a halt, almost hitting her.

'Christ!' she yelped. 'Watch what you're doing, will you?'

And then he stuffed a piece of paper into her hand, and sped away.

Annie stood there, looking at the piece of paper.

Ah shit. No, no, no. Not now. Please, not now.

She stepped back on to the pavement and unfurled it. Numbers. Not many. She stood there and slowly she deciphered the code. It said: *Come at once.*

Annie screwed the note up, the *pizzino*, and flung it to the ground where it was quickly trampled underfoot.

I can't, she thought. *Not right now. I'm sorry, but I can't.*

And once again she stepped into the road and followed Jackie Tulliver, the useless drunk – and also the only hope she had.

Night was closing in on them as they went to the address of one of Jackie's 'contacts'. The rain was swooshing down and the wipers were working overtime in the taxi. On the way, they passed the Palermo and Annie stared out at it. Earlier in the day, she'd passed it and the police tapes had been up, an officer had been there standing guard on the door. Now . . .

'Stop! Stop the damned car, will you?' she said.

'What the . . . ?' asked Jackie, who'd been half-dozing, almost ready to sleep off his latest boozing session. Now he snapped awake and stared at her as the cab driver pulled in to the kerb.

Annie slapped payment into the driver's hand and was out of the car like a long dog. She ran over to the Palermo and stood there, staring.

The police tapes were gone. There was no officer on the door. Instead, there was a white van parked outside and men were bringing out boxes of stuff. Annie saw clothes she recognized, a pink fluffy cushion perched on top of one of the bulging boxes. It fell to the pavement, soaking up wet dirt and grime. Someone bent, snatched it back up, stuffed it back in the box.

'Holy *shit*,' said Annie under her breath, and hurried inside.

40

'What's going on?' bleated Jackie. 'I thought you wanted—'

Annie wasn't even listening. She shot off inside the club, blundering past the removals men, almost running past Pete the barman, and then she hared across the club floor and up the stairs, nearly knocking over another bloke coming down with another full box of Dolly's belongings. She barged into the flat and stared around in disbelief.

They'd stripped it. The rug with Dolly's blood on it was gone, and all her little ornaments. Everything. From the bedroom next door she could hear men laughing, a radio playing Whitney Houston, who was blasting out 'One Moment in Time' as they disassembled Dolly's bed, cleaned out her bedroom, trampled on her memory.

In the middle of the sitting room stood Caroline, Gary's latest squeeze. She saw Annie there and her mouth formed a cat's-bum pout of dislike.

'What the fuck are you doing?' demanded Annie.

'What does it look like?'

Annie felt like she'd had a gutful. She barrelled forward and grabbed the front of Caroline's dress. Caroline let out a squawk of surprise. Annie's eyes bored into hers from inches away.

'It looks like you're taking the piss,' said Annie. '*That's* what it looks like. This is Dolly's home, you silly tart.'

'*What* did you call me?'

'You heard. Would you jump into her grave this fast, you cow?'

'You'd better let go of me,' said Caroline, writhing against Annie's grip as Jackie walked into the room.

'Hey! Ladies, no need to get rough now . . .' he started, waving his hands around. It was the most animated Annie had seen him since she got back, and that angered her all the more, that he was defending this stupid *bint* who thought she could swan in here and turn Dolly's memory to ashes in the blink of an eye.

'Shut your trap, Jackie,' Annie shot back at him over her shoulder. She gave Caroline a shake. 'And you! Explain yourself.'

'Explain *what*?' spat out Caroline. 'Gary said I was going to take over here, and that's what I'm damned well doing, OK? I'm just cleaning out all this old crap.'

'Old crap?' Annie's eyes glinted with rage. 'You cheeky little pisser! This is *Dolly's* place.'

'This *was* her place,' corrected Caroline. 'The Bill have said they've got all they need in here, and we can clear it out. I've got the decorators coming in tomorrow, got to get shot of all this fucking pink tat first.'

Suddenly the rage drained out of Annie like someone had released a valve. Dolly was dead, and actually? This bitch was right. Things were moving on. But to think of this prancing little clown in here running the show, riding roughshod over all that Dolly had so painstakingly built up, it stuck in her gullet to even think of that. But what could she do? Precisely *nothing*.

'You say Gary gave you the word on this?' asked Annie coldly.

'Damned right. And he got his orders straight from your old man.'

'*What?*' Annie stared at her. 'Max has been in touch with Gary? Since Dolly got shot? When?'

'Couple of damned days ago. Gary filled him in on what happened, and asked if I could step in. Mr Carter said yes. You going to let go of this dress? You're creasing the fabric.'

'I'll crease *your* fucking fabric in a minute,' snapped Annie. 'You never heard of the word "respect"? Dolly's only just cold, and you're in here already. It's not right.'

'It *is* right, your damned husband says it's OK and he owns the place. So what the hell you're beefing about, I really don't know. Take it up with him.'

I wish I damned well could, thought Annie. Her head was reeling. Max had phoned Gary, and if that was the case maybe he'd also called the Prospect villa. She'd check that when she got back to the hotel. With a disdainful flick of the wrist she released Caroline, who staggered back a pace.

'You're fucking berserk, you are,' said Caroline, brushing down the front of her dress. 'Gary always said you were, and he's right. Having marriage troubles, he said. You and Mr Carter. And meeting you? I'm not surprised.'

Marriage troubles? Since when had Max and her been having marriage troubles? This was the first she'd heard of it.

Jesus, Max, what's going on with you? Where the hell are you?

'Life goes on, you know,' said Caroline, brushing past her and past Jackie, and going to the door of the flat.

'Yeah.' Annie turned and gave Jackie a bleak look. 'Just not for Dolly.'

Caroline kept on walking. Annie could see she didn't give a shit. Life had just bounced her a big result; she'd caught herself a nightclub manager and now she was going to step into Dolly's shoes and have the running of the

Palermo. Probably she'd get Tony and the Jag to queen it around town in too. No wonder she was so made up with it all.

Sickened, Annie stood there as Caroline vanished back downstairs. Jackie looked at the floor.

'It's fucking sad,' he said. 'About Dolly.'

'Yeah,' said Annie, thinking that she'd like to kick Gary Tooley's balls up around his ears somewhere. 'Ain't it just. Come on, let's go see this fucking contact of yours.'

41

'It's years since I've been in a nightclub,' said Redmond, looking around at the lush gold and brown décor of the Blue Parrot as Gary greeted him in the foyer. 'We owned some, you know. My family. Back in the dim distant past,' he said in that almost hypnotically soft southern Irish lilt.

And they were all burned to the ground, he thought.

'Really,' said Gary Tooley, uninterested.

Redmond took his time looking over this strange storklike individual. He was too tall, too thin, his hair swept back and coloured a bright blond. His eyes were the eyes of a killer; pale, uncaring. Redmond recognized a kindred spirit, someone who could be every bit as vicious as himself.

'So,' said Redmond after they'd shaken hands. 'This information you've got for me . . .'

'Yeah. You'll be amazed,' said Gary. 'Come on up.'

He led the way up the stairs at the side of the big room, escorted Redmond into an office, closed the door behind them. He sat down behind the desk, while Redmond sat in front of it. Then Redmond sat there and stared at Gary Tooley expectantly. Gary swallowed; he seemed all of a sudden nervous.

Well, he should be, thought Redmond. Gary Tooley ought to remember that the Delaney gang had shoved hard at the

Carter territories, had been almost more trouble than could be handled. The Carter boys had been tough; but the Delaneys had given them a run for their money.

'So?' said Redmond, when Gary didn't speak.

'I've been getting calls,' said Gary.

'From who?'

'Whoa.' Gary sat back in his chair, sprawled, tried to re-establish just whose office this was, who was in control here. There was something about Redmond that chilled and intimidated him. But they were here to do business. That was all. Redmond had been out of the hard game for years. Even so, he still looked like a cold son of a bitch who'd pull your throat out through your ears if you upset him.

'Whoa?' echoed Redmond. His thin lips tilted in a lop-sided smile. 'Would you like to explain just what you mean by that?'

'I *mean* let's not rush this. There's the question of pay-ment first.'

'Payment?' Redmond's smile broadened but it didn't touch his eyes. 'For what?'

'For the information. It's pretty hot stuff, I can tell you.'

'But you *can't* tell me. Apparently. Until I pay you money.' Redmond stared at Gary and thought of old enemies. 'Has Max Carter told you to do this?'

'No. No way. This is all my own work.'

'Mr Tooley, I need a suggestion of what you're talking about.'

'All right.' Gary sat back, hooked one long leg over the other. Considered for a moment. 'Suppose I shared with you some information I've held for a long, long time. About you. And about your sister, Orla.'

Redmond went very still. He had no idea where his twin was, or what had happened to her. They had parted ways back in the seventies, and so far he'd felt no driving urge to hook up with her again. He hoped she was well, and happy, wherever she was, but being Orla, tormented soul that she'd always been, he doubted it.

'Go on,' he said.

'Someone's been in touch with me and has told me things that concern you, and her.'

'Like what?'

'Can we negotiate first? Agree a price?'

'No. I need more.'

'It concerns an accident. A crash. Back in the seventies.'

Redmond stared at Gary but he wasn't seeing him. Suddenly he was back there. The plane plummeting from the sky. The icy waters closing over his head, the panic, the pilot strapped dead, drowned, in his seat at the controls . . .

'What about it?' asked Redmond.

Gary smirked. 'That got your attention.'

'I said, what about it?'

Gary took a breath and said, very slowly, leaning forward in his chair: 'It wasn't an accident.'

He saw the impact his words had on Redmond. Saw the pale face blanch even whiter as the words sank in. Gary leaned back again in his chair and said: '*Now* can we talk money?'

42

They talked money, lots of it. Five thousand for information, five thousand to discover that there had been no fuel leak; five thousand to find that Constantine Barolli the Mafia don had ordered sabotage, had wanted both Redmond and Orla dead.

'And there's more,' said Gary Tooley, clearly gloating now. 'This old cunt keeps phoning here, talking about past times, and she's hinting at something more. Something *incredible*.'

'And what is that?' demanded Redmond.

Gary spread his long-fingered hands. 'That I don't know yet,' he lied. 'But I will. I'll worm it out of the crazy old bitch and then we'll talk again, yeah? Agree another price for the additional information?'

Redmond smiled. It was the smile of an alligator before it snaps its jaws shut on its prey.

'Of course,' he said.

After the meeting, Redmond went home to his new rented house.

'Good day?' asked Mitchell, who had replaced the old housekeeper after his troubles with the church. Mitchell had worked for Redmond years ago, he could cook – after a fashion – and he was handy in any sort of fight, however nasty, so he was always useful to have around. Redmond had been booted out of his grace and favour home, although that didn't concern him much. Years ago he had salted money away all over the place, the proceeds of lorry hijacks and shop robberies; he was minted. He could do as he pleased. He did miss all those willing little acolytes from the church, but what could you do? There were always women, if you wanted them. Right now, he didn't.

'Yeah, good,' he said, and doggedly ate the meal Mitchell had prepared to keep his strength up, although he felt sick with excitement and his insides were churning.

Constantine Barolli had planned to kill him, and his twin.

And for what? Because Barolli had the hots for Annie Carter, of course. And who wouldn't? She was – had always been – magnificent. Strong, ferocious – a lioness. You had to admire that.

It was a miracle that they had survived that crash.

The Mafia boss had wanted them dead.

And Gary Tooley had said there was more information to come.

Redmond wanted that information *now*.

He finished the meal, hardly even registering what he was eating, and went upstairs to his bedroom. There he sat on the bed for a while, then he stood up, stripped off his jacket and his shirt, and went to the mirrored wardrobe. Turning slightly, he saw the marks on his back, the freshly healed scars there. He opened the wardrobe door and took out a brown cardboard box, three feet long by four inches wide, removed the lid, and lifted out the kidney-shaped piece of rubber and the cat o' nine tails hidden there.

He was wicked and he knew it.

He'd disgraced the church.

Disgraced himself.

Self-flagellation was the only cure, the only thing that

cleansed him and made him feel better. So he lifted the woven-leather handle, marked brown with dried blood – *his* blood, and the blood of some of those women before Sally Westover, those poor little acolytes of his with their puny soft backs striped with the marks of the whip, the way he liked them, whimpering in pain and fear and adoration.

He put the rubber between his teeth. Then he lifted the whip out, and swung it back, and struck, hard.

The pain was exquisite, cleansing him, scouring his troubled soul.

43

Limehouse, 1960

Dolly became a fixture around Celia's knocking shop. She cleaned, she ironed, she chatted to the girls, and what little remained of any childlike innocence quickly fell away. It became her task to keep the bedrooms tidy and the bedding fresh, to make sure every room was ready for action.

It was her job to make sure there were plenty of tissues and packets of French letters beside each bed, and that there was always a full bottle of baby oil and a tub of Crowe's Cremine, which was a theatrical make-up remover and perfect for lubrication. In Aretha's room she also made sure there was a stock of rope and leather straps – and she regularly whopped the Dettol over a couple of old tasselled camel whips that someone had brought back from a Moroccan trip.

It always astonished Dolly, the diversity of the men who came through the door of the knocking shop. Cavalry officers, dustmen, bowler-hatted civil servants – the search for sexual satisfaction knew no social boundaries. And mostly they were well-behaved. But one night they weren't, and what happened then stuck in Dolly's memory and just wouldn't budge.

'I told you I don't do that,' Ellie was shouting.
Dolly came out of her room and stood on the landing.

'No! For fuck's sake, what are you—'

Darren came out of his room, quickly pulling on a robe. 'What's going on?' he asked.

'It's Ellie,' Dolly said, and Darren stepped forward and knocked on Ellie's closed bedroom door.

'Ellie? You all right in there?'

No answer came back.

Darren went to the banister, leaned over and shouted: 'Celia!' Then he went back to Ellie's door and tried the handle. The door was locked. They could hear Ellie crying.

'Shit!' said Darren, kicking the door. Then he hammered on it again. 'Open this bloody door!' he shouted.

Celia was standing on the bottom stair. 'What's up?' she called.

'Ellie's got trouble,' said Darren. 'The door's locked, I can't get in.'

Celia said nothing, just went to the phone on the hall stand and dialled quickly. Dolly didn't hear what she said, but no sooner had she spoken to someone than she put the phone down again and hared up the stairs. She banged on Ellie's door.

'Ellie? You all right in there? Come on, unlock the bloody door.'

'I can't!' came back Ellie's shaking voice.

'Why can't you, for God's sake?'

'He won't let me.'

'Well, he'd better bloody let you or there's going to be trouble. You all right?'

'He hit me.'

There was a muttering of a male voice from behind the door.

'Oi!' yelled Celia. 'You! Arsehole! You want to go beating girls up, do you? Come out here and try it on one who can take it then!'

170

'*Fuck off!*' *yelled the punter.*

'*You shit, you get out here. This is my house!*' *returned Celia.*

'*I said fuck off!*'

From down below came the sound of a key turning in the front door and a gust of cold night air came in; with it came two red-haired men built like barn doors. Dolly had never seen the Delaneys before. Celia always spoke about them in hushed tones, like they were gods or something, set apart from the rest of shambling humanity. Now, as Dolly saw them come running up the stairs toward her, she thought they were just bloody terrifying.

'*What's going on?*' *asked the one in front, who had the air of being in charge.*

'*Mr Delaney, one of my girls is having trouble. The door's locked,*' *said Celia.*

'*Pat, get it open,*' *he said, and they all stood back as Pat, massive and mean-eyed, took a kick at the door lock. It instantly juddered open, and he pulled a tyre iron out from under his mac and charged in, his brother following.*

'*What the fuck's this—*' *started the man sitting on the bed, who was in shirt and Y-fronts.*

Ellie was sitting on the other side of the bed nursing her jaw, her face wet with tears.

'*I'll show you what the feck it is,*' *said Pat Delaney, and yanked the man up and smashed a fist into his nose. Blood spattered out of it as he staggered away, then the one in charge caught him and held him as Pat started whacking his middle with the tyre iron.*

Once the man sagged and all the fight left him, the one in charge flung him to the floor, and Pat waded in again, thwacking the iron down again and again, landing blow after blow to the man's face until all Dolly, peeping in from the hallway, could see was a wet bloody mask.

Finally, the Delaneys hefted him up, grabbed his trousers and jacket, and bundled him and his belongings down the stairs and out the front door. Celia, who had followed them down, closed the door softly behind them. The house was quiet again, but for Ellie's soft sobbing.

Celia came back up the stairs and looked at the bloodied carpet in Ellie's room.

'Get some soap and water and take care of that, will you, Doll?' she said to Dolly, then she and Darren went in and sat either side of Ellie on the bed.

'You all right then, Ells?' asked Darren, putting an arm around her.

'Yeah,' she said. 'He kept on about having a French polish, and I told him I don't do that, I've told him a dozen times before, and tonight he just went bloody mad and wouldn't listen.'

'Never mind, Ellie, it's over now. Tory and Pat Delaney have sorted him out good and proper. He won't come back again,' said Celia, patting her shoulder.

'What's a French polish?' Dolly asked Darren later, when they were just turning in for the night and peace was restored.

'A blow job,' said Darren.

'Oh.' Dolly knew about blow jobs. She could understand Ellie's aversion.

'Night then, Doll,' he said, and went back to his room.

Dolly went to bed. She lay there in the dark thinking about the man who'd had his face smashed in because he wanted a French polish, and the Delaneys that Celia paid protection money to. Now she could see why. They'd worked that bloke over like they were tenderizing a piece of meat. It had taken her some while and a lot of elbow grease to get the blood stains out of the carpet.

She had always thought that men worked against you – the exception being Darren, who was too interested in his own sex to ever bother the girls. But tonight had taught her a lesson; sometimes men could work in your favour, too. She turned over, plumped up her pillows, and slept more soundly than she had in a long, long while.

She caught Celia alone in the kitchen next day.

Celia looked up at her young worker through a haze of ciggie smoke. She was turning the pages of the Daily Mail, reading about all the bookshops selling out of Lady Chatterley's Lover on publication day. 'What?' she queried.

Dolly sat down at the table. 'I've remembered his name, that pimp who duffed me over.'

Dolly closed up the paper and took another deep drag on her ivory holder. 'That's good. What's he look like?' she asked.

'He's tall and thin. Bony. Dark-skinned. There's a big scar here.' Dolly ran a finger down her left cheek. 'And he wears these flashy shoes with silver eagles on the toecaps.'

Dolly would never forget the eagles. One of them had been imprinted on her thigh for days after the beating he'd given her. You could make out the beak and even the feathers, he'd kicked her that hard.

'Is that right?' Celia exhaled a plume of smoke. 'And his name?'

'I'll start on the bedrooms,' said Dolly, standing up. 'It's Gregor White.'

'Right you are,' said Celia, and went back to her paper.

44

Gregor White knew the trouble with brasses. The trouble was, you had to be on their backs day and night. Keep them on their backs, too. Fail to do that, and the lazy cows would slope off to the Lyons Corner House or the coffee shop or the local Wimpy and stuff their faces with cakes and burgers and get a big arse on them and turn the punters off and then where would you be? Fucked, that's where.

Discipline was Gregor's watchword when it came to whores. You had to rule them with an iron fist, these women. That was all they understood, because basically they were scum, but they were lucrative scum, you must never forget that. Provided you kept a good eye on them, reined them in when necessary, landed a punch or two in the right place (which was never the face, punters were so picky) your income was secure.

And this was why Gregor was pissed off one night at around eleven o'clock to find that two of his best payers, Julie and Charmaine, were not on their usual corner where he expected them to be. He knew this because he was looking out of the window of his toasty-warm flat over the newsagents and from there he could see the corner – and where the fuck were they? Granted, it was foggy out there, and bloody cold, but they were used to it, they'd been doing it for years. This just went to prove that what his dear old mum had told him on her deathbed was true – you couldn't depend on a bloody soul.

Angry, muttering under his breath, he pulled on his silver toecapped shoes, his favourites, and his tailored jacket, and then he pounded off down the stairs to find out what was occurring. The cold hit him like a knife and he pulled his jacket around him, shivering. Bastard women, he'd have to discipline them over this. And then he was going to give each of them a stiff talking-to.

He stalked to the corner and looked around. Traffic drifted past, fog lights cutting a swathe through the pea-souper, all the streetlights wearing shadowy mustard-yellow haloes. The fog dampened all sound, stifled the traffic noise – it felt quite spooky out here. He paced around, looking up the road and down it. No sign of them. No sign of anyone.

'Fuck it,' he muttered.

'Got a light?' asked a voice behind him.

He spun around, startled. He hadn't heard anyone come up. The fog was drifting, thick as cobwebs; he could feel the dampness of it on his face, seeping into his clothes. Fuck this for a game. There was a bulky man wearing a mac and with a hat pulled down low over his face standing right there under the sickly, soupy glow of the street light. He was holding a cigarette.

'Yeah,' said Gregor, distracted because he was looking for his bitches, who had vanished, apparently, and by fuck, by God, he swore he was going to mark their card good. Give them both a swift kick up the cunt. And then he was going to get back indoors in the warm.

Gregor pulled out his gold lighter, the one he'd had initialled; he liked his nice threads and he liked his accessories too, his eagle-tipped shoes, his gold initialled bracelet – he had a lot of style and he liked to show it.

Gregor flicked the lighter and a flame erupted, illuminating the other man's face. Green eyes, he thought. That was rare, wasn't it? That was the last thing Gregor thought and those mean green eyes were the last thing he saw. There was the slightest puff of movement behind him and then there was a crashing pain in his head. Then there was only blackness.

45

Limehouse, 1962

Time passed and Dolly grew up. Once past sixteen, Celia asked if she'd like to earn some more wedge, become a working girl like the others here; Celia would hire a cleaner to take over Dolly's duties, what did she think?

'What – do the man-and-woman thing?' asked Dolly, shocked.

'Fuck the punters, yes.'

'Oh no. I don't think so.'

'Your decision. Up to a hundred sovs a night, though.'

'How much?'

'You heard me. The money's damned good,' said Celia. 'Not to be sniffed at. Maybe set yourself up, do something with your life, something different one of these days with money like that behind you. What do you think of that?'

Dolly looked blank. The money sounded great. But to start all that again . . .

'Think it over,' said Celia.

Dolly did, long and hard. She went and sat on Darren's bed and asked him what he thought of the idea. Darren was nice and he had style, and Dolly – who didn't – admired that.

She did try. Sometimes she got the home dye out and coloured her straight mouse-brown hair – but she ended up

177

with a yellowy blonde mop that looked hellish with her pink-toned skin. Thinking to improve it, she then permed it, and she had nice curls for a little while before her tortured barnet rebelled and took on the dull brittle texture of horse hair.

Ah yes, she tried. Didn't see the point, really, but she did. She let her roots show on occasion, bit her nails. Truth to tell, she knew she looked a bit of a mess most of the time. Yeah, Darren had style all right. And so did Celia. Dolly thought sometimes that she'd give a lot to be as polished as them, but she was realistic enough to see that it just wasn't going to happen.

'I wondered when she was going to get round to asking you, with Cindy and Tabs moving on. I should bite her bloody arm off,' Darren told Dolly, squinting his large blue eyes as he primped his glossy blond hair in the mirror, then carefully adjusted the peach chiffon scarf around his neck.

Grinning, he blew a kiss at his reflection and turned to Dolly. 'Wake up, Doll. This is a nice place. I've never worked in better. Madam down there looks after us all, she don't work us to death either. Gives us breaks, makes sure we're kept safe, insists on the clients washing themselves first and using French letters. This place is properly run.'

Then Dolly went in to Ellie's room where Ellie was loading six 45 rpm records on to the retaining arm of her little red Dansette. Dolly told her about Celia's offer while they sat on Ellie's bed and listened to 'Stand By Me', then 'Crying', and then Patsy Cline was wailing on about falling to pieces when Ellie said: 'Do it.'

Ellie shook out a couple of Player's cigarettes from a packet and passed Dolly one. She struck a match and lit them both up. 'Lay down any ground rules first, though. Celia knows I don't do the French polishes – the blow jobs – never have, don't like that at all, and she makes sure the clients know it. Anything you really draw the line at, tell her.'

'I'm not sure,' said Dolly, pulling a face as she exhaled smoke. She liked smoking. It calmed the nerves, even if it did turn your fingers yellow. And she was remembering the time when the punter had disregarded Ellie's wishes, become obsessive and dangerous, and they'd had to call for the Delaney mob to do a dark alley job on the stupid cunt.

'The money's bloody good,' said Ellie.

Dolly thought it over. It wouldn't be like all that had happened in the past, with Dad. She would be in charge, that was the difference. And this time, should anything untoward happen, there was always the Delaneys to fall back on. She liked the thought of that, very much.

Thoughts of what happened years back always made her feel depressed. She tried not to think about it, but she didn't always succeed. Sometimes, she still caught the bus and went down the end of the street where she had grown up. She watched for Dad going to work, and she saw Sarah and the boys, growing up now, in big school, and little Sand bumbling about the place. She couldn't talk to them, couldn't even know them any more, because they would ask why did she go, and she couldn't tell them, couldn't even speak of it.

She didn't see Mum, but no surprises there; Mum was probably banged up in the funny farm by now, a permanent resident instead of a part-time visitor. Thinking of Mum was the worst thing of all, because she ought to feel sorry for her but she couldn't.

She mulled Celia's offer over for a couple of days, then thought of the money and all that she could do with it out in the big wide world some day in the future when she was no longer so scared as she was right now, scared like she had been ever since the man-and-woman stuff had started with Dad. So she said yes.

★

It wasn't so bad. All she had to do, she discovered, was what she had always done in the past – just take herself off somewhere in her mind while it happened, let that familiar old blankness settle over her and then, wallop, two minutes and it was all over and the customer was off out the door.

By the time she hit nineteen, she had a pretty good stash of loot put aside in the bottom of her wardrobe but she had no idea what to do with it. Dreams, plans, those were for other people. Unlike Ellie, there was nothing she objected to with the clients because she was never actually there *while it happened. So she did the lot. The blow jobs, the full sex, the hand jobs, anal, even some tying up and whipping (although most clients preferred to go to the more experienced Aretha for those services) and she even accommodated the Golden Rainers who liked to piss on a woman for some weird perverted reason of their own.*

'Oh, I seen worse than that, girl,' said Aretha. 'One of my boys? He likes to eat my . . . well, I think you get the picture.'

Nothing was off limits to Dolly, because she never felt it, was never truly aware of it happening. Somewhere, deep in her core, she knew that something had been killed in her; something that had once been alive and well was now dead and rotten.

'Smarten yourself up a bit, will you, Doll?' Celia asked sometimes when the blackness descended and Dolly's scruffiness reached a new low.

Dolly kept up with the home dye but her hair did look frazzled. Sometimes an inch of dark root showed through. She chain-smoked and didn't eat good food, only rubbish, so her skin was bad and she had to slather thick make-up on it to make it look passable.

Celia nagged Dolly sometimes about her appearance, but the truth was she didn't much care what she looked like because what was it for? The punters, who climbed on board and used her? Fuck them. If they didn't like it, they knew what they could do.

Despite the bad memories it conjured up, she still made the occasional bus trip to her old home, just to stand at the end of the street, watching. She didn't know why. It was something she felt she had to do, a compulsion, beyond her control. Common sense said leave it. The past was dead and it should stay that way. But every so often she'd get the urge to go back there and no amount of reasoning with herself could stop her.

Then one day – the day when she realized hell had opened up – she stood there at the end of the street for over an hour. That day she saw no boys, no Nige, no Dick, no little Sand trying to jump over the front wall and falling on his arse as usual, no Mum. What she did see was Sarah, her little sis, now fourteen years old, coming out of the door with Dad, and going out the front gate.

She saw Dad's arm draped around Sarah's shoulders. Saw his springy bow-legged walk, and felt her stomach heave.

But the worst thing? When she thought about it afterwards – and she couldn't stop thinking about it, try as she might – the very worst thing was Sarah's face. It was turned up to her father's and Dolly saw clearly that it wore an expression that was cowed but at the same time pitifully hopeful. Dolly's heart stopped in her chest as she saw it. Sarah's face said: I'll be good, Dad, so please don't hurt me. I love you, Dad, why do you hurt me?

And in that instant, sick beyond words, sick to her stomach, Dolly knew.

46

Dolly had her own worries, her own private concerns, but she wasn't completely cut off from the rest of humanity. She went downstairs one morning and into the kitchen, and there they all were: Celia, Darren, Aretha and Ellie, all sitting around the table with untouched cups of tea in front of them, all looking like they'd lost a tenner and found sixpence.

Dolly stopped inside the kitchen door and stared at them. Celia hadn't even lit a fag, hadn't even put one in her ivory holder. It lay on the table in front of her, unused, beside an unopened packet. It was like they were all in suspended animation. They didn't even look up at her.

'What's going on?' she asked, gazing around at their still, frozen faces.

Celia was the first to respond.

'Oh! Doll,' she said, and seemed unable to say more.

'What is it?' asked Dolly, taking her usual seat. She gave a tentative smile. 'What's happened then? Somebody died or something?'

Celia gave a slow dip of a nod. 'Yeah. Something like that, Doll.'

'What?' Dolly had been joking. The smile fell from her face. 'You know the Delaney boys?' said Aretha.

'What about them?' said Dolly.

'We got the news ten minutes ago. Can't take it in really,' said Celia.

'What is it?' Dolly's mouth was dry. Whatever it was, it was bad. Really bad. She could see that.

'Tory Delaney's dead.'

'Tory . . .' Dolly frowned. Tory was the one in charge of the Delaney gang they paid protection money to, the one who'd come in here with his hair-trigger-tempered brother Pat and sorted out that punter who'd been beating on Ellie.

'He's been shot. Outside the Tudor Club in Stoke Newington,' said Celia, whose face was pale with shock.

'Four times, they reckon,' said Darren. 'Three in the chest, one in the head. Nobody knows who did it, but we're all thinking the Carters.'

Dolly knew the Delaney and Carter gangs were at loggerheads – had been for years. But this . . . this was going to bring open warfare on to the streets. And if Tory was dead, who was going to be in charge of the Delaney gang now? Who was going to take revenge for Tory's murder?

'Redmond will take over. He's the eldest. Not Pat – he hasn't the brains for it,' said Celia.

'Redmond? That's the one with the twin, ain't it?' asked Aretha.

'That's the one. Redmond and Orla. Redmond's a thinker. Christ, I've only just got used to dealing with Tory. Tory was always a bit of a hothead, but Redmond? He's a cold fish. Cold right through, that's Redmond, that's what everyone says,' said Celia.

'Wasn't there another son? Younger still?' asked Ellie.

'That's Kieron, the painter. No, he wouldn't be into dirty games like the others. He's kept himself apart from all that,' said Celia.

Dolly tuned them out; she was still thinking about seeing Sarah and Dad on the street, still reliving it, still seeing little

Sar's face. She felt powerless and terrified whenever she thought of Dad. She couldn't face him, she couldn't bear it.

But oh God. Sarah!

'Dolly! Wake up girl, stick the kettle on, will you? This tea's stone cold,' said Celia.

Dolly tuned back in. She stood up and did as Celia asked, feeling a cold shiver run right up her spine. Things were changing here at the knocking shop, and she hated that.

47

Dolly would never forget the day Annie Bailey showed up on Celia's doorstep. It was not long after Tory got himself shot to death, and the rumours were rife. Max Carter, Max Carter, that's what everyone was saying. Max Carter did it. He was guilty as sin. And then there were other rumours, even more shocking ones; Max Carter had got married the day after Tory Delaney's death, but on the night that Tory had been killed Max Carter had also bedded his soon-to-be bride's sister. Somehow, this had become known to the Bailey family – and the shit had hit the fan big-style.

'Christ, that bloke's been busy,' was Darren's opinion, shared with all the girls at the kitchen table. He made a fanning gesture with his hand. 'I've seen him, you know. This Max Carter person. Hot as hell, that one. Shame he's straight. That man is gorgeous.'

'Do you think it's true? That he did all that?' asked Dolly, fascinated.

Darren shrugged. 'Who knows? Could be. He don't give a shit for anyone, that man. He's been shoving the Delaney boys for months now and I reckon it's about time they shoved back. And the girl? This Annie Bailey sort? He'd do that without a moment's thought.'

And then, this exotic-looking girl arrived – Celia's niece, by all accounts – and Celia Bailey took her in. Despite all her worries about Sarah and Dad and the changing situation with the Delaneys, Dolly glimpsed Annie and thought, Just look at her. Talk about Lady Muck.

Dolly herself was no beauty, and when she saw beauty in others she resented it. Annie was dark-haired, tall, with bone structure any girl would kill for and a stately, upright way of carrying herself. She had fabulous dark green eyes and a great body, shown off by a brief white PVC mini-mac and white kinky boots.

'That's her,' *Aretha said to Dolly and Darren, as Celia led Annie up the stairs.*

'Who?' *They looked at her in confusion.*

'Jeez, keep up will you? That's* her.' *Aretha leaned in so that Celia shouldn't hear them gossiping away down in the hall.* 'That's Annie Bailey, that's Ruthie Carter's sister, that's the one who was fucking Max Carter the night before he married Ruthie, the night they also say he killed Tory Delaney. Christ, don't you know anything? Her mum threw her out when she found out about it, and Celia's taken her in. Bet that went down well with dear old Mum, don't you?'

'She's a working girl then?' *asked Darren, eyes like saucers.*

'Nah, Celia's her aunt, her father's sister. I don't suppose anyone else would have her after what she did.'

'This Annie's sister took it bad then?' *said Ellie.*

'Bad?' *Aretha gave a guffaw of laughter.* 'Ruthie Bailey told their mum straight off, I heard, and the mother went crazy and kicked Annie Bailey's high-toned arse straight out on to the street. They ain't got a clue she's come here. Celia and the mother don't talk, haven't for years. Word is, Ruthie Bailey – no, Ruthie Carter – is taking to drink just like the mother, she's that upset about it all.'

In the days that followed, Dolly watched Annie. She carried herself like a queen. Which of course she wasn't. Dolly knew that. She was no better than any of the workers here, she was a tart, surely? No, she was worse than that. She'd fucked her brother-in-law, betrayed her sister. She was the lowest of the low.

One evening, Dolly went up to the room where Annie was hiding out, keeping out of everyone's way.

Guilty as sin, thought Dolly as she went up the stairs. Ellie's Dansette was playing Cliff Richard, and Darren and Ellie were in there, singing along, both of them out of tune like a couple of cats howling on a roof; they couldn't carry a tune in a bucket. They were all at a loose end tonight except Aretha, who was banging away with a client like a good 'un. It was raining; that always put the punters off.

Dolly was about to go and join Ellie and Darren when she saw Annie heading into her room.

'I know you,' said Dolly, pausing there. 'Word is, you fucked your sister's bridegroom the night before the wedding.'

Annie hesitated. After a moment she said in a low husky voice: 'Whatever the "word" is, I've got nothing to say about it.'

'Oh, go on,' crowed Dolly. 'I could do with a laugh.'

'Fuck off,' said Annie Bailey.

'I'm only taking an interest.'

'Who asked you to?'

Dolly's smile dropped from her face. She moved in closer. 'I could tell you the things I've heard,' she said.

'Such as?'

'They say your sister's on the bottle. Took it all bad.'

Annie's face remained blank. 'Says who?'

'Says everyone. You know, you ought to be nicer to me,' said Dolly. 'I could get word to your sister that you're living in a knocking shop. How would that go down? You wouldn't be so

fancy then, would you, with her thinking you were making your living flat on your back.'

Annie slapped her, hard. Dolly stood for a moment, shocked, transfixed by the nerve of this cunt, then she launched herself at Annie, flinging the door wide and knocking the taller woman back on to the bed, clawing at her hair. Annie hit her again, even harder, and Dolly let out a screech of surprise, trying to get her nails hooked into Annie's face.

Annie grabbed Dolly's wrists and pushed her back, and then there were shouts and Darren and Ellie were there, yanking Dolly off. Dolly was shrieking and spitting, but between them they managed to drag her out of Annie's room and back on to the landing.

'You'll be sorry you did that,' screamed Dolly.

'What the hell's going on out here?' asked Aretha, joining the gathering on the landing wearing a very small white towel.

'They were fighting,' said Darren, both shocked and excited.

'Well, pack it in,' hissed Aretha. 'I've got a solid-gold punter in there and he's getting nervous. He thought the sodding Old Bill were out here raiding the place.'

Darren tossed his blond head and took a step back. Through the half-open door he glimpsed a man tied face-down to Aretha's bed. There was a whip on the floor. The man's naked buttocks were striped with pink lines.

'Nice arse,' said Darren.

'Get your thieving eyes off it,' advised Aretha, stalking back into her room. 'Keep it down, OK?'

'Come on, girls,' said Ellie with an encouraging smile at Dolly and Annie. 'Shake hands and make up, all right?'

Dolly took aim and spat neatly at Annie's feet.

'You'll be fucking sorry,' Dolly promised, and she went off to her room, slamming the door behind her.

48

As Dolly saw it, there was nothing else she could do. Forget Her Royal Highness Annie Bailey coming in here queening it over all the mere mortals, that was nothing. It soured Dolly's mood, but her mood was sour anyway, after what she'd been through and what she'd seen.

Dad and Sarah, walking down the street.

And – oh God – the expression on Sarah's face. That haunted Dolly. Made her wake in the night, moaning in terror for her little sis. Sometimes, she succeeded in blanking it from her mind, but it always crept in, always came back and tormented her.

Supposing what happened to me happens to little Sar?

The baby came into her brain again, the dead baby with Dad's face.

No. She couldn't allow it. She couldn't let Sarah go through the same horror. She wouldn't.

So one morning when Celia was alone in the kitchen, having her 'elevenses', Dolly went in there, closed the door behind her and said to Celia: 'I have to talk to you.'

Celia was making tea, squinting past the thin spiral of smoke coming up from her posh ciggie holder. 'All right, Doll. You want a cuppa?'

Dolly shook her head and sat down at the table. She'd

barely kept down her breakfast; she couldn't face tea, not right now.

'What's up then?' Celia asked with a brisk smile, coming to the table with her cup and saucer and sitting down.

Dolly took a breath. She didn't know how to start.

Celia looked at Dolly's face. 'In your own time, lovey,' she said more gently. 'What is it then?'

Still, Dolly could barely form the words. She felt like they would choke her.

'What is it, you want to come off the game?' Celia sipped her tea. 'That don't matter, Doll. Don't you fret. You can dust around, get the bloody Hoover out, it ain't the end of the world. You're one of the family now, we won't turn you out.'

'It's not that,' said Dolly, but she was touched.

'Then what? Come on, I won't bite.'

'Celia . . . when we first met, when I was out on the streets . . .'

'Yeah. Go on then.'

'I was on the streets because I couldn't stay at home any longer.'

'Right.'

Dolly bit her lip, looked down at the table. She felt a hot wash of shame sweep over her; whenever she thought of being back there, she felt again the humiliation of it, the embarrassment, the awful guilt.

'Take your time,' said Celia, watching Dolly's face with concern. 'Whatever you got to say, you won't shock me, Doll. And I won't judge. You must know that by now.'

'It started when I was nine, nearly ten,' said Dolly, her mouth dry while she could feel sweat breaking out on her brow.

'What did?'

Dolly took a big breath and began to speak. As she spoke, Celia's forgotten fag burned down to nothing in its ivory holder, the ash dropping unheeded on to the table. Dolly spoke for almost a quarter of an hour, and when she was finished she looked like someone had whipped all the life out of her.

'Holy Christ,' said Celia when silence fell at last. 'You poor little cow. I always wondered what had gone on with you, Doll, but I didn't think of that. The rotten bastard.'

'There's worse,' said Dolly.

'What the fuck could be worse?'

'He's doing it to my little sis now. To Sarah.'

'How do you know that, Doll? You been back there?'

'I stood down the street . . .' Dolly hesitated, searching for the right words. 'I saw him, how he was with her. And I saw her face. I know it's happening, Celia. And it's got to stop.'

Celia noticed her fag had gone out. She scooped the ash up, put it in her Capstan ashtray, shook out another cigarette from the packet, stuck it in the ivory holder and lit it. 'Fucking hell, Doll, what a shocker.'

'Celia.' Dolly's chest was tight with tension; she felt she was going to be sick, having to tell all this; it was like living it all over again. 'We got to get the Delaneys involved with this.'

'Yeah.' Celia nodded. 'Sure we can do that. They can give the old cunt a shot across the bows, make sure it don't happen any more.'

Dolly's face was hard all of a sudden. 'No. That's not good enough. Not nearly good enough.'

'Doll . . .'

'He has to die,' said Dolly.

49

It happened when the railway workers were taking a carriage needing repairs into one of the far sidings. Arthur Biggs was at the controls of the big steam engine, backing it up, his mate the fireman on the footplate with him. Further back, the senior guard, the signalman, the porter and a pointsman were chatting to the shunter, Sam Farrell, who was directing operations in his usual Big-I-Am manner, sending hand signals up to the driver, saying all was well.

Sam was relaxed and in charge. He loved being in charge, and he was blankly astonished when the senior guard, one of his oldest work pals, grabbed his arm and kicked him behind the knee, taking his legs from under him.

'What the fuck you doin', boy?' he demanded, falling on to the track, grazing his hands and knees.

Wincing with the pain in his leg – Jesus, that kick had been hard – Sam knelt there and looked around. None of the others were shouting a protest, they weren't saying to the guard, 'Hey, what's up with you?' They were just watching, and their faces were grim. What the hell was going on?

Sam scrabbled back to his feet, ready to come out swinging at the senior guard. And then he saw that the engine, belching steam and chugging hard like the deafening breath of an ancient monster, hadn't slowed down.

'What the f—' Sam started.

He knew – everyone knew – that once the driver couldn't see the shunter's hand signals, that was the safety feature, that was when Arthur was supposed to shut her off, slap on the brakes. But Arthur hadn't done that. The engine was still backing up; it was coming straight for Sam.

He screamed as he saw clearly what was about to happen. And then the engine's massive weight smashed into him, flattening his chest and stomach, shattering his ribcage, whipping the air out of Sam in an instant, sending blood spurting out of his mouth in a torrent. His scream was cut short as his heart was squeezed to nothing and stopped beating.

'Fuckin' hell,' said the senior guard, going pale as Sam's blood spattered thickly down on to the tracks.

Arthur slammed on the brake and then him and the fireman came running back. They stopped short as they saw Sam Farrell pinned there, his head tipped forward on to his caved-in, blood-soaked chest. A ghastly odour was rising from Sam, the open-drain odour of a burst stomach and mangled intestines. The driver turned away from the sight, gagging at the smell, and heaved up his breakfast on to the platform.

The senior guard looked at the fireman. Then he glanced around at the other men there.

'We're all straight on what we say?' said the guard. 'He slipped, and by the time he got back up it was too late, the engine crushed him. It was an accident. All right?'

The fireman spat on the ground. 'Good riddance to bad rubbish,' he said.

The train driver couldn't speak. He staggered away and sat down on the hard concrete. He couldn't believe they'd done it, but they had.

They'd killed Sam Farrell.

50

When she came into the kitchen at teatime, the first thing that struck Sarah was that Nigel was crying. Sarah had never seen Nigel cry before. It alarmed her. And even more alarming, a pair of policemen were sitting at the kitchen table with Mum, who was looking blank-faced as always. Dick wasn't racing around like he usually did. Sandy sat and stared at the kitchen table.

'What's happening?' she asked, but Mum only looked up, then back down again, saying nothing.

One of the two Old Bill said: 'There's been a very bad accident, your mum's upset.'

Sarah looked at Edie. Mum didn't look upset. She just looked the same as always: disinterested.

Nigel burst out through his tears: 'Dad's dead, Sar! He's bloody dead.'

Sarah pulled up a chair as her legs were about to go. She fell into it, stunned, and looked at the policemen.

'There was an accident,' said the one who had spoken before. 'On the railway. An engine crushed him. I'm so sorry.'

'Was it . . . quick?' asked Mum.

All the kids turned and looked at her. Mum hardly ever uttered a word these days; this was unusual.

'Very quick, you can put your mind at rest on that.'

'He didn't suffer?'

'No. He didn't.'

Now Edie started crying too. 'Ah God, poor Sam,' she gasped.

Sarah sat there at the table and looked at Nigel snuffling into his handkerchief and Mum wailing away, and thought, Why can't I cry?

She really ought to. It was expected. Even Dick and little Sandy were looking on the verge of tears. She thought of Dad, dead, and still the tears refused to come and she was irritated at herself for not caring as she should.

Didn't she care at all that her dad was dead?

Deep in her heart she knew she didn't.

The only thing she felt was relief.

Redmond Delaney phoned Celia Bailey later that same day.

'It's done,' he said.

'Good God.'

'A terrible accident.'

'Right.'

'Tell your girl there.'

'I will. And . . . thank you, Mr Delaney.'

'It's a pleasure,' he said.

51

London, 1994

Jackie's 'contact' turned out to be no bloody good – just one of his drinking buddies looking to tap up Jackie's new source of income for a fiver or two. Feeling she was being milked like some prize heifer, Annie left Jackie there in disgust and got a taxi back to the hotel.

When the taxi pulled up, she paid the driver. The red-liveried doorman opened the cab door for her, asked if she'd had a good day. She hadn't. She'd had the day from hell – they were *all* days from hell right now – but she smiled and told him yes, and thanked him and went into the cosy reception, resplendent with bowls of red carnations, and into the lift and up to her room. She was barely through the door when the phone rang.

'Mrs Carter? I'm sorry to disturb you but there is a police detective in reception asking for you, a DCI Hunter.'

'Send him up,' said Annie, shrugging off her coat and plugging in the kettle.

A minute later, there was a knock at the door. Hunter stood there, looking more sober-faced than ever. Annie stood aside and he came into the room. She closed the door.

'What is it?' she asked hopefully. 'You heard something about Dolly?'

'No, Mrs Carter, I've heard something about *you*.'

'Tea?' asked Annie.

'No, thank you.'

'Well, go on then. What is it?' Annie gazed at him curiously.

'DS Duggan says you tried to bribe her to get information.'

Annie stared at him straight-faced. 'Really? She's mistaken.'

'Oh. Is she.'

'I spoke to her, yes. Told her I was keen to help in whatever way I could. But bribery? She must have misunderstood me.'

'You think so?'

'Yeah. I do.'

Hunter watched her closely. 'You know what? I think she understood your meaning perfectly well. I think you offered her money, and she refused.'

Annie shrugged. 'Nah. As I say, she must have misunderstood.'

Hunter stepped forward so that he was almost nose to nose with Annie.

'Understand *this*, Mrs Carter,' he said quietly. 'If I hear one more report of you trying to coerce a police officer in that way, you'll be inside a cell quicker than you can say knife. Is *that* understood.'

'Yeah, fine.' Annie nodded. 'Any news then? On the case?'

'Nothing yet.'

'Do you want to know if *I* have any news, on the case?'

'Mrs Carter. If you don't share any information you

might have with me, then you are impeding an investigation and that is a very serious offence.'

'I know that. And I told you I'd share. Of course I will.'

Hunter eyed her sceptically. The woman was deep, unknowable. Utterly mysterious. Married to a man who'd evaded the law over many years, linked to the American Mafia.

He didn't like these Scottish visits of hers, they made his detective's nose twitch with interest. He'd looked into them, curious, but they'd led nowhere. When she went up there, she always departed from London Heliport, sited by the Thames and opposite Chelsea Harbour, and was usually taken to a private residence outside Edinburgh. From there? He had no idea. Yet.

'Tell me what you know,' he said, and started walking around the room, twitching the huge moss-green tasselled drapes at the floor-to-ceiling window aside to stare out at a sodden Kensington Park. In the foreground, trees whipped about in the wind. The rain sheeted down, fogging the view of the palace over on the far side of the park.

'Her father got her pregnant way back, years ago,' said Annie. 'There. Is that new information for you?'

Hunter turned his head and looked back at her. His mouth was pursed with distaste.

'Are you *sure* about that?' he asked.

'Certain.'

'Christ, that's horrible.'

'It's the truth. And . . .' She hesitated, but telling the Bill couldn't hurt Dolly now. 'She had someone organize a hit on her old man.'

Hunter sent her a sharp glance. 'Who?'

Annie shrugged and said nothing. She wasn't about to finger Redmond Delaney to the cops, not now, not ever. She wasn't a grass and she wasn't a fool, either.

Hunter let the curtain drop. He came back across the room to where she stood. 'Tell me all about Dolly Farrell,' he said.

Annie had to swallow hard to get the words out. 'There's not much to tell. Dolly was a tart. She worked in a whorehouse. That was *after* her father did that to her when she was a young girl. After that happened in her own home, where she was supposed to be *safe*, I imagine anything else was pretty easy.' Annie sat down on a bulky pink Chesterfield sofa. Dolly would have loved it, this sofa. She felt sick, talking about Dolly this way, knowing how Dolly would have hated anyone knowing about the past she'd tried so hard to bury.

'Later in life, she worked for my husband, and for me, managing clubs. She was good at it. Got on well with the staff, was tough enough to deal with any problems. She'd seen it all, done it all. Nothing fazed her, nothing shocked her. Not surprisingly. I suppose the lines get sort of blurred, when you've had an experience like that.'

'So . . .' Hunter was watching Annie's face '. . . despite her early setbacks, she was a woman to reckon with.'

'Dolly was strong. She had to be, to survive. Stronger than anyone I ever knew.'

'And she got on well with the staff.'

'Have you heard different? I certainly haven't. The one thing I do know? Everyone who worked for her *loved* Dolly.'

'That's what I've been hearing too.'

Annie ran an agitated hand through her hair. 'I just thought . . . well, I had this thing stuck in my head and I thought that this awful thing happening to her . . . getting shot, being killed . . . I just thought that it could be coming from anywhere, couldn't it? A punter she upset, a supplier, a member of staff, who knows?'

'I keep coming back to the idea of a lover,' said Hunter.
'Dolly didn't have lovers. She didn't rate men at all, and
God knows that is no surprise. She had no kids, no family
that she wanted to know of, no nothing. Her friends were
her family. Me, and Ellie.' Annie swallowed hard. 'That's
all she had. And I suppose she must have been lonely
sometimes, but that never occurred to me when she was
alive. Poor cow.' Annie shuddered and looked at Hunter.
'Or maybe it could be coming from somewhere in her
past. She had a *horrible* past.'

His eyes held hers. 'Leave it to the police, Mrs Carter.'

'Of course,' said Annie. 'I'll do that.'

52

'You said there was more,' Redmond growled down the phone at Gary Tooley.

Days had passed since their meeting. He was beyond impatient now.

'There *is*. I know there is. But the old bint, you don't know when – or if – she's going to call again. She's crazy, unpredictable. I have to wait.'

'I paid you five grand,' said Redmond.

'Yeah, and I gave you the stuff you wanted for that.'

'It's not enough.'

'Tough.'

'What use is that information to me? Barolli's dead. This mad sister of his? Let the old bitch suffer and die at her own pace. Do I care?'

'I don't know what you want from me. I've told you—'

'I want more. You said there would be more, and I want it.'

Gary heaved a sigh. 'As I said—' he started, and Redmond slammed the phone down.

Gary put the receiver back on the cradle with a satisfied smile. He hoped he wasn't pushing this too hard. In fact, he already *had* the information Redmond wanted, but

Gary wanted him hungrier, willing to part with even more dosh this time.

Ten grand, he was thinking.

Yes, Gary already knew these things, but he was holding on, keeping his powder dry, building up Redmond's interest and anxiety until he was *desperate* for a word on all this. Gary was playing a long game. Oddly, that batty old cow Gina Barolli hadn't phoned him for a while now, but that didn't matter – he *had* what he needed. That crazy-eyed cunt Delaney might be snapping at his heels, but he could handle him.

He was sure of it.

Ten grand for the big one, for the best and most shocking thing of all.

The news that Constantine Barolli was *alive*.

53

Annie lay in bed that night and thought about Dolly's past. She fell asleep and dreamed of chasing a murderer through a church with Hunter, and then the murderer morphed into Darren, who had been her friend, camp as a row of pink tents and dead, *long* dead. Then he was laughing and joking with Ellie as they both sang along to 'Summer Holiday'. At first they were in the church and then the church became upstairs in Auntie Celia's old knocking shop.

Halfway through the song, the flesh started to melt off Darren's face and Dolly popped her head around the door – not Dolly as she had been then, a rough and uncouth brass, but the Dolly she had been just recently, well-groomed, middle-aged.

Dolly told them it was the heat coming off the lines, nothing to worry about, but Darren just kept melting like a candle, his eyes vanishing under strings of waxen flesh, his cheeks dissolving, his mouth slanting to one side like a stroke victim's, and the music just went on and on, pounding into her head, louder and louder, and then Annie woke up abruptly, panting, sweating, shooting up in the bed to stare wild-eyed into blackness.

She flicked on the bedside light, pushed her hair out of her eyes and looked at the big empty bed and wished that

Max was here with her. You got used to a person being there, and Max's presence had always been so reassuring. With him around, you felt nothing could go too badly wrong. Without him . . .

Christ! Where is he? What's going on?

Earlier, she had tried the Prospect villa number again; still, he wasn't there. And he hadn't even phoned home.

Anxiety gripped her. What if he was planning to leave her, and the next time she saw him it would be just so he could tell her goodbye? The terror of that crushed her chest like a vice. More than anything she longed to go home, to go back to being in Barbados with Max, happy, unworried.

But she had to stay here in London. She was *needed* here. Dolly's death could not go unpunished and the truth was she didn't trust the law – not even Hunter, who had been useful in the past, had even once pulled her cut and bleeding from a near-terminal wreck – to handle the job of tracking down Dolly's killer.

She knew she was needed elsewhere, too: the *pizzino*, the note, hastily passed to her in the street. *Come at once.*

Well, she couldn't. Not now.

They know, she thought. *That's what this is. Everyone knows.*

And . . . oh shit, Max knows too.

She reached for a bottle of mineral water, poured herself a glass and drank half of it down in one swallow; she was parched. She looked at the bedside clock; a quarter to four in the morning and already outside the traffic was starting. Soon it would be daylight and the birds would sing and London would come heaving back to her feet after the night's rest and start her frenzied daytime dance again.

But Dolly would still be dead.

Annie squeezed her eyes tight shut.

Ah, Jesus, why her? Come on, God, if you had to take somebody, why'd you have to take Dolly?

There were no answers.

It was just the heat coming off the lines.

Crazy, crazy dreams. What the hell did *that* mean?

She had no idea. She lay back down, flicked off the light. Thought of old friends, dead friends. Darren and Aretha and Billy . . . and now Dolly had joined them.

They're up there now, in heaven, singing 'Summer Holiday' . . .

That thought at least made her smile. Her eyes closed. This time, she slept and the nightmares stayed away.

54

Annie left the hotel next morning and got a cab over to Ellie's. The cleaners were in, hoovering up the debris and collecting champagne corks from the excesses of the night before.

Annie went upstairs and walked straight into Chris.

'Hi, Chris,' she said.

He just grunted. Avoiding her eyes, he swept past her down the stairs. Annie walked on into the kitchen. It was all shipshape again, although the dresser with its crystals was gone. Everything else was neat and tidy, as Ellie liked it. Ellie herself, elegantly dressed in a navy skirt suit and white blouse, was sitting at the table drinking tea. When Annie appeared, she missed her mouth and slopped tea on to the table.

'I see I'm still getting the bum's rush off everyone,' said Annie with a grim smile.

Ellie grabbed a tea towel and wiped at the table's surface. She was scowling – and, like her husband, avoiding Annie's eyes.

'Ellie,' said Annie, sitting down opposite.

'What?' Ellie wasn't looking at her, she was still dabbing at the wet patch, trying to prevent a mark on the wood.

'You're supposed to be my mate.'

Ellie glanced up. Her big moon face went pink. 'I *am*

your mate,' she said, and turned her attention back to the tabletop.

'Then tell me what's going on. I've had the cold shoulder off you, Tony, Steve, Gary – everyone except Jackie Tulliver, and that's only because he's a useless waste of space and he sees me as one big fat wad of walking cash to provide the next drink for him. Tell me, Ellie. Tell me what the hell it is.'

Ellie shrugged and looked unhappy. 'I can't help you,' she said.

'You mean you won't.'

Ellie's eyes darted up and met Annie's. 'Will you leave off? I mean I bloody *daren't*. Don't you get it? Having you here put me in bother with people – they damned near wrecked this place just because I said I'd let you stay. You're *trouble*, Annie. And I don't need trouble. I've had enough of all that. All I want's a quiet life. That's all. No bother, no aggro.'

Annie decided it was time to put the screws on. Ellie had always been the weak link in the strong chain of friendship with her and Dolly. Ellie was the self-centred one who would pull the ladder up and say fuck you when the going got rough. 'If you came to me in trouble, I'd help you,' she said.

'Yeah, you say that.'

'I mean it. I need a friend, Ellie, and at the moment I'm on my own.'

Ellie stood up and put her cup and saucer into the sink. She turned quickly, and this time she looked Annie square in the eye.

'Look, I don't want to have to say this to you, but I have to so I'm going to say it, straight out, no sugar coating. Just piss off, will you? For my sake. Just go away. I can't help you, I've got nothing to say to you, just *leave me alone*.'

55

Annie walked out of the club feeling sick and bereft. Ellie had washed her hands of her. She had one friend dead and the other not giving a fuck.

Not that she blamed Ellie. Ex-tarts were always of the nervous variety, she knew that. They'd seen the rough end of life and when they escaped from the game they didn't want anything except normality, the comfy old fire and slippers routine. How could you blame them for that? Annie knew she'd be exactly the same, in those circumstances.

A bike shot past and then a long dark car swerved into the pavement with a screech of brakes. Horns hooted, taxi drivers hollered out of their windows and waved their fists. Annie kept walking, thinking about Dolly. She paused in front of the car to cross the street; Jackie had said he'd meet her in the next road. And then suddenly there were two big men standing on either side of her and one of them was shoving something that felt like a knife into her side.

She winced and shouted: 'What the fuck?' in surprise and pain, and the knife dug deeper.

'In the car,' said the one with the knife.

She looked up into a plug-ugly big dish of a face with a nose dotted with blackheads, mean piggy eyes and thick curling black eyebrows that met in the middle.

I know you, thought Annie.

He jabbed the knife deeper into her side, hard enough to hurt.

'Don't fuck me around,' he warned, nudging harder and harder, pushing into her. His mate moved in closer too. Annie flashed him a glance. Taller, shaven-headed, his darkly tanned face pitted with adolescent acne. His face was like stone, without expression.

Jesus, I'm in trouble here.

Between them they shoved her into the back of the car. Eyebrows got into the back with her while the bald one went round to the front and slid behind the wheel. The whole time, Eyebrows kept up the knife pressure on her side.

Gonna have a bruise there, she thought.

'You don't want to do this,' she said, her voice breathy with panic.

'Shut up,' said Eyebrows.

'No, listen. You *really* don't.'

Eyebrows stared at her. 'I *said*, shut *up.*'

Annie shut up. She was aware of her mouth drying to ashes, of her heart rate accelerating crazily with fear.

'Can you tell me what the fuck's going on?' she managed to get out.

Eyebrows turned a dark cold look on her. 'Shut up,' he said, and the way he said it made her freeze. 'You make me say it again, you'll be sorry.'

The car was in motion, swerving out into the traffic; more honking of horns, more taxi drivers shaking their fists.

Help me, thought Annie, but there was no help to be found. She thought she saw Jackie, ambling along the pavement on the other side of the road, but he was there and then gone; the car moved fast, leaving Jackie far behind.

As usual, she was on her own.

They stopped beside a warehouse down by the docks. Annie was watching Eyebrows nervously, but as he got out he flicked the knife shut and slipped it into his pocket. Baldy got out too and the pair of them dragged her from the car.

Annie decided she had to front this out.

'You don't know what you're playing with here,' she said to Eyebrows. And, ridiculously, she heard the next phrase coming out of her own mouth, a phrase she openly laughed at when it was uttered by politicians, film stars, people who were so far up their own arseholes that they had lost all sense of reality. 'Do you know who I am?'

Eyebrows just looked at her. Baldy gave a slight smirk.

'Yeah,' said Eyebrows. 'We know exactly who you are, and *what* you are too. That's why we're here.'

'I'm warning you—' started Annie, but the words were cut short when Eyebrows slapped her hard across the face.

She flew backward as if shot from a cannon. The stinging pain of the blow shocked her. She grabbed at her face as if to check it was still attached to her head. Couldn't believe it. This *fucker* had the nerve to hit her – *her*, Annie Carter. She drew in a gulping breath. Her eyes were watering.

She started to speak again, and then Eyebrows came in close and punched her mid-section and all the breath went from her body in a huge *whoosh* of exploding air. She fell to the ground and lay there, unable to draw breath, her mind floundering in shock, her body clenched, her stomach a fiery ball of agony.

You bastards! You can't do this! I'm Max Carter's wife, are you fucking mental . . . ?

Her mouth formed the words but she couldn't speak. She had no breath to speak *with*. Groaning, face screwed up in pain, she tried to crawl away, thinking *this can't be happening*, and then Eyebrows kicked her hard in the ribs and there was pain, *unbelievable* pain. She felt something give; something that had been solid inside her was broken, and she went face-down into the gravel and the mud, the rain washing her hair into the dirt, covering her expensive clothes with yellow slime.

Then there were more kicks, and she was crawling, trying to get away, but it wasn't possible. They were following her, both of them, kicking her, and in the end it was easier to just stop moving and hope that it would end.

It *did* end, eventually. In this century or the next, she wasn't sure.

But not before she'd prayed for oblivion, even for death, just to make the pain go away.

Help me, someone.

But no one came.

PART TWO

56

'You again? Look, OK, I've got what you want, but it's going to cost you,' said Gary when Redmond called in unannounced at the Blue Parrot one night.

Gary took Redmond up to the office, away from all the punters and the dancing girls and the noise of the DJ's decks thrumming out 'Sledgehammer' by Peter Gabriel; Gary loved that song.

All right, he hadn't expected an actual visit from Redmond, and he *certainly* hadn't expected that he'd bring along a big shaggy dark-haired sidekick with a look in his eyes that said he'd kill his own granny for a fiver, but he had this sorted, *he* was the one in charge.

'This is Mitchell,' said Redmond. 'He helps me out.'

Gary gave Mitchell a nod. Mitchell didn't nod back.

'Now listen,' said Redmond, still talking reasonably, sweetly. 'The time has come for you to stop dicking me about and tell me. What information do you have?'

Gary sat back in his chair behind his desk and pursed his lips. No way was he going to let Delaney rush this. *He* had the whip hand.

'It's very *expensive* information,' he said.

'How expensive?'

Gary thought of the ten grand, and hiked it a bit. Delaney would want to haggle, anyway.

'Fifteen,' he said.

'Fifteen *thousand*?' Redmond raised his eyebrows. 'You can't be serious.'

'I'm very serious indeed,' Gary said, and the track downstairs changed to 'West End Girls'.

Redmond was shaking his head. He stood up and came around Gary's desk. Gary didn't like people doing that, he felt like a king on a throne behind that desk, he didn't want oiks shoving around behind it.

'Hey—' he started, but he didn't have time to finish.

Redmond grabbed the front of Gary's bespoke tailored shirt and hauled him to his feet and hissed into his face: 'You great long streak of piss! You think you've got the measure of me, do you?'

'I—' started Gary again, wondering where these delicate negotiations had gone wrong. This wasn't in his plan, not at all.

'Five grand,' said Redmond, and to Gary's horror he whipped out a knife and held it against his throat. 'That's what you'll get, and that's generous. If I don't decide to cut you to ribbons instead.'

'Hey, that's—' gulped Gary.

'*Five*,' said Redmond. 'Right here. Four days' time. And you tell me the rest of it.'

He let go of Gary's shirtfront and moved back around the desk. Mitchell opened the door, and they left the room.

Gary sagged in his chair, shaken, aware that his palms were clammy.

Jesus!

That guy was a maniac.

Gary stared at the closed door, and touched a trembling hand to his throat. He'd thought he could handle Redmond Delaney, but looking into that crazy cunt's eyes? Now he wasn't so sure.

57

There was a mad jumble of impressions running through Annie's head. Muddy yellow gravel and then wetness on her face, the rain, the *fucking* endless rain. Crawling again. Then collapsing into the wet grit beneath her, her fingers clawing into the gravel, her whole body clenching against the agony in her middle.

Something broken in there, for sure.

And then nothing. Blackness. Which was OK, which was pretty damned good really. But did it last? No. Soon she was back again, and this time there were voices, men's voices, the sway of motion, she was back in a car and then a rush of air and she was on the ground again. Consciousness faded out, then in. Now there were people talking again, above her. Hands lifted her and she fell, and someone snapped: 'Careful!'

She clawed at the ground and it was smooth, it was tarmac this time, not yellow grit, and she felt sticky hanks of wet hair hanging in her eyes when she opened them. She was lifted again. A crazy cacophony of sounds and cars zipping past, feet away; hands touching her, voices, more voices, and she was struggling to break free, to get away before they started on her again, but she was too weak to move.

'Don't,' she whispered.

Then she was out of it again, she was gone.

'. . . and no real internal injuries, she's been . . .'

Voices. One female, one male.

Annie kept her eyes closed. She felt groggy, without strength.

'Five milligrams,' said someone close to her head.

Then she was gone again, blackness sweeping up and over her like a cloak.

Some time later, she was back. An hour may have passed, or a second. Or a year. She didn't know. She half-opened her eyes and there was a bed, she was in a bed; there were five other beds nearby, all occupied, and there was a reception desk at the end of the row of beds, nurses in uniform, chatting, laughing, as if everything was normal.

Hospital, I'm in hospital.

She drew in a shuddering breath. It hurt like fuck. Her hands went to her midriff. She felt wide adhesive stuck there, stretching over her ribs and right round to the centre of her back. Into her mind came Eyebrows and Baldy, kicking her while she lay helpless on the ground.

Bastards.

'You're back with us then,' said someone.

Annie turned her head a little and was instantly aware of pain in her neck, an aching muscle-deep pain that spiralled down to her arms, to her legs. She gulped, tried to find her voice. She felt drugged, enfolded in layers of cotton wool. They'd given her something, of course they had; without it, she reckoned the pain would be much, much worse. She looked at the young blonde nurse at the end of the bed.

'Only one fractured rib – you were lucky,' said the nurse. 'I'm Gemma. You were in a pretty bad way when they brought you in on Saturday. How are you feeling now?'

'Shitty,' said Annie, not feeling very lucky at all.

Gemma smiled. 'We've sedated you to help with the pain. But there's nothing major – just the rib, and that'll pretty much mend on its own, it's not too bad a break. You'll find you'll be able to shower in a few days with the strapping on, and in a couple of weeks that can come off. Take some ibuprofen for any discomfort. Six weeks' time, you'll be right as rain. Could have been a lot worse,' she said cheerfully. 'Could have punctured a lung. What happened? The old man's team lose the match then?'

Annie gulped again. 'Something like that,' she said. *Six weeks?*

'The police want to speak to you,' said Gemma. 'When you're ready. They always do with assaults. You might want to do that. Press charges. Make him think better of it next time.'

Press charges, thought Annie. How *quaint*.

'Who brought me here?' she asked.

'Some men dropped you off in the car park. What were they, your brothers or something? They didn't want to hang around, anyway. They grabbed one of the ambulance crews and left you with them. Me? I hope your folks have gone back and given the old man the pasting of his life.'

It hurt to lay on her back, she felt she couldn't get her breath. Painfully, with the nurse's help, Annie manoeuvred herself on to her side. Then she closed her eyes, and let the darkness take her again.

When she awoke, the windows across the ward showed that night had come. People were talking, and a woman in a dark green tabard was wheeling a tea-trolley up near the nurses' station. Annie rang the bell and after a moment a nurse came – not Gemma; this one was a brunette.

'I need to go to the loo,' said Annie, and started to swing her legs off the bed. Instantly she felt her head swim, felt the grey fog descend. Her whole midriff was a hard ball of agony.

'Whoa, easy!' The brunette dashed forward and caught her before she collapsed to the floor. She eased her back on to the bed. 'Too soon for that,' she scolded mildly. 'Tomorrow, maybe. We'll see. I'll fetch the bedpan.'

Annie lay back on the pillows, winced, turned on her side again and thought: *Those bastards!*

They had reduced her to this; her, Annie Carter, mob boss, madam, Mafia queen. And here she was, confined to bed and having to shit into a bedpan. A slow seething anger started to coalesce in her beaten, aching guts then. Eyebrows and Baldy. She *knew* them.

And now? They'd be sorry.

58

The brunette was right; next day, Annie felt a little better. The night had been bad. When she turned over, the pain woke her and then there was too much noise to get back to sleep, people talking and laughing, people crying out, some mad old lady trying to get into bed with one of the other women in the ward and the nurses having to come running. Annie didn't know what time that happened, maybe three; and then when things died down again, when they'd ushered the old dear back to her own bed and finally she *did* sleep, there was another nurse, at six in the bloody morning, nudging her awake to take a painkiller.

Christ, I've got to get out of here.

She was given a brisk bed bath at nine, and then breakfast was wheeled in. She didn't touch it. Felt sick to her stomach to even look at food, to even *think* about it. And then at eleven, DCI Hunter and DS Sandra Duggan came to see her.

'Oh Gawd, look what the cat's dragged in,' she moaned, closing her eyes. When she opened them, they were still there; Hunter looking solemn, DS Duggan looking suspiciously pleased to see her come to this.

'What happened, Mrs Carter?' asked Hunter, ignoring her remark. 'Ask too many questions or something?'

Or something, thought Annie.

'The nurse tells me that you have bad bruising and a cracked rib,' he said.

'Give that boy a coconut,' said Annie, propping herself up a bit, wincing.

'Who did it?'

'Two men. Don't know their names.'

'Could you describe them?'

'No.' A vision of Eyebrows and Baldy flashed into her brain. She could describe them perfectly well, but she didn't have to. 'I couldn't. It all happened too fast.'

'The nurse said you were left in the hospital car park.'

'I got nothing to tell you,' said Annie tiredly.

'Hm,' said Hunter. 'You're sure?'

'Positive,' she said, and closed her eyes.

'You want us to notify anyone for you? Any relatives?'

Annie thought of Ruthie and shook her head. Whatever was going on, it had already brought grief down on Ellie's head, and her own. She didn't want Ruthie getting dragged into the mix too.

'You can tell Mrs Brown at the Shalimar. If she's interested. And the hotel I'm staying at, they must be wondering what the fuck's going on.'

She gave him the hotel's name and address and closed her eyes. When she opened them again, Hunter and Duggan were gone. And she needed to get to the loo; no way was she using a fucking bedpan again. She levered herself to the side of the bed and her head started swimming like a bastard. She tottered to her feet, grabbed at the metal headboard and just about stopped herself going sprawling to the floor.

'You want to take it easy, love,' said the gummy elderly woman in the next bed. Her teeth grinned from a glass on the bedside table. 'Call the nurse, she'll help you.'

Or sit me on that ruddy contraption again.

Annie ignored the advice and somehow got to the foot of the bed. 'Where's the loo?' she asked the woman.

'Over there,' she said.

Annie launched herself across the room, and with her head reeling, her guts in pain and her legs unsteady, she made it. In the loo, she did what she had to do and then washed her hands and looked at her reflection.

Jesus, the state of you! she thought.

Her face was grey-toned, as if her warm Barbadian tan had never been. She was sheeny with sweat, her eyes dark-shadowed with anguish. The hospital gown was the least flattering thing ever made in the whole of creation. She turned away in disgust, and staggered back to the ward, back on to the bed, which had felt like a hard stony horror all night, but now felt like absolute bliss. She fell into it, dragged the covers over, and fell asleep.

59

Tonight, Dave Waterman was going to get laid. Sabrina, one of the dancers at the Blue Parrot where he worked as a doorman, had been giving him the come-on for weeks now, and they'd gone on one date, then another, and now it was the third date, and that was pay-off time, was he right or was he right?

He grinned at himself in the mirror as he splashed on the old Paco Rabanne, spruced himself up for the big event. Granted, he was no oil painting. He had a big dish of a face and nothing seemed to shift those blackheads on his nose, but he was big in all the departments that mattered and he worked out, kept himself fit – needed to in that job, all sorts of nutters out on a weekend spraying champagne at each other and sniffing lines of coke in the bogs, you had to be able to handle yourself.

He waggled his thick eyebrows and hummed along to the radio, it was the Quo, he loved them. Wondered if he should get something done about those eyebrows, met in the middle, that was a bad sign, wasn't it, meant you had a short fuse? Well, he *did* have a short fuse, that much was true. He hoped Sabrina was going to put out tonight, or he'd be *very* annoyed.

The doorbell rang and he grabbed his jacket and tore off down the stairs, opened the front door; she was early.

It wasn't Sabrina, though.

Dave stared at the two men standing there. They were very well-groomed, wearing identical smiles, and one of them held a snub-nosed automatic in his hand. Dave felt his bowels turn to liquid as he stared in disbelief at the gun.

'Hi,' said the one holding it. He sounded American. 'We're takin' a little trip. Come on.'

Evan James was looking in the mirror too, and thinking that having acne as a kid had scarred him badly, but that was also *good*, because his bald head, mean eyes and scarred skin meant that he looked ferocious, and he was.

He'd just been in the showers at the boxing club, and he'd had a good bout tonight, beaten the crap out of his opponent, and his trainer had said he could almost go pro, he was that promising.

Now here he was, drying off, getting dressed, stuffing his shorts and gear into his bag and trotting off to the door of the club, calling out cheerio to the kids pounding the punchbag, but they were intent, head down, training hard, and didn't hear him, and that was OK.

He went outside into the early-evening rain and trotted over to his car, and it was then that two well-dressed men approached him. One of them showed him a gun.

'What the fuck?' he said aloud, staring at it, mesmerized.

'Let's take a ride,' they said.

'Hit him again,' said the one who seemed to be in charge of proceedings, the one with the American accent and the gun in his hand.

The other one hit Evan again, as instructed. Evan's bloody head, which was already looking like a squashed watermelon, bounced around on his shoulders. He was tied to a chair in the depths of Smithfield meat market, and Dave Waterman was beside him, *also* tied to a chair, and looking pretty well done over, his features damned near unrecognizable, so Sabrina wasn't going to get laid tonight, not by Dave anyway. Not tonight, and not, he was beginning to suspect, at any time in the future either.

'This is nothing personal, guys,' said the American. 'This is just a lesson in *manners*, you understand me? And also, a lesson in who not to pick on, not *ever*.'

Neither man responded. Blood and urine was dripping on to the concrete floor.

'Let's wrap this up,' said the American.

60

When Annie woke again, Dolly was standing beside the bed. She started to crack a smile, and then she realized that this was in fact impossible because Dolly was stone-cold dead on a slab somewhere. She blinked, shoved herself up against the ghastly hospital pillows.

Ellie.

It was Ellie, not Dolly. How could she have confused the two? Ellie was standing there wearing a powder-blue skirt suit, clutching the metal end of the bed and biting her lip as she looked at Annie.

'I shouldn't be here,' said Ellie.

Annie cleared her throat. Ellie was wrestling with some big internal problem, so she gave her a moment.

'I really bloody shouldn't,' said Ellie. 'But the police, that Hunter person, he told me you were in here. What the hell's happened to you? He said someone worked you over, I couldn't bloody believe it, and fuck it, I *shouldn't be here.*'

'But you are,' Annie pointed out.

'Is it true, what he said?'

'Yeah, Doll, it is.'

'Doll? What you calling me Doll for? I'm Ellie. Did you take a knock to the fucking brain or something?'

Annie shook her head. For a moment, she truly had

thought it was Dolly standing there. Stupid. Her head was fuddled with painkilling drugs, that was all.

'No, I . . . I dreamed Dolly was standing there. And I'm drugged up to the hilt. Sorry, Ellie.'

Ellie glanced around as if expecting a ghost to appear; she looked genuinely spooked.

'What happened?' she asked.

'Two blokes decided to give me a kicking.'

'But *why*?'

'No idea.'

'Chris would be spitting blood if he knew I'd come here,' fretted Ellie, looking left and right like her husband was going to appear out of thin air and give her a bollocking.

'Why's that?' asked Annie.

Ellie was back to biting her lip again. 'I can't say.'

Annie gazed at her, hard-eyed. 'Can't or won't? Look. You're here. So it's time to shit or get off the pot, Ellie. Tell me what you've heard about me.'

'I can't,' she said, desperately shaking her head. 'I'm really sorry, but I *can't*.'

Annie sat up straighter. 'Draw the curtains, Ell. Give us some privacy.'

Her face unhappy, Ellie drew the curtains around the bed. Annie eased the covers back, winced, and swung her legs to the floor. 'Get my stuff out of that locker, will you?' she asked.

'Why . . . what are you doing? You can't just do that, you can't just walk out of here – you have to be signed out, the doctors have to see you, they won't—'

'Oh, shut the fuck up,' snapped Annie. 'And pass me my clothes.'

Ellie hesitated, then did as she was told. As she turned to the bed, Annie grabbed her wrist. It was a hard clench, startling Ellie. She'd come in here thinking Annie looked weak as a kitten but she should have known better. Annie Carter was strong at the core, and that was where it mattered.

'Tell me,' said Annie.

Ellie shook her head dumbly.

'Tell me, or I'll tell Chris you came here.'

'You wouldn't!'

'I would. You know it.'

'It's none of my business . . . '

'You got that right. It's *my* business though, isn't it? If people start beating me up and targeting my friends and treating me like dirt, it's very much my business.'

All the colour left Ellie's face suddenly. 'Oh Jesus, you don't think *Dolly* . . .? God, could it be that? Because of you, because of what you've done?'

'I don't know. Because you won't tell me what's happening, and I think you know.'

'It's all over town,' said Ellie, hopelessly shaking her head.

'What is?'

'Oh God . . .'

'Ellie!' Annie tightened her grip.

'They're saying that you've been making a fool out of Mr Carter.'

'*What?*'

Ellie nodded. 'They're saying – and this is crazy, right? This is *mad* – they're saying that Constantine Barolli didn't die. That he's alive. And that you've been seeing him behind Mr Carter's back.'

Annie froze.

'But it ain't true,' said Ellie with a little disbelieving laugh, 'is it? It *can't* be true.'

Annie just sat there, staring at the floor.

'Is it?' asked Ellie again.

Annie didn't answer.

Ellie's smile died on her lips. Now her mouth was hanging open. She shut it slowly as she stared at Annie. 'Oh. Dear. God,' she said.

Annie looked up at her friend's face. 'Ellie . . .' she started.

Ellie began to shake her head wildly. She waved her hands in front of her face, making *no, no, no* gestures, as if warding off something evil.

'Don't you dare say it! Don't tell me a damned thing, because if it's true, I don't want to know. I don't want to get involved. What, you think I'm out of my tree or something?'

'You're the only friend I've got left, Ellie,' said Annie.

Ellie was still shaking her head. '*No!* Count me out on this one. Count me *right* out. You think I'd cross Max Carter? You're off your bloody head.'

'Ellie—'

'No!' shouted Ellie, and she twitched the curtain to one side and was gone.

61

'All right, Boss?' asked Gary as Max Carter came out of the arrivals gate at Gatwick and strode over to where he stood waiting.

All around them, families were hugging, mothers greeting daughters, couples embracing, throngs of taxi drivers holding up boards with names of travellers. The tannoy droned on in the background, and the noise of voices and incoming aircraft was deafening.

Gary took a look at Max's angrily set face and thought, *Shit. Better tread careful here*.

'Do I look fucking all right?' snapped Max, shoving his hand luggage at Gary.

Gary put his face straight, twisted it into a fake look of sympathy. Inside, he was triumphant. That cow Annie. He'd been waiting years to get the knife in on that bitch, and now he'd succeeded.

'I know it's bloody rough. And I didn't want to tell you. But shit, what could I do? You *had* to know.'

'Yeah,' Max said.

'I would have spared you this if I could,' said Gary. 'You know that.'

'Yeah. I do.'

'So no shooting the messenger, OK, mate?' said Gary with a sad, sorry smile.

'No,' said Max, slapping Gary's shoulder. 'None of that. You've seen her then? She's still here?'

'Too right. She came back when Dolly Farrell got done. I told you about that.'

'Yeah. Fucking tragic. Right.' Max sighed and straightened. 'Let's get the fuck out of here, shall we? We got places to go, things to do.'

62

Annie left the hospital, hailed a cab and made her way back to the hotel in Kensington, ignoring the odd looks from the driver as he took in her mud-spattered clothing. As she paid him from the back of the taxi, the usual red-uniformed hotel doorman opened the cab door for her, his smile freezing for an instant when he saw the state she was in; then it was back in place. Stupidly, he asked if she'd had a good day. But it was his job to be pleasant to the guests, she knew that, even in the face of disaster.

'Fine,' she smiled, and walked into reception, pausing there to talk to the familiar receptionist, who also did a double-take as she saw the yellow mud stains on Annie's clothing.

'Any messages for me?' Annie asked, still smiling but in anguish. She wanted to lie down, really quickly, because her middle was throbbing hard and she felt sick. She clutched at the reception desk to hold herself upright.

'Oh! Are you all right? We were told you'd been admitted to hospital. We were worried about you.'

'I'm fine. Messages?'

'Messages?' The girl behind the desk looked puzzled.

'Yeah, for me.'

'No, but . . . you were checked out over an hour ago.'

'What?' Annie stared at her blankly.

The girl nodded, referred to her list, then looked up again.

'He took your things . . .'

'Who did?'

'Yes, it's right here – he checked you out, said you'd been called away on business, and he paid the bill for your stay. I'm so sorry, haven't you seen him . . . ?'

'*Who?*'

'Well . . . Mr Carter, of course. It was Mr Carter.'

Annie wandered out of the hotel and away down the street in a daze. *Max is here. And he knows. Everyone knows.* Then Jackie Tulliver ambled up.

'*There* you are,' he said, wafting alcohol fumes all over her. He wagged a finger at her. 'You want to keep me informed, you don't want to just go wandering off like that. Where you been?' Jackie's eyes went up and down her body. 'And what the *fuck*? You been in a mud-wrestling contest? What's all this?'

Annie ignored him; she kept walking.

'Only, you know, for back-up purposes. It's always useful, having someone keeping watch.'

Annie kept walking.

Jackie skipped along beside her, his dirty-denim-clad legs struggling to keep pace.

'You don't tell me what's occurring, how am I to know? You been in a fight? You want to take it easy, let *me* take the strain—'

Annie stopped walking and spun round so suddenly that Jackie almost bowled into her. She grabbed the front of his moth-eaten denim jacket and shook him, hard. Then she stopped. It hurt like fuck, shaking him. And he wasn't worth the effort, or the pain.

'Listen,' she spat out, eyes mad and cold with rage, 'you

fucking lowlife son of a bitch! Let you take the strain? Last time I needed your back-up, you were too busy trying to find an off-licence to give a fuck where I was and what was happening to me. When I was being hijacked by two thugs, where were you? Oh yeah – I *saw* you, on your way to the offy. So don't give me any of your ruddy smarm, you little tosser – and don't give me any of that bullshit about back-up. You're fucking *useless*, and you just proved it.'

'Hey! No need to get abusive,' said Jackie, dusting down the front of his jacket like she'd ruined the line or something.

'You heard anything about Max being back in town?' she demanded.

'What? No.'

He was telling the truth, of course. Jackie Tulliver, who had once known everything that was happening on these streets, now knew nothing because no one included him. After all, what was the point? He really was useless.

'I don't know why you're bein' mean to me when all I'm doin' is tryin' to help you,' he whined.

'Shut. Up.'

'Well, I don't think there's any call for that,' he sulked.

'What, for telling the truth?' Annie glared at him. She rummaged in her coat pocket, found a fiver and flung it on to the pavement. '*There's* what you're after, right? Some cash to buy the next lot of booze. Well, there it is. Use it and stay the fuck out of my face.'

63

Jackie scuttled away, but not before he'd bent and snatched up the fiver from the ground. Annie watched him go, disgusted. He'd been one of Max's best, and now look at him – not even the dignity left to argue the toss with her. Not even the dignity left to refuse the money, tell her where to stick it. If he'd done that, she might have thought there was some hope for him. But he hadn't.

She walked on, with no idea where she was going to go or what she was going to do. Her broken rib and bruised body ached with every step. Her head ached too. People passed her on the pavements and the traffic roared through her throbbing brain like a nightmare. Once, a place of refuge would have been obvious: Dolly's. But not now, not any more.

He knows.

The thought pinged into her brain and lodged there like a cold metal spike, before sinking to the pit of her stomach and stabbing her with icy dread.

Oh Christ, it's true. He knows.

A two-stroke motorbike rushed past, the blank black helmet turning her way. Then bike and rider roared off, weaving in and out of the traffic up ahead. A white van pulled into the kerb and two men in navy boiler suits got out. Annie thought they were going to go into the audio shop she was passing in front of, and she went to step around them. They stepped in front of her. She stepped aside again. They blocked her way. Suddenly she thought of Ellie's place, wrecked.

Six men in boiler suits, hadn't someone told her that?

Yeah. They had.

Annie stopped walking. *Oh Jesus, please, not again.* She looked from one to the other of the men, total strangers to her.

'Look . . .' she said, dry-mouthed, thinking that she couldn't take another beating, she just couldn't.

'Get in the front,' said one of them.

'Wait . . .' said Annie.

He took her arm and pulled her out into the traffic, then when there was a gap in the flow he opened the passenger-side door and pushed her oh so gently but still very firmly inside the front of the van. He got in, and the driver did too, neatly pinning her between them. No knives in evidence this time, but these were hard men, people who wouldn't think twice about using force if they had to.

'Listen, I don't know what this is about, but you've got the wrong person,' she said quickly. 'You don't want to do this. Believe me. I have friends. Dangerous friends.'

They didn't answer.

Annie gulped as the driver started the van and steered it out into the traffic. 'Wait! It's true, what I'm telling you. You'll be sorry you did this.'

Neither one of them answered.

Annie fell silent, her heart hammering.

There was nothing else to say.

64

They drove her to the East End. As they wove through the streets she recognized the area and thought: *No, it can't be. Can it?* But they carried on, and soon she knew the road, she knew the house, she recognized the little Victorian terrace.

Oh shit.

The house had a powder-blue door and a teensy front garden with a chequered pathway leading up to it. She'd walked up it in the past, maybe a thousand times. The driver parked the van, and the other one took her arm. With the same gentle firmness he'd employed before, he helped her down from the van, then he closed the door and took her round to the pavement. The driver opened the blue-painted wrought-iron gate, and together they escorted her up the pathway to the house.

The driver rang the bell.

Presently, the door opened and the squat bulk of Steve Taylor stood there. He looked at her, briefly took in her mud-stained state, then he looked at the two men and held the door wide. With nowhere else to go, Annie stepped into the entrance hall of Queenie Carter's old domain. The house was empty – it had been empty for years – but for a big table and twelve chairs upstairs in the front bedroom, where Max and her and all the boys had once met up and discussed business.

Steve went on upstairs, and the driver nudged Annie that way too. She went up, feeling as if she was ascending the gallows.

He knows, he knows, repeated that panicky little voice in her brain.

Someone had done the unthinkable, broken the code of silence. But *who*, for God's sake?

The driver and the other one came up too, hard on her heels so she had nowhere to run. When Steve reached the landing, he knocked on the first closed door he came to, and then pushed it open. He stood aside, so that Annie could enter first.

Oh Jesus . . .

Annie braced herself and stepped inside the room. There was the table, just as she remembered, and the chairs. Gary was seated in one of them, Tony in another. Another man stood at the window, his back to the room.

'Blimey. Looks like a fucking courtroom in here,' said Annie. She glanced around at them all, a bright smile masking the awful fear that was gripping her guts. She felt almost unable to move, she was so frozen with apprehension.

'So who's on trial?' she quipped.

The man at the window turned and stared at her. Black hair, deep tan, dark navy-blue eyes and a piratical hook of a nose. Her husband.

Ah shit, she thought.

'Looks like you are,' said Max Carter.

65

'Hi,' said Annie.

Max didn't say another word. He just stared at her.

'You want us to step out on the landing, give you a bit of privacy?' asked Steve, directing the query to Max, not her.

Max nodded. One by one they rose and left the room. Gary gave Annie a smirk as he passed by.

'How are your two boys then, Gary?' she asked, quick as a flash.

He paused. 'What?'

'The one with the eyebrows and the bald one. Your doormen. They OK?'

He hesitated. *Knew* that she was on to him, that he had ordered that going-over after she'd cut up rough with his girlfriend at Dolly's. She could see it in his eyes.

'They're fine,' he said.

'What the fuck's all this?' asked Max irritably.

Annie turned to her husband with a bright smile.

'Nothing! Just me and Gary having a little conversation,' she said, and her eyes were resting on Gary's face again, telling him this wasn't over, this wasn't finished, not by a long shot.

'Fuck off, Gary,' said Max.

Gary went, minus the self-satisfied expression. Annie

was delighted to have wiped it off his face. It made the hot twinging pain of her broken rib more bearable, just to see that shadow of emerging fear on his ugly mug.

She watched the door close behind Gary, then turned to Max.

'Where the hell have you been?' she asked. 'And what are you doing, checking me out of hotels without my say-so?'

Max's eyes narrowed to angry slits. He shook his head.

'Oh, no. That won't wash with me, you ought to know that. Turning the tables, making out *I'm* the one in the wrong? I don't think so.'

'I'm just asking, that's all. You left Prospect without a word, not even a note. What was I supposed to think?'

Annie saw his eyes flash over her, take in the dried mud on her skirt suit.

'Am I supposed to give a shit what you think? I had some calls from Gary saying that something was going on, so I went and checked it out.'

Yeah, he knows.

Annie could feel her heart beating very fast. She could hear Max's boys talking in hushed whispers out on the landing. She felt sick now, really sick and terrified. She swallowed hard and managed to get the words out.

'Checked it out where?'

'Sicily.'

'What was it all about then?' she asked.

'About you,' said Max. 'And about Constantine Barolli.'

Annie could only stare at his face. 'Constantine? What about him?'

Max crossed the room and came and stood in front of her, very close. Annie forced herself not to take a step back. Fury radiated off him like heat from a fire.

'He's not dead, is he? He's alive.'

'Max—'

'Don't "Max" me. You *know* he's alive.'

'Look,' said Annie desperately. 'I couldn't tell you. I couldn't tell *anyone*.'

He grabbed her upper arms, bringing her still closer, cutting off her words. She felt the jolt of it all through her abused body; her damaged rib gave a red-hot spasm of protest that made her wince. His face was so close to hers that she could feel his breath on her cheek. This was the man she loved, Max Carter; she had grown so close to him that she hardly knew where she ended and he began. Now he was glaring at her with total hatred, and it chilled her to the marrow.

His head dipped down and she felt a shiver as he whispered in her ear.

'Now you have to scream,' he said. 'Loudly. Make it good, so they hear it.'

'Wha—?' Annie's eyes met his as his head drew back.

Without warning he shoved her backwards. She hit the wall hard, off-balance, and her broken rib set up a shriek all of its own. The pain was severe, and Annie screamed.

'Again. Louder,' said Max.

'You *bastard*,' she choked out, realizing what this was for; so that he looked the big man to the men out on the landing. So that they heard her being disciplined, and thought he was top dog, no question, tough as old boots for giving his lying old lady a thorough going-over.

'Do it,' he said, and shoved her against the wall again. It wouldn't have hurt, not really, but her already beaten body felt it all and she screamed again in real anguish.

'*Shit*, you *bastard*,' she panted as he let her go. She sagged there, feeling bile rising in her throat, feeling sick with the pain. She felt a prickling of cold sweat break out on her brow and wondered if she was going to pass out cold.

'You utter fucking . . .' she gasped out, her voice trailing away to nothing, glad of the wall now because it was all that was holding her up.

He grabbed her chin, turned her face up to his. Out on the landing, all was quiet. They were listening. Just as he'd intended.

'So he's alive?' Max's voice was a low, angry hiss. 'Well, not for very fucking long – and that's a promise. I'm going to *finish* that cunt. And you know what? Then I'm going to finish *you*. But right now, there's just one thing I want off of you.'

'What? *Ow!*' said Annie as the pain lanced through her mid-section again.

'Oh, don't give me that,' he muttered by her ear. 'I barely touched you. Don't milk it.'

'What do you want?' asked Annie, gasping the words out, thinking that yes, she was going to faint, she felt that rough now, that shaken up.

'A divorce,' he snapped. 'We're through, you hear me? This fucking marriage is over.'

Then he let her go and surged past her, out the door, slamming it hard shut behind him.

66

Annie staggered away from the wall and slumped down into one of the chairs at the table. Her head was humming, her heart was crashing around in her chest, and she thought, *That's it, I'm going to pass out now.* She heaved in air and put her head between her legs, which set up a fresh surge of agony in her middle. She stopped like that for a long time. Wincing, hurt, shocked, she straightened up again, feeling a little steadier.

Jesus, he knows, he knows . . .

The panicky phrase kept boomeranging around her head. Max knew about Constantine, and he wanted to divorce her. Of course he did. That was why she had made sure he would never know. But somehow it had all gone wrong. Now he was thinking all sorts, and accusing her of things, and this was where they'd landed up. Scuppered. Finished. Max wasn't the type to make empty promises, either. He *would* kill Constantine. And then he would kill *her*.

'Oh, Christ,' she wailed, and slapped a hand over her mouth because she wasn't going to give those clowns on the landing any more satisfaction.

She could hear them out there, talking in low voices. She thought that Max had gone straight out and down the stairs and away, she'd heard the front door slam after him; but Gary, Tony and Steve were still there.

Front it out, she thought. That was all she ever did.

Dolly was gone.

Ellie had washed her hands of her.

Chris, Tony, Steve, all once her friends, were now judging her, hating her.

And worse, far worse than any of that, Max. Max had turned against her, caught her out in this monumental deception. And he was going to destroy both Constantine and her. She totally believed that.

She stood up, steadying herself with a hand on the table. She tottered over to the closed door and took another breath.

Steady, she thought. *You ran these streets once. You were a Mafia queen.*

Yeah, once . . .

Annie opened the door. The three men, all of them massive and scary, turned and stared at her. She stepped out on to the landing, closing the door behind her. She moved past Tony, past Steve, and there was Gary, barring her way to the stairs.

'You got something to say to me?' she asked him.

'Yeah. What was that bollocks about my boys?'

Annie shrugged, very cool. 'I said it to them and I meant it. They shouldn't have done what they did. I warned them.'

'You're in no position to warn anybody about anything,' he sneered. 'The boss is spitting mad at you. You're *finished*, girl.'

'Oh, shut the fuck up and mind out the way,' said Annie, shoving past him.

Gary lunged at her, arm raised. Annie teetered on the top stair, clutched at the banister, thinking *This is it, he's going to knock me arse-backwards down those stairs, all the way to the bottom*. Then Steve stepped forward and grabbed Gary's upraised hand, forced it down.

'This fucking bitch, I *told* him what she was like, but would he listen?' burst out Gary, his face puce and his eyes fastened on Annie.

'Calm down, you cunt,' said Steve. 'This ain't our fight. Let *him* put it right, any way he wants.' Then he turned to Annie. 'You'd better go.'

Annie didn't need a second telling. Feeling like she'd escaped by the skin of her teeth, she turned and went down the stairs and out the door.

67

Because she couldn't think what else to do, she went to the Holland Park house and opened it up. Outside the front door, on the top step, were her bags and suitcase, dumped there.

Yeah, like I'm about to be dumped, she thought miserably.

Hunter was there too, just getting out of his car.

'Mrs Carter,' he said. 'Feeling better then? I went to the hotel and they said you'd checked out, so I wondered if you might come here.'

'Right,' said Annie, uncaring. Her world had crashed around her, she didn't give a shit about anything right now.

'In fact they said Mr Carter checked you out.'

'He did. Yes.'

'I take it he's here with you?'

'Yeah. That's right,' lied Annie. She didn't want to start explaining the perilous state of her marriage to anyone. It hurt too much.

'That's good,' said Hunter as she climbed up the steps to the house. 'I'm questioning Dolly Farrell's brothers and sister at the moment, if you're interested.'

Right now, Annie wasn't. She didn't answer.

Hunter stared at her curiously, then said: 'I'm glad Mr Carter's with you, anyway. You might need a little moral support.'

Annie paused and looked at him. 'Why?'

'We're releasing Miss Farrell's body. Mrs Brown is arranging the funeral for this Friday.'

Oh shit, she thought.

Inside the house, it was deathly quiet. Having said goodbye to Hunter at the door, she crossed the big, empty, echoing hall with its black-and-white chequered marble floor tiles, passing beneath the vast chandelier. All the tables and chairs in the hallway were shrouded in white dust sheets. She dropped her ruined bags and her suitcase, then opened the study door and went inside, tossing more sheets aside and sitting tiredly down in the gold leather captain's chair behind the desk. Her heart was racing, her mouth dry. She wished she drank, because if ever drink was called for, it was now.

Max knew, and he wanted a divorce.

A divorce.

She slumped there behind the big Moroccan leather-topped desk and let her head sink into her hands. Her rib twinged painfully as she leaned forward, and in frustration and irritation she picked up the bone-handled paper knife that had once been Constantine's, and flung it to the floor.

Christ, what a mess.

Her brain flashed back to the fury in Max's eyes, the way he'd spat the D word at her. She shuddered as if caught in a blast of cold air. He meant it, too. She knew that.

But he don't know it all. He only knows part of it.

Would he give her a chance to tell the rest? She doubted it.

She was still sitting there an hour later when the doorbell rang. She heaved herself to her feet and went and answered it. Jackie Tulliver was standing there.

'Now where the fuck you been? You keep vanishin' like you do, how am I supposed to stay in touch?' he asked, his voice indignant as he bustled inside.

Didn't I tell him to sod off?

Annie let out a weary sigh and closed the door behind him. 'What the hell do you want now?'

'Hey, I'm workin' hard here, on your behalf. Findin' out things. Doin' some business, greasin' some palms.'

'Did I ask you to?'

'I'm not the sort of person who quits on a job,' said Jackie.

No, not when there's some beer money in it, thought Annie.

'Y'see, the way I see it *is*, my job is to take a load offa your shoulders, help you out, smooth your path through life.'

'Right,' said Annie. 'So start doing that. Ellie told me that, years ago, Dolly asked the Delaney boys to knock off her dear old dad.'

'She what?'

Annie clutched her head. It hurt to think. Her brain ached. She felt like her head was almost coming off.

Dolly wanted her father killed.

Well, had Ellie's words really been such a big surprise? After what he'd done to her, it was only what he'd deserved, the dirty old bastard. She thought of the Delaney clan, arch-enemies of the Carters, who had ruled the Limehouse streets back in the fifties and sixties. Tory, the eldest, and Pat his second-in-command. Then, later, the twins: Orla and Redmond.

Tory was dead, shot in Stoke Newington.

Pat? He was dead too, his bones mouldering somewhere out in the depths of the English Channel.

The youngest of the family, Kieron, was long gone. And Orla, she was gone too.

The only living member of the family was Redmond. Annie had seen him five years ago, on the Essex marshes. Had thought almost that she'd dreamed him, but no, he'd been real, he'd been there in the flesh and he'd claimed to have put aside his evil ways – but had he?

Redmond would know exactly what had happened, all those years ago, to Dolly's father, and that might even lead them to the person who'd killed her.

'Jackie?' she said.

'Yeah, what?'

'You've got to find Redmond Delaney.'

'Fuckin' *hell*,' said Jackie.

'Do it,' she said, and went to sluice some of the mud, sweat and hospital stench off her skin, dig out some clean clothes and stuff another load of painkillers down her throat.

68

Next day Annie took a cab over to the Shalimar, passing the Palermo on the way and getting the driver to stop there.

Things were being unloaded from the back of a large van; Caroline was moving into the flat over the club, obliterating all memory of the woman who had once lived there.

Isn't she worried by the thought of a murder having been done there? wondered Annie.

Obviously Caroline wasn't. Maybe Caroline was so ambitious that she would even consider murder to clear a path for herself. Who knew?

'OK, drive on,' she said, and the driver took her on over to the Shalimar.

One of the cleaners let her in; no bouncers in yet, it was too early for that. She went through the nearly empty club and up the stairs to Ellie and Chris's flat.

'Hello?' she called ahead, not wanting to surprise anyone. Chris was already pissed off with her, and Ellie too.

Down below, the Hoover started up just as she reached the kitchen door. Chris was sitting at the table, reading a paper. The front page showed French troops pouring into Rwanda.

'Hi, Chris,' she said.

He looked at her with a mixture of embarrassment and surly dislike.

'Now what the fuck?' he asked.

'It's OK, Chris, I'll take it from here,' said Ellie, appearing at her shoulder.

Chris stood up, folding his newspaper. He brushed past Annie, then she and Ellie went into the kitchen. Ellie closed the door while Annie sat down at the table.

'Look,' said Ellie, her face set. 'I *told* you—'

'I didn't mean to just show up, but I had to see you,' interrupted Annie. 'The police told me you're organizing the funeral.'

Ellie's face relaxed into sad lines. She let out a sigh, her shoulders slumping.

'Yeah. That's right.'

'Christ, it's the pits. *Dolly's* funeral.'

Ellie came over to the table and sat down opposite Annie. Her brows drew together. 'Yeah. It's bad. Like a nightmare. And you know what? I'm thinking, if that can happen to Dolly, who everybody loved so much, then what about me? Is this about you? I know you got trouble. Am I a sitting duck here? Or is this about the clubs, the *Carter* clubs? Is someone making a point? Is this a takeover bid? You get all sorts in here these days, pushing drugs, you know. I could be in serious bother.'

'You've got Chris here with you. Dolly had no one.' Annie swallowed hard, thinking of Dolly, alone in the flat, and of someone climbing the stairs to kill her. 'Look, Ellie – I want to help out. Any way I can. With the funeral.'

'There's no need.'

'I want to. The headstone. Flowers. Anything.'

'God, I don't know. I don't even like you being here. Mr Carter—'

'I've seen Max. I saw him yesterday.'

Ellie's eyes widened. 'Fuck! Did you?'

'Yeah. I did. And there's trouble. *Big* trouble. You're right.'

'Chris said it was something about the Mafia bloke you were married to once. The one who died. He wouldn't say more than that.'

Annie looked Ellie straight in the eye. 'Ah, what the hell. He didn't die, Ellie. He's alive.'

Ellie went pale. 'What I told you in the hospital? I meant it. I *don't* want to know the details. I got enough going on, without that.'

Annie slumped forward, then winced and straightened. 'Yeah. I understand.' She looked up at Ellie. 'So the funeral's Friday?'

'Yeah,' said Ellie, and told her what time, and where.

'I'll be there.' Annie pushed herself wearily to her feet. 'Meantime, if you want anything, need anything, just give a shout. I'll be at the Holland Park place, you've got the number.'

Ellie stood up too. 'No offence, but the last thing I need is your help. You're bad news around here, ain't you heard? The best thing I can do is keep clear. For *all* our sakes.'

Annie went back to Holland Park, feeling even more like Billy-no-mates. Well, had she really expected Ellie to change her mind and lay out the welcome mat, be friends again?

She paid the cab at the door and went inside the house. It was huge, empty, echoing; the chequered floor threw back her footsteps as if mocking her, while over her head, the chandelier worth a fortune dangled, massive and glinting with crystal droplets.

Mafia money.

Hadn't Max once told her that the police never rested

over Mafia money? Well, this place was *built* on Mafia funds. Constantine had owned this house; then he'd passed it on to her after his 'death'.

She went into the study, threw aside another dust sheet and sat down on a big tan leather Chesterfield. She kicked off her shoes and gingerly lay down on the sofa to rest her aching body. But her mind refused to be still.

Constantine's death . . .

Only Constantine *wasn't* dead. She'd known it for years, and kept it to herself. *Omerta* was the code the Mafia lived by, and that extended to Mafia queens too. No one ever broke that code. Secrets were never to be shared, not with loved ones, not with a living soul. Not even with husbands. Not even with Max Carter. She'd sworn an oath, unbreakable. She'd had no choice but to be quiet.

The parcel bomb, planted on the night of Lucco's wedding.

Ah shit.

She would never, ever forget it. She relived it in her dreams sometimes. A night full of laughter and celebration, that had quickly turned into a screaming, howling wall of grief.

Montauk, Long Island.

A soft summer night in the States.

A night of terror.

69

Montauk, Long Island, USA, August 1971

It started with the explosion. Or, rather, it finished. Annie's life with Constantine Barolli, her married life with him, finished right there, on the day of his eldest son Lucco's marriage to his dull little second cousin Daniella from Sicily.

It was a hot August night and the party was clearly going to go on into the small hours. The mariachi band was playing, the oceanfront house in the millionaire's playground of Montauk was heaving with happy, laughing guests.

Annie stood alone on the deck, just a little light spilling out from inside the house, not much, and she thought of that later, realized that her eyes had played tricks on her. She was standing in the darkness by the edge of the terrace, and she was five months' pregnant with Constantine's child, and she was tired; she was relishing the cool breeze blowing in off the Atlantic Ocean, which stretched out, black as oil, to the lighter grey of the horizon.

Then the French doors opened and Constantine stepped out.

He smiled at her and picked up a present from the pile on the trestle tables just beside the door. Later, at ten o'clock, Constantine, the Godfather, the Silver Fox, would hand out the presents to Lucco and his new bride; but for now he was smiling at Annie and shaking the present as he lifted it from the table.

'Hey, wonder what's in this one?' he said, and then it happened.

The explosion. Sudden, shocking; a mind-crippling upswelling whumph of sound and sensation.

She felt herself blown off her feet, lifted over the rail and dumped on to the sand of the beach, all the air punched out of her. She couldn't hear, and her brain couldn't offer up any logical reason for why she was lying there, staring at a seashell while black things rained down around her, scorched things, and fire was erupting on the balcony above her; the whole deck was quickly turning to matchwood.

To the world at large – more importantly, to the FBI and to other rival families and to those who worked even more closely against him – that was the point at which Constantine Barolli died.

70

London, January 1989

It was Alberto, Constantine's youngest son and now Il Papa, the Godfather, the head of the Barolli family, who finally broke the news to Annie during one of their rare, brief, secret meetings. Alberto was on the run from the FBI, but sometimes she was passed a note, a pizzino, and then he appeared. Sometimes he even brought his girlfriend – Annie and Max's daughter Layla – with him, a rare treat and something Annie lived for, and she was disappointed to find that on this occasion Layla wasn't present.

Slowly, Alberto started to talk. He laid it all out. He talked and Annie sat there, listening but not believing what she was hearing. When he had finished speaking, she asked him to say it all over again. He did.

'This is rubbish,' said Annie.

'Annie—'

'You're . . . what the hell are you saying? You're telling me Constantine's not dead,' she said at last, feeling like she was going to scream or cry – probably both.

'That's what I'm saying,' Alberto nodded.

Annie put both hands over her mouth. Her eyes were wide with shock.

'Hey . . .' said Alberto, springing to his feet, coming over to her, hugging her tight.

Annie flinched away from his embrace, shaking her head. She gulped, blinked, and dropped her hands into her lap. On one of those hands – her right – there was a small white scar on the palm. She stared at it, numb, not believing any of this.

He was alive?

She tried to speak, and couldn't. Tried again.

'You're telling me,' she managed at last, 'that for all these years, you've known this?'

'Yeah.' Alberto sat back; a storm was about to break over his head, and he knew it.

'You've known, and you didn't say something?'

'Omerta.' He shrugged.

'What?'

'Our code of silence. The Don spoke, and I had to follow his orders. Those are the rules of Cosa Nostra, Annie. Nobody breaks the code, ever. Dammit, you of all people, you know that.'

Annie was shaking her head now, over and over, thinking, This is crazy, this can't be true.

'No. He's dead.' She swiped at her face – there were actual tears running down her cheeks; she wiped them away and glared at Alberto, the stepson she adored, who'd been an ally and a friend to her for almost twenty-five years. At this moment, she was staring at him as she would stare at a hostile stranger. 'I saw him die.'

Alberto leaned forward, sighing, clasping his hands between his knees. His face turned toward her and he stared at her with those laser-blue eyes – his father's eyes. Constantine's eyes.

'The man you saw die wasn't Constantine Barolli,' he said.

'No, that's not possible, I spoke to him when we were getting dressed, I was with him all day . . .' she was protesting.

'Papa was with you all day, but the man who walked out

on to the deck and died there was not him. That was the actor we'd hired to take his place. We groomed him, trained him, dyed his hair silver, he even got the voice just right. Poor bastard, all he knew was that it was a family joke he was being paid to carry out on the wedding day. Some joke, uh? When that man died, the Don was already gone, out of the house and away.'

Annie was still staring fixedly at his face.

'You've had a shock,' said Alberto.

'A shock?' A bitter laugh escaped Annie. She clutched at herself as if feeling cold. So many years, he'd been gone. They'd spirited him away and an innocent man had died in his place, and they'd kept Constantine's wife, who had lost his baby, who he was supposed to have loved, in total ignorance.

'I wanted to tell you,' said Alberto.

'Sure you fucking did.'

'I did. I swear. But you know Papa – he could detach, real easy. The Feds were closing in on him. He made the decision to go, and he carried it out. He was like that, you know he was. He could be cold, ruthless.'

Annie nodded. 'You're pretty ruthless yourself. You saw me back then. I was in pain, mourning him. And you just let it pass.'

'I had to. I told you.'

Annie jerked to her feet and started pacing around the room, still hugging herself, her movements agitated. Suddenly she stopped and stood in front of Alberto.

'You fucking bastard,' she said flatly.

'Hey . . .' He stood up, reached for her.

Annie twitched away. 'Don't even think about it! You kept this from me! You knew it and you didn't say a word.'

'I couldn't. Believe me.'

Annie paced some more. She stopped again, right in front of him.

'Why now?' she snapped out. 'Come on, I'd like to know. Why not keep the stupid bitch in her cage forever?'

'He never saw you like that. Never,' said Alberto.

'Fuck it, who gives a shit, wasn't that his attitude? He was safe and well, so who cares?'

'He did care.'

'Bullshit,' she said.

'And now . . .'

Annie stopped moving. She stared at his face. 'And now what?' she prompted.

'Now he wants – he needs – to see you.'

71

London, June 1994

At about nine o'clock Annie went down to the kitchen, looked in the fridge, which was empty, and the freezer, which was empty too. She closed the freezer door, switched off the light and left the kitchen and went back into the drawing room with its big sandstone hearth and tapestry-covered Knole sofas.

Yawning, exhausted and achingly lonely, she yanked the curtains closed against the remaining daylight. Later, she would sleep in the master suite at the top of the stairs, in what had once been Constantine's bed.

She wished Max was here, but he wasn't, and if he *was* he would probably rip her head off and beat her with it, and she might as well get used to that idea. She thought again of the cold hatred in his eyes when they'd confronted each other at his mum's old place.

I'll finish him, and then I'll finish you.

He wouldn't forgive her, and he would never forget.

At ten, Annie went upstairs to the master suite and eased her aching body into bed. The thought of what Alberto had told her about Constantine still haunted her. For a long while after Alberto broke that news, she had been convinced that she was going insane.

But no.

She wasn't imagining the whole thing. It had happened. And the worst part? She could share that knowledge with nobody. Not even Max. *Particularly* not Max, because, if he knew, then he would search out Constantine, find him, kill him. And she *couldn't* break the code.

Now, Max knew.

So Constantine was under threat. And so was she.

What would Max's next move be? He said he'd been to Sicily, so he'd spoken to someone in the inner circle of the family there, and they had broken the code, told him more than they should. Who, though? She didn't think that Daniella, Lucco's bride, had ever been privy to that sort of information. Daniella was a lightweight, not to be entrusted with such a burden.

Annie stared at the ceiling and thought: Gina.

It *had* to be Constantine's sister Gina. Who else would have been told, apart from her? No one. And for years she had kept the secret, respected its gravity. Until now. Why *now*? What could have happened to make her betray the family and give out such information to strangers?

She didn't know. Couldn't believe it had happened.

Gina was sound, an insider, *family*.

Dislike her though she did, Annie had to admit that Gina was the last person she would have expected this from.

She reached out, turned off the light.

72

She didn't know what woke her; some suggestion of movement, some slight noise. Her eyes opened and it was still dark, but the blue-toned moonlight was visible through the curtains, casting a ghostly shaft of light on to the floor at the foot of the bed.

She turned over, sat up. Wished she'd thought to bring a glass of water in here with her, but she'd forgotten. Her brain was scrambled, she was miserable and her midriff ached with every breath she took. Sleep had been blissful, and she hadn't wanted to wake up. The way she felt, she hadn't wanted to wake up *ever*.

But she had, in the middle of the night, because . . .

Because someone was in here with her.

Her senses were instantly alert. The floorboards creaked in this room, and that was what she'd heard, she was sure of it.

Someone's killed Dolly and now they're coming for me.

She took a gasping breath in and flicked on the bedside light. *No, no, it was just my imagination, it was nothing, it was . . .*

There was a man sitting in the chair in the corner of the room.

'Holy *shit!*' Annie yelled, floundering back against the pillows. Her bruised and bandaged mid-section cried out a protest and she clutched at it, wincing; it hurt so much that tears sprang into her eyes.

She blinked, stared; it was Max.

'What the *fuck* . . . ?' she demanded.

'Did you forget I had a key?' he said. 'And you didn't set the alarm, that was careless.'

Yes, she had forgotten he had a key. And the alarm? Yes, that was careless, but then she was in shock over Dolly's death, and Max's discovery of her sins, and she was shattered and hurt, and she wasn't going to tell him a damned thing about any of that.

Annie hauled the sheets up to her chin and stared at him. 'What, have you come to give me another bollocking?' she challenged.

'I might do. You bloody well deserve one.'

'I would have tried to explain the other day if you could have been fucking bothered to let me. But no – it was more important to you to show what a big man you are in front of your boys.' Annie sneered. 'Lacking your bleeding audience now, aren't you? Haven't got the boys outside the door listening in this time. Bet that gave you a thrill, playing the big I-am, putting the little woman in order. Give you a hard-on, did it?'

'You really do push your luck,' he said.

'I'm all out of luck. Haven't you heard? My husband wants to divorce me, my best mate's taken a bullet in the head, and everyone's acting like I should be ringing a bell and shouting "unclean".'

'Maybe you should.'

'Yeah, maybe. But I'm your wife and you owe me.'

'What? I owe you fuck-all. You've been creeping around behind my back screwing that flash Yankee arsehole . . .'

'No.'

'*Yes.*'

'No. Look. I had to keep the secret. I had to honour the code.'

'Bollocks. Maybe now – without an audience – you might just explain to me what the fuck's been going on?'

Annie frowned and sighed. 'Me and Constantine.'

'No, you and the Pope. Yes, I mean you and Constantine, or is there any other cunt I should know about as well?'

'I wouldn't know where to start.'

Max came and stood beside the bed and stared down at her. He moved quickly, stealthy as a cat. But he'd forgotten the floorboards, she reminded herself. He ought to have remembered that.

'Try starting at the beginning,' he said.

'I don't even know where that *is* any more.'

'Let's think about it.' He put his hands on his hips and considered. 'Oh yeah. How about when he was supposed to have died, and didn't? That seems like a good place.'

'I didn't know about that until Alberto told me,' said Annie. 'I thought he was dead. I really did. Until then.'

Max cocked his head to one side. 'Is that another fucking barefaced lie?'

'It's true. Constantine swore him to secrecy until then.'

'And then suddenly he decides to tell you. You sure you didn't know all along?'

'You're joking. I didn't know *anything*. I thought he'd died. Damn it, I saw it happen. At first I couldn't believe it. But then Alberto said that he'd had to do it. That they'd put in a double, an actor, to pretend to be Constantine because there had been rumours of a hit coming.'

Max was silent for a long while, watching her face. 'All that time, I thought you and Alberto. I thought it was him you were sneaking off to see on your "business trips". I was *sure* there was something going on. And you know what? Turns out I was right. Only it wasn't the son you were seeing, was it? It was the father. You *cow*.'

'No.' Annie gulped. 'Look. You don't know the real story.'

'All right, so tell me. And you'd better bloody make it good. What happened after Alberto broke the news? And *when* did he break the news?'

'Five years ago.'

Max was staring at her as if he didn't even know her. 'Five fucking *years*?'

'*Max*—'

'Five years, and you didn't tell me a thing?'

'I couldn't.'

Max's face was set with fury. 'All right. Go on. Then what?'

'Then?' Annie sighed tiredly. 'He told me Constantine wanted to see me.'

73

'You've been lying to me, straight-faced, for years,' said Max, shaking his head in wonder.

'Lying? No. That's bullshit. I just didn't *tell* you, that's all.'

'Oh yeah. The Mafia "code". Your fucking "*omerta*".'

'That's right.'

'What a shitload of bollocks. You didn't tell me you were seeing him. You fucking well *deceived* me. How the hell can you say you didn't? You bloody did.'

'I had to. The code—'

'Fuck the code. And fuck *you*.' Max dragged his hands through his hair then rubbed them over his face. He walked over to the wall, turned, walked back to the bed and stopped there, staring down at her.

'And what the hell happened then?' he asked. 'Supposing I believe a damned word of it, that is. You heard the tale about that concubine who kept spinning tales for the Sultan to stop him cutting her head off?'

'*The Arabian Nights*,' said Annie, and shot a sour smile at him, even though her heart was hammering with dread. 'Damn, you mean you've actually read a book in your life? News to me.'

Constantine had devoured books. Max? She had never seen him pick up a book of any description, not once. Two such different men she had fallen in love with. Max so fiery, and Constantine so controlling.

'Is that what you're doing? Spinning tales to save your neck?' asked Max.

'Do I have to?'

Max paced around the room, hands in trouser pockets, eyeing up the rugs, the four-poster bed, the big carved-oak dressing table. Then he stopped and looked at her sitting there in the bed, grey with exhaustion, big shadows under her eyes.

'People in this town expect me to discipline you,' he said. 'Severely.'

'For what?'

'For *what*? You serious? You been sneaking off to see another man for *years*. A man you were married to. A man you jumped into bed with when I was off the scene.'

'Are we really going to have *that* conversation again? It happened years ago, Max, and I thought you were dead.'

'Everyone expects me to make you suffer.'

'As I already said – for what?'

'You seriously expect me to believe that you saw him again, met up with him – and you *didn't* sleep with him? Why else would you carry on seeing him, and not tell me?'

'I couldn't tell you. I couldn't tell *anyone*.' Annie sighed heavily and swiped a hand over her face. 'Those are the Cosa Nostra rules. I don't know how you found out about him. You never would have, from me. I swore a blood oath, Max, and that means something.'

Annie held out her hand, showed him the white scar on her palm.

'You see this?' she said.

'What about it?'

'That's where Constantine cut me. When I married him, I married into the Mafia way of life too. It's a serious commitment. He cut my hand and burned a picture of the saint and let the ashes fall into my cupped hands, and he said that if I ever betrayed that oath, then I would burn in hell, just like the saint was burning.'

'And you *believed* that shit?'

'It was an oath, Max. A blood oath. I would have thought that you, with all the people who work for you, would understand that.' Annie stared at him. 'So who gave him away?'

'It was his sister,' said Max.

Annie's attention sharpened. She'd suspected it, but she found it hard to believe that Gina would betray her brother. 'What, Gina? Really? You're joking.'

'That's the only sister he had. Yeah, Gina.' Max started pacing again, shooting her hostile looks as he did so. 'She lost her marbles and started making phone calls. They went to Gary at the Blue Parrot. From then on I knew.'

'God, I bet he was pleased when that happened,' said Annie. 'He's moving his girlfriend into the Palermo to take over management there, did you know that?'

'I knew it. And why not? Dolly Farrell's gone.'

'Gone? Someone killed her.'

'I know that too. Your mate Hunter's been on to me, asking what I know.'

'And do you know anything?'

'Should I?'

'She was shot, Max. Someone *shot* her dead.'

'Not me.'

'Did I mention you?'

Max shrugged. 'Maybe she was keeping bad company.'

'Everyone loved Dolly.'

'Not *everyone*. Case in point – she's dead.'

Annie closed her eyes tight, rubbing at them with her

fists. 'Look, can we go on with this in the morning? I'm tired, I need to sleep.'

'No, we fucking can't. It couldn't have been just one visit. How many times did you see him behind my back?'

'There was more than one visit,' admitted Annie. 'There were quite a few.'

'You cow,' said Max, and came to the bed, very sudden.

He moves fast, she thought. *Don't I know that, better than anyone?*

Suddenly he was leaning over her, and his hand was on her throat. It wasn't squeezing, she took some comfort from that. His eyes might be blazing mad as they glared into hers, but his hand wasn't squeezing and it could, easily.

'Max . . .' she tried to get out, but she couldn't speak. It came out a groaning wheeze.

'Shut up,' he snapped.

Their eyes locked. Then, as suddenly as he'd grabbed her, he let her go. Annie's hand flew to her throat. Max started pacing the room again, his movements tense with anger. Suddenly he stopped and turned to her. He paused. Seemed about to say something. Then he went out of the door, slamming it shut behind him. She heard him go off down the stairs, cross the entrance hall. The front door closed with a bang.

He was gone.

74

'You sure you're up to this? You look fucked,' said Max.

The day of the funeral had dawned bright and clear. Annie turned as she and Max stood momentarily alone beside the hearse outside the Catholic church. She stared at him. Last night he'd been ready to throttle the life out of her; her throat was bruised. Yet today he was asking if she was up to playing her part in this, carrying her oldest friend to her final resting place.

'I'm surprised you care,' she said.

'Don't flatter yourself,' he said coldly. 'I just don't want you dropping the fucking thing, that's all, and making a cunting spectacle out of the lot of us.'

Annie glared at him. 'She carried me plenty of times. And I'm going to carry her now. I won't drop her.'

Tony joined them, ignoring Annie, nodding to Max.

'If we're ready . . . ?' asked the undertaker, and his two co-workers slid Dolly's coffin out of the hearse.

Max, Tony and Annie joined the other three black-suited men and lifted the coffin on to their shoulders. Pain clamped down on Annie's rib, but she could do this: she had to do this one last thing for Dolly, who had helped her so much in life. Steadily, moving together, the six of them walked the coffin along the gravel path and into the church.

Inside, it was full of people, there wasn't a spare pew to

be found. There were white lilies all around the altar and when they brought in Dolly's coffin everyone rose to their feet and watched as they carried it up to the front of the church and placed it carefully on the dais.

Drawing to one side between Max and Tony, Annie saw Ellie and Chris up near the front, and glancing back she saw Hunter, without his accompanying DS today, standing near the back; he was watching the crowds, just as she was. Their eyes met, and he nodded a faint greeting.

Then she turned her attention to the mourners right at the front of the church on the right; there was a woman there who, from the back, could almost pass for Dolly. She had the same rounded shoulders, the same puffball of blonde hair, the same firmly planted way of standing.

Doll?

No, it wasn't Dolly. Dolly was in that box, about to be consigned to the earth. As the ceremony began and the first hymn was sung, Annie kept her eyes on that little group up the front of the church. The woman's head kept bending as she dabbed at her eyes. Beside her, there was a man, not very tall, his build similar to the woman's. He squeezed the woman's arm a couple of times, tried to comfort her.

Dolly's brother? Dolly's sister?

The hymns went on, and the prayers, and then – at last – it was over. They carried the coffin outside, and as the organ music played on, everyone left the church to assemble at the edge of the newly dug plot, the earth decorously covered with Astroturf so that no one would see what lay beneath.

'Ashes to ashes, dust to dust . . .' intoned the priest.

Annie didn't pay attention to the words. She focused on the coffin. She'd known her friend for years, but she hadn't been aware that Dolly was Catholic. Not that it mattered.

Annie's opinion was, so long as you didn't scare the horses, you could worship however and whoever you liked. What difference did it make?

Her eyes scanned the crowds huddled around the grave. That woman again . . . pale, blue-eyed . . . she had to be a sister, a niece, something. And the man. Definitely a relative. And Dolly had never ever mentioned her relatives. Yet here they were, at least two of them, attending her funeral.

Annie's heart seemed to freeze as she met Max's cold, accusing gaze. He was standing away from her now, among his boys: Chris, Gary, Steve, Tony. The sight of them there in black coats, all of them big and very intimidating, gave her a deep, visceral shudder so hard that her bruised and strapped-up middle throbbed. And it wasn't just them giving her evils: when she looked around at the crowds, she could see people staring, pointing, whispering.

Suddenly, she didn't feel safe. She felt like these people might turn on her like an angry mob, because she'd crossed the line; they believed she'd done the dirty on Max Carter, and he had more clout in this town than she would ever have. These were *his* people, not hers.

She was relieved when the whole damned thing was over and the crowds began to disperse. She kept her head down and got back on to the gravel path and headed for the lychgate. She walked straight into DCI Hunter.

'Hello, Mrs Carter,' he said.

'Hi, Hunter. Here looking for murderers?'

'Something like that. You?'

'Just getting my friend buried.' Annie thought it was coming to something when you started bumping into a copper and felt pleased to see a friendly face. Once, she'd ruled these streets and everyone had respected her. Now, she knew she could fall down dead on the pavement and they'd just step over her body. Or piss on it.

273

Hunter gave a sigh. 'It's tough.'

'It's worse than that,' said Annie sharply. 'It's bloody awful. Listen, did you check out the CCTV in the club?'

'I did. The stairs aren't covered by the cameras inside. Why would they be? If anyone misbehaves, it'll be in the main body of the club, not up the stairs.'

'The outside ones then?'

'Nothing out of the ordinary. Nothing at all.'

'The club closed at one in the morning. Someone must have called after that, to kill Dolly.'

'Really? What if they arrived earlier, while the club was open? Blended with the crowds going in, snuck up the stairs, kept her there until everyone else had left, then did the deed?'

'Do the staff say she was upstairs? Not down in the bar?'

'They confirm that she was upstairs from ten o'clock onward. The bar manager Peter Jones knocked on the flat door just after one to say he was cashing up, and Dolly said OK. Next morning he found her dead.'

Annie was frowning at the ground. Then she looked up at Hunter's face. 'Thanks for that. It helps, you know. Hearing the details. Thinking that maybe we can solve this.'

'Mrs Carter,' he said flatly, '*I* can solve this. Not you.'

'You really think so?'

'Yes, Mrs Carter. Never doubt it. Can we talk about your Edinburgh trips?'

'What?'

'The trips to Edinburgh from the heliport?' Hunter pulled out a notebook and thumbed through. 'Yes, here we are. The taxi service from Edinburgh airport confirmed that on a few of your trips you were going to a house not far outside the city, and the house is owned by a company that trades through a series of tax havens.'

'I just stayed there sometimes, that's all.' Annie kept her face blank.

'And sometimes you flew direct to the Highlands. To a place called the Mouth of Hades, I believe.'

'It's just a place I like to stay at.'

'I see.' Hunter snapped the notebook closed. Then he looked around. 'Is it my imagination, or are you getting some disapproving looks?'

Annie knew she was. People were staring at her with angry faces. Again she felt that spasm of insecurity; that sensation of no longer being safe on these streets, the streets where she used to stride around like a queen.

She nodded to indicate the woman who looked like Dolly, the man who seemed to share the same genetic profile. They were lingering beside the grave. 'You seen those two? You know who they are?'

'I do. That's Sarah Foster, née Farrell. And that's her brother, Nigel.'

'Dolly's brother and sister?'

'Exactly.'

'I never knew she had close relatives. She never mentioned them.'

'Have you spoken to them?'

'No. Have you?'

'Yes, briefly.'

'And?'

He shook his head with a smile. 'Police business, Mrs Carter,' he said, and turned and walked away. Then he paused. His eyes swept over the milling crowds and then resettled on her face. 'You don't seem to be flavour of the month around here right now. So be careful.'

75

Annie watched him go, then turned back toward the grave-side. Over to the left, she saw Max still there, in a tight huddle with Steve, Chris and Tony. Gary was gone. Ignoring them all, she went toward Sarah and Nigel. On the way there, a group of eight people, men and women, approached her, their faces grim, their eyes accusing. She was jostled, and she heard the words *traitor bitch* hissed at her. Someone spat at her feet, spattering her legs with phlegm. Shocked, she shoved and pushed her way through them and emerged shakily on the other side.

Gathering herself, she took a breath and then walked on to meet up with Dolly's relatives. She held out a hand that wasn't entirely steady and said: 'Hello? I believe you're Dolly's brother and sister? I'm Annie Carter. I was a friend of hers.'

Up close, Sarah's resemblance to Dolly was even more pronounced. She did have the same posture, the same sloping well-padded shoulders, the same tough stockiness of frame. But this woman had never hit the dye bottle like Dolly had, crisping her hair to the texture of straw; this woman's was a soft mousy brown fashioned into an old-style set-and-shampoo which did nothing for her pallid features. Her eyes were light blue, reddened with tears. She wore an unflattering and overlong black coat with a silver spider brooch high up on the lapel. Her mouth was thin, her lips trembling. She looked at Annie's hand and seemed to debate as to whether or not she was going to shake it. Then she made her mind up, and did. Her grip was limp, and damp.

'Did she ever mention me?' asked Annie.

The woman shook her head. Annie was staring at her, thinking it was weird, to see Dolly's features on this woman's pale, set face – and yet it was obvious this woman was no Dolly. She looked timid, introverted, and Dolly had never been either of those things. Annie found herself wanting to shake the woman, to say, Come on, Dolly, show yourself, I know you're in there.

Stupid.

'We never saw Dolly,' said Sarah in a low lisping voice.

Annie watched her curiously, waiting for explanation. When it was obvious she wasn't going to get any, she turned her attention to the man standing there. Dark brown eyes on this one, but again – Dolly's features. That hot surge of exasperation was overwhelming now, the need to shake some life into them. The man looked no more animated than the woman. He had the look of someone permanently undernourished, with a thin mouth, sunken cheeks . . . and yet, there it was, in the stance, in the build, sometimes even in the expression of the face, fleeting, there one moment, gone the next; an echo of Dolly Farrell, her friend.

'Dolly left home when she was thirteen. She never kept in touch,' said Nigel. His mouth thinned into a prudish line. 'We heard she became a prostitute.'

Maybe that had something to do with her own father fucking her in the first place, thought Annie, feeling an upsurge of anger at Nigel's disapproving tone.

Perhaps these two dour little creatures didn't know

anything about what the father had done. And was now really the right time to bring it up? She didn't think so.

'She was the salt of the earth, Dolly,' she said. 'The best friend I ever had.'

'Well, we wouldn't know about that,' said Nigel with a sniff of disapproval.

I don't like you, thought Annie.

Ah, but that was unfair. She'd only just met these two; it was too soon to decide that they had no balls, no guts, no drive and no feeling; Dolly had had all that and more. Once again it crashed in on her: the realization, the terrible knowledge of what she had lost. She swallowed hard and said, 'She never talked about her family. Is it . . . are there more brothers and sisters?'

'We have a younger brother, Sandy.'

Then why isn't he here too? wondered Annie. It was like drawing teeth, trying to get a word out of them. 'Couldn't he come?'

'He's in a home,' said Sarah. 'And Dick's in New Zealand.'

'And your parents . . . ?' asked Annie, thinking of the father – that bastard.

'Mum passed last year. Dad died years ago. An accident on the railway.'

'He worked on the railways? I never knew that.'

'Oh yes. Started out in the signal boxes but then he went on to be a wheeltapper, and a shunter.'

That meant precisely nothing to Annie. 'Shunter? What's that?'

'They connect the engines to the carriages. Dad's accident was about five years after Dolly left home,' said Nigel accusingly, as if Dolly being there could have prevented it.

'What happened?' asked Annie.

They looked at her in dual disapproval. They didn't like

giving out personal information, or any damned information at all, she could see that; but fuck it and fuck *them*, she wanted to know.

'He was crushed,' said Nigel. 'By one of the engines. It was a terrible accident. People don't realize how dangerous it can be, working on the railways. Accidents happen all the time.'

Or more likely it was an act of God, thought Annie, thinking of the dirty old goat mauling Dolly about.

'I'm sorry to hear that,' she lied. People were still passing by, staring at *her*. Hunter was right. She had to be careful.

Nigel and Sarah both nodded morosely, and stood there looking at the grave.

'Now Dolly's with Dad,' said Nigel after a pause. 'In heaven. If she repented of her sins before she died.'

A shiver went through Sarah, so intense that Annie stared, wondering if the woman was going to collapse, fall right into the open grave and land, *thunk*, on her sister's coffin.

'Yeah,' she said, thinking that Dolly was bound for heaven for sure.

But the father . . . ?

That old bastard was cooking over a low light in hell, with Satan turning the spit. And a fucking good job, too.

76

They told Annie there would be a wake – cake and sandwiches and cups of tea, nothing fancy – back at Sarah's place, and she would be welcome to come if she wanted. She didn't think she wanted to spend one more second in this joyless pair's company, but she took the address anyway.

Then she went back along the gravel walkway toward the lychgate. A large crowd of mourners had gathered there. She looked around for Ellie, but she seemed to have gone. She felt a shudder, thinking of Dolly lying in the cold earth, alone. Soon the gravediggers would come and fill in the hole and that would be it; Dolly would be gone forever.

Feeling apprehensive after that little tussle with the group near the grave, she walked on, head held high, but at the back of her mind was the kicking she'd got off Gary's thugs, the unrelenting soreness of her broken rib, and she thought, *I don't want any more of that.* She had thought Max and his boys had it in for her, for sure; but the fact that the bad news about her had already reached the wider population was chilling. She made a mental note to dig out her can of Mace when she got home. It wasn't much, but it was something, at least.

Maybe she wouldn't have the chance to *get* home and

do that, though. The mob by the gate turned and watched her coming, their eyes unfriendly.

Christ, I could be in real trouble here.

Her footsteps slowed and finally she stopped walking. Then there was movement closer to her, all around her, and she turned, startled. She had been so focused on a possible threat at the lychgate that she'd missed another. Tony had appeared on one side of her, and Steve came up in front of her. Her head whipped round and she started to turn further, but there was Chris, grim-faced, right behind her. No Gary. There was that to be thankful for, she supposed.

Oh fuck . . .

Her heart lodging in her throat, she spun back round to the front and there was Max, standing right beside her like a brick wall and looking at her blank-faced.

She was closed in.

She was *trapped*.

Please no, not again, please, please . . .

'Just keep walking,' said Max.

What else could she do? She had four big men surrounding her and an angry mob waiting for her at the gate. Her stomach clenched with terror, she did as he said. No good making a break for it, they'd catch her easily. And frightened though she was, she wasn't about to give any of them the satisfaction of seeing *that*.

She kept her head up, and somehow got her trembling legs to move forward. As she moved, so did the four men surrounding her. As one body, they walked to the lychgate, and the now silent, watchful crowd parted in silence to let them pass.

The four of them walked her right to the car, a black Jag. It gave her a pang, just to see it. This had once been her car, the car Tony had chauffeured her about in, but it had passed to Dolly. Now Dolly wouldn't use it any more. Tony got behind the wheel. Once, back in the day, Tony had been the jockey, the wheelman on heists pulled by the Carter gang; he could do things with a car that would make your eyes water. Turn the damned thing on a sixpence. Chris slid into the front passenger seat. Steve got in the back, and Annie was pushed in after him; then Max got in. And it was then it hit Annie, the truth; that her husband had just rescued her, put a steel wall around her to get her out of the church grounds and away.

'Max—' she said, turning toward him.

'Shut the fuck up,' he said.

'Max—'

'I *said*, shut up.'

And having said that, he turned away from her and stared out of the window, jaw set.

Tony gunned the engine and drove them back to Holland Park.

She shut up. Tony drove on, through the steadily hardening rain. When the car pulled up outside her house in Holland Park and Max dragged her out, she thought maybe he'd go and leave her there. But he didn't get back in. He slammed the door shut, and the other three men shot off in the Jag.

'Come the fuck on then,' he said, and grabbed her arm and hauled her up to the steps to the big imposing navy-blue doors of home.

77

Once inside, Annie went on unsteady legs across the hall and into the drawing room. She peeled off her coat and dropped it on to the carpet, then slumped down on a Knole sofa and put her head in her hands.

'*Shit*,' she said with feeling.

Max was pacing about again. Suddenly, he stopped in front of her.

'Oh, you think those at the church were scary? You ain't seen fuck-all yet. What in the name of . . .'

His words trailed away and he started his restless pacing again. *Not* a good sign, she knew that. Then he was back in front of her. 'You low-life cow. I don't know why I bothered to do that. I must be off my fucking head. You've been cheating on me with that flash Yankee *bastard*—'

'I haven't.'

'Oh, for fuck's sake!' Max's eyes were blazing. 'You admitted you've been seeing him. What, you been playing tiddlywinks or something? Or chess like in that film? Or have you been doing what we all *know* you've been doing? That is, dancing the horizontal tango with that American *prick*.'

Annie sat there, head bowed. 'You said you wanted a divorce,' she said slowly.

'What?'

'A divorce. That's what you said. So what the fuck? What's the use of all this? You want a divorce, you got one. Simple as that.'

Max lunged forward and yanked her to her feet. Every ache in her body started setting up a protest, and Annie let out a yell.

'Oh, don't give me that, I ain't even touching you. Do you know the lucky escape you've just had? That was a fucking lynch mob there at the church, all out for your blood, and I had to walk you out of there with a body-guard of three blokes who were none too sure they wanted to bother. They did it because I told them to, that's all. And that made me look like the world's worst fucking fool.'

Annie stared into Max's eyes from inches away. It had taken her a while to realize it, but he hadn't been trying to intimidate her at the church by surrounding her in that way. He'd been *protecting* her. And when he'd cornered her at his mum's old house, he hadn't been planning to hurt her; it had all been for the benefit of the three men waiting outside the door. He'd told her to scream, and she had. In actual pain, although he hadn't known or intended that.

Annie started to smile.

Max glared at her. 'What?' he snapped.

'I love you, Max Carter,' she said, wincing as her dam-aged rib set up a riotous ache. 'Every macho, hot-headed bit of you.'

'You *what*?'

Annie pushed herself free of his grip. She dragged her hands through her hair and stared intently into his eyes.

'For God's sake *listen*,' she said. 'This is *me*. This is not rumour. This is not someone talking in the pub after too many sherbets. I'm telling you that I never slept with Constantine when we met up again. I saw him, yes. But sleep with him? No.'

'You must think I came upriver on the last banana boat,' he sneered.

'No, I think you're smart. I *know* you are. When you stop behaving like a jealous arsehole and start thinking, you'll work it all out.'

Max stood there staring into her eyes for a long time. Then he said: 'You know what? I don't have to think about it, I can just beat it out of you.'

'But you won't do that,' said Annie. 'The great Max Carter, beat a woman up? Nah. That's never going to happen.'

'Oh, you think so.'

'I *know* so.'

Max's eyes narrowed. Then he turned away from her, walked a few paces, came back.

'And while I'm working all this out, what are you going to be doing?' he asked.

'Finding Dolly's killer,' said Annie.

'Yeah? On streets where everyone wants you strung up from the nearest lamp post? That'll be a neat trick.'

'One word from you would change that.'

'Yeah. If I could be arsed.'

'I need some help,' she said.

Max raised an eyebrow. 'I heard you *had* help. For what it's worth. Jackie Tulliver. That cunt's a drunk these days, what use is he to you – or anybody?'

Annie remembered that Max hated drunks, and would never tolerate them anywhere near him. He'd been scathingly harsh in the past about her mother, Connie, who'd been a useless alkie and so – in Max's eyes – beneath contempt.

'I wasn't thinking of Jackie,' she said.

Max's eyes widened. 'Oh, have a day off. Me? No

bloody way. You've made me look enough of a fucking idiot already.'

'No, not you.'

'Who then?'

'I want Tony. I want my driver back.'

78

After Max left, Jackie showed up. Annie guessed he'd been skulking about outside, just waiting for Max to go before he showed himself. Maybe the man had *some* pride left, after all. Didn't want his old boss to see the state he was in.

'So what's next?' he asked when she let him in and led the way back across the hall and into the drawing room.

'For you? Hopefully a bath. And a shave, would that hurt?'

'Hey, no need to get personal,' he whined.

Annie sat down and looked up at him. 'What happened with your mother?' she asked.

Jackie flinched as if she'd struck him. 'What you talkin' about that for?'

'She died, Steve told me. What was it then? Heart? Cancer?'

Jackie stood there, looking at the floor. 'I ain't talkin' about this.'

'Maybe you should.'

'I don't *want* to.'

'Why? She died of old age, I suppose? People do die, Jackie. It's sad, but it's part of life. Unavoidable.'

'I don't want to talk about it. What's next, that's what I came to say. Not to talk about things I'd rather not discuss, OK?'

Annie drew a breath. After today, and seeing Max again, she felt tired out, literally wrung dry. She longed to get some more painkillers down her then fall into bed and sleep. If Jackie didn't want to talk about what was bugging him, fair enough. She didn't have the energy to push it. Instead, she would move things forward on what happened to Dolly.

'Dolly's brother and sister.' Annie picked up her bag, pulled out a scrap of paper with Sarah's address on it. 'This is her sister Sarah's address and her married name. I don't know Nigel's address. I want you to find out everything you can about both of them. Talk to them, if you can – although I think you'll find they don't say much. Tell them you were a friend of Dolly's and you're in bits. Work their emotions if they've got any, which I doubt. Don't mention you're doing this for me, OK?'

Jackie's thin shoulders slumped and he glanced at Annie. 'You know what? I *did* like Dolly. She was straight as a die. A nice person.'

'Dolly was the best.' Annie was silent for a moment, fighting down that horrible black wall of grief again. 'That's your first job, then. All right? There's another brother, Sandy, he's in a home. I'll find out where and see if there's any chance of getting any sense out of him. And there's another brother, Dick – don't know anything about him yet. Except that he's living abroad. The father had an accident years ago on the railways, he was a shunter. So maybe the Delaneys *didn't* carry out Dolly's wishes. Anything you can find out about that would be good. What are the narks saying to the Bill?'

'Nothin'. Precisely fuck-all.'

'Keep pushing on that.'

'Jesus! What am I supposed to do in my spare time then?'

'You got anything on Redmond Delaney yet?' she said.

'Still lookin'.'

'Well, hurry the fuck up, will you? I want him found. The rest of the Delaney mob are toast, but I know for a fact that he's still walking. Don't approach him. Just find him. And go easy. I want to talk to him in person.'

'That whole family's poison.'

'They're all dead, Jackie. All except Redmond. How hard can it be?'

'All right, all right! I'm on it. What the hell do you want to talk to him for?'

'Dolly wanted her old dad hit, remember? Ellie told me that Dolly approached the Delaney mob to do the job for her. So my thinking is, was that "accident" really an accident? Who knows? As Redmond's the only one left, I'm hoping *he* does.'

Annie reached for her purse, thumbing out a few twenties. She handed them to him. 'I don't want this going on drink, you got me? I want everything about Dolly's family you can find. They're Catholics – check the parish records, dig up anything and everything. This should be enough to get you started.'

Jackie nodded and took the money, folded it and stuffed it into his jeans pocket. He turned away from her and went to the door. Then he paused.

'You sure about this Delaney thing? You open a wasps' nest, you're gonna get stung, you know.'

'Do it,' she said.

Jackie nodded again, his hand on the doorknob.

'Something else?' asked Annie when he hesitated.

'She was crossing the road,' he said and when he glanced up she saw tears in his bloodshot eyes. 'My old mum. Too slow, see? Arthritis in the hips. Far too slow. Boy racer comes through, takes her out. Bounced fifty feet, *smack* on to the pavement. Dead the minute she hit the ground.'

While Annie sat there with her mouth open, wondering what to say, Jackie slipped out through the door, and was gone.

79

Next morning, Tony was there with the Jag. She answered his knock, and he looked like he wanted to be somewhere, *anywhere*, but here, talking to her.

'Morning, Tone,' she said.

He grunted. As always, he was immaculately dressed in a sharp navy-blue suit, white shirt and dark tie. Bald as a coot, ugly as sin and tanned to a turn, eighteen stones of muscle sporting twinkling gold crucifixes in each big cauliflower ear. He smelled good – some sandalwood-based aftershave. Once her staunchest supporter, he was looking at her now like he wanted to spit in her face.

Without a word he turned away from the door and led the way down to the car. He opened the back door, and she got in. Then he closed the door behind her, and slid behind the wheel.

'Where to?' he asked.

So that's the way it's going to be, she thought.

She told him the address, and without a word he edged the car out into the flow of traffic and drove her there.

'Wait for me,' she said when they arrived. Without waiting for a reply – she didn't think she was going to get one anyway – she got out and went up the front path to the Foster household.

It was a neat little terrace, one of a row of identical

houses, and the whiteness of the curtains and the pristine condition of the front step, the rampant health of the plants in the hanging baskets on either side of the door, all screamed that this was the home of someone who was careful to make a good impression on the outside world. Annie lifted the highly polished brass dolphin door-knocker and banged it, hard, twice. She waited. Half-hoped that Sarah Foster née Farrell would be out. *Drains and radiators*, she thought. Some people drained you – like Sarah and her charmless, repressive brother Nigel – and others radiated warmth, like Dolly.

But all too soon the door opened and there was Sarah, wearing a tobacco-brown knitted woollen skirt that had never been in fashion and never would be, a thin lambswool cardigan in a washed-out shade of lavender and a lemon-coloured blouse. She stared at Annie with a fixed and immobile expression.

'Oh – it's you,' said Sarah, sounding neither pleased nor put out by it.

'Can I come in?' asked Annie.

'What for?'

The woman had no social skills. No charm. No *chutzpah*. But this was Dolly's sister and somewhere inside she must have a grain, a tiny seed, that resembled Dolly.

'I'd like to talk to you. About Dolly,' she said.

'It's not very convenient. I've had the police round asking questions, and *people* . . . '

Jackie Tulliver would probably be one of those people, Annie guessed. Christ knows what this buttoned-up little article would make of *him*.

'And if you don't mind I would rather not discuss the subject any more.' The thin voice, the repressive mouth, everything served to irritate Annie, but she ignored that, fought against it. She had to keep her tongue under control here, or she'd never even get to first base.

'This is your sister we're talking about,' she reminded Sarah.

'I know that.' Two dull red spots appeared high up on the pallid cheeks.

'Then spare me a few minutes, because I would like to know what was going on with her, what happened, how she came to be killed like she was.'

For a moment Annie thought Sarah was going to slam the door in her face. But that would show a bit of passion, a bit of feeling, and she didn't think Sarah had it in her. Instead, she opened the door a little wider, then her hand apathetically dropped to her side. Without a word she turned and walked off along the hallway. Taking this for an invitation, Annie followed. She closed the front door behind her, and followed Sarah into a tiny pin-neat box of a kitchen.

'You'd better sit down then,' said Sarah gracelessly, seating herself at a tiny, old but clean grey-laminate kitchen table.

Annie sat down. It was dark in the kitchen, not much daylight seeping in through the north-facing window. The place felt chilly and smelled faintly musty, although outside it was supposed to be summer.

'Thank you for this,' said Annie. The woman wasn't about to offer her any refreshments, and she was starting to read this bloodless little creature now; she couldn't expect any warmth from her, not even a tiny bit.

Sarah shrugged. 'Say what you've got to say,' she said.

'Had you seen Dolly recently?' said Annie quickly, in case Sarah changed her mind and asked her to go.

'No. We didn't keep in touch.'

'How about Nigel? Your brother?'

The thin mouth got even thinner. 'Nigel wouldn't lower himself. He knew what Dolly was.'

'So your dad died in an accident on the railway,' said Annie.

Sarah went pale but said nothing.

'The driver of the engine that hit him, was he named?'

'No. I don't think so.'

'But did your family know who he was?'

'I know nothing about any of this,' said Sarah.

'What about Dick, or Sandy?'

'Dick's abroad. New Zealand. I told you. And Sandy's an invalid.'

'In what way?' Annie half-expected Sarah to tell her to mind her own business.

But Sarah said: 'He was never strong. Had some strokes. He's not much better than a vegetable.'

'I'm sorry. What home's he in?'

'I don't want you bothering him.'

'I won't bother him. Can you give me the name of the home?'

For a minute it looked as if Sarah was going to say no. Then she said: 'Sunnybrook. It's up Watford way.' She gave Annie the name of the road. 'But I don't want you upsetting him. He's not right. Don't tell him about Dolly. He's got troubles enough, without that.'

'I won't,' said Annie. 'Nigel said Dolly left home at thirteen. Did she not tell you she was going? She was the oldest, that right? And then there was Nigel, then you? Then Dick and Sandy?'

'That's right. Dolly didn't tell anyone she was going. She was wild, Dolly. Bad to the bone, Dad always said. After she left us.'

'He didn't like her?' It took a real effort on Annie's part

not to say that he had a damned nerve saying anything about Dolly, when he was such a low-life arsehole.

Sarah shrugged. 'For a while she was his favourite. Then she went, and *I* was.'

The prim mouth lifted at the corners. This was a little victory to the woman, Annie could see that.

'So you don't know who the driver was, when your dad had the shunting accident? That must have been awful for the driver, that responsibility. Killing someone like that. You sure you don't know his name?'

'No,' said Sarah. 'I told you. I don't.'

'Didn't *you* like Dolly?' asked Annie.

'She was all right. Until she went to the bad.' The lips tightened again, assuming an irritating Puritanical look. 'We're a good Catholic family, always have been. For her to do things like that, *disgusting* things . . . well, we could never forgive anything like that. Excuse me a moment,' said Sarah, and stood up and left the room.

Annie heard her go up the stairs, heard the landing boards creak, heard a door shut. She sat there and waited, looking around at this plain little kitchen and thinking how well it suited the woman who lived here. Sarah was married – so where was the husband? There were no photos on display. Maybe in the sitting room . . . ?

There was movement upstairs and then Sarah came back down and into the kitchen again. She sat down and stared at Annie.

'How did Nigel find out what Dolly did for a living?' asked Annie.

Sarah looked blank.

'If you never kept in touch, how did he find out?'

'Oh! Nigel found out through an acquaintance. I won't call him a friend. This man went to places like that, *disgusting* places, and he said he'd seen Dolly there.'

'Did Nigel tell your dad that?'

'Dad was already gone when Nigel found out about her.'

But this was your sister, thought Annie.

She thought of her own sister, Ruthie, who had forgiven her everything, anything, even when she had been beyond all hope of redemption. Ruthie even now would welcome her with open arms, but Annie had no plans to contact her. Better to keep her distance, keep Ruthie safe.

Suddenly there was the sound of a key turning in the lock at the front door. It opened and closed, and then thin repressive little Nigel came into the kitchen. Sarah looked at the floor. Nigel stared straight at Annie.

'What are you doing here?' he asked in his reedy voice.

'I'm here to see Sarah,' said Annie. 'Just for a chat. And to offer my condolences.'

'You say you're Dolly's friend? What were you, another one of those *tarts* she liked to mix with? I don't like you coming here. You've just come to fish about in things that don't concern you.'

'Dolly's death concerns me,' Annie replied. 'I heard your dad was a bit of a bastard, that right? Mistreated Dolly?'

Nigel looked like his head was going to explode and blow clean off his narrow sloping shoulders. His face went brick-red and his whole body tensed.

'Get out!' he shouted.

Annie stood up, dwarfing Nigel by a foot.

'Good of you both to turn up for the funeral though,' she said. 'Even if she *was* a tart.'

Nigel puffed himself up like a toad. 'We went to the funeral out of respect for the dead, but I'm telling you right now – a woman like that? She was no sister of mine.'

80

Tony drove her back to Holland Park. It wasn't a pleasant trip. In years past the silence between them had been companionable, but today it was charged with stifled aggression. Yet she supposed she was safe with Tony; Max had told him to behave, and he would. She hoped.

She couldn't even be sure of Max, not now. He'd believed what he'd been told about her, and he seemed to believe it still. At any moment he could turn on her, and if he did, she was finished. She'd suspected he was having an affair, but she'd been miles off. In fact he'd been tracking Gina Barolli down, and Gina had broken the Mafia code, betrayed her brother. *Why?* Annie wondered, and then she thought of Constantine as he was these days, and thought that she might know the answer to that.

Tony pulled up outside the house, got out of the driving seat, opened her door. Looked the other way while she got out.

'Tone?' Annie said when he was about to get back behind the wheel without even saying goodbye.

He paused. Cocked an eyebrow, waited.

'Our tame coppers – you said you were going to talk to them. Anything? I got Jackie on it too, by the way. And he's turned up nothing.'

He shook his head. 'Nah. They ain't heard a thing.'

'Right. Tone . . . ?'

'What now?'

'None of it's true. I've told Max and now I'm telling you. *None* of it.'

His expression didn't change. He didn't believe her.

Annie let out a sigh. 'Come tomorrow at one, OK?'

Tony nodded, got back behind the wheel, and drove away.

Annie deliberately didn't set the alarm that night. If he was going to come, if they were ever to get past this, then bring it on: she'd risk his rage, she'd take that chance. But Max didn't show.

To cheer herself up she spent the next day indulging in some retail therapy. It was Saturday and she could have used some company after this grim week. She could have met up with Ellie, if only Ellie hadn't decided that she was too dangerous to talk to. So she kicked her heels up and down Bond Street and then went home alone with a silent Tony at the wheel and sat in solitary confinement into the evening before deliberately not setting the alarm again and then going to bed.

He won't come, she thought miserably. *He's done with me. All right, so he's keeping me safe – for now – for old times' sake, but he won't come again. He's had enough.*

And then, at about one in the morning, she woke up, switched on the bedside light, and he was there.

'You didn't set the alarm again,' said Max, rising from the chair in the corner of the room and coming over to the bed.

'Didn't I?' asked Annie, pushing the hair out of her eyes and yawning.

'Careless.'

'Yeah. Wasn't it.'

'So get the fuck on with it. Go on with what you were saying,' he said.

Annie frowned. 'What was I saying?'

'Don't play dumb. You were going to tell me, Scheherazade, about your first visit to that shit Constantine.'

'Oh. That.'

'Yeah, that.' He sat down on the side of the king-sized bed and stared at her, sitting there all rumpled from sleep with her hair all over the place and the thousand-thread-count sheets pulled up to her chin. 'So come on. Let's see how good a storyteller you *really* are. What happened then?'

'Max, I'm tired.'

'Tough. Tell me what happened next, and by Christ you'd better make it good.'

81

Annie drew in a breath. It made her rib ache like a bastard, and she pulled the sheet higher – no way did she want him glimpsing the strapping and the bruises around her middle and thinking she was going for the sympathy vote, playing the poor-little-wounded-wifey card.

'All right. I'll tell you. Alberto took me up to the Scottish Highlands that first time. It was January 1989. Five years ago. He chartered a private flight out of the heliport. Sometimes we flew straight to the castle . . .'

'A *castle*,' said Max. 'That bastard never did stint himself, did he.'

Annie went on as if he hadn't spoken. 'Sometimes I stayed in a house outside Edinburgh. We had to be careful. We were always watching, making sure no one joined up the dots.'

Max's eyes were intent on her face. 'Yeah, me included, right? What was it like, this castle?'

'The locals called it the Mouth of Hades. It's an actual castle. It's got a big tower – battlements, don't they call them? Yeah, battlements. There's a courtyard in the centre, and a helipad. Big steep stone sides to the place. On one side, there's nothing beneath it but sea. Two hundred feet down, a sheer drop to the water. It looks grim.'

'Go on then. You got there, then what?'

'The housekeeper met us, Mrs McAllister. Took me up to this room in the tower, through all these old stone passageways with tapestries and suits of armour. And then in the evening . . .'

Annie stopped talking, her eyes on Max's face.

'Go the fuck on. What then? You met up with *him* and fucked his brains out? Yes?'

Annie shook her head. 'God's sake, Max, will you listen? Mrs McAllister took me into this dining hall. Alberto had made himself scarce. And yeah, that's when I saw Constantine. That's when I knew he was alive.'

Max said nothing. He just sat there, arms folded, face set in angry lines.

'Five years ago! And you know what? He was pretty much unchanged. Or at least he seemed to be.' Annie could see Constantine in her mind's eye. Back then he had still been the Silver Fox, broad-shouldered, narrow-hipped. There was still the mane of startling white hair, those piercing blue eyes. A few more wrinkles around the eyes. No silver-grey Savile Row suit, though: now he wore slacks, and an open-necked shirt.

'You still fancied him,' said Max.

'No, I didn't.'

'Bullshit.'

Annie shook her head. 'All the way there, I'd been wondering how I would feel when I saw him again. And in that instant, I knew.'

'Knew what?'

'That it was all gone.' Annie passed a tired hand over her face. The sheet slipped a bit, and she grabbed it quickly, pulled it back up to her chin. 'Everything I'd ever felt for him, it was as if it had never been. There was simply nothing left. Nothing at all. He thought we could just pick up where we'd left off. But I lost it, shouted at him that it was all finished, done, all in the past.'

Max puffed out his cheeks like an angry bull and stared at her. 'Oh, come on. You really think I'm going to swallow *that*?'

'It's the truth, Max. I didn't feel anything for him . . . except pity.'

'Pity?'

'He'd escaped the threat of a hit back in the seventies. He'd given the Feds the slip. But really, do you think he was free, stuck up there in his Highland castle? He wasn't. He might just as well have been banged up in Fulsom Prison in the States, because he was in prison anyway. He barely went out of the door. And when he did, he was scared to fucking death that someone was going to spot him, recognize him, dob him in.'

'He changed his name then?'

'He calls himself David Sangster these days.'

Max stood up, started his nervy pacing around the room again. 'Does he, by God. And you had a nice little chat, did you, the two of you?'

Ignoring the sarcasm in his voice, Annie said: 'Oh, we did. I told him in no uncertain terms that it was over, that it had been over for years. He'd bailed out, left me. And I had moved on, I'd survived, what else could I do? And I told him I was leaving, coming home, first thing in the morning.'

'Yeah?' Max paused, hands in trouser pockets, and looked at her. 'And what did he say to that?'

'He said I wasn't going anywhere.' Annie took a gulping breath. 'He said that, if I left, he would give the order to have you killed.'

82

Max was silent for a long time, staring at her face.

'You *what*?' he said at last.

'The man was lonely. Desperate. I think . . . I think he realized what he'd tossed away, all those years ago, and when he saw I wasn't going to play ball, he lashed out. He threatened you.'

Max was nodding, grim-faced. 'Oh, that's clever,' he said.

'Clever?' she echoed faintly.

'Yeah, it is. So you did it? You spread your legs for that git because you *had* to, right? To save me. How long did it take you to think *that* one up?'

Annie stared at him in outrage. 'You *shit*,' she snapped. 'What, you think I'm playing you? That I've cooked up his threat to you so I could just say, "Oh, I had to sleep with him, I couldn't help it"?'

'Got it in one,' he snapped right back.

'You're wrong. *So* wrong. I spoke to Alberto next morning – after a night *alone*, I might add – and told him what his father said. Alberto spoke to him. And Constantine backed down. He apologized for saying it, and he said that even if I couldn't agree to . . . well, to be *more* than that, at least we could be friends.'

Max stared at her in disbelief. 'Just supposing any of that hogwash is the truth . . .' he said.

'It is,' said Annie.

'Yeah, yeah. Just supposing it *is*, and there was no fucking involved, only *friendship*, my *arse* . . .'

'You asked for the true story and I'm giving it to you.'

'So you stayed friends. Played Monopoly in the afternoons, or poker. Or did he poke *you*?'

Annie didn't dignify that last crack with a response. 'I don't play poker. As you well know.'

'Oh, you play all sorts of games, I know *that*.'

'Meaning?'

'Meaning you're not setting the alarm deliberately. Meaning you've been expecting me, and you knew damned well I had a key, you remembered that, don't deny it. You want time to work on me. You're spinning these tales and hoping I'll fall for them.'

'Well, at least you're *getting* tales. You're getting some information. Which is more than I ever got from you, by the way,' said Annie, flinging one of the pillows aside in frustrated anger. It hurt, and she stifled a wince.

'What the fuck does that mean?' he demanded.

'You cleared off without any explanation. You were fed evil bloody lies by Gary Tooley – who's always hated me, you know that – and you ran off to Sicily without ever once thinking of talking to me first.'

'You'd have denied it,' said Max.

'Well, of course I would, because what you're thinking, it's not even the bloody *truth*. That's not the point. The point *is*, it was "all boys together", as usual. You believed your old mates over me. And that's a fucking insult, Max Carter. I'm your *wife*. And meanwhile, do you know what *I* thought was happening?'

He shook his head.

'I thought you were having an affair.'

'You what?'

'You heard. We see them all the time on Barbados, don't we? Men of your age with women twenty years younger. We've even laughed about it. The way these girls just happen to turn up when they think a soft target's in view, a man in his forties or fifties with loads of cash on the hip. Well, you bastard, I thought the joke was finally on me.' Her voice trembled on those last words.

Max was silent, looking at the floor. Then he said: 'So. You went back there, to him, many times?'

Annie nodded. 'Two, three times a year. Sometimes more.'

A muscle was working in Max's jaw. He looked mad enough to hit someone. 'Yeah. When you told me you were here in London or going to the States to call in at the Annie's club in Times Square.'

'On the way there, I'd call in on him. Sometimes on the way back.' Annie stared at Max, so closed-off from her, so distant from her. 'The man was *lonely*. There was no spark left there between us. None for me, anyway. None at all.'

'But for him, it was different. He wanted you back.'

'Yeah. He did. But I made it clear that wasn't an option.'

'Really.'

'Yeah, really. Max – he was shut up in that place. Sometimes he played golf with other big-time crooks who also had to hide away to stay free. But in fact, seeing them, talking to them, seeing the fear in their eyes, you realize that none of them are free at all. They daren't move, they're so afraid of the law catching up with them and putting them in the slammer. Well, guess what? They're already there.'

'All that bloody time . . .' Max was shaking his head

now. 'You were up there, with him, seeing him, and you didn't say a fucking word.'

'I couldn't. You know that. And if I could have? Even then, I wouldn't.'

His head whipped round and those intense navy-blue eyes held hers. 'Why not?'

'Why *not*?' Annie gave a thin laugh. 'Because you'd have gone up there and killed him.'

'But you're telling me now.'

'Only because you've found out anyway. And have I told you the exact location? I don't think so.'

'Gary will tell me that. And even if he don't, I'll track the bastard down. If it takes years, I'll do it.'

'Maybe. But you've had time to think now, yeah? To think, and to calm down. And maybe to get together some faith and trust in your own wife, for God's sake.'

'When she's played me for a mug.'

'Max – I haven't.'

'Yeah, you have.'

'So divorce me then. Only you don't name him as co-respondent or whatever the fuck they call it – you *never* name him, OK? Think about it. Because on paper? He's dead. And because Alberto's still alive, and he's with Layla – and Layla means the world to you, I know she does. So you mustn't stir up anything that involves them. You *can't*.'

'Piss off,' said Max furiously, and stood up and left the room.

Annie watched him go, her face creased with anguish.

This time, he wouldn't come back. She knew it.

83

Jackie Tulliver turned up at the house on Sunday, clutching several sheets of paper, looking pleased with himself and slightly less drunk than usual.

'You would not *believe* the stuff I've found,' he said as Annie showed him into the study at the front of the house. Then he paused and glanced nervously around. 'Mr Carter not here then?'

'No, he's not.'

'Right! Look at this lot.' Jackie spread the sheets out on the desk. Annie saw copies of birth and death certificates, copies of newspaper cuttings. 'Checked out the parish records, got the copies. And the woman at the local newspaper was very helpful. Nice lady. Showed me how to work the microfiche thingy and everything. Helped me work the fucking photostat machine too, those things are a bastard. Look.'

Annie looked. Jackie had been busy; there was a lot here to look through. She picked up a death certificate.

'That's Dolly's dad. Samuel Farrell. Look here.' Jackie shoved a copy of a newspaper clipping toward her and there it was:

Tragedy of Local Worker

Samuel Farrell of Limehouse died yesterday in a tragic accident on the railway. Mr Farrell worked as a shunter for many years but suffered fatal injuries when he fell and was trapped between an engine and a carriage. The driver is being treated for shock.

'He shouldn't have been there,' commented the driver, who has asked not to be named. 'I thought it was all clear.'

Mr Farrell leaves behind a wife and five children, who are devastated at his loss.

'What do you know about shunters?' asked Annie as she stared at the obit, her mind buzzing.

'Nothin'. You?'

'Not a damned thing.' Annie looked at him. He smelled OK today. He'd made a bit of an effort, she could see. Taken a bath. Even had a shave, although his hands were so unsteady that he'd nicked himself with the razor. Bits of tissue dotted his face like white measles. But he'd tried.

'You went to see Sarah?' asked Annie.

'That cold-blooded cunt. I said I knew Dolly, I was upset at her death, and you know what? The twat didn't even offer me a cup of tea. Said she'd rather not discuss it, went to shut the door in my face.'

'But you didn't let her.'

'Course not. Stuck my size nines in, didn't I, got the old waterworks goin', said I was so upset, I'd come miles, could I just have a drink of water? And she bought it.'

'And . . . ?' she prompted.

'And nothin'. She don't give out much, that one. Half-way through what was a pretty one-sided conversation, she went upstairs to go to the loo, then by the time she came back downstairs the brother had pitched up. I'm guessin' she phoned him. She seemed relieved to see him, anyway. Like I was a danger to the old tart or somethin'. I mean, do I look like a fuckin' rapist?'

'Nope,' said Annie. 'She did the same thing to me. Looks like she don't even take a shit without his say-so.'

'Exactly. And he ordered me out, thin little stick of a cunt he was, so I went. So not much gained there, really.'

'Hey, Jackie?'

'Yeah?'

'You done well, boy. Never mind about the brother and sister, they're bloody hard work, I know that. But all this? This is good stuff, this will help.'

'Good,' he said, chewing his lip. 'That's what I wanna do, I wanna help.'

'So how's it going with Redmond Delaney?'

'I told you. I'm workin' on it.'

'Jackie?'

'Hm?'

'You're not pissing me about, are you? You *are* trying to find him?'

Jackie squirmed. 'He's an animal, that man, you do know that, don't you? Had a real cold look in his eye back in the day, like he'd chew your heart straight out of your chest and swallow it, still beating.'

Yeah, but he's a priest now. Or at least he was, the last time I saw him. Wouldn't a priest have turned his back on wicked ways?

She hoped so. But this was *Redmond Delaney*. And you could never be sure about him. Still – he was the only link left to Dolly and her nonce of a father. So she *had* to speak to him.

'Look – find him. But I want you to be careful around him. You hear me, Jackie? Take it easy.'

'And what are you goin' to be doin'?' asked Jackie.

'This and that.' Annie fished in her bag and handed him a small wad of fivers. 'Here you go.'

The fivers were quickly snapped up. Jackie tucked them into the pocket of his battered denim jacket. Then the bell rang at the front door.

'Leave all this with me,' said Annie, and showed him out. Standing on the front doorstep was DCI Hunter. Jackie gave him one startled look and then shot past him like a whippet. Hunter's eyes followed Jackie down the steps, then he turned.

'Spare a minute?' he asked Annie.

'Sure. You working weekends now?'

'On murder cases, I always do.'

He stepped into the hallway like a nun entering a crack den, looking around at the chandelier, the marble tiles, the showy ostentation of great wealth.

Mafia money, thought Annie.

She knew that's what it was, and so did he. Crime had paid for this place. Crime had paid for a whole lot more, too. More than he would ever know. She led the way into the study, and Hunter followed.

'Am I interrupting anything?' he asked, glancing at the papers.

'No, nothing,' said Annie, scooping them up and neatly shoving them into a drawer.

'Mrs Carter?'

'Yeah?'

'I've had another complaint about you.'

Annie looked at him in genuine surprise. 'From who? I haven't done a bloody thing.'

'A Mr Nigel Farrell says that you've been calling at the home of his sister, Sarah Foster, harassing her.'

'*Harassing?* That's a bit strong. I went to see her, sure, to give her my condolences.'

'She says you were asking about personal details, and she found it all very intrusive and distressing.'

'Oh. Well then, I'm sorry. I was just chatting, that's all. About Dolly. You know.'

'Yes, I do know, Mrs Carter. Or rather, I know *you.*'

'Meaning what?' Annie was glad now that she'd over-come a momentary urge to show him the papers Jackie had brought her. She was glad now that she'd swept the papers out of his sight. If he'd seen the death certificates and newspaper clippings, he'd have freaked for sure.

'Meaning, leave it.' Hunter's dark eyes grew hard. 'Just butt out, Mrs Carter.'

'Noted,' said Annie with a shrug.

'I hope it is noted, because the next time we have this conversation, I promise you, there'll be a formal charge and a night in a cell to look forward to. Don't push it.'

'Also noted,' said Annie. Well, she'd been in a police cell before. No big deal there.

'This is an official warning, Mrs Carter.'

Annie gave him a radiant smile. 'Noted,' she said again.

84

Annie went out, got a few supplies in, phoned ahead to Sunnybrook, then took a very interesting call from Jackie Tulliver.

'About Redmond Delaney . . .' he said.

'What about him?'

'You thought he was a priest, right?'

'Yeah.'

'Dream on.'

'What?'

'He was defrocked about a year ago.'

'For what?' All sorts of nasties went crawling through Annie's brain at that point. She knew both Redmond and his twin Orla had been a target for abuse from his brothers Tory and Pat. She knew too that the abused sometimes become abusers in their turn. 'Not kids?' she said.

'Kids? You're joking. No, it was a shitload of his female parishioners. Sounds like Redmond was like the Pied Piper to 'em, only using his dick instead of a flute. Liked to beat the crap out of them, too. Enjoyed it, they say.'

'Anything else?'

'Not yet, but I'm on it – I'll keep you posted.'

'Go easy.'

'Easy's my middle name.'

*

Annie was sitting in the big gold-leather-padded porter's chair in a corner of the hall at one, waiting for Tony. When the bell rang, she got to her feet and answered the door with a smile.

'Hiya, Tone,' she said.

Tony just turned and led the way to the Jag. Opened the back door. Annie got in. He waited a moment while she settled herself, then he closed it. Got behind the wheel.

'Where to?' he asked.

Annie pulled the slip of paper with the address out of her pocket and handed it to him. He glanced at it, said: 'OK,' put the car in first, and they were off.

'Nice day,' said Annie.

Tony grunted.

'That's what I like about you, Tone. No annoying fucking small talk.'

He didn't comment; he knew she was taking the piss.

'Can I just say something?'

'You can say anything you like,' said Tony, his eyes on the road. 'Mr Carter's asked me to do this, so I'm doing it.'

'Under protest, right?'

'That's right.'

'I thought you knew me, Tone.'

'Yeah.' His eyes flicked up to the mirror, met hers, then flicked away. 'I thought that, too.'

Annie said no more. Tony might be doing this under protest, but if Max had told him to do it, then he would, and he would provide major back-up if she needed it, whether he approved or not. She settled back and enjoyed the ride, inhaling the scent of clean polished leather and Tony's pungent aftershave.

It was almost like the old days.

Except it wasn't, and would never be again, because her whole world was in ruins and her marriage was over.

*

Sunnybrook was an imposing Victorian brick mansion with fancy fretworked eaves. Its frontage looked on to a tarmac car park and the drive up to the house was half a mile long. Once the home of a wealthy family, it had been sold off and converted to a nursing home.

Someone had thrown a lot of money into the conversion, Annie could see that the minute she walked in through the crisply red-painted doors. The carpet was also red, and immaculately clean. The woodwork on the vast staircase was old, well-buffed mahogany. It smelled fine in here, of polish and air freshener, and there were fake floral arrangements dotted about the place to brighten the look of it.

A brisk young woman with a dark ponytail and wearing a light blue smock instantly appeared.

'You're Mrs Carter?' she asked.

Annie said yes she was.

'I'm Helen. This way then,' she said, and took her up in a lift two floors, to Sandy Farrell's room.

As they travelled upward, the girl said: 'I look after Sandy. He's not been at all well. He's had three really serious strokes, and I'm afraid they've left him unable to speak. But we do communicate.'

How? wondered Annie, her heart sinking. Was she wasting her time coming here? She'd phoned ahead, made sure it was OK to visit, saying she was a friend of the family – well, she was a friend of *Dolly's*, so it was more or less true. Sarah had told her not to break the news to Sandy about Dolly, and she had no intention of doing that. Why the hell would she burden him with anything so tragic?

'Hiya, Sand,' said the girl, leading Annie into the room.

Fuck, thought Annie as she met Sandy Farrell for the first time.

He was sitting lopsided in a high-backed chair beside a hospital bed, wearing pyjamas and a dressing gown. He couldn't be much over forty, but he looked weak as gnat's piss, with sharp cheekbones jutting against yellowish skin. His hair was crew-cut, pale brown fading to grey. His eyes were like Dolly's, exactly the same shade of blue. There the similarity ended. Dolly had been robust, a little bulldog of a woman. This man, with his twisted mouth and vacant stare, was just the opposite.

'Visitor for you,' said Helen. 'This is Mrs Carter, she's a friend of your family's.'

Nothing.

There was a lovely view out of the window, a big emerald lawn in front of a forest of dark pines, but Sandy wasn't looking at that; he wasn't looking at *anything*. He was just staring at the wall, making no sound, no movement.

Jesus, thought Annie. *Poor bastard.*

Helen, still smiling, took a small notebook out of her pocket, and a pencil, and indicated that Annie should sit on the bed beside her. Annie did. Then Helen said: 'Will you say hello, then, Sand? How about an H?'

Sandy blinked once with his left eye.

'And an E?'

Another blink. Same eye.

Helen turned her smiling face on Annie. 'You see? We can chat like this.'

Annie took a breath. *OK then.* 'Hello, Sandy,' she said.

There was no reaction, nothing at all. But he'd just said hello to her, so they *were* talking. In a way.

'Sandy, I wanted to ask you about your dad. I know there was an accident. On the railway.' Annie turned her head and looked at Helen. 'Is this OK? I don't want to upset him.'

'Sandy?' asked Helen.

Sandy blinked his left eye.

'That means it's all right,' said Helen. 'But why do you want to know about that?'

'Sandy's sister Sarah told me about the accident, but she didn't want to talk about it. I'm hoping Sandy will.'

Helen frowned at Annie. 'I'm not sure . . .' Then she looked at Sandy.

'All I want to know is, does he know the name of the train driver. That's all.'

Helen sat poised, pencil in hand. 'I'm not sure about this. If it upsets Sandy at all, then I'm stopping. All right?'

'That's fine,' said Annie.

Helen nodded. 'A?' she said to Sandy.

Sandy blinked his left eye.

'B?' asked Helen.

Nothing.

Helen carried on, right through the alphabet until she came to R.

Sandy blinked. Helen wrote down AR.

She went through the alphabet again and came to T. Sandy blinked.

'Arth,' said Annie. 'Arthur?'

Sandy blinked his left eye.

'And his surname?' Annie asked.

'A,' said Helen. Nothing. 'B?' Sandy blinked his left eye. 'B then,' said Helen. 'A, B, C . . .' Helen talked on until she reached I, then Sandy blinked. Helen carried on, and finally they had it. The name of the driver at the controls of the engine on the day of Sam Farrell's death was Arthur Biggs.

'Is there anything else he can tell me?' asked Annie.

Helen started again. 'A?' she asked. Nothing. 'B? C? D?' Sandy blinked his left eye.

'D then. A? B? C? D? E?'

Blink.

'DE. A?'

Another blink.

'A again?' asked Helen. 'B? C? D?'

Sandy blinked his left eye.

Annie and Helen stared at the notebook.

Helen had printed there in capital letters: ARTHUR BIGGS.

Below that, she'd printed DEAD.

Annie stared at it, and then looked at Sandy and said one word: 'How?'

Sandy came back with the answer. Annie gazed at the notebook.

It said HANGED.

85

After visiting Sandy, Tony drove Annie to a Camden back street. They went up to a sixties block of flats via a series of metal walkways and arrived at the second floor, stopping when they came to a door with purple paint peeling off it in strips. There were claw marks at the bottom of the door. They both looked at it and thought *cat owner*.

Annie knocked.

Seconds later, a young man with a high-coloured face, blond hair and baby-blue eyes came to answer it, clutching a large green-eyed ginger tom.

'Oh!' he said, looking at the pair of them.

'Pete? Pete Jones? Do you remember me?' asked Annie.

'Mrs Carter! Oh God, yes. Sorry. Yes. Of course it's you.'

'Sorry to bother you on your day off . . .' she started.

'No! Not at all. Come in, come in, sorry about the mess . . .' and Pete Jones, bar manager of the Palermo, stepped back, let them come in, hastily depositing the cat outside on the landing. 'That's Benj,' said Pete. 'Never get a cat. They're adorable but they rip everything to shreds. Come in, sit down.'

It was neat inside the flat, and pristine-clean. Annie and Tony sat on a ruby-red fabric sofa and Pete sat down opposite in an armchair, looking flushed and flustered.

'Can I get you a drink?' he said. 'Tea, coffee? Anything?'

'No thanks.'

'Pete's anxious eyes rested on Annie's face. 'God, this must be so hard on you, so awful. This whole thing with Dolly. I'm so sorry.'

'You found her,' said Annie.

'I did. Yes.' Pete made a flapping motion with his hand in front of his eyes, which suddenly reddened. 'Sorry, sorry. I keep thinking about it, and every time I do, it's just . . . it's just so upsetting.'

Annie stared at him in sympathy, thinking he'd had a terrible shock and he didn't seem like the toughest of types, either. It must have knocked him sideways, finding Dolly like that.

'Can you talk about it?' she asked. 'I know it's difficult for you, but if there's anything you know, anything you can tell us that might help catch whoever did this, it would be good.'

'I know. The police have been round and asked me all about it again, but what can I say?' Pete swiped a tear away from his eye and shook his head. 'It was horrible. She usually opens the front entrance before eleven, to let in the bar staff and the cleaners, and I'm always first on the doorstep – we always used to laugh about that. I'm a punctuality freak. So there I was, it was a quarter to eleven, and the doors were still locked.'

'And that was really unusual,' said Tony.

'Yes. Very. I rapped, but there was no reply, so I used the key she'd given me for emergencies and let myself in.'

'What then?' asked Annie.

'God, it was awful. *Awful,*' said Pete, and had to stifle a sob.

There was a loud scratching noise from outside the door.

'That's just Benj,' Pete said with a faint, tearful laugh. 'He's ruined that fucking door, the little bastard.'

'Go on with what you were saying,' said Tony.

'There's not much more *to* say. I let myself in, I went up the stairs and called out to her, asked if she was OK, but there was no answer.'

'So you went in,' said Annie.

Pete just nodded, lips compressed, fighting back more tears.

'Then,' he said, sighing, trying to compose himself. He passed a hand over his face, and Annie saw that his nails were bitten down to the quick. 'I tried the handle and it was unlocked. So I went in. And I found her.' Pete's face crumpled again as the tears flowed. 'She was *dead*,' he managed to say, and then he just sobbed his heart out.

86

Redmond Delaney was always interested in Annie Carter. He'd had Mitchell watch her when she came back to England, and she did that quite frequently. She was a pet project of his; he liked to think of her as a butterfly trapped under glass so that he could watch her at his leisure.

Redmond was very curious about her trips north of the border. What was so fascinating to her up there? And he wondered – given that she'd been *married* to the Mafia bastard at one point – if she had known about Constantine Barolli's plan to kill both him and his sister back in the seventies.

He was irritated that Gary Tooley hadn't come up with the goods yet on this next big secret. Him and Mitchell had gone to the Blue Parrot to get the information and pay the five thousand (Redmond wasn't sure if he was going to pay Gary or cut him yet; the cunt had seriously annoyed him), but guess what? Gary was suddenly out of town. This made Redmond think that Gary was just tweaking his tail, upping the ante.

That *prick*.

'He's back again,' said Mitchell.

'What?' Redmond was sitting in his living room, and Mitchell was standing at the window, nudging aside the closed curtains. It was night-time.

'The dirty little creep in the crappy car. Annie Carter's follower,' said Mitchell. He glanced at Redmond. 'Now *your* follower too, it seems. He's parked up outside, watching the house again.'

Redmond stood up, went over to the window and looked out. There was a car there. Inside, dimly, a match flared as Jackie Tulliver lit a cigar.

Redmond ground his teeth in annoyance. The Tooley business was irritating enough, and now this. His years spent as an East End Face had made him anxious about people tailing him, tracking him, following him. He was the last Delaney standing and there was a reason for that; he was the toughest, the smartest, the fastest to react. Much as he admired Annie Carter, he was not so keen on this lapdog scruffy cunt of hers watching his house.

He'd done a little watching of his own, though; he knew Annie was back in her Holland Park house, and Mitchell had seen her talking in the street with the man out there in the car.

'Jackie Tulliver,' Redmond told Mitchell. He'd recognized him from years back as a Carter boy. 'He's working for *her*.'

That night, Redmond lashed himself with the whip again, because he was having thoughts, *impure* thoughts. Nothing new there. Really, they'd done him a favour, kicking him out of the priesthood, he just wasn't suited to it. He thought of all those lovely parishioners and got quite excited, quite *agitated*. And then he whipped himself harder, and got angry at the thought of those Carter people, Tooley and Tulliver, arsing him about. And mixed up in it, as usual, was Annie Carter, fabulous and unflinching as she strode about creating mayhem.

Panting, naked to the waist, he put the whip back in its

box and went to his bedroom window and looked out. And there he was, that little fecker Jackie Tulliver, sitting in his car smoking oversized cigars and having the brass neck to be watching *him*, Redmond Delaney.

Redmond wasn't happy.

He wasn't happy *at all*.

He snatched up his shirt and dragged it on, glorying in the stinging pain as the cuts on his back stuck to the fine material. He wasn't having this. He was going out there, right now.

87

Max was back again that night. Annie woke up, switched on the light, and there he was, in the same chair, looking at her. Her heart leapt. After last time, she'd been sure that was it: finished. But he was here. He was back.

'Do you *ever* set that bloody alarm?' he asked when she pulled herself into a sitting position and tucked the covers up to her chin.

'Sometimes,' she said.

'But not right now.'

'Got it.'

'Because you're expecting me.'

Yes, she had hoped – prayed, even – that Max would come back tonight. She had doubted it; but here he was. She'd had a tiring, stressful day, visiting Sandy and then Pete Jones; then she'd phoned Hunter with the news that the train driver involved in Dolly's father's accident all those years ago was dead.

'So what?' Hunter had asked her.

'So *this*: Arthur Biggs hung himself. He couldn't live with the guilt.'

After that, her rib had been aching so much that she'd had to lie down and rest. Now, here Max was, piling on the pressure. But she was glad he was here. He'd come back, and that meant that maybe she could dare to hope.

'You want to go on with it then?' he said. 'What you were telling me? Not that I believe a word of it.'

'Where was I?' *Please believe me*, she thought, staring into his eyes. *I love you, I need you, I want you so much,* please *don't let this be the end of it.*

'You said you and he were going to be "friends",' he said mockingly.

Annie let out a sharp sigh. 'Has Gary told you exactly where Constantine is yet?'

'Gary's out of town right now.'

Good, she thought. 'So you really want to know what happened next?'

'I'm here and I'm bloody well asking. So after that first time – when he said he was going to get a hit done on me – Alberto stepped in and Constantine backed down and said you'd be friends instead. Very fucking likely, I don't think. So you went back. You felt sorry for the cunt.'

'Yeah. I did. But . . . it was a problem.'

'In what way?'

'He behaved himself for a while. And then he started trying to get me drunk.'

Max's eyes narrowed as he stared at her face. 'What, he was trying to get you pissed and have you over the table, that's it?' asked Max.

'You have such a delicate way with words. But yeah. I think he was.'

'You barely touch a drop, though. And when you wouldn't drink . . . ?'

'He got moody.'

'I bet he did. Did he try that much?'

'Couple of times.' *Maybe ten, maybe twenty.*

'And then he gave up?'

Annie nodded.

'OK, then what?'

'What do you mean?'

'I knew Constantine Barolli. He might have *appeared* to have given up, but my guess? He hadn't.'

'You're right,' said Annie.

'So what happened next?'

'He started wheeling out the hookers.'

'What?'

'Women. Very expensive call girls. I'd go in to dinner, and there they'd be. Half-naked or even performing sex acts on him. Right in front of me.'

88

Max was quiet for a long, long time, then he got to his feet and came over to the bed. 'And how did *that* go down?' he asked. 'With you?'

Annie felt anger rising. She was tired, edgy, and here he was again with the inquisition. Yes, she wanted him back. She *needed* him. But this? Right now? It was too much.

'How do you think?' she asked.

'That's what I'm asking. Did it bother you, seeing him with other women?'

Annie reached out for her robe, awkwardly pulled it on, and swung her legs off the bed, sending him a glare as she stood, tied the sash, pulled the robe tight around her, right up to her bruised throat.

'Why the fuck would it bother me, Max? I told you: all that was dead and gone. Just like *he* should have been.'

'Yeah, so you keep saying.'

'And I mean it.' Annie went over to the dressing table and started angrily pulling a brush through her hair. 'Can't you get it through your skull? We were *finished* years ago. He was just a lonely, desperate man and . . .' she hesitated, her hand pausing on the brush. 'You don't understand what it was like. How things changed over these past five years, how *he* changed.'

Max came up behind her and his eyes locked with hers in the mirror. 'Meaning what?'

Annie put the brush down. 'I don't want to talk about this now,' she said.

'Well, fuck your luck. *I* do.'

Annie turned, confronting him. She let out a sigh.

'What?' he asked. 'Come on.'

'I saw a change come over him,' she said. 'He loved reliving his old glory days, when he was *Il Papa*, sending Lucco and Alberto out, his *caporegimes*, to pass on his orders to the *capos* and the foot soldiers on the streets of New York. He liked to talk about his family back in Sicily, all the things that had happened over his lifetime. As time went on, he changed a lot. The hookers didn't come any more. He stopped trying to get me drunk. He just wanted to talk – about the past, mostly.'

'And . . . ?' he prompted.

'Over five years I saw it happen. He didn't take care of his appearance any more. He became vague. A bit confused. Max . . .' Annie looked at him earnestly. 'The thing you seem to have forgotten here? He's thirty years older than me. When I married him, New York was scandalized because of the age gap, but he was still a young, vigorous man. And now he's old, Max. You know what he wanted from me, more than anything, at the end of the day? He wanted my company.'

Max was silent, his eyes on her face.

'It shocked me, realizing he was growing old,' she went on. 'But I couldn't miss it. His shoulders started to stoop, his hair was growing thinner. He liked to talk, sometimes he liked me to read to him. That crack you made about playing board games? Sometimes, that's what we did. Chess, or card games. Just passing the time. Things like that.' She frowned. 'And then *it* happened, and I realized what was going on with him.'

'What?'

'We were clearing the chessboard one day and he said to me, "You were never much of a player, Gina."'

'He mistook you for his sister?'

'He did. I said to him, don't you mean Annie? And then he said that he'd *said* Annie, what was I talking about. He got very angry. Almost aggressive.'

'Go on.'

'The next time I visited, he called me Maria – that was his first wife's name. I queried it again, and he got angry again. He said what the fuck was I talking about? And then he asked me where Nico was, he said he kept asking that housekeeper woman where he was, but she didn't know.'

'Nico?' Max frowned. 'Who the fuck's Nico?'

'Nico used to be Constantine's right-hand man. He died in the early seventies.'

Max stared at her. 'That was the one who hid Layla when she was a kid, right? The one who got hit outside the Palermo.'

'Yeah,' said Annie sadly. 'That's him.'

'You're saying Constantine's been going senile?'

'That's *exactly* what I'm saying. And that's what makes what *you* think so fucking stupid. At the beginning, yeah, maybe he tried it on. Or thought he would. But within a couple of years, that was right off the agenda. I *pitied* him, Max. I went there to keep him company because it was clear how lonely he was. Alberto couldn't visit very often, it was too risky. So I went there. The castle, all that grandeur, it was just another prison. And I was just a visitor.'

Max's eyes narrowed as he stared at her face. 'So it was all very close, you and Constantine up there playing cards and discussing ancient history.'

'It was OK for a while, yes. I hated the deception, Max, I really did. I wanted to tell you. I couldn't.'

'So you say.'

'I *do* say. It was pitiful to see, Max. He was forever asking after people who died long ago, forgetting they were dead. And there were other things: a change in his character, a shortness of temper. He just wasn't Constantine any more. And then, six months ago, it got to the point where he didn't know me at all. He barely spoke to me, and if he did it was to ask, "Who the hell are you?" He's not the Don any more, he's just a confused old man.'

Max said nothing.

'It seemed pointless to keep going there, so I stopped. And now . . .'

'Now what?'

'He's asked to see me again. He wants me to go.'

'Like fuck you are,' said Max, and grabbed her wrist, spinning her round to face him and pulling her in close against his body.

Annie gasped in surprise. His grip hurt, it was so hard. 'I know you don't believe me, but—'

'Don't I? Maybe I wouldn't believe that shit about him losing his marbles, if I hadn't seen his sister.'

Annie's eyes widened in realization as they stared up at his face. 'That was it then? I couldn't work out why Gina would have done that, broken the code. So *that's* why.' She shook her head sadly. 'Could that be a family thing? Passed down, father to son, mother to daughter . . . ?'

'I don't know. Maybe.'

'I know you don't want to hear this,' said Annie. 'But you know what? It's heartbreaking to see him like that. Once he was so powerful. Now he's just . . . nothing. You've no idea.'

'Yeah, I have. Remember – I saw Gina.'

'You're hurting my wrist.'

Max stared into her eyes for a long time, then he let her go. Annie went back over to the bed, sat on the side of it, pulling her robe in tight around her.

'I really can't tell you anything else,' she said tiredly.

'What, and you think I'm leaving it there? I haven't finished with you yet. Not by a bloody long chalk.'

89

Max came over to the bed too, sat down on the edge of it, and looked at her.

'What?' she asked.

'So first he tries to force you to stay, then he starts trying to get you drunk, and then he was showing you what you were missing?' said Max. 'And then . . .'

'Yeah.'

'. . . you're telling me he got confused. Lost it. Like his sister.'

'That's right.'

He was silent, watching her face. It was unnerving. Then he said: 'So what's with the sheets? And the robe?'

'What?'

Max flicked a finger at the robe she was holding up to her chin. 'This. Every time I've been in here, you've done this. Pulled the sheets – or this damned thing – up like a Victorian virgin, like I haven't seen everything you've got to show about a thousand times before.'

She couldn't answer that. The only truthful answer was that she was trying to hide the bruises and the strapping from him; she didn't want or need his sympathy.

'You were so angry, the first time you came in here,' she said with a shrug. 'I just felt . . . defensive, I suppose. Under threat.'

'But now you don't?'

'Not so much, no.'

'Because you think you've softened me up.'

'I don't think that.'

'Yeah, you do. Sitting there with those big innocent eyes.'

'Max – I *am* innocent.'

'Then you've got nothing to worry about, have you. So let go of the robe.'

Annie sighed and let the robe go at her throat. Max's eyes went there and stayed there, on the faint finger-shaped bruises. 'Shit. Did I do that?'

Annie nodded.

'Untie it,' ordered Max.

Annie looked at him in consternation. But what the hell. If she refused, he'd only rip the damned thing off her, she knew it. Slowly, deliberately, she untied the sash on the robe so that it hung loose.

'Take it off,' he said.

With a heavy sigh, Annie slipped the robe off her shoulders. She sat there, naked, while his eyes roamed over her.

'What the fuck's *this*?' asked Max, staring at the strapping around her ribcage and the purple bruises above it.

'It's . . .' Annie started, wondering what the hell she could say. 'I fell. An accident,' she said. She didn't want to go into all this, not now.

Max stared at her face. Then his gaze dipped again to the strapping. He reached out, touched the bruised skin above it.

'Some fall,' he said. 'What's the damage?'

'Yeah, it was. It cracked a rib.'

Max stiffened. 'Holy shit. When I slapped you up against that wall at Mum's old place, you had this then?'

She nodded again.

'That must have hurt like a bastard.'

'It did. But not as much as having you think I'd been fucking around.'

His hand drifted up, cupped her right breast.

'Max . . .' she said.

'Shut up,' said Max, and his other hand took the left breast, cupped it, rubbed against it. Annie's nipples sprang erect and a low-level ache of desire started in the pit of her stomach. When the phone began ringing, she could have hurled it across the room. Max stopped what he was doing. After a moment to steady herself, Annie reached out gingerly and picked the damned thing up.

'Hello?' she said.

'I've found him,' said Jackie's trembling voice. 'I'm not . . . I don't . . .'

'Slow down, Jackie. Take a breath. Tell me where.'

'Essex way.'

The last time she'd seen Redmond, it had been on the Essex marshes.

'Give me the address.' Annie pulled a writing pad and pencil off the table and on to the bed. 'Go on.'

Jackie sounded breathless, panicky. 'Here's the address, it's . . .'

Jackie spoke quickly and Annie wrote it down. He sounded sober, and the stark terror in his voice alarmed her.

'Where are you, Jackie? Right now?'

'I'm in a phone box outside. It's dark, there's a wood on one side, it's out in the sticks. I think . . . I thought I saw something move just now. Over the other side of the road. I'm sure it was him, and he sort of stared over here, and he *grinned*.'

Annie felt a shudder of unease go straight through her as she pictured Jackie standing there like a sacrificial goat with Redmond Delaney stalking around outside. She clamped down on her own rising anxiety and said clearly: 'Jackie. Get back in the car. Lock the doors. Get the fuck out of there. '

'I dunno, maybe I'll sit it out a bit longer, but I don't know—'

'Jackie. Listen to me. Get out of there.'

'Oh shit. Oh holy fuck.'

'What?' Annie's fingers clenched so hard on the phone that it hurt. Max was watching her, frowning. 'Jackie, what? What's happening?'

'It *is* him. He's coming over.'

'Oh *shit*,' said Annie, and Max snatched the phone.

'Jackie? You heard what she said. Get out of there,' he said.

Annie was craning her head close to Max's to hear what was going on. They both heard a sound like a kiosk door being opened – and then a scuffling and a hideous, nerve-prickling noise. Tough-nut Jackie Tulliver was screaming like a wounded baby.

'Jackie!' shouted Annie, but there was no answer. The scream died away to a thin cry, and then there was silence except for the steady muted background noise of a car engine running nearby.

'Jackie?' said Max into the mouthpiece.

Nothing.

90

Max put the phone back on to the cradle, looked at the address she'd scribbled down, then picked up the phone again. Waited.

'Steve?' he said. 'We just had a call from Jackie Tulliver, he's in the shit. Go to . . .' Max reeled off the address. 'He was in his motor, watching Redmond Delaney's place, but it sounds like Delaney dragged him out of a phone box near there.'

Annie eased herself off the bed and started putting on the clothes she'd worn yesterday.

'What are you doing?' asked Max.

'Coming with you.'

'No, you're not.'

Annie stopped moving. 'Yes, I am. I asked him to find Redmond.'

'Why, for fuck's sake?'

'Because it was the Delaney mob who Dolly asked to do a hit on her dad. Turns out he died in a railway accident, but I'm thinking, was it an accident? I don't know, but Redmond can give answers to that. Max, this is *my* mess, not yours.'

Max let out a sigh. 'Well, hurry the fuck up then,' he said.

*

When they got to the address Jackie had given them, Steve was already there, standing beside Jackie's old car. The empty phone kiosk was ten yards away. There were large detached houses on this side of the road, and a dense stretch of oak woodland on the other. Jackie's car engine was still running, headlights blaring; the driver's door was open, the light inside the car was on. Steve took out a heavy-duty torch from his own car.

'There's no blood in here,' said Annie, peering into the car's messy interior. Jackie's car reflected its owner's character; outside it was OK, but inside it was littered with sweet wrappings, empty beer cans, carrier bags and inches of dust, leaves and other crap.

'I'll have a look around,' said Steve, and went off first to the phone booth and then into the wooded darkness on the other side of the road.

Annie looked at Max. 'What if Redmond took him inside the house?'

'Why would he do that? Just as likely Steve's going to trip over Jackie, stiff as a board and stone-dead any minute, back there.'

'Christ.' Annie shuddered. If Jackie was dead, then it was her fault. 'You heard Jackie screaming, same as I did.'

'That might not have been Delaney.'

'Bullshit.' Annie leaned against the warm bonnet of the car, her legs shaking. Her hands were shaking too. That soul-chilling scream had sent a bolt of fear right through her – fear for Jackie. Taking a handkerchief out of his pocket, Max wrapped it around his fingers and leaned in and switched the engine off, then took the keys out of the ignition. The lights went out as Max closed the car door and locked it, wiped the keyhole, pocketed the keys. Annie pushed herself away from the car and started walking.

'Where you going?' said Max.

'Where do you think?'

Max came and placed himself in front of her. 'No, you're not.'

'Look – if he did this—' she started, stepping around him.

Max grabbed her arm. 'You don't know he's done anything.'

'I know he's fucking evil. I know *that*.'

Steve came back, the torch throwing a wavering cone of white in front of him. He reached them and flicked off the torch. 'Nothing,' he said. 'The phone was off the hook, that's all. No sign of a struggle.'

'He could be inside the house. We can't just *go*,' said Annie, shaking her head as if to clear it. 'Jackie's done what I asked, he's found Redmond. We're *here*. So you can do what you fucking well like, but I'm going over there and I'm going to speak to him.'

Redmond himself opened the door. Not a housekeeper, not a servant, not a henchman – although there was a man coming in through the back door into the kitchen at the end of the hall when they arrived at Redmond's house. He was tall, stooping, dark-haired, scruffy and mean-eyed.

Annie was instantly struck by how little Redmond had changed since she'd seen him last. He still had those killer-cold green eyes, that long, pale, perfectly symmetrical face, the neatly trimmed red hair. Last time she'd seen him he was wearing a priest's cassock; this time he was in dark slacks and an expensive-looking cream shirt. He was devastatingly attractive as always.

Annie thought of all that he had been in the past, and all that Jackie had told her about Redmond and the female parishioners. And she was suddenly very glad that she had

Max and Steve standing right behind her. The sight of Redmond gave her the dry heaves.

'Mrs Carter! And Mr Carter, I see. And a friend too. What a pleasant surprise,' said Redmond smoothly.

'Cut the fucking bullshit, Redmond,' said Max, before Annie could open her mouth. 'Where's Jackie Tulliver?'

'I sent Jackie to find you,' said Annie.

'Did you?' Redmond looked perfectly composed, the picture of innocence. 'Please, come in.'

Feeling like a fly stepping on to a spider's web, Annie crossed the threshold of Redmond Delaney's home.

91

Is Jackie in here somewhere? she wondered. The same thought was obviously crossing Steve and Max's minds, because Steve said, 'Mind if I take a look around the place?'

Redmond shrugged, seeming perfectly relaxed. Whether he said yes or no, it was obvious Steve was going to do it anyway. 'Of course. Although you won't find your missing friend here, I'm afraid.'

Steve didn't reply, he just left the room. They could hear his footfalls as he climbed up to the first floor, could hear the old boards creaking as he moved about up there.

'Please – sit down,' said Redmond.

'I'll stand, thanks,' said Max. He planted himself against the wall beside the door and pulled out a gun and pointed it in Redmond's direction.

Redmond's eyes opened wide in surprise, but he made no comment.

'This is Mitchell,' said Redmond, as the stooping man came into the room, sent a long look at Max and the gun, and took up a position on the other side of the door. 'He keeps house for me. Sees to things. You know. Mrs Carter . . . ?' Redmond indicated a seat on the other side of the fire.

Annie sat down, and so did he. The atmosphere in the room was suddenly thick with a palpable air of menace.

'What did you want to find me for, Mrs Carter?' asked Redmond.

'My friend's been killed. Dolly Farrell,' said Annie bluntly.

'Killed? What, you mean an accident?'

'No accident. She was shot in her flat over the Palermo club. She was managing it for us, for the Carters.'

'I see. I'm sorry for your loss, Mrs Carter, but I don't understand how you expect me to help with this.'

'You knew Dolly didn't you?' asked Annie.

'Oh, from years back. She was an acquaintance, occasionally an employee, back then.'

'In the Limehouse knocking shop,' she said, remembering that Redmond's language was always formal and polite. He might be an arsehole, but you'd never guess it when you spoke to him.

'That's correct,' he said.

'Her father abused her.'

Redmond was silent for a long while. Then he said: 'Yes. I knew about that.'

'And Dolly asked the Delaney family to do away with her father.'

'Yes, that's right too.'

'Only my friend Jackie's turned up stories of an accident on the railway where Dolly's dad worked. And I just wondered . . . was it an accident?'

'What does any of that matter now?'

'It matters because someone might be upset at what happened to the old tosser. They might have gone looking for revenge. They might have targeted Dolly. *Did* the Delaneys organize that "accident"?'

'God moves in mysterious ways, his wonders to perform, Mrs Carter.' Redmond gave a chilling smile. 'Yes, your Aunt Celia brought Dolly Farrell to me, wanting me to do something about her father. She explained the situation – it was quite distressing. A kiddie fiddler. A filthy nonce. Is there anything lower? Anything worse?'

Annie shook her head. No. There wasn't. 'So . . . what happened?' she asked.

'I said, "Let his co-workers decide his fate. Let's tell them what he is, what he's done." Of course they were in uproar. You can rely on the masses for hysteria, I find. One person on his own? Not so bad. An angry group of people? Lethal.'

'And so?' Annie prompted. She could hear Steve upstairs, going from room to room.

Fuck it, Jackie, where are you?

But she kept her focus on Redmond. She had to hear the rest of this.

'They all agreed, all of Sam Farrell's railway workmates, that he was scum and must go. Arthur Biggs was the train driver, but he was reluctant. He said the guilt would be on his shoulders, *he* was the one who would back the engine on to Sam Farrell; even if all the others swore it was an accident, *he* was the one who would do it.'

'He objected?' said Max.

'Strenuously,' said Redmond. 'But his co-workers rounded on him and said he had to. So . . . he did.'

Christ, thought Annie.

'And so,' said Redmond with a sigh, 'the people who had once been Sam Farrell's friends attacked him, and the locomotive backed into him. Crushed his chest and stomach as flat as a pancake. Killed him.'

'And then Arthur Biggs was so tormented with guilt that he hung himself,' said Annie, thinking of what Sandy had told her, and that she had to find the Biggs family and speak to them.

'Did he? I didn't know that.'

Steve was coming back down the stairs in his size elevens, the treads creaking under his weight as he did so. He caught Max's eye, shook his head, and then went off further along the hall and started looking in the downstairs rooms. Mitchell sent a look at Max; Max stared him down. Mitchell left the room, went along the hall toward the kitchen.

'Tea, anyone?' asked Redmond, and he stood up.

'No thanks,' said Annie and Max together.

Then all the lights went out.

92

Utter blackness descended. Annie froze in her chair. Something brushed by her leg, there was a scrabble of movement, and then someone grabbed her arm. She let out a shriek.

'It's me,' said Max, and then Steve was in the room and the wavering light of the torch was blinding Annie. Steve cast the beam around. 'That other geezer shot past me out the back door,' he said.

So – no Mitchell.

Steve cast the torch's beam around the room.

And no Redmond, either. He was gone.

'That bastard makes my skin crawl,' said Max as he started the car and drove them back to Holland Park.

'Me too,' said Annie. She wasn't convinced that Redmond had told them the complete truth about what had happened to Sam Farrell. Redmond was a game player. You couldn't trust a word that came out of his mouth.

Steve had searched everywhere in the house and the grounds, but Jackie wasn't there. So where the hell *was* he? And what had made him scream that way? Annie shivered to think of it, what could have happened to him. All right, he was a walking disaster, drunk and disgusting most of the time, but he'd been making an effort to shape up over

344

this last week or so, and he'd been on her side when no one else seemed to be.

She thought of Redmond, sitting there like butter wouldn't melt. But she *knew* that bastard of old, just like Max did. That cool polished exterior hid a squirming worm-fest of nastiness that could be unleashed at a moment's notice. Priest, pervert or crook, Redmond's basic personality never changed. He was disturbed, and disturbing, and there was history between them. Bad history. Annie could never forget that it had been Constantine who had tried to kill both Redmond and his twin sister Orla back in the seventies. And it had been Annie's own daughter, Layla, who had finally put a stop to Orla's sad, twisted life.

'Are you going to come in?' asked Annie when Max pulled up outside her house.

'What, to hear more tall tales?' Max sighed.

Annie looked at him in exasperation. Before Jackie's phone call, Max had been about to make love to her. She knew it. Now he was cold again.

'We can talk,' she said. 'Can't we?'

Truthfully, she didn't want to be alone, not after this evening, not after hearing that godawful scream and staring into Redmond's expressionless eyes.

He shrugged. 'If you want,' he said, and got out of the car.

Annie got out too, shutting the door after her, crossing the pavement, starting up the steps. There was something, a bundle of rags, something like that, near the door, lit by the carriage light over it.

'What the f—' she started, coming to a halt as her feet met a puddle of dark oil.

They had found Jackie.

93

Jackie could almost have been asleep. He was sitting, legs sprawled open, his back to the navy-blue double doors of the house, his head slumped forward on his chest.

He's asleep, she told herself. Or drugged? She was hoping against hope that this could be true.

Max passed her where she stood frozen on the steps. And then she realized. It wasn't oil at her feet, it was *blood*, and it had flowed down the steps from Jackie's body. Unable to move, too *shocked* to move, she watched as Max crouched down by Jackie, lifted his head and then . . .

'Oh, holy *shit*!' said Annie, her hand flying to her mouth and bile surging into her throat. Jackie's neck had been slashed open and his shirtfront was soaked through with blood. She could smell the coppery stench of it now; it hit her in a wave.

Max let Jackie's head fall back down on to his chest. It was like releasing a puppet's strings, Annie thought. There was no life left in Jackie; he was dead.

'Stay there a minute,' said Max, and got out his key and opened the door.

Jackie fell back across the threshold and lay there, inert. With Annie's body blocking anyone's view from the road, Max dragged Jackie into the hall, then motioned for Annie to come on in. She did, stepping around the dark waterfall of blood, gagging, her feet leaden, her heart pounding dully in her chest.

She closed the door behind her, flicked on the hall lights and looked down at Jackie. The brilliance of the chandeliers only served to highlight the awful pallor of his face, the deep wound across his neck, the half-open lids showing filmed-over eyes that saw nothing.

'*Shit*,' she moaned.

Max was crossing to the hall table, snatching up the telephone. She didn't even listen to what he said, her mind was spinning out of control and all she could think was that this was down to her. All evening, she'd been afraid of something like this, and now here it was. Jackie had helped her – and he'd died for it.

Max returned to her side, took her arm. There was blood all down his shirt and on his jacket. 'Come on, let's go in here,' he said, and guided her across the hall and into the study, shutting the door firmly after them, turning on the lights.

'Chris and Tone are on their way,' he said.

Annie nodded. This had happened before here, this procedure. A clean-up. A dead body shipped discreetly out and disposed of. Which meant no Christian burial for Jackie Tulliver, just a trip out into the depths of the English Channel or down into the concrete foundations of a new building or a motorway bridge.

'Oh God,' said Annie, sitting down behind the desk and sinking her head into her hands. She looked up at Max. 'Do you think Redmond . . . ?'

'Dunno. Would he have had the time? What about his creep of a mate, that Mitchell sort. He'd been up to something, before he came in the back door. Could be that this is his handiwork.'

'I can't believe this.'

347

'Shit happens,' said Max.

'Is that all you've got to say? Jackie's *dead*, and you say "shit happens"? That poor little bastard, he was mourning his mum and drinking to numb the pain, and all your lot, all you rotten fuckers, you turned your backs on him because you thought he was a loose cannon and not to be trusted.'

Max gave her a long look. 'He *wasn't* to be trusted. He turned into a drunk. You can't ever trust drunks.'

'I think he would have got himself back on track, with some help.'

'Well, *that* ain't going to happen now.'

'Christ, you're a bastard.'

'Just stating the obvious.' Max came over, leaned on the desk, stared down at her. 'For what it's worth, Jackie Tulliver was a good friend to me back in the day. I'm sorry he's dead, and sorry it was this way and not peacefully in his own home. But shit *does* happen, and we're going to deal with it.'

There was a heavy knock at the front door then; Max straightened and went to answer it.

'You can stay in here,' he said over his shoulder. 'You don't have to see this.'

'No.' Annie shoved herself upright on shaky legs. 'I got him into this. So whatever there is to see, I'll see it. OK?'

'OK,' said Max, and opened the door into the hall, where Jackie lay dead.

Annie braced herself, and followed.

94

Chris and Tony came into the house wearing rubber gloves and old clothes that would later be burned. Gently they cleared Jackie away, wrapping his corpse in a tarpaulin sheet then carefully wiping the hall floor clean afterwards. With that sorted, Chris switched off the porch light and Max doused those in the hall while they cleared up the steps outside. When they were done, Tony stepped out, leaving the door open, looking up and down the street. Then he came back in, nodding.

All clear.

Together Chris and Tony hoisted Jackie outside, and Max closed the door behind them, locked it, and came back across the darkened hall to where Annie stood in the doorway of the study, light spilling out behind her.

'Been a hell of a fucking day,' he said.

'Yeah.' Annie felt both sick and numb, still unable to take it in. Jackie was *dead*.

'Come on. Bedtime,' he said, and took her arm and led her upstairs to the master suite.

Annie didn't think it was possible, but she took a couple of painkillers and then she managed to fall asleep after an hour or so of lying awake, staring at the ceiling. Max had gone off to the next room, the one with the connecting door into the master suite. *He* wouldn't have any trouble getting to sleep, she knew it. The whole world could be coming off its axis, and Max Carter would never panic.

Her mind kept replaying it: Jackie sitting there dead, propped against her front door like a discarded rag doll. And the blood. The *smell*.

Jackie had been watching Redmond, and Redmond could kill or give the order for it just for sheer pleasure, she knew that. Her mind kept churning it all over: Dolly dying and now Jackie, and those two grey little souls standing by Dolly's burial plot, her brother, her sister. And Sandy, all that he had told her. And Dick, in New Zealand. Or – was he?

Ellie, who didn't want to know her any more . . .

The mob by the lychgate at the funeral, who would have done her serious damage if Max and his boys hadn't been there . . .

She drifted into a light, restless sleep, and only woke when she knew he was in the room. She sat up, reached for the light. Max was there, in the chair again. Fully dressed. Watching her. She pulled the sheets up to her chin and stared at him.

Max's eyes were on the sheets. 'Yeah, let's talk about that,' he said. 'The strapping. The bruises. You said a fall.'

Annie let out a tired sigh and said, 'All right. I lied.'

'Oh? Well, there's a bloody novelty. So what really happened?'

'Gary had a couple of his boys give me a going-over. All thanks to you.'

'You what?'

'You heard. They grabbed me, took me dockside and gave me a kicking.'

'Gary OK'd this?'

'He hates me. Always has. It must have made his day,

this story that I'd been fooling around with Constantine. Probably thought I'd run away, never to be seen again. But instead I read his tart Caroline the riot act. So he arranged for me to be taught a lesson. I guess he thought you'd be pleased.'

Max's face was grim. 'I'm going to have a fucking word with him. And these two goons of his, do you know them? Can you describe them?'

'No need,' said Annie.

'Why's that?'

'Because it's been taken care of.'

'By who?'

'By Constantine. Well, by Alberto really. I expect they're sleeping with the fishes now – ain't that what they say? Something like that.'

'So . . . you're being watched by the Mafia. Watched *over*.'

'That's right.'

'So he really is your friend.'

'He really is. In his way.'

'You don't sound too sure about that.'

'It's complicated,' she said. 'But Alberto keeps an eye on me.'

Max stood up, stretched, came over to the bed and sat down on it. 'So Alberto's giving the orders now?'

'I told you. Things have changed. Constantine's not the man he was.'

'It all sounds very cosy. You and Constantine, playing cards.'

'Yeah, it was OK – until he'd start asking after Nico, or thinking I was his sister, or his first wife.' Annie shook her head. 'Oh God, what a night it's been. What a fucking *day*, come to that. Poor bloody Jackie. What are we going to do?'

Max stared steadily at her face. 'You know this Dolly thing? You could be fooling yourself with all this bad-past bollocks. It could have been random, it could have been something stupid, something right here and now.'

'Like what, for instance?'

'A punter she turned out. A supplier who tried to short-change her. Who knows?'

'It's possible,' said Annie, looking doubtful. 'I'm still thinking about Dolly's brother, the one who gave me the name of the train driver. Arthur Biggs. He killed himself.'

'I heard the police gave you a warning.'

'Yeah. So?'

'So perhaps this would be a good time to back off, let them handle it.'

Annie was shaking her head. '*No*. No way. If I did that, what's it all been for? Jackie's dead, it's my fault, and what's more he died for no reason – because I quit? You're joking. I started this, and I'm damned well going to finish it.'

'You're such an obstinate cow.'

'Hey – you always knew that.' Annie felt sick, weary, stressed to hell. 'Max, I'm dog-tired. Let me sleep.'

Max's eyes locked with hers. 'Alone?'

Just say you want to stay with me, she thought. She wanted him so much, but if he still doubted her, if he still thought she was lying over her visits to Constantine, then what was the point?

'I'm getting used to it,' she said, and he didn't argue. He went through the door that led into the adjoining twin suite and closed it behind him, leaving her alone once again.

95

Late next morning she found Max down in the kitchen, in jeans and rolled-up shirtsleeves, staring into the empty fridge. He turned his head as she wandered in, yawning, rubbing her head, wearing an old short pink silk nightshirt. Sleep had made her feel better, even if it had been patchy. She was still devastated over Jackie's horrible death and still shaky after the trauma of it, but she felt a little stronger now.

'Have I said this before?' said Max. 'You're not very domesticated.'

Annie leaned against the kitchen table and looked at him. 'Have I said this before? Neither are you.'

'I'm starving.'

Jesus! Just last night he'd been clearing an old mate's remains away, now all he could think of was his stomach!

'There's a deli down the road.' Annie went to the built-in espresso coffee machine, part of a big kitchen revamp that had been done years ago. 'Shit, I never did learn how to use this thing. Rosa knew how, I don't.'

'So no coffee *and* nothing to eat.' Max shut the fridge door. 'Perfect. You sleep OK?'

'Fine.'

She hadn't. Dreams of Jackie had haunted her, all night. Poor bloody Jackie. She'd woken up often during the night, panicking, half-vomiting with shock and dismay as it all came back to her. More than anything, she had wanted to go into the adjoining room, to climb into Max's bed and feel his warmth, his strength, envelop her. But he was still angry, and she could see his point. She felt bad about the whole Constantine thing; how could she climb into bed with him when she'd done that, deceived him that way?

'What?' she asked, when he continued to stand there, staring at her.

'Nothing.' Max came over and stood in front of her. For a long moment he just stared at her silently. It was unnerving. Then his hand went to the front of the nightshirt and popped open a button.

Annie put up a hand in surprise. 'Wait. Just *wait*. What the fuck happened to the divorce?'

'It's on hold,' said Max.

'For how long? Until you get the fact that I'm telling the truth through your thick head?'

Max wasn't listening. 'How long have you had this? It's nice. Have I seen this before?'

'Stop that. I *said*, what about the divorce?'

'And *I* said, it's on hold. For the moment,' he said, and popped open another button.

'Oh, only for the moment? What the hell's *that* supposed to mean?'

'It means what it says,' said Max, slipping his hands inside the shirt, touching cool naked flesh.

Annie drew in a gasping breath, stirred by his touch yet not wanting to be. Hating him for his power to move her. 'You're such a bastard.'

Max stared into her eyes from inches away. 'You do realize you're still in the doghouse.'

'Got that message loud and clear.'

'I *ought* to kick you to the kerb, keeping secrets like that from me,' said Max, fiddling with another button until he lost patience and tore it loose from its moorings. It rolled across the kitchen tiles and *tinked* against the base of a cupboard.

'Steady,' said Annie, but her heart was racing and her nipples were hard as rocks. He still wanted her, and oh Jesus, she still wanted him, so much.

'Steady? Don't give me "steady", you cheeky mare,' said Max, grabbing her hips and lifting her up on to the table. He unbuckled his belt, undid the button on his jeans. 'Get the fucking thing off, hurry up.'

Annie pulled the nightshirt off and flung it to the floor. Max's eyes went again to the bruising at her throat, and to the strapping on her rib and the bruises there, beginning to turn yellow. Annie lay back on the table with a shaky sigh.

'Don't worry about that, I'm all right,' she said. After all she'd been through, all the horrors of Jackie's death, and thinking that she could still have lost Max for good, she *needed* this. Yes, she was mad at him for doubting her. But she was still crazy about him. 'Hurry,' she gasped out, and Max did, shoving his jeans down to free his cock. Annie guided him in eagerly.

'Christ, that's good,' he said, leaning over her, his hands on either side of her head, his hips thrusting in a hard fluid rhythm, fucking her over and over again until she felt almost delirious with desire.

'Oh God – Max,' she moaned, feeling her climax starting to build, her eyes locked with his.

'Jesus,' he said, and came, shuddering, just as she did, pumping into her ever more frantically, almost hurtfully, like he really did want to punish her, to make her suffer.

All too soon he pulled out, straightened his clothes, rebuckled his belt. He scooped the nightshirt off the floor and handed it to her as she sat up, dazed from the speed of what had just happened. He'd made love to her. Maybe everything was not completely lost, after all. She felt a tiny twinge of what could almost be hope.

'Come on then,' said Max brusquely, turning away from her. 'Get dressed, we'll eat out. After that, I'm going over to have a word with Gary, if he's back.'

'Can I come?' asked Annie, thinking that Max's tone of voice was telling her that she wasn't completely forgiven, not yet. But it was a start. And if he was going to give Gary the right royal bollocking he so richly deserved, she wanted a front-row seat for *that* event.

'Why not?' asked Max.

After breakfast in a local greasy spoon, Max drove them over to the Blue Parrot, but Gary wasn't there.

'He is back, though. Probably with that bird of his at her place, the Palermo,' said one of the cleaners sniffily.

'He's not very well loved by his workers, is he?' commented Annie as they went back to the car.

'Well, it ain't a fucking popularity contest,' said Max.

They carried on over to the Palermo, with Annie wishing that she *hadn't* got herself invited along to this little shindig, because going back to the Palermo, to Dolly's old place, was going to creep her out for sure and she was already shaken up by what had happened to Jackie.

She steeled herself as they neared the place, telling herself not to be stupid, it was just a *place*, and there were no ghosts, only memories. She was so busy giving herself a pep talk that she was surprised when Max spoke.

'What the hell?' he said.

Annie glanced at him, and then ahead. There were four police cars in front of the Palermo, headlights flashing. The red double-doors were wide open and uniformed police were moving about on the pavement, talking into radios.

Max parked the car and they got out and started walking, only to be stopped by a burly policeman whose female colleague was busy stringing up police tapes around the entrance.

'No entry, I'm afraid, sir,' said the man to Max.

'I own the place, I'm Max Carter,' he said.

The policeman turned, searching the nearby faces until he found the one he was looking for, a dour individual in plain clothes who was accompanied by a plain skinny girl taking notes.

'Hunter,' called out Annie.

DS Sandra Duggan turned and gave her a look that could have curdled milk. Hunter walked over, and his sidekick came too.

'What's going on?' asked Max when he drew level. 'We're here to see Gary Tooley.'

Hunter didn't ask who Max was. He *knew*. He'd spent quite a few years trying to pin Max Carter down in some misdemeanour, *any* misdemeanour, but Max had always eluded him. Running various protection rackets all around the East End, taking tributes from shops, restaurants, brothels and snooker halls paid well, allowing Max to set up three nightclubs that had grown over the years from cabaret halls to discos to lap-dancing hotspots.

Hunter gave them both a nod. 'Mrs Carter, Mr Carter, I'm pleased you're here because I would have been getting in touch with you shortly anyway, and this saves me a trip. I'm afraid there's been a serious incident.'

'What sort of incident?' they both asked at the same time.

'It's another murder,' said DCI Hunter.

96

This time, Annie didn't have to ask to be let in. This time, Hunter turned, with DS Duggan at his heels, ducked under the tapes and led the way straight into the club, across the club floor where men in white coveralls were hauling bags and bits of electronic equipment. Max and Annie followed.

'Done?' Hunter said to one of the SOCO team in passing.

He nodded. 'Just about.'

Hunter led the way up the stairs and, with a horrible feeling of déjà vu, Annie followed. But he didn't go into the lounge, he carried on until they reached the flat's one small bedroom, which was tucked away at the back of the building. A woman was dismantling photographic lights there; a tech was tucking a camera away in a flat aluminium case.

'Stay at the door,' said Hunter to Max and Annie, while he stepped into the room, avoiding the markers the tech people had laid out as points of special interest.

Annie caught her breath and held it as the stench of fresh blood hit her nostrils. She felt her stomach contract, felt vomit creep up in a choking wave into her throat. Gary was stretched out on his back on the bed, the sheet pulled up to his waist. Above that, everything was red. His eyes were bulging out of his head, there was livid bruising on his cheekbones and one of his eyes had swollen half-closed. His face was puce and his tongue protruded grossly from between his thin lips.

At his neck, there was a deep cut; and blood – lots of it.

'Jesus,' said Annie, appalled. It felt too hot in the little room; she felt sweat pop out of her pores. She was forced to draw in a quick, shaky breath, and got a mocking look from DS Duggan.

The blonde woman in white coveralls who was crouching over Gary's corpse looked first at Hunter and Duggan, then at the two civilians they'd brought in with them.

'The owners,' said Hunter. 'Max and Annie Carter. You can speak, it's OK. Estimated time of death?'

'Round about midnight,' said the woman. 'An hour or two either side.'

'And . . . ?'

'A knife,' said the woman. 'Smooth, not serrated.' She leaned in, prodded with a gloved finger at the gaping wound that was Gary's neck. 'Applied with a lot of force. Probably a man's work, not a woman's. Cut right through the windpipe, sliced the carotid artery too. Very nasty. And these bruises on his face? They were administered pre-death. He was beaten quite badly and then slashed.'

This is like what happened to Jackie, thought Annie with a shudder.

'Where's the girl?' she asked.

'What?' said Hunter.

'The girl – Caroline. The one who's taken over as manager here. I'm assuming that if Gary was here, then he was with her. Unless she was away somewhere and he was keeping an eye on the place?'

'I'll talk to the staff,' said DS Duggan, and left the room.

'Excuse me,' said the blonde pathologist, and followed her out.

Hunter, Max and Annie stood there, looking at the dead man. True, she'd never liked Gary, but Christ, he hadn't deserved *this*. Yeah, he'd been a bastard, and he'd had her done over, put her in hospital. Annie's eyes narrowed. But no. This wasn't the usual style of her Mafia watchers. It was far too public.

Redmond and his sidekick. It had to be one of them, or both. Didn't it?

But why? She could get Jackie, just about. She could understand that. Jackie had been trying to trace Redmond, and he'd made it clear he didn't want to be traced. That was on her, all Jackie's suffering and his death, it was her fault and she was going to have to soak it up. But why Gary? What possible connection could there be between Redmond and him?

'Can I ask you a question?' she said to Hunter.

'You can ask.'

'Did Pete the bar manager actually *see* Dolly Farrell on the night she was killed? You said he spoke to her, but did he see her? Or did she call out through the door?' Annie was annoyed with herself that she hadn't thought to ask Pete this question when they'd visited him.

Hunter stared at her. 'He said he spoke to her; that's all. I'll check with him. If the two of you have any ideas about who did this, now is the time to share them with me.'

He looked from Max's face to Annie's, then back again.

'Obstruction of the law is an offence,' said Hunter.

'We're aware of that,' said Max. 'Look, I've known this bloke for Christ knows how long. But how he wound up like this? I've no idea.'

'Then if you'll excuse me . . . ?' Hunter nodded to the door.

They took the hint, and went out of the flat and back down the stairs. DS Duggan was talking to two of the white-clad techs there, and she gave Annie a sneering look in passing.

'That girl don't like you,' said Max as they went out into the fresh air.

'No kidding,' said Annie.

They got into the car and Max drove them back to Holland Park, stopping off at the Shalimar because he needed a word with Chris.

'Coming in?' he asked Annie as he pulled up.

'OK,' she said, doubting she'd be made welcome.

But she was surprised. When they got upstairs, Ellie met them out in the hallway.

'Christ,' she said when she saw Annie. 'I'm glad you've turned up.'

'What?' asked Annie. Max and Chris had vanished into the office.

Ellie lowered her voice. 'I got someone here wants to talk to you. She's fucking hysterical and she's gripping my kitchen table like it's a life raft, and she won't let go. All she keeps saying is she wants to talk to you.'

'Is it Caroline?' asked Annie.

'Who?'

'Caroline. Gary's girlfriend. The one who took over the Palermo from Dolly.'

'No. Why would it be? It's that funny little stick of a woman from the funeral. You know – Dolly's sister, Sarah.'

97

'He did things to Dolly,' said Sarah.

When she saw Sarah in Ellie's kitchen, Annie thought that Ellie had been right, she *was* clutching the table as if letting go could sweep her away, into madness. Ellie and Annie sat opposite her, and they closed the kitchen door firmly.

'You're safe,' said Annie, because she thought it would calm Sarah down.

'Nowhere's safe. I thought I was safe at home,' said Sarah, and her pale blue eyes looked wild. 'So did Dolly. But she wasn't, and neither was I.'

'I'll put the kettle on,' said Ellie, and stood up and went about the business of making tea.

'Nigel said I should never speak of it. He said it was all in my imagination, and Dolly was bad and going straight to hell. He loved Dad, you see. Worshipped him. But now this . . .' Sarah's voice trailed away. 'He said it was filthy, disgusting, what she turned into, and then I told him that it had happened to me with Dad, and I said maybe it had happened to her too, and that was why she left. He was so mad when I said that. Furious. He said I ought to shut my dirty mouth. He said it shamed the whole family, me making things up like that.'

'But now Dolly's been killed.'

'Yeah.' Sarah's eyes met Annie's; tears started to roll down her pale face. 'It haunts me, all this. The bad stuff he did.'

'Your dad.'

'Yeah. Him.'

'Dolly had to leave home because of it,' said Annie. 'Did *you* leave home?'

'No. I stayed. Looked after Nigel and Dick and Sandy. Helped Mum around the place. Did what Dolly used to do. And then *he* had the accident on the railway. And it was all sort of OK, after that.'

'Except I don't suppose it was, not really,' said Annie.

'It was our secret shame, our family. Mum half off her head, and Dad doing *that*.' Sarah gulped. Ellie placed a mug of hot sweet tea in front of her, and she let go of the table and fastened her hands around the warmth of that instead. 'I've got the cutting from the paper. I kept it all these years. Like confirmation, I suppose. Like it was in black and white, and that was good, that *proved* he . . . he wasn't coming back.'

Ellie put down two more mugs of steaming tea and a plate of biscuits. Sarah let go of her mug long enough to scramble in one of her raincoat pockets and pull out a yellowed scrap of paper. She shoved it across the table to Annie.

Annie unfolded it; it was nearly torn down the middle, from being folded up for so long. She read:

Railway tragedy

Samuel Farrell, who worked as a shunter on British Rail, was killed in a freak accident late yesterday. He leaves behind a wife and five children.

Annie read it, refolded it, shoved it back across the table. It was similar to the piece that Jackie had discovered and given to her. Sarah put the paper back in her pocket and clung on to the warm mug once more.

'Nigel said I shouldn't speak of it, not to anyone, that it was all filthy lies, but I have to now. *He's* long dead, our dad, and now poor Dolly is dead too. I suppose what he did to her sent her the way she went, into the way of life she led. I don't think it was her fault, although Nigel says it was, that we're all responsible for our own actions.'

Nigel's got a bloody lot to say for himself, thought Annie.

'She was always good to me, Dolly,' said Sarah.

'She was a diamond,' said Ellie.

'To think of her ending that way, I don't like it. And I just wanted to tell you, if there's anything I can do, *anything*, you've only to say.'

Nigel's not going to like this, thought Annie.

'Thanks,' she said.

'I got married, you know,' said Sarah. 'But we divorced. Because I couldn't be a wife. I couldn't do *that*. I couldn't do anything.'

98

When Sarah had gone, Annie went along to the office. Chris wasn't there any more but Max was, thumbing idly through a set of accounts. He looked up as she came and stood in the doorway, arms folded.

'Profit margins good?' she asked.

'Always,' he said, with that glinting, piratical smile that *still* made her stomach flip, annoyingly. It would be best, she thought, *not* to be infatuated with her husband if he was going to kick her arse out the door. Which he probably was, she thought in a sudden rush of gloom. So they'd had sex. So what? That proved nothing. She knew he was mad at her. Mad enough to spit, mad enough to take their wedding licence and tear it into tiny shreds, set light to the bits and chuck the ashes in the Thames.

'So where's Caroline gone?' Annie asked him.

'That's what I was wondering.' He stood up. 'Let's see if we can find out.'

'Suppose Gary *was* a Mafia hit,' said Annie, as Max drove away from the Shalimar.

Max threw her a look. 'Unlikely. And too much like what happened to Jackie.'

'But not completely out of the question.'

'I dunno. What makes you think that?'

'God, I don't know. I feel like my head's coming off.' Annie closed her eyes tight, opened them, then said: 'Gina was losing her mind and phoning Gary, and Gary was passing the glad news on to you about Constantine being alive and me visiting him. Maybe they're thinking Gary is a loose thread that needs tying up.'

'Yeah, but if that's right then we're *all* for it, ain't we? You *and* me. You, because you know where he is. Me, because I might get it out of you – if I haven't already got it out of Gina.'

Annie stared at him. If Max *had* got it out of Gina, then wouldn't he have acted on that information already? Gone up to Scotland and done something drastic? He didn't have that info, she was sure of it. She was pretty certain that Gary had died before he got around to passing it on to Max.

'You haven't. Have you?' she asked, to be sure.

'Nope.' Max accelerated toward a delivery van that was blocking their path, then swerved out and overtook with a honk of the horn.

'Christ. You still drive like a fucking lunatic,' said Annie, her right foot automatically stamping on a non-existent brake, her hands clutching her seat.

'You can get out and walk if you like.'

Annie loosened her grip as he veered around an obstacle. She dragged her hands through her hair. 'All right, this doesn't *look* like Mafia style, but who really knows? As for any threat to us, forget that. That's rubbish. Alberto wouldn't have it. We're Layla's parents.'

'Fucking Redmond. That sick bastard just *won't* die like the rest of that family.'

'Maybe Redmond found out that Gary was getting calls off Gina,' said Annie. 'Maybe he found out the content of those calls. When Constantine arranged that "accident" way back for Redmond and Orla – maybe Redmond knows about that. Maybe he even knows Constantine's still alive. Maybe he was trying to beat Constantine's whereabouts out of Gary before he realized Gary didn't know, and finished him.'

Max threw her a sombre look and swerved the car into the pavement. 'Maybe he *did* beat Constantine's whereabouts out of Gary. And *then* he finished him.'

Annie looked at Max in horror, but they didn't have time to talk about it, not now.

They'd arrived at the Blue Parrot.

99

Inside the club, things were hotting up for the evening. All the girls were in, getting ready, and a hush fell over them as Annie stepped into the doorway of their dressing room while Max carried on into the office.

'I'm looking for Caroline,' she said. 'She's not at the Palermo. Do any of you know where she is right now?'

There was a long silence. Then one of them, a tall corn-gold blonde, her eyes alight with interest, said: 'Is it right, what we've been hearing on the news? That Gary Tooley's dead?'

'Yeah, it's right.'

'Christ!'

'He was *such* a bastard,' said another – shorter, dark-haired, pouty-lipped. 'I heard he got knifed or something.'

Max stepped into the doorway behind Annie and she felt a seismic shift in the girls' postures and attitudes. Breasts pushed out, stomachs in. Smiles suddenly super-bright. Irritating. 'So you don't know where Caroline is?'

'I got her old home address out of the book in the office,' said Max to Annie.

'We ain't seen her,' said a girl with Schiaparelli-pink streaks in her ash-blonde hair and dangling pearl earrings that brushed her equally pearly shoulders. 'Not that we *want* to. She was after Gary from the get-go, she was bloody shameless. Thought she was better than the lot of us, she did. Started queening it about the place after he slipped her one.'

'Girl, *you* were after him too,' the blonde reminded her with a smirk. 'You're just mad because she got him and got bumped up the ladder to take over the Palermo after Dolly Farrell got done.'

The pink-and-ash girl blushed. The blonde had hit a nerve. 'And look how *that* turned out,' she shot back. 'Dolly Farrell's dead, Gary's dead. You ask me, that place is *cursed*.'

'You know what I think? I think it could have been Caroline up there in Dolly's room who answered Pete,' said Annie when they were back in the car. 'Maybe she was there talking to Dolly, telling her to fuck off out of it and let her take over the club. Maybe Gary had hinted to Dolly that she ought to be put out to grass and let his fancy piece be in charge, and Dolly – being Dolly – would have told them both to go fuck themselves.'

'You seriously think Gary or Caroline could have done the job on her?' asked Max, flicking her a glance as he drove them over to Caroline's old place.

'Yeah. Maybe a combined effort. And by the way, where's Tone? I thought I said I wanted my driver back.'

'You did. But why bother Tone when I'm right here?'

'Yeah, driving like a ruddy maniac. Tone's steady, I like him driving me. This isn't Formula fucking One.'

'Shut it,' said Max, but he was grinning.

They went back to Holland Park. When they got there, DCI Hunter and DS Duggan were on the doorstep, waiting for them.

'Problems?' asked Annie, coming up the steps with Max

following, thinking that just last night Jackie had been propped right here against the door, dead. It made her shiver with horror all over again.

'Thought you'd like to know,' said Hunter. 'Pete Jones the bar manager *didn't* see Dolly that night. She shouted through the door.'

'So . . .' said Annie.

'So possibly it wasn't Dolly Farrell who answered. Quite possibly it was another woman in there with her.'

Maybe it was Sarah and now she's just acting all shook up to throw us off the scent, thought Annie.

But she didn't think so.

Maybe Caroline?

And then she thought of Nigel, with his high-pitched, almost womanly voice.

100

When they got to the block of flats in Stepney where Caroline lived before she started jumping Gary Tooley's bones, they went up to the second floor in a piss-stinking lift, then past graffiti-clad concrete walls and along a covered walkway strewn with dead pot-plants and grimy lines of washing. When they reached the flat door, Max hammered on it. Nobody came. Max hammered some more. There was a murky window beside the door, but they couldn't see in; the curtains were closed.

'No one here. Was this her parents' address?' said Annie.

'No, she shared it with a flatmate. I remember Gary saying so.'

'Well, the flatmate ain't here then.'

'Let's see,' said Max, and stepped back and kicked the door. It juddered back on its hinges, the lock shattered. 'After you,' he said, standing aside.

Annie stepped straight into a grubby-looking living room. It wasn't exactly Ideal Home Exhibition territory in here. There was a cheap sofa, with a dirty red-and-blue woven Indian rug thrown over it. Hectically patterned carpeted floors that had seen much better days. A Bush TV with an inch of dust on top. A scratched and stained teak G-Plan coffee table cluttered with empty cider cans and the remnants of last night's takeaway meal. Not a lot else.

'I can hear something,' said Max, pushing in front of Annie and moving along a dingy hall. He toed open a door and there was a bedroom, thin purple curtains still pulled closed, a crumpled bed and a dark-haired girl half-sitting up, looking in surprise at the two who had just busted their way in here.

'What the fuck . . . ?' she wondered, rubbing her eyes and then her sleep-matted brown hair.

Annie looked around at this shit-hole and tried not to inhale. There was a crack pipe on the bedside table, burned-out matches, another cider can. The bedding smelled stale. The girl was blinking at them as if they'd landed from Mars.

'Hi,' said Annie. 'And you are . . . ?'

'What the *fuck* . . .' demanded the girl again, her tone turning angry.

'We're looking for Caroline. Used to be your roomy, right?' asked Annie, as Max moved off further along the hall. She could hear him opening drawers, looking in cupboards.

'Yeah, she did, but what the fuck are you doing in my flat? Get the hell *out*, right *now!*'

Max came back. 'The other bedroom's empty,' he told Annie. 'Nothing in there at all. I suppose all Caroline's stuff was still in the wardrobes over at the Palermo? The police checked that?' He looked at the girl in the bed. 'You – did Caroline leave stuff here? Has she been back? Have you seen her in the last couple of days?'

'I ain't seen Caroline in *months*,' said the girl. 'She's too hoity-toity to talk to me now. Moved on up, kicked all her old mates aside. Got herself a nightclub manager, I heard. Too good for the likes of me now. And I ain't been able to find another girl to share. The landlord's tearing his hair out for the rent, but what can I do? I ain't got his money.

Is that it? He sent you to get it? Well, good luck with that, because *I don't have it.*'

'We're not here for the rent. So you haven't seen Caroline?' asked Annie.

'No.'

'Really?' asked Annie. She moved closer to the bed. The girl in it leaned back, sensing trouble as she stared into Annie's eyes. Annie grabbed a hank of dirty hair and shook the girl's head about. It made her damaged rib shriek, but she didn't care.

'Hey! Come on!' yelled the girl, squirming.

'Only, if I find out you're lying, you see that pipe there?' said Annie. 'I'm going to get this bloke here to shove it up your arse sideways. And that, I promise you, is going to hurt.'

'I ain't lying! Let go of me, you raving *nutter.*'

'Sure?' Annie picked up the pipe and eyed it.

'Sure!'

'Damn, that's a shame,' said Annie, and moved suddenly. Pain gripped her middle as she pulled the girl's head over to one side, shoving hard at her shoulder, and flipping her over like a landed fish. The girl let out a piercing yell that was instantly muffled by the pillows. She looked at Max. 'Stick this thing up here, will you?'

'Look, just *hold on*!'

'For what? Fucking *Christmas*? I don't think so.'

Max came over and picked up the pipe.

'No! Don't. All *right*. I saw her today. This afternoon. She came here. Let me up, you cow, I can't *breathe*!' It was a yell of pure terror. 'Just *stop*, OK?' she panted. 'There's no need for this, I saw her. Just *stop.*'

Annie stopped. She released her hold on the girl and the girl pulled her head out of the pillows and scrabbled back against the headboard. She eyed Annie like she was unhinged.

'You're both *mad*,' said the girl, her voice shaking.

'Remember that,' said Annie.

'All right! She said not to tell, but what the hell, it's my arse on the line, not hers. Caroline said it had all gone tits-up at the club and she was leaving. She had some clothes here and she took them, she looked scared to death – I mean really, honest-to-God, shit-scared – and she said she was going to her folks' place and not to say anything and I wouldn't see her again anytime soon.'

Annie exchanged a look with Max.

'Where's her folks' place?' he asked.

'Ibiza,' said the girl.

101

'Fuck,' said Max on a sigh as Annie picked up the pay-phone.

'What?' she asked, dialling. They were squished into the phone box outside the block of flats, it was raining, and Annie was doing something that Max would never, ever do.

'We don't call in the Bill,' he said, for the third time.

But Annie shook her head. 'In this case? We *do*. They can get straight through to passport control at Gatwick and stop her. By the time we get there to do it, she'll be gone.'

'Something going on, you and this "Hunter" dickhead?'

'*What*?'

'You heard. You seem very pally with him, is all I'm saying.'

Annie stared at him. 'Oh sure. I've been fucking his brains out, him *and* Constantine.'

Max looked grim. 'Not funny.'

'Am I laughing?' Annie clamped the receiver to her ear. 'Yeah, hello? I need to get a message to DCI Hunter, it's urgent. Is he there?'

Hunter was. Annie relayed the information they'd just received to him, put the phone down and looked at Max.

'They'll stop her,' she said.

'All right. So now what do *we* do, genius?' They extracted themselves from the phone box and as they did so a cyclist zipped up and stopped right beside Annie. No *pizzino* this time. A slim man, dark glasses, helmet. Could be anyone.

'What's this?' asked Max.

'Constantine's been asking for me.' Annie looked at the cyclist. A thin, fit young man, totally anonymous, speeding through the London streets delivering messages on the order of his masters. 'I can't come,' she said to the man. 'Not yet. Soon. Tell them.'

The cyclist gave the briefest of nods and shot away, weaving through the traffic; almost instantly, he was out of sight.

They went down the cop shop to see what developed. It was a long, long wait, but eventually Hunter arrived with DS Sandra Duggan, and she was holding on to the arm of a swearing, struggling Caroline. When Caroline saw Annie there, she spat at her feet and surged toward her. 'You *bitch!*' she yelled.

Hunter grabbed the girl's other arm, and they carted her off into the depths of the nick, kicking and screaming insults at everyone around her.

'Well, that worked out well,' said Annie. She turned to Max. 'Can you get someone down here to pick her up when she comes out? Then have them bring her over to my place, OK? We can have a chat.'

102

It was Tony who brought Caroline over to the Holland Park house when the police eventually released her. By that time it was gone eleven at night, and a lot of the fight had gone out of her. She looked pale, exhausted and scared when Tony ushered her into the study at the front of the house. Annie was there, sitting behind the desk, and Max was standing nearby. Tony manhandled Caroline into a chair beside the desk and then retreated to the closed door, where he placed himself, an impenetrable wall of muscle.

'They give you a hard time, down the nick?' asked Annie.

Caroline said nothing, just looked at her with eyes full of hate.

'Witness to a murder, taking off like that? You can see they wouldn't be pleased.'

'I didn't see anything,' said Caroline quickly.

'That what you told the Bill?' asked Annie.

'It's the truth.'

Annie stared at her. 'Not so hot then, jumping into Dolly's shoes before she was even cold?'

'Shut up, you cow,' spat Caroline.

'Tell us what you did see,' said Max.

'Nothing. I told them and I'm telling you.'

'We're not the police,' said Annie.

'I *told* you.'

'Tone?' Annie looked up at him. 'Come over here and break a couple of her fingers. Just the little ones, we don't want to cut up *too* rough yet.'

Tony lumbered over. Caroline shot out of her seat like she'd been launched from a cannon.

'What the *hell*?' she wailed, scooting up against the desk, eyes wide. 'What did you say?'

'Oh, come on,' said Annie. 'Way I see it, you deserve a few breakages. The way you moved in on Dolly's patch? You got to admit, that was nasty.'

'It was Gary's idea, not mine.' As Tony approached, Caroline edged around the desk until she was on the same side as Annie. Max was over by the bookcases, watching with arms folded. Now Tony was on the other side of the desk. 'Wait,' said Caroline, scuttling behind Annie's chair. 'Just *wait*.'

'Why? Are you going to stop bullshitting and tell the truth?' asked Annie. 'What scared you enough to make you run for the airport? What did you see?'

'I told the police—'

'Yeah. Nothing, right? And as I told you, we're not the police. We don't have to go by the rules. Go ahead, Tone.'

'I didn't—' Caroline let out a yelp as Tony came round the desk. She darted for the other side, but Max had moved and now he was blocking her path. 'Oh, come on . . .' she said, half-laughing, a scared, disbelieving little sound, as Tony came up behind her.

'Do it, Tone,' said Annie, and Tony grabbed Caroline's arm, gripping her hand, which she instantly pulled into a fist. Tony prised out her smallest finger and held it on the desk's edge.

'No!' Caroline screeched.

Annie looked at her. 'You really think he won't?'

'Shit, don't, please . . .' Sweat was popping out on Caroline's face. 'I don't, I can't . . .'

Tony brought his fist down hard. It hit the desk, just an inch from Caroline's finger. She let out a strangled scream.

'Next one hits the target,' he warned, taking aim.

'I can't . . .'

'You can,' said Annie, her eyes hard as they rested on Caroline's face. 'What did you see?'

Caroline threw back her head and let out a sob. 'I saw him do it!' she said, and fell to the floor. Tony released her hand and she sat there, crying hard, cringing, both arms over her head.

Tony looked at Annie. She nodded, and he moved away.

'Tell us,' said Max, and Caroline finally started to speak.

103

'I was so fucking scared,' said Caroline in a small voice. 'I was *terrified*.'

'What happened?' said Annie, looking at the girl with a mixture of pity and irritation. She *did* look shattered; none of her former aggression was in evidence now. 'Get up off the bloody floor, for God's sake.' Annie flicked a look at Tony and he hauled Caroline back to her feet, half-carried her around the desk, and deposited her into a chair.

'I was in bed, it was late, and Gary was in the sitting room watching the TV when there was a knock at the door and he let someone in. A man. I heard his voice. The bedroom door was half-open, I couldn't see who it was, not then. I didn't take any notice really. Not at first.'

'Go on,' said Annie when Caroline paused, rubbing her hands over her face.

Caroline gave her a look, a remnant of her usual attitude. 'If you tell the Bill all this, if they ask me about any of this, I swear, I'll say you're lying, that I never said it, that it's not true. I don't want to get involved.'

'OK. That's fair. Go on.'

'They were arguing. Just raised voices at first, and then they started shouting. I mean, it sounded *vicious*. And then . . . oh fuck . . .' Caroline stopped, clutching at her face, her eyes tormented; remembering.

'What?' prompted Annie.

'Then there were sounds like fighting. Something hit the wall. Christ, it was frightening. All the yelling and swearing, and then they were actually *hitting* each other, and then they were out in the hall . . . it reminded me of when I was growing up, and Mum and Dad would be knocking seven kinds of shit out of each other. It was scary. So I . . .'

Caroline stopped talking.

'Yeah? You did what?'

Tears slipped down Caroline's face. 'I did what I did when I was little,' she gasped out, grimacing. 'I thought that whoever was there with Gary, I thought they were so angry they were going to *kill* him, and if they did, then who was in the flat too? Me. And then they would do me too. And so . . .' Caroline heaved in a sob. 'So I hid. I hid in the wardrobe. It had these louvre doors though. So I saw it. I saw it *all*,' she said, and broke into a fresh wave of tears.

'What did you see?' asked Max.

Caroline swiped a hand across her runny nose and threw him a glance with tear-reddened eyes. 'If I hadn't moved when I did, you know what? I'd be dead. I'm sure of it.'

'What did you see?' he asked again.

'They were in the hall, grappling with each other, *snarling* at each other like dogs, and then they fell in through the bedroom door, and then I saw this bloke, he had Gary on the bed, and . . . oh shit . . .' Caroline's voice trailed away. She wiped tears from her face with a shaking hand and looked at Annie. 'Gary was pretty good to me. All right, he could be an arsehole, but can't they all? He didn't deserve *that*.'

'What?' asked Annie.

'That man cut his throat. And I saw it, I can't get it out of my head, *I saw it*! There was blood and Gary was screaming and choking, making these sounds like a butchered animal, it was . . . it was . . . just horrible. *Horrible.*'

For a long while the only sounds in the room were Caroline's sobs. Then Annie said: 'The man who did it. You saw him through the louvre doors, right? Can you describe him?'

Caroline's hands clawed into her scalp as she nodded. 'Yeah, I did. I saw him.'

'What did he look like?' asked Max.

'Tall.' Caroline sniffed and wiped at her nose again with the back of her hand. 'Not as tall as Gary. And pale. White like a ghost. And *grinning*, sort of, while he did it.' Caroline shuddered hard and hugged herself.

'Anything else?' asked Annie.

'Yeah. There is.' Caroline's head was nodding like a metronome now. 'I've been having nightmares about it ever since. The look on his face. Like a demon or something. Like he was *enjoying* it.'

'What colour was his hair?' asked Annie.

Caroline looked at her with haunted eyes.

'Red,' she said.

104

They let Caroline go, and then the three of them stood in the study in silence. Finally Max spoke.

'I'm thinking about Gina and the phone calls to the Blue Parrot.'

'What about them?'

'Gina knew where her brother was living, didn't she? She must have. What if she did tell Gary? She was mental. I spoke to her, the poor old cow didn't have both oars in the water. Raving about how you were still Constantine's wife, not mine. Saying he was still alive. She could have said all that and more to Gary on the phone. So maybe Gary knew where Constantine was.'

It was Annie's turn to pace the room, skirting around Tony, who stood silent, watching.

'Sounds like Redmond did Gary,' she said.

'Penny to a pinch of shit,' said Max, nodding. 'Fucker's a psycho.'

'Over Constantine's whereabouts?' Annie stopped in front of Max and locked eyes with him. 'Jesus, do you think Gary was playing with fire, trying to get money or something off Redmond, doing a trade? He knew that Constantine was behind the plane crash that should have killed Redmond and Orla back in the seventies. Did he give that piece of information to Redmond, maybe *sell* it to him, as a little taster, and then Gina comes on the phone raving about Constantine being alive and where Constantine's living these days, and Gary thinks, *I can make some bigger wedge here, better than I did before.* Maybe Gary tried to milk Redmond? And maybe Redmond snapped and killed him over it.'

Max folded his arms and stared at the floor, thinking. 'Redmond's no fool. I don't think he would top Gary until he had that information – if he was so desperate to get it.'

'Caroline said he was beating the crap out of him beforehand.'

'Yeah.' Max's head raised and he looked grimly at Annie. 'So it's possible he beat it out of him and then killed him. In which case, right now – Redmond knows where Constantine is.'

Annie considered this with a sense of dread. She considered also that Redmond could have cornered her, forced the location out of her just like he had with Gary. That he could have done with her exactly as he had done with Gary and with poor bloody Jackie. The thought brought her out in a cold sweat.

'Why didn't he do you?' wondered Max, echoing her thoughts. 'He could have.'

Tony spoke for the first time. 'I think Redmond Delaney has a thing for Mrs Carter. Weird as that may sound.'

Annie looked at Tony in surprise. 'Oh, *really*? He left me to die once. You forgotten that?'

Tony shrugged. 'He's a twisted, cold-blooded bastard. Who knows how his brain works? But for sure, he *could* have done you over and got it out of you. And he didn't. Just saying.'

'He likes playing cat and mouse with people,' said Annie with a heartfelt shudder.

'So what now?' asked Max.

'We get someone over to Redmond's place. See if he's there. He won't be, I'm sure of it, but we should check. And then . . . '

'Then what?'

'I have to get up there,' said Annie. 'If Redmond knows, then he's going for Constantine.'

'And I'm supposed to care about that?'

Annie looked at him in exasperation. 'He's Alberto's father, and if Alberto suffers then so does Layla, have you thought about *that*?'

'So you ride to the rescue? Redmond's had a day's start. He's probably whacked Constantine already. And frankly, do I care? OK, once he and I, we worked together. We had a mutual respect. But that sort of went for me, when he fucked my wife.'

'I thought you were dead. And so did he.'

'Yeah, yeah. And not content with *that*, you've been flitting back and forth to Scotland whenever you've come back here, visiting that shit and not telling me. No, I hope Redmond *has* done the business on him. I'd like to pat that fucker on the back over this.'

'I explained that,' said Annie. 'You *know* I did. Fuck's sake! I've got to get up there and I need some back-up with me. Steve and Tone.'

'And me,' said Max.

Annie looked at him, startled. 'No,' she said firmly.

But Max was determined. 'Look. If we're right, Delaney's already there and he could finish the job off properly. He could do you too, if you pitch up – even if you think you have got a free pass where he's concerned. Don't kid yourself. The man's a *psycho*. You don't know *what* he's going to do.'

'Max . . .'

'Don't "Max" me. You're not going up there without me.'

Annie stuck her hands on her hips. 'I'm not going up there *with* you.'

'Why's that?'

'Because you want Constantine dead. Because even if Redmond doesn't finish the job, you will. I know you. You'll *kill* him.'

'I'd be doing the cunt a favour, holed away up there, losing his fucking faculties in a five-star prison. But Delaney's probably already sorted that problem out for me.'

'Christ, Max . . .'

'Forget it. I'm coming too.'

105

Annie made the call and they took off five hours later from the heliport in the usual six-seater Agusta 109 Grand helicopter. The pilot, a big ice-cool Yorkshireman, knew her of old; he'd worked for 'David Sangster' for years. The chopper's two lines of three passenger seats were camel-coloured, butter-soft leather armchairs, each with its own drinks holder and headphones that piped soothing music. The cabin was lined to prevent too much noise, in a toning shade of cream.

As the rotors began to spin, Annie looked across at Tony and Steve, who were both plugged in to Chopin. Max had drafted them in, in case there was trouble. She was sure there would be, if Redmond was involved. One of Steve's security boys had been out to Redmond's place, and she'd been right: the house was deserted, not even that weirdo heavy Mitchell was there. The place was shut up tight, everything dark.

But even now, they could be wrong; Redmond could be anywhere, not at Constantine's. Annie hoped that was true, she really did. But at the back of her mind, she doubted it.

As the craft lifted into the air, Max, sitting beside her with one spare seat to his left, said:

'There's no way to get a message to him? To Constantine – or Alberto, if he's in no fit state?'

Annie shook her head. 'They contact *me*. It's never the other way round. I have no telephone numbers, no email addresses, nothing.'

'How many times have you done this trip now?'

'Too many,' she told him.

'And who owns this damned thing?' Max waved a hand, taking in the luxurious cabin interior. 'Or is it rented? Must cost a fucking mint.'

'It's owned by Constantine – or rather, "David Sangster" – through a network of corporations that winds up in Liechtenstein or the Caymans, somewhere like that.'

Annie took a breath, glanced over at Steve and Tony sitting there like a pair of overlarge bookends, headphones on, arms folded and eyes closed. 'Redmond's going there to kill him, isn't he?'

Max looked grim. 'Well, let's put it this way. If Redmond hasn't done for the bastard, then I will,' he said. 'That's a promise.'

'Max, I told you. He's old now. He's old and he's confused and he's scared. He doesn't deserve it.'

'Bollocks.'

'And what about *me*, then?'

'What?'

'Where does that leave me? Where does it leave *us*?'

Max looked away. 'Christ knows,' he said, and fell silent.

Annie gazed out at the black sky, the rushing lights skimming by beneath them, and felt sadness engulf her.

He wouldn't forgive her.

Yeah, they'd made love. Hot, passionate love.

But really?

It could have been for the very last time.

106

Half an hour later, they were there. Against the purple-dark night sky lit only by a dazzling full moon and a sprinkling of stars, they could see the castle's towering black outline as the helicopter sped over the sea toward it. At the last moment the craft lifted, and they could see the lights outlining the circular landing pad in the courtyard within the castle keep.

The pilot guided the helicopter down on to it, battling a fierce headwind that was coming in off the ocean. It touched down with barely a bump. Steve and Tony ditched the headphones, and everyone unfastened their seat belts. The rotors slowed, and stopped, then the pilot came and opened the door, helping Annie down. She stood there, her hair whipping across her face in the breeze, and looked around at the castle's tall forbidding walls and wondered with a shudder of foreboding where Redmond was, right now.

'There's a door,' she told Max. 'Over here.'

'Does someone usually come out to meet you?' he asked.

'The housekeeper, Mrs McAllister.'

'Then where is she this time? She must have heard us arrive. And supposing Delaney's here, how the fuck would he get in? This place is a fortress.'

'There's a path up from the beach below the headland,' said Annie. 'It's a slog, but it's no trick to get in. You ring the bell, and Mrs McAllister opens the gate down there or . . .'

'Or what?' asked Max when she hesitated.

'Redmond could afford to hire a helicopter. You saw his house. My guess he's got a lot of gang money stashed away, so this would be no big stretch for him. Maybe his pilot landed round the headland, or even right here in the courtyard. Maybe Mrs McAllister thought it was me or Alberto coming in, came out to meet us, and got the shock of her life.'

Steve and Tony were alighting from the helicopter. Annie led the way over to the door Mrs McAllister usually emerged from. But she wasn't there this time, and that was odd. Max was right about that. Annie felt a threadworm of fear crawl up her spine. But it was too late now for second thoughts. The pilot was getting back behind the controls, firing up the rotors. Within a couple of minutes, the helicopter had lifted off the ground, spun around, and was gone, away into the night sky.

'So, no welcome party,' said Max as they stood beside the door.

'I hope she's OK,' said Annie.

'She's probably not,' he said, and gave a nod to Tony, who twisted the circular handle on the old door. It opened, and Tony pushed through, into the body of the castle.

107

Now Annie was glad she had taken the time on previous visits to familiarize herself with the castle's layout. They climbed the steep flight of stone stairs that were so old the centre of each step was worn away by several inches. Wild, kilted highlanders with small ceremonial daggers, *sgian dubhs*, tucked into their socks would have climbed them in centuries past. Now, it was her and Max, Steve and Tony.

At the top of the flight a corridor opened out, stone flags on the floor, suits of armour lining the long in-curving wall. They walked silently on, then Annie indicated a left-hand turn, down more steps; Max pushed open the door and they stepped into a brightly lit and modern kitchen.

In the middle of the room, gagged and tied to a chair, was Mrs McAllister, her eyes wide with panic. When she saw Annie, she started making noises. Annie held a finger to her lips. *Quiet.*

The woman stopped making noises. She stared as Steve appeared, then Tony, and her eyes nearly popped out of her head when she saw they were holding guns. Moving stealthily, Tony went to the left side of the room, Steve to the right.

Annie looked at Mrs McAllister and mouthed, *Anyone in here?*

Mrs McAllister nodded frantically.

Shit, thought Annie.

Max moved forward. *Where?* he mouthed at the terrified woman.

She turned her head and indicated a door. A walk-in larder, Annie knew. Big enough to conceal a man, easily. The door was slightly ajar. Tony went in close, and Steve crossed the room quickly.

Annie held her breath.

Tony nodded to Steve, then threw the door open and dived inside, Steve right behind him.

There was no one in there. Steve shook his head at Max. Max moved over there while Annie stepped forward and quickly ripped the tape from Mrs McAllister's mouth. The woman winced and opened her mouth to speak, and Annie held up a hand urgently: *Shush. Quiet!*

Inside the larder there were stacks of provisions, canned and jarred goods; nothing else. There was a tatty old strip of carpet on the floor. Tony threw it back. They were looking at a closed circular trapdoor with a disengaged bolt on one side.

'Where does that lead?' Annie whispered to Mrs McAllister, busy tugging the ropes that bound her loose.

'I don't, I couldn't, he came in here so fast and I didn't know what to do . . .' she babbled.

Having freed the ties, Annie came round to the front of the chair and grabbed Mrs McAllister's shoulders. 'You're safe now. Where does it lead, that trapdoor?'

'Down into the cellars. We use them as wine cellars now, but once upon a time they were dungeons.'

Max looked at Mrs McAllister. 'One man. Just one. Sure?'

She nodded shakily.

Steve reached down and flicked the bolt shut. 'Well, he won't come up that way,' he said.

'But there's got to be another route up from the dungeons,' said Annie. 'Mrs McAllister, when this man came in here and tied you up – how long ago was that?'

'About half an hour, I suppose.' Mrs McAllister was a tough old bird, but she was choking back tears. 'It seemed longer. He came in a helicopter, I thought it was you . . .'

'And you're sure he was alone?'

'I didn't see anyone else.'

'So he could be anywhere in the bloody castle by now,' said Max.

'What did he look like, this man?' asked Annie.

Mrs McAllister drew in a sobbing breath. 'Pale. Sort of smiling. He looked *crazed*. And he had red hair,' she said.

108

They left Mrs McAllister in the kitchen. The trapdoor was bolted shut and she was strong enough to shove a largish butcher's block across the kitchen door when they'd gone back out into the corridor, so she would be out of danger there.

Wish we *were out of bloody danger*, thought Annie as they went on along the corridor, Tony and Steve throwing open doors on either side of it, stepping in, stepping back out. The silence in here was eerie. And now they were fast approaching the hall where Constantine had wined and dined her over the years – and an assortment of high-priced hookers too – while he still had wits left to do it.

She hoped Constantine wouldn't be in there. She didn't think he would be, but if he *was*, then Max would shoot him, beat Redmond to the draw. Once, she had hoped that Max could have let it go, the animosity he felt over her relationship with Constantine; now she knew he never would.

Steve was reaching for the door handle, and Annie's stomach was crawling with dread. *Don't be in there, please don't be in there . . .*

Steve opened the door, dived inside. Tony followed, then Max, then she walked in too – and there he was.

The breath caught in her throat.

Constantine, sharp-suited, narrow-hipped, broad-shouldered, wearing the silver-grey suit to match his silver hair. He was standing in front of the roaring fire, facing away from them, staring into the flames.

Then she turned and saw the gun in Max's hand.

109

Hearing the commotion in the doorway, the man standing by the fire turned and looked at the four interlopers.

'Stepmom?' he said to Annie.

Of course it wasn't Constantine. Constantine wasn't like this any more, he wasn't the Silver Fox, he wasn't the Don. The man who stood before them now very definitely was.

It was Alberto, Constantine's youngest son.

As they all stood there staring at each other, two massive Latino men in dark suits emerged from the shadows at the side of the room, pointing guns at them.

'It's OK,' said Alberto quickly, raising a hand to them. They stopped moving, kept watching. 'It's Annie Carter. And her husband Max.'

Annie hurried forward and hugged Alberto. 'Christ, you gave me a fright. For a minute I thought it was your father, standing there. Thought I was seeing things.'

'No, just me,' he said, smiling; but the smile looked strained. He stared at Max. 'Hi,' he said.

'Golden Boy,' said Max, letting the hand holding the gun fall to his side.

Annie shot him a furious look. Max would never be cool with Alberto, particularly not since Alberto had linked up with Layla, their daughter. She turned back to her stepson.

'What's happening?' she asked. 'We found Mrs McAllister tied up in the kitchen.'

'You *what?*'

'Redmond Delaney's in here somewhere. He's after Constantine. Didn't you hear us coming in on the chopper?'

Alberto looked blank. Then he shook his head. 'We haven't heard a thing. These walls are three feet thick, you forgotten that? Delaney! For God's sake. How did *that* happen?'

'One of ours gave the game away,' said Max. 'Told Redmond that your dad organized the hit on him and Orla back in the seventies, told him Constantine's still with us. Bit of a fucking shocker, to be honest. And your aunt spilled the beans over this place, so he knows where to find your father. The Delaneys don't do forgiveness. Redmond's come for blood.'

'We've got Papa under guard upstairs,' said Alberto. 'He's safe.'

Not for long, thought Annie. *Not if Redmond can get through. And if Redmond can't, then Max will.*

She was aware that if she announced Max's sworn intention to Alberto's men, then Max would be toast. So she couldn't. But somehow, she had to try to find a way to stand between Constantine – who was helpless now, more to be pitied than feared – and two people intent on killing him.

Somehow.

If only she knew *how.*

'He's been asking for me,' said Annie. 'Hasn't he.'

'That's right.' Alberto gave a sad smile. 'He's been remembering you these past few weeks. But I don't suppose it'll last. He's getting worse. Much worse.'

'Layla's not here, is she?' asked Max sharply.

'Layla's safe,' said Alberto. 'She's a thousand miles away.'

'Let's get up there and see him then,' said Annie.

110

They crept up the stairs where the upper floor opened out on to a big stone landing hung with tapestries that once had been bright and glorious reds and yellows but were now muted to pink and ochre; there were lights up here, but they were faint, and there were too many shadowy corners for a madman with red hair to hide in. Annie didn't like it at all.

As they turned a corner and approached the master bedroom, she breathed a sigh of relief. There, sitting in a chair on guard outside Constantine's bedroom door, was a bulky minder. They went closer and Alberto signalled to the man, but he didn't look round.

A look passed between Alberto and Max. Then as a group they all moved forward again. Steve put a hand out to the minder, touching the man's shoulder, and he slumped sideways in the chair and hung there over the arm of it, unconscious. As he did so they could see a bloody egg-shaped lump on the back of his head. Annie felt a chill of dread. Somehow, Redmond had got in close enough to strike.

Alberto put a hand to the man's neck, feeling for a pulse. He found one, nodded; and looked at the closed door leading to the bedroom. His father was in there. And so – without a doubt – was Redmond Delaney.

Alberto started forward but Max caught his arm. 'Is there another way in?' he whispered. He knew it would be suicide for the first person who walked through that door.

Annie spoke, very low. 'There's a secret passageway leading up from the hall. It opens in the bedroom, a false bookcase – I can show you.'

'How long?' Max asked her.

'Three minutes, if we run,' said Annie.

Max glanced at his watch and then looked at Alberto. 'Three minutes,' he said.

'In three minutes my father could be dead,' said Alberto urgently.

'Less than that and you could be, too,' Max hissed. 'This bastard don't take prisoners. Not that I give a stuff, but my daughter thinks the sun shines out of your arse, so go with it, OK?'

Alberto paused. Looked at the door, at Annie, at Max. 'Three minutes,' he nodded, and checked his watch.

Max and Annie ran.

111

'Christ, when was the last time anyone used this thing?' Max whispered to Annie as they opened the concealed door into the spiral staircase that led up to the master bedroom. He was leading the way with a pencil torch, swiping thick cobwebs away as he charged up the stairs. There was a faint smell of rat urine burning their noses, and the ancient stones were green with moss. Even though it was the height of summer, it was bone-chillingly cold in here.

Annie was following, trying to stay calm. As usual under pressure, Max was clearly having fun, but all she could think about was what would happen when they reached the top, and what they would find when they stepped out into the bedroom itself.

Constantine, lying dead on the bed, his throat slashed like Gary's and Jackie's?

Or Redmond, looming over him, just about to do the deed?

And if they managed to stop him, what then? Max had his own agenda, and that was dangerous. If he tried to kill Constantine, she had to find a way to stop him. Constantine was no rival to Max. But if Max went ahead with his promise and he succeeded, for certain Alberto would be forced to kill *him*, and that would destroy her, break her heart – and Layla's too. She couldn't let that happen.

They reached the top of the stairs and there was the door. On the other side of it, there would be the fake bookcase, nothing to give them away. So they had the element of surprise on their side. Annie remembered once marvelling at the books in that case right beside the bed, how convincing they appeared; they gave every appearance of real books when they were anything but. She had read to Constantine sometimes in the last year or so, sitting beside his bed; and he had joked sometimes, get another book, that one's crap, and he would indicate the bookcase. Once she went there and tried to pick a book out from the others; but the book she selected was nothing, just blank pages inside a gold-blocked cover.

Max stopped, breathing hard, looking at his watch.

'Minute to go,' he mouthed at her as she stood there on the top step, heart pounding, breath coming in shallow gasps.

Max kept the penlight trained on his Rolex, and slipped the gun out of his pocket. Annie's eyes met his.

'No prisoners,' he said. 'You stay here.'

'No fucking way,' she said.

'I *said*, you stay here,' he repeated.

'And I said, forget it.' She looked at the watch. 'Three minutes are up,' she said, and that was when they heard the gunshot.

112

Annie, standing right behind Max, felt him stiffen and then push forward. He shoved the bookcase open and sprang into the room beyond, gun raised, looking down the barrel as he scanned the bedroom.

Over Max's shoulder Annie saw Alberto and his two men surging into the room through the main door. There was the fireworks smell of cordite in the air and a man was lying on the floor near the bed with most of his chest shot away, a gun near him on the carpet, and blood all over the place. Annie looked in horror at the face of the dead man. But it wasn't Redmond. It was his sidekick, Mitchell.

Then she looked at the old man sitting up in the bed. Constantine was holding a big smoking Magnum in his shaking, age-spotted hand, and his face was twisted in triumph.

'Fucker came in here and thought he'd get the draw on me?' he asked the assembled company. 'No chance. I always keep this right under my pillow.' He shook the gun in his hand. Looked around at Alberto, the two men with him. Then he turned his head and saw Max.

'Nico! You old bastard, I've been looking for you,' he said with a happy grin, looking straight at Max. 'Where the hell have you been?'

Alberto moved quickly forward and took the gun from

his father's hand. He looked sharply at Max. 'So Redmond didn't come alone. He had company.'

Twisted and clever, that was Redmond. Annie knew it. Cold as ice and sick with it. He'd let his accomplice barge in the front door, let him take the hit. And himself . . . ? Suddenly it was all clear.

She started to turn, but it was too late. Annie felt something cold, metallic, press into the skin of her neck. 'He's here . . .' she managed to get out.

Then from behind her, there came a voice. It whispered in soft southern Irish, very close beside her ear.

'Yes, Mrs Carter. He certainly is,' said Redmond.

And then she felt the pressure of the knife harden, nearly cutting off her air, and knew that this time there would be no second chances, no reprieves. She was about to die.

113

She tried to speak and couldn't. Clever Redmond had laid low and simply followed them on their run up the stairs of the secret passage. She could see Max standing there, all his attention riveted to her and the monster standing behind her. She could see Alberto, raising the gun he'd taken off his father. And the other two – everyone was watching, everyone was still, wondering what to do now.

'Put the guns down,' said Redmond.

No one moved.

'Put them down, or I slit her open right now. It's messy. And really – do you want to risk that, any of you?'

Annie watched as first Max and then Alberto threw the guns on to the floor. Alberto turned and nodded to the two men behind him, and they too dropped their weapons. Constantine, his expression bewildered now, watched from close by on the bed as Redmond nudged her, straining painfully back against the front of his body, further into the room.

'Back up, Mr Carter,' he said, and Max did. 'You too,' he said to Alberto, and Alberto instantly did so.

'Well, this is interesting, wouldn't you say?' Redmond looked around the room at them all. 'Bit of a stalemate, yes? But now listen: all I want is *him*.' Redmond nodded to Constantine. 'The rest of you?' he shrugged. 'Not interested.'

The pale grape-green eyes met Max's. 'Not even interested where you're concerned, Max Carter. Old days, we were enemies, weren't we? Competitors, really.' He gave a chilly smile. 'Think you may have accounted for a brother or two of mine, but can I prove it? No, I can't. And do I give a shit? To be honest, no. I don't. Now – all that needs to happen is that you all leave the room. That's all. I'll keep Mrs Carter here, as insurance. And when I'm done, I'll let her—'

Out of the corner of her eye Annie saw Constantine move, lunging over the bed toward Redmond. She saw the flash of a blade in his hand as he plunged it into Redmond's flesh. Redmond buckled to one side and looked down in pained amazement at the knife that was deeply embedded in the side of his thigh.

An agonized high-pitched shriek came out of his mouth, deafening Annie. His hand jerked against her neck and the knife bit hard into her flesh. She felt the stinging pain of it and thought *that's it, I'm dead.*

Constantine pulled himself back straight in the bed and as Redmond tottered, off-balance, eyes screwed shut in agony, Max dived flat to the floor, grabbed his fallen gun and fired, shooting low and getting Redmond in the other leg. Redmond shrieked again and went down, dragging Annie with him, choking off her air. The knife grazed her skin deeper, trailing a fiery line of pain behind it.

Max came to his feet in a rush and whacked Redmond on the head with the handgun, hard. Blood flew as the blow opened Redmond's scalp like a crushed fruit. Finally his grip on the knife at Annie's throat loosened and he collapsed.

Max hit Redmond again, then grabbed the knife out of his hand as he keeled over, dragging Annie to the floor with him. Max pulled her upright, shoved her roughly away from Redmond and, eyes blazing with hate, he aimed the gun at his old enemy's head.

Now Redmond was blinking dazedly up at him, blood stinging his eyes from the head wound. He was wincing with the pain of his wounded legs and panting for air.

Alberto came forward and touched Max's arm. 'No,' he said. 'This one's ours.'

His two men grabbed Redmond roughly and hauled him up; he couldn't stand. Dragging his feet behind him, blood cascading down both legs, he was hauled across the room.

'Do it properly this time,' said Max.

One of the men was yanking back heavy brocade curtains at the window. He threw the window wide open. A strong gust of salty air swept in and Annie sagged on to a corner of the bed, a hand to her bloodied throat. She watched in horror as she realized what was about to happen.

Below this window there was nothing but a two-hundred-foot drop to the rocks and sea below.

She saw the realization hit Redmond, too.

'No. No!' he yelled.

He fought like a mad dog, but he was weak from blood loss and shock. Redmond was lifted off his feet and thrust out to dangle from the window, his hands clawing at the stonework, his bloodied face a rigid mask of terror. His eyes met Annie's. She thought she would never forget the look on his face. And then the men simply let go, and he vanished, crying out a slowly dwindling yell of despair, until he struck the rocks and was silent at last.

114

'Maria? Are you all right?' Constantine asked Annie.

Annie shot Max a look. *You see? He thinks you're Nico, and he thinks I'm Maria.*

'I'm fine,' she said.

'Thank God,' he said, his voice trembling with emotion, and grabbed her hand and kissed it. 'That bastard, did he hurt you?'

Annie shook her head. She glanced up at Max, standing there in silence, taking this all in.

Constantine looked over at Alberto. 'Your mother's OK, son,' he said.

'Yeah.' With a sad sigh Alberto moved closer to the bed while his two henchmen hefted Redmond's dead minder up on to the window sill, shoving and pulling until he too went spiralling out and down on to the rocks. Then they closed the windows, dragged the brocade curtains closed, and left the room, shutting the door behind them.

'You and I should have a talk,' said Max to Constantine. 'We've got a lot to catch up on, wouldn't you say?'

'He's tired,' said Annie quickly, her eyes pleading with Max. *Don't kill him.*

'Let them talk,' said Alberto, taking Annie's arm. 'It will do Papa good. All this mess? We'll clear it away later. No worries.'

No worries?

Annie stood up and let Alberto lead her from the room. She glanced back, and there was Max standing with a gun in his hand looking down at Constantine. She was terrified for both of them. Max could kill Constantine, who was helpless now, not the man he was, couldn't Max see that? And if he did . . . oh Christ, if he *did* then Alberto would never let Max out of here alive.

115

'Remember the old days, Nico?' Constantine was smiling, his eyes vacant. He'd just killed one man and maimed another, and he was no more concerned than if he had squashed a gnat. 'Sit, sit!' said Constantine, patting the edge of the bed.

Mental or not, this is one dangerous old cunt, thought Max.

Max pulled up a chair instead, giving himself some distance, and kept the gun in his hand for insurance. If Constantine could hide a bloody great Magnum pistol and a knife under his pillows, then he could have other weapons hidden, too.

'Remember all those times we had together?' said Constantine, heaving a fond sigh. 'When we were young foot soldiers, getting *agita* off our women for being so wild? What times we had, Nico. Chasing the coin, having sit-downs with the other people when there were turf disputes, we were on top of the world.'

'I'm not Nico, I'm Max,' he told him. 'Remember? Max Carter.'

Constantine looked puzzled. 'But . . . I don't understand. You were dead. That woman, that other one . . .'

'Annie.'

'I helped her find her daughter when you'd been hit. Abroad somewhere, in Europe.'

'You did.' Max thought about this: yes, he did owe Constantine a debt of gratitude. And he hated that. He thought of this old cunt trying to seduce *his* wife, trying to get her drunk, tormenting her with sex shows.

'I never see her these days,' said Constantine. 'Annie, I mean. Maria comes and visits me. You know what I wish?' Constantine lay back on the pillows and for a moment he looked ancient, ready for the tomb.

'No. What do you wish?' asked Max.

'I wish I could die now,' said Constantine, closing his eyes wearily. 'This life? It ain't all that, my friend. You get old and you ache and you forget things. Nothing tastes good. You don't even want a fuck. It's pathetic.'

Max stared at the face of the man who had once been so powerful, so fearful. Now, he was nothing but a shell. There was nothing for Max to do except what he'd come for. To kill Constantine, to finish him once and for all. To have revenge on the guy who'd stepped into his shoes with Annie and made her deceive him for so long.

Now was his chance. He had the gun in his hand, it would be a simple matter to pull the trigger and finish it at last; end the old godfather's sad remnant of a life.

The eyes opened, still blue, but no longer sharp. They were milky; faded with age. The head turned on the scrawny neck and Constantine looked straight at Max.

'You understand what I'm saying, don't you, Nico?' he asked.

'Yeah,' said Max, not bothering to correct him this time. 'I do.'

'That's what I would like,' said Constantine.

'You could have done it,' said Max. 'You had the gun, the knife. So did you really want it that much?'

Constantine shrugged. 'Maybe I could. Nothing's right any more, Nico. You're the only friend I have left in the world, you'll look after Maria for me, I know that. You swear that, don't you? I've been waiting for you to come and now you have, it's time. If I know you'll do that, then I'm ready and there's nothing else left for me.'

Max cleared his throat. Stupid to feel choked up, but he did. 'Yeah. I swear.'

'OK.' Constantine raised a tired smile. 'Then, I tell you what. Put the gun on the bed and go and look at that tapestry over there. It's a good one. French, you know. The best. Cost a fucking fortune like everything else in this damned cold hole of a place. When they come in, you can tell them I snatched the gun off you.'

Max stood up. Carefully, he placed the gun on the bed near Constantine's right hand.

And now I'll turn my back and the crazy old cunt will shoot me, thinking I'm some old enemy.

Ah, fuck it. Max turned away from the bed and took two steps away to look at the tapestry, all sewn in faded rose-pinks, greens and golds. Nymphs and cherubs, angels and demons, all writhing together in pink fleshy chaos.

He's going to shoot me.

Max could feel the skin between his shoulder blades crawling as he waited for the hammer-blow of the gunshot. He wouldn't hear it – you never heard the shot that killed you. And thank God for that.

Thirty seconds after he turned his back on Constantine, the shot rang out, deafeningly.

Max flinched at the noise, and spun back toward the bed.

The gun lay in Constantine's open hand. There was a head wound and blood – not much. Actually Constantine looked quite peaceful, lying there. Max stood and listened to the commotion start outside, to running footsteps coming closer. He sat down in the chair again, feeling neither satisfaction nor pleasure.

It was just *done*, that was all.

Constantine – finally, at long, long last – was dead.

116

'So what happened? Really?' asked Annie as they sat in the dining hall an hour later.

Max looked at her. They were alone in the room and it was cold, no fire burning in the hearth. Upstairs, Alberto was coming to terms with losing his father. The others were cleaning up. Mrs McAllister had gone to her room, shattered by the night's events. Down in the kitchen, she hadn't heard the gunshots. Alberto had assured her that the trouble was over, told her to go to bed, there was nothing to worry about.

'Really?' Max looked at Annie. 'I'll tell you. He snatched the gun off me and shot himself. It was a happy release, for God's sake. The poor old sod was fucked, anyway.'

'You didn't encourage him to do it?' Annie's eyes were narrowed with suspicion.

'No. It's done. Let it rest. How's your throat?'

Annie shrugged. There was a thin angry red line on her neck, but what little bleeding there had been was stopped, crusted over.

'I'm fine,' she said. 'It's just so bloody sad, what's happened here tonight.'

'It had to happen,' said Max. 'He thought I was Nico, and he seemed to be waiting for Nico to appear. When he did, he could rest.'

The door opened and Alberto came in. He looked strained and pale, but composed. He crossed to where they sat and slumped into a chair and put his head in his hands.

'Jesus, what a night,' he groaned.

'I'm sorry, Alberto,' said Annie. 'Really.'

Alberto looked up at her. 'Why be sorry, Stepmom? We lost him quite a while ago, didn't we. That wasn't my father up there, rambling on like some sad old fart. Fucking incontinent and not holding his fudge. Eating baby food. Not recognizing people. Even me, you know that? Last week, he asked who I was. No . . . it's better, what happened tonight. And Max? You mustn't blame yourself for it. It was kinder, really, that it ended that way.'

'So now what?' asked Max.

'Now?' Alberto heaved a sigh. 'Now I make the arrangements for the funeral. Bury David Sangster once and for all. Constantine Barolli is already long dead. And you know what? I think it would have been better, really, for him if he had truly died when that bomb went off in Montauk, instead of the poor sap who died in his place. That would have been a better end for a great man, don't you think?'

'If there is anything we can do . . .' said Annie.

'There's nothing,' said Alberto with an attempt at a smile. He stood up. Looked at them, sitting there. 'It's been a tough time. Losing Aunt Gina, and now Papa.'

'Gina?' asked Annie. She glanced at Max, who looked blankly back at her. 'I'm sorry. I didn't know that.'

'And now I guess you've resolved your differences, you two?' said Alberto.

'Is there *anything* you don't know about?' groaned Annie.

He smiled. 'Very little. Stepmom, two abductions in the space of a week! I was scared for you. My people saw to the first two guys, but the second lot . . . I told them to hang back on that one. Had a feeling they were your people, Max – the ones in the boiler suits?'

'They were,' said Max.

'Thought so.' Alberto glanced between them. 'I hope you can resolve this.'

'I've explained everything,' said Annie.

'And been believed? I hope so.'

'I hope so too,' said Annie, and looked at Max, but his face told her nothing.

'I'll get your transportation fixed up, get you back to London.'

'How's Layla?' asked Max.

Alberto relaxed a little. 'She's happy and she's well.' He walked over to the door and paused there. 'And she's pregnant,' he added, before leaving the room.

117

Next morning Annie awoke in the master suite of the Holland Park house, to find Max sleeping beside her. They'd started off in separate bedrooms, but some time during the night he'd obviously decided he wanted to be in here, with her. As she stared at him, so peaceful, his navy-blue eyes opened and looked into hers.

'Hi,' he said.

'Hi,' said Annie.

After a moment, Max stretched, yawned and then pulled her in against his naked skin.

'Did all that just happen?' he murmured against her hair.

'It did. And it's over now,' she said, cuddling in close against him. Her rib protested, but she didn't care. She'd missed this close contact with him so much.

Yeah, but has he forgiven you? Have you won, or lost?

'You went to Sicily to see Gina,' said Annie. 'You didn't . . . ?'

'Oh, come on. She was sick, frail. It was her heart. It just gave out.'

'Right.'

'And did Golden Boy *really* say he's knocked up my daughter?'

Annie disentangled herself, moved to the edge of the bed and slipped on her robe. 'I'll make some tea,' she said.

An hour and a half later, DCI Hunter was standing on their doorstep with a new companion at his side. This one was male, tall, and not at all sour-faced like DS Sandra Duggan had always been whenever she was close to Annie Carter.

'Mrs Carter, I just wanted a word,' said Hunter. He half-turned to the younger man with him. 'This is DS Nolan.'

Annie nodded to the handsome, bright-eyed young man and opened the door wide. 'You'd better come in then,' she said, and they followed her and Max inside the house. Annie led the way to the drawing room and indicated that they should sit. Max stayed at the back of the room, standing by the door.

'Where's DS Duggan then? I miss her smiling face, I really do,' said Annie.

Hunter gave her a look. 'On a training course. DS Nolan's filling in.'

'What's this about?' asked Annie, sitting down.

'We've been checking the telephone records at the Blue Parrot and the Palermo club and the Shalimar. The Blue Parrot received a lot of international calls. Some from Barbados, but others too.'

'Where did these other calls come from?' asked Annie, but she knew.

'Sicily,' said Hunter.

'The Palermo had some calls from Barbados to Miss Farrell.'

'That was me, phoning Doll.'

'None to the Shalimar at all.'

Annie and Max exchanged a look. Poor old Gina

Barolli. Losing her marbles and telling secrets to Gary. Who tried to cash in, like the grasping bastard he was – and found himself in too deep, falling foul of Redmond Delaney.

'What you were saying, Mrs Carter,' Hunter went on. 'What Sandy Farrell told you . . .'

'About the train driver,' said Annie. 'Arthur Biggs?'

'Who took his own life,' said Hunter.

'He couldn't live with the guilt,' said Annie. 'Sam Farrell's death was *murder*. Redmond Delancy told us what happened. It wasn't an accident. All Sam Farrell's co-workers were told what he was, what he'd been doing to his daughters, and they ganged together in a mob and killed him. And really? I don't blame them.'

'A dirty business,' said Hunter.

'Yeah,' said Annie, thinking that it wasn't finished, not yet.

When Hunter and his DS left, she phoned Tony and told him what to do.

118

It took Tony about five days to get the information, calling in favours from numerous contacts and then just waiting while they dug around. The records were old, archived, and his contacts told him that some had – mysteriously – gone missing. But there was enough to piece it together. All they needed was an address, really, and they got that, and passed it on to Tony. Tony passed it to Annie, and they got in the Jag and he drove her over there, to a large council estate full of weary-looking identical pebble-dashed cream houses, many of them with old sofas and fridges in the front gardens. The roads around the estate were littered with burned-out cars.

A young woman answered the door to them. She was mousy blonde, anorexic-thin, wearing a pink T-shirt and tight-fitting ripped jeans. Annie put her at about twenty years old, and hard-faced.

'Yeah?' she asked, seeing Annie standing there with Tony behind her.

'The Biggs family live here?' asked Annie.

'Nah,' said the girl, and went to shut the door.

Annie stuck her foot in it.

'You mean they don't?' she asked.

'Get your fuckin' foot out my door,' said the girl.

Annie shoved forward and the girl teetered into the

hallway. Annie grabbed her by the throat and pushed her back against the wall. Her rib protested, but she ignored it. Tony came inside too, and stood there watching.

'The Biggs family. I've asked you politely, but there are other ways. They live here?' said Annie.

The girl squirmed. 'What the fuck's *wrong* with you? I said no, didn't I. They used to live here, sure, not any more.'

'And they moved where?'

'That was *years* ago. When my mum and dad moved in here, I was ten.'

'And they moved where?' repeated Annie.

'Gawd, how would I know? There was some sort of family scandal, I know that. They were a bad lot, something happened and they moved away, got out of the area.'

Annie glanced around the hall, wondering if Arthur Biggs had topped himself right here; hung himself from these very stairs.

She let the girl go. 'You've been very helpful. Thanks.'

When they left the house, Tony went to one side of it, Annie to the other, and they started knocking on doors. Did anyone remember the Biggs family that used to live here? No one did. Time had closed over the scandals of the past. Tony went on knocking, and Annie was getting pissed off with the whole thing when he came and fetched her.

'Got something,' he said. 'And by the way, saw your mate Hunter going into the old address just now. His car's parked up over there, see? Reckon they're on the same track as us – don't you?'

Nine doors along from the old Biggs home, a grey-haired woman with large bulging brown eyes was leaning eagerly out of the front door. When they approached, she smiled and ushered them inside, straight into a tiny lounge with chairs and a TV. Most of the room was taken up by a bed, and in it lay a very old woman, sunken-cheeked, white-haired, but beautifully clean and turned out lovely in a mint-green bed jacket tied with ribbons at her wrinkled throat.

'Mum?' shouted the woman who'd come to the door. 'These people are asking about the Biggs, you remember them?'

The old lady cocked her head and stared at her daughter. 'Biggs?' she said in a cracked voice.

'You remember, don't you? The old man hung hisself, there was an accident on the railways. He was a train driver.'

'Course I remember Biggs,' said the old lady.

'Take a seat,' said the daughter, who was pushing seventy. The old girl in the bed had to be ninety-five if she was a day, but she was sharp.

Annie and Tony sat down.

'These people are friends of the family, they want to find out where they've moved to,' said the daughter, shouting.

'Bad do, that was,' said the old lady. 'Broke the wife's heart when he did that to hisself. She passed on not long after he did it. His married daughter found him, you know. Let herself in with her key one morning and there he was. Hanging from the sodding hall stairs. She had to go and wake her mother up, tell her.'

'God, that's awful,' said Annie.

'This your fancy man?' asked the old lady, smiling toothlessly at Annie, at Tony.

'Mum!' said the daughter. 'That's not your business.'

'No, this is my friend,' said Annie. 'Do you have an

address for the married daughter? Any contact details?' she asked, thinking that the old lady would say no.

'Of course I have,' said the old woman scornfully. 'I get a hundred and twenty cards every Christmas. My daughter Susan and me keep in touch with all our old pals, and Clarry Biggs is on her list. Or Clarry *Jameson*, as she is now. Clarissa, posh name that, always called her Clarry. Susan and her went to school together.'

'Can we have her address then? Please?'

119

Clarry Jameson, married daughter of Arthur Biggs, lived in Wimbledon near the Common. Her house was a detached Edwardian with deep bay windows. The house looked tired, the paintwork was neglected, the eaves rotting in places, but the front garden was well kept. It was colourfully planted with marigolds and red begonias around a lovingly striped square of emerald-green lawn. There was an unflashy Ford motor in the driveway and an air of peaceful suburban gentility lay over the small cul-de-sac.

The front door was wide open. Tony knocked at the door, and a thin, weary-looking man with a long solemn face and sand-coloured hair peppered with grey came up the hallway from the kitchen and stared at them both standing there.

'Hello,' said Annie. 'We're looking for Clarry Jameson.'

The man's features seemed to stiffen. 'What for?' he asked.

'We'd like to speak to her,' said Annie.

He heaved a sigh. 'You're not reporters, are you?'

'No,' said Annie. 'Why do you say that?'

'Oh, we've had people round here before, trying to dig up the past. Asking about my father-in-law and the rail accident. That happened *years* ago. But you know what? It never seems to go away. I'm just making some tea. You might as well come in.'

Inside, the place was a mess. Unwashed cups and dishes were stacked on the draining board, and the dust was thick on every surface. The carpet was stained and didn't look like a Hoover had ever troubled it.

'I don't do a lot of housework,' said the man, sticking the kettle on to boil. 'I'm out in the garden, mostly.'

They sat down in the dirty kitchen and Annie said: 'Clarry – your wife? – she's not here?'

'Clarry? We agreed to separate a long time ago. Her nerves were bad, you see. After *it* happened. Couldn't stand all that wailing and weeping. Christ, comes a point you just got to try to move on.'

Another dead end.

Annie sighed. 'So where does she live then?'

'Live?' The man looked sad all of a sudden. 'She don't live, Clarry. She never got over finding her dad like that. Turned her head, shot her nerves to pieces.'

'What happened?' Annie was getting a bad feeling about this.

'She took two hundred paracetamols. After we'd agreed to go our separate ways. She saved 'em up and just whopped 'em down in one go. I found her dead upstairs on the bed when I came home from work. Terrible shock, it were. And she had the letter in her hand.'

'What letter?'

'The confession. The one her dad left when he topped himself. Saying it was him, he murdered a shunter called Sam Farrell. He said how sorry he was. All old news now, ain't it. None of it matters a toss any more.'

'Did it say anything else?' asked Annie.

'It did. It said as how one of the big gang bosses of the time – not the Krays, but one of *those* types – got wind of

Sam Farrell doing something to his daughter and gave the order for it to be carried out.'

'Mr Jameson, can we *see* this letter?' asked Annie.

'Nah. Burned it. Long time ago. Old stuff, see? You got to let it go. Let the past stay dead.'

Annie was silent for a while, thinking. Then she said: 'Do you have children, Mr Jameson?'

'Just a boy. Peter.'

'Does he live at home?'

'Nah, moved out. He works in a club up West called the Palermo. Lap-dancing or some such thing. He runs the bar, done well for himself.'

Annie felt her whole body turn to stone as he spoke those words.

There was no Peter Jameson working the bar at the club – but there *was* a Peter Jones, and he had found Dolly dead.

'Did he ever see that letter, Mr Jameson?' she asked.

'Peter? Sure he did. We both did.'

'Do you see him much these days?' asked Annie, feeling her throat go dry as dust, feeling the aftershock of discovery still jolting through her.

'Hardly ever,' said Mr Jameson.

120

'What do you mean, he's gone?' asked Annie when they went from Wimbledon over to the Palermo.

She was in the main body of the club and it was all business as usual: the dancers were getting ready, the DJ was pumping out 'Venus' by Bananarama from the decks, the bar staff were polishing glasses and bringing up cases of drinks and snacks from the cellars, but there was no sign of Peter Jones.

And now the acting bar manager, a very efficient dark-haired woman who was wearing thick black false eyelashes and who was *also* acting as overall manager now that Dolly was dead and Caroline was off the scene, was telling her that Peter Jones had not shown up for work for a week. They had hired a replacement to start next week; she'd sorted it.

'Is he still at the same address?' asked Annie.

'Yes, he is. We phoned, but no answer.'

'And what's your name?'

'Vanda Pope.'

'Right. Thanks, Vanda. And just double-check for me, will you? There's no Peter Jameson works here?'

Vanda went off upstairs and came back within five minutes. 'No, there's no Peter Jameson works here, sorry.'

And they were off, Tony at the wheel, over to the tiny back-alley flat in Camden accessed by metal walkways.

They went up to the door, with purple paint peeling off it in strips, and Tone put his boot to it. It juddered open and they walked in. The flat was neat, clean, and completely empty. No clothes in the wardrobes, no personal belongings. Peter Jones had cleared out.

Annie walked around the flat. She kicked the sofa. Walked away. Went back, and kicked it again.

'That whinging little bastard,' she said, her voice cold with hatred. 'He must have changed his surname by deed poll to cover his tracks. He killed her for revenge,' she said flatly. 'He planned it. Got a job on the bar in the Palermo so he was close enough to do it. Got hold of a gun from somewhere, and he fucking shot her.'

'Looks that way,' said Tony.

'Pete's grandfather died because of what Dolly set in motion against her father. Pete's mother died too, because she found her dad dead and couldn't get it out of her mind. It was one big fucking tragedy all round, Tone, and his family was ruined by it.'

'Yeah,' said Tony.

Annie paced around the room. 'That little fucker sat there with us and cried like a girl. He wasn't sad for Dolly, he was scared for himself. Well, he bloody should be. I want him found. I want him dealt with.' She stopped pacing and looked at Tony full in the face. 'I want it like you said, Tone. No cells, no cosy TV, no nothing.'

'We'll see to it,' said Tony, walking over to the door. He looked down. On the cobbles below, behind the Jag, another black car had just pulled up and DCI Hunter was getting out of it with his new DS in tow. Annie joined him, looked down.

'They're on it,' said Tony.

'Yeah. Looks like.'

'You going to tell them what we know?' said Tone.

Annie thought. 'Why not? They might find him.'

'I'm hoping we find him first.'

'I'm hoping we do, too, Tone.'

Tony held the shattered door open for her. 'Breaking and entering,' he said sadly. 'Old Bill's not going to like that.'

'We found it that way. *We* didn't break. Or enter. We just stood here in the smashed doorway and looked inside, right?'

'Good plan,' said Tony, and smiled. 'After you, Mrs C.'

Annie went out of the flat feeling like a weight was gone from her shoulders. They knew Dolly's killer now. All they had to do was finish him.

On the way back down to street level, they met Hunter and his new handsome young sidekick coming up.

'Is he up there? Peter Jones?' asked Hunter.

'Nope. And I suppose you know—' started Annie.

'That he's really Peter Jameson? Yes, Mrs Carter, we do. Son of Clarissa Jameson, née Biggs, the grandson of Arthur Biggs who ran a steam engine into Sam Farrell, Dolly Farrell's father, and killed him.'

'You might find the lock's gone on the door,' said Annie as she carried on down, Tony following.

'Oh, big surprise,' said Hunter, but he was almost smiling as he climbed on up the stairs.

121

Annie had Tony drive her over to the cemetery next day. She bought roses on the way; pink, Dolly's favourite colour. Then she went alone to the freshly filled grave. Someone had put up a wooden cross; it would take time for the ground to settle, months before a proper headstone could be erected. Which was OK. Now that they had a handle on who had robbed Dolly of life, everything else would follow at its own pace.

They would find Pete Jones. Peter *Jameson*.

And then . . . Dolly would be avenged.

'We're on it, Doll,' she whispered under her breath as she stood and looked at the cross there. 'Don't worry. We're going to find that arsehole.'

'Talking to yourself?' asked a female voice behind her.

It was Ellie.

Annie gave her a sarky look. 'No good talking to *you*, is it?'

Ellie stepped forward, looking sheepish. 'Chris says it's all OK now. That you and Mr Carter have sorted it.'

Constantine's dead, if that's what you mean.

She still wasn't sure that Max had forgiven her for keeping to the code like she'd sworn she would. But wouldn't he have done the same? She knew he would.

'I suppose we have,' said Annie.

'Well, good. I'm pleased,' said Ellie, impulsively linking her arm through Annie's. Ellie looked down at the grave. 'It's so bloody peculiar. Thinking of Doll in there.'

'She's at peace now,' said Annie.

'If you believe in all that,' said Ellie.

Annie wasn't sure whether she believed or not. But she hoped Doll was somewhere else; somewhere *better*.

'Chris said it was Pete Jones,' said Ellie.

'That's right.'

'That son of a bitch.'

Annie bent, wincing at the pain from her broken rib. It was getting better, but still there. She emptied the dead flowers Dolly's sister Sarah had placed there from the vase, and put the pink roses in there instead. She placed the vase carefully on the grave.

'Hurts still, does it?' asked Ellie.

'Not too bad. Got lots of painkillers. Another month, I'll be able to get this strapping off. Can't wait. It's awkward showering with the damned thing on.'

'What you going to do now then? Go back to Barbados? Or stay on? I mean, you and Mr Carter, it's all OK now, ain't that right?'

'Dunno. I might stay for a while.' *We haven't got Peter Jones yet. And Max? I just don't know.*

'Oh. So it's like that, is it?'

'I don't know *what* it's like, Ellie. That's the truth.'

'Well, if you do stay on, why don't we make a date then? Drink a toast to the old cow's memory, eh? Next Thursday at the Ritz.'

Annie turned and looked at Ellie. For the first time in a fortnight, she actually felt like smiling. 'It's a date,' she said.

122

At the entrance to the cemetery gates, Ellie went off in a cab and Annie was just getting into the Jag when DCI Hunter pulled up.

'Mrs Carter,' he said.

'Something up?' she said.

'Nothing at all. Don't worry – we're going to find Peter Jones, I promise you that.'

'And bang him up for – what? – ten years, twelve? What does he plead – insanity, the balance of his mind disturbed by family tragedy? Then he's out, and what about Dolly? She gets a longer sentence than that. And so do we. All the people who loved her.'

'It's justice, Mrs Carter,' he said.

It stinks, thought Annie. *It's not good enough.*

She had all the boys out looking for the little shit, and their contacts were on the alert now. Added to that, she'd had a word with Alberto, and the Mafia street people were watching out for him, too. He wouldn't get away with it. She was going to make certain of it.

'Can I ask you a question, Mrs Carter?' said Hunter.

'Shoot.'

'Who exactly is David Sangster?'

'What?' Annie was poleaxed.

'David Sangster. The David Sangster who is on the

board of the company that owns the house on the outskirts of Edinburgh, the one you stay in sometimes. And the castle you visit in the Highlands, he owns that too, I'm told. I've checked out all the other directors, and they're kosher, but Sangster? He's a bit more interesting. Lots of paper trails, all leading nowhere. So I repeat, Mrs Carter – who is he?'

Annie was silent for a long, long time. Then she smiled, sadly.

'He was a friend of mine,' she said.

'Was?'

'Yeah, he was.' Annie took a breath and turned away and walked over to the Jag. She paused there as Tony opened the door for her, and she looked back at Hunter. 'But he's dead now,' she said, and got in.

And he's going to stay dead, she thought, as Tony got behind the wheel and started the engine.

123

When she got back to Holland Park, she found Max in the study, behind the desk. Chris was in there too, and Steve. All conversation halted when she showed up and stood in the open doorway looking at them.

'What's this, a board meeting?' she quipped, breezing in, thinking, stuff them; they'd intimidated her once, they weren't ever going to do it again.

'Sort of,' said Max.

'Anything I should know about?' she asked, looking around at the three of them and seeing that something had changed.

Now, Steve looked directly at her, not avoiding her eyes. And Chris, who hadn't addressed a single civil word to her in a fortnight, was smiling ruefully.

'Hunter's just phoned,' said Max.

'Oh?' Annie held her breath.

'They've picked up Pete Jones. He was getting on a ferry in Portsmouth when they collared him.'

'*Shit*,' said Annie. Yes, she could almost feel some sympathy for the little bastard. His life had been so wrecked by the fallout from Sam Farrell's sins and Dolly's revenge that he had been driven to murder. But she hadn't wanted the Bill to get him. His arse belonged to *her*. She didn't want prison, rehabilitation and release for him. She wanted this closed up, done with.

Chris and Steve stood up and came to the door. Annie stepped aside.

'Mrs Carter,' said Steve, passing her with a polite nod.

'Mrs Carter,' said Chris, and winked at her.

Annie closed the door on them both, heard them go off across the hallway and out the front door.

'Blimey, what did you say to them?' she asked.

'Not a lot,' said Max, standing up and coming around the desk.

'Bit different to the treatment I've been getting.'

'They thought you'd screwed me over.'

'I know.' Annie stepped further into the room. 'And now, knowing the full story, what do *you* think?'

Max stared at her.

'God's sake, say something,' moaned Annie, wishing he'd come to her, hold her, take the fear away, the awful fear that she might be losing him.

'I think that you kept an oath you swore to keep. You honoured that oath, even when it came back and bit you in the arse. Even then, you kept it. When a lot of others would have given it up.'

'It sure didn't do me any favours,' said Annie.

'Even so. You kept it.'

'You say that as if it's good.'

'Loyalty's a good thing.'

'Max, I'm sorry,' Annie burst out suddenly. 'I wish I could have told you. I wanted to. I couldn't do it. Not just because of the oath. I was too afraid of what your reaction would be.'

Max moved closer until he was within touching distance.

'I was mad as hell at you,' he said. 'When I left Gina Barolli's place, I wanted to wring your bloody neck.' His eyes dropped to the bruises at her throat. 'I nearly bloody did it too, didn't I. Sorry.'

'What changed your mind?' She couldn't believe it; he'd apologized.

'You did. Being so tough, so bloody-minded, so certain you were in the right.'

'I *was* in the right.'

Max stepped closer. He let out a breath and gripped her waist with both hands and pulled her in, very gently, so that their bodies touched.

'One thing,' he said.

'Oh? What's that?' Annie linked her arms around his neck. She kissed his chin, then his cheek, then his mouth, nuzzling in against him, inhaling his scent.

Max eased her back a bit, grasped her chin, stared her straight in the eye. 'No more fucking secrets. Not now, not ever. Are we agreed?'

'Agreed,' said Annie.

'Swear?'

'I swear. I really do.'

'Good.' He pulled her back in and kissed her, hard. 'Time for bed, then,' said Max.

'It's two in the afternoon,' said Annie, starting to smile.

'Shut up,' said Max with a grin, and lifted her into his arms.

'Ow! Watch the damned rib,' she said.

'I *said*, shut it.'

EPILOGUE

1995

Pete Jones was just going out into the prison exercise yard, lined up with a load of other cons, all jostling each other, talking, telling jokes, taking the piss, all of them waiting for the gates to be opened.

He'd been handed down a twelve-year stretch for doing Dolly Farrell, but he reckoned he'd be out in eight and it was worth it because he'd done it, he'd got even with that bitch for what she'd done to his family. He'd loved his mum, couldn't ever get over losing her. And Grandpa, his death had been for what? Just so some vicious cow could get her revenge on someone. None of it should ever have touched his family, but it had, and he was glad he'd made her pay the price for that.

The sun was shining. He couldn't wait to get out in the yard, kick a ball about, stretch his legs. Stir wasn't so bad, once you got used to it. Bit rough, and you had to watch out for the queers after a slice of your arse in the showers, but not too bad. No cats, though. He missed Benj, but Benj was all right, Dad was looking after him. He was sorry about this prison business for Dad's sake. But he'd get out, make it up to him. Put all this shit behind the both of them.

Then someone shoved him from behind. He turned.

'Easy,' he complained, seeing a hard, dark-eyed face close to his own.

'This is for Dolly Farrell,' said the man, and plunged a knife straight into Pete Jones's heart.

He died instantly, collapsing to the ground, an image of Benj the last thing he thought of before he kissed goodbye to this world and headed for the next. His murderer moved on, and was quickly lost in the crowd of other cons.

Later that day, one of the cons made a call out to a mate.

'It's sorted,' he said, and put the phone down.

The man he'd phoned went out, down the pub, saw *another* man. 'It's sorted,' he said.

Next day, Steve Taylor made a call to Barbados. When Annie Carter came on the line, he said: 'Hiya, Mrs C. Tell Max that business he wanted seeing to? It's done.'

Annie was silent for a moment. Then she said: 'I'll tell him.'

She put the phone down, looked out of the big picture window of the villa at the crystal-blue Caribbean and the azure of the cloudless sky above it, and thought, *There you go, Doll. Hope you're safe in heaven now, babe, with the angels.*

Then with a light step she walked out on to the sunlit terrace to join Max.